Lucifer's Redemption

VERA FOXX

FOXX FANTASY PUBLISHING

First paperback edition: July 2022

Book design by: GetCovers.com

Publisher: **Foxx Fantasy Publishing LLC**

Thanks and Dedication

Thank you so much to **Tabitha Marko** and **Jamie Kidd** to whom this book is dedicated to. Without their help in editing such a piece, I don't know if it would have ever made it to print!

Contents

Dear Reader

This book doesn't have your normal heroine. Uriel is immature, hidden away from the world, and blissfully unaware of the danger around her. Then she meets Lucifer, her darkness to his light.

There are acts of age play submissive and dom in this book if you are familiar with BDSM. All acts are consensual complete with two virgin gods with a bond pulling themselves so tight it is ready to snap!

Again, strong alpha male, an innocent submissive and hilarious moments to get you laughing. If this doesn't seem like a book for you, might want to stop here.

Happy Reading!

Incerpt

"I'm Lucifer." The voice made Uriel shudder involuntarily. It was then, that Lucifer realized who she might be to him. Glancing back at his mother, Ember nodded her head frantically, but there was no smile on her face, just worry.

"I'm the Goddess of Innocence; what are you? Everyone has been asking me for my title; I think I should ask you too!" Uriel giggled.

For once, Lucifer felt embarrassed. He wanted nothing more than to strike fear in those around him, but with this small woman, he didn't want that. "It isn't important." He adjusted his collar. Uriel stared back blankly for a moment until her head popped up.

"Ok!" Putting down her empty plate with extra honey from her dessert, she took his hand and shook it frantically. "Nice to meet you! I'm going to see what the kids are doing outside! Oh, you tickle!" She almost snorted and left without a care in the world.

Lucifer was left standing frozen in shock. Those 'tickles' were the tingles his mother warned him about. There was no doubt in his mind that the innocent goddess was his mate.

Hades and his true mate, Ember, gripped each other, waiting for Lucifer to say something, anything. A good minute passed by before the uneasy crowd parted, and Lucifer walked out the door and into the garden, following the strange woman who pranced out the door.

Chapter 1

Lucifer

In the boughs of hell, the smell of burning skin and flesh pierced my nose into the night. With such heat, many would think that the flames would cast light upon the tattered souls, but it doesn't. Black magic reeks around every corner of Hell, leaving behind a bittersweet taste of fear as the tortured souls hope their torture is done for the day.

It *never is. Their torture will never cease.*

Just because night has fallen in Hell with the deep-red sun dusting the rusty-colored grass as it sets for the evening, it meant nothing. The screams of the night, the howls of pain from twisting a soul into odd positions, gave me strength. For every fear that popped to mind, my hands made it a reality.

Blue, red and white flames, hot enough to melt any earthly metal, swept across my nails. The flame jumped from side to side as if it were a small doe jumping through an ominous forest. One touch could induce pain for weeks, yet to me, it is just the sweet burn of menthol across my chest. Breathing deeply and smelling the skin crisp under me—which everyone here deserved—fueled my lust for destruction.

Anger rose within the depths of my gut at how humans, supernaturals, and whatever else the damn gods decided to create had me fixing their dirty work. The ones that turned away from the light sought revenge among their own kind, hurt the innocent, and craved to rule over the weak like cows for slaughter.

I am the God of Destruction, the bringer of death and despair. I will not just destroy buildings, the soil, and the physical bodies, I will destroy their minds, twisting them in ways they could not fathom possible. They will scream for me to extricate myself from their mind as I contort their deepest fears into reality. I will only laugh at their pathetic cries of absolute terror.

They are mine to control; my father, Hades, deemed it so. The torture, the destruction, and the ending of a soul were the greatest high I could ever get. No matter how much my mother embodied the kindness and empathy that she tried to teach me, the Fates had already chosen my path: destruction.

Another whip of the silver chains slashed through yet another damned werewolf alpha. The clacking of my footsteps rang as I sauntered to the middle of the cold metal platform. The alpha's head was bowed, his hands chained behind his back, and blood dripped from his brow. His wolf, just as evil as he was, panted in the back of his mind, suffering from the wolfsbane gas.

No creature would go unpunished.

"Your mother has been in labor for eight hours, and yet you still waste time beating this pathetic wolf." My father's leather shoe stepped in the deep-red trail of blood flowing into the grate. "She would be most disappointed to know you didn't wait for your sibling's arrival along with the rest of the family."

My lip curled in amusement. *Little does he know, the only screams I did not want to hear were those of my mother. She was too perfect.*

Born a wolf, she endured years of torment after being sold into a trafficking ring at a strip club and forced to work as a waitress and a maid. Father found her, and eventually, they mated. Mother became the first werewolf supernatural to be mated to one of the Twelve, the Original Gods of 'Olympus'—as the humans called it.

"She would be furious, wouldn't she?" I chuckled. My father grabbed a rag from a nearby hook, tossing it to me to wash the blood from my bare torso.

Mother mated one of the most powerful gods of the Celestial Kingdom. Once soul-bonded, she inherited his god-like qualities. Her gift of empathy was enhanced, and she gained the ability to pair souls like Selene, the Moon Goddess. It was the biggest uproar across the realms. Now, Selene had been granted time to find her own mate, the old-fashioned way, by being a wolf herself.

"Let's go back, hmm?" Father slapped my bare back. "I know the fire roars inside you to destroy. It is part of who you are, but don't let it control you. There needs to be a balance." He sighed, rubbing his chest.

"That balance will only come if I get a mate, and I don't need one." I let out a harsh breath, hitting the alpha once more with my chain, knocking him to the ground.

None of the females I had ever met had given my soul ease. They all wanted power, sex, or a title. My mate wouldn't be any different, no matter how much my mother lectured me.

The alpha's grunts and cries no longer excited me. Now my thoughts traveled to the idea of always being alone.

It was better that way: to be alone.

"I think you forget everyone is paired with someone." Father walked with me off the platform. "As the son of Ember, the Goddess of Empathy and Bonding, you should know that." The crowd that watched the humiliation of the alpha at his knees faded. His fear left the arena as blackness became his next torture. He was no longer allowed to see the light and was forced to remain alone.

Loneliness was the only way to survive in this world. Mates will continue to bring you down. My father, once known to be a monster in everyone's eyes, had now softened into a regular family man. That was good for him, but I could never be the person he is now.

There are days I could not control my lust for inflicting pain and suffering on my next victim. The grip of the whip in my hand and the sound of my claws ripping across someone's chest made me groan with pleasure. Burying myself in a part of my father's work was my new normal. Running as soon as Hell's sun crossed the tops of the blackened forest and not returning until the blood-red moon was high in the sky.

It was all I needed.

Large bursts of cries came from the room next door. My mother's screams finally ceased, but not those of my new sibling. Loki, my younger brother, still of adolescent age, was hiding from his latest nanny. We had been through fifteen in the past three months. Many were killed or quit while attempting to corral the God of Mischief.

"Master Loki! Where are you?" the nanny squealed.

It was another demon mistress trying to get into my suit pants. Every single one of the lust-hungry demonesses in their short damn skirts.

"Oh, Master Lucifer, have you seen your brother?" Her eyelashes fluttered towards me, flashing her sharpened fangs which damn near sparkled.

Yeah, he's under my damn seat. Rolling my eyes, I stood up and moved to the couch.

"There you are, Loki!" She squealed in excitement like she enjoyed the job.

Did she forget I inherited my father's ability to read the minds of his creations? Crossing my arms over my chest, I silently counted in my head.

Ten... nine...

"Yep, here I am. Will you please help me out?" Loki's sweet, childlike voice trailed to her ears symphonically. The red demoness smiled, reaching her hand down and planting her rear up, seductively, in my direction.

Four... Three...

I watched as Loki reached out his hand. Once her fingers touched the tip of Loki's finger, a giant hellhound spouted from his body, knocking the chair over. A half-second later, her shrill scream was silenced as Loki's hound ripped through her vocal cords. Blood splattered on the floor, and I groaned in annoyance at the mess Mother would surely complain about. Taking a black handkerchief from my suit pocket, I wiped away the blood absentmindedly from my shoe.

"Did you see the look on her face!" Loki squealed excitedly from the closet on the other side of the room. "Look at that, already turning to dust!"

Cerberus, Father's constant companion besides Mother, walked by the waiting room. He shook all three of his heads before continuing his stroll down the hallway, clearly not amused by Loki's tricks.

Loki's giggles filled the room, his arms holding his stomach to contain his breakfast from this morning. "Oh, come on"—Loki looked at me with a smile plastered to his face—"that was comedic gold!"

My head laid back, hitting the wall. Loki grabbed a broom from a nearby closet, sweeping up the dust that was his former nanny.

"Do you have one of your wing feathers stuck up your butt? Is it permanently embedded around your sphincter or something? Even for a destroyer, you are utterly depressing."

I stood up, slipping my hands into my pockets, walking past the mess of dust scattered on the floor. She would respawn in Father's demon pool to be re-summoned, pardoned, and sent back to the demon's cities. That was the only reason Mother had not locked Loki in his room for the next century—not that he wouldn't get out; he was smart.

One had to be smart if they were going to be a trickster.

My feet lightly tapped along the red carpet leading to Mother's room. The cries from my new sibling had softened, leaving Mother's gentle humming. I fixed my black tie, leaning back on the wall next to the door. Several moments later, the doors opened as a team of doctors and nurses walked out. The door stayed open enough for me to listen and peek at my parents who had a few moments alone with the newest addition to Hell.

"I worry for him," Mother spoke to Father. "I've tried everything. I even tried to coddle him as a baby, but his sternness, his seriousness... I can barely get him to smile, even at me, anymore." My mother sniffed faintly.

"I do as well. Are you sure that you cannot see his mate yet? I'm sure that would calm his beast."

"No," she whispered. The baby made a sucking noise, and Mother hushed her back to sleep, still nursing.

"My theory"—Father wrapped his arms around Mother, staring down at the baby in her arms as his finger traced the chubby cheeks already filled with milk—"still stands. I think Kronos' blood is running in his veins."

My hand gripped my chest with my back now flat against the wall. Kronos, my grandfather, was evil upon evil, and here I was, teeming in his blood. Kronos ate his children, including my father. It was rumored he had no heart, and not even his poor wife could calm the fury inside him.

Kronos is still trapped in Tartarus, but could he be planning something with me? If his wife could not calm him, how could a mate possibly calm me? It wouldn't; it couldn't.

Many times, I heard Father bring up Kronos. Even when I was a child, I heard his worry. Now that I am older, I can feel more power running through my veins. Looking at my hands, I gripped my fists.

I must not let it control me. I must not let my heritage decide my fate. The fate that one day, I may have to cease to exist.

I should increase my twelve-hour days of torturing to eighteen, letting out every bit of the rage inside me. I would die if anything happened to my family, especially my mother. Sweet angels, my mother—if anything happened to her, I'd rip out my own heart, over and over, for all of eternity.

My mother was the one woman I truly loved. I would be so much worse if I hadn't been raised by her. She refused to let nannies take care of me because she noticed I was different, noticed I had a sick way of destroying everything in my path. My anger, the tantrums, they grew so much, and she has yet to yell at me or punish me physically. Who knows what I would have grown up as if she had done that to me?

"Lucifer? Is that you?" My mother's voice trailed into the hallway. Loki ran in front of me, jumping on the bed right beside her, smiling gleefully at the baby in her arms.

"Come, Lucifer. Come and say hello to your new sister." Mother's eyes were tired, her breath labored from the pain she must be feeling. Father only looked on to his newest addition. "Her name is Lilith." Loki tapped her nose. In return, a small bubble of milk escaped her pouty lips.

"She's beautiful, Mother," I spoke calmly, gazing into her half-slit eyes. My sister lifted her head to look at me, only to close them again as she nuzzled back into Mother's chest.

"So, when can I play tricks on her?"

Mother glared; Father was not too happy either as his black smoke trailed out of his body. "Never! Just like your older brother. I mean it, Loki!" Mother stated firmly, pursing her lips.

"Awe, that's cause Luci can't take a joke!"

My teeth gritted. *I fucking hate that name.*

Fire welled in my fist. Loki squeaked before running out of the room in terror. He has felt a punch in the gut from me before, and he wouldn't want it again.

"Lucifer." Mother grabbed my flame-free fist. "It's alright. Calm down, love." I took deep breaths, letting the fire abate in my fists.

I need to stay away from Lilith, Loki, and the rest of my family until I learn how to control myself.

Chapter 2

Uriel

"That was terrible!" I plopped my head on my gigantic, fluffy, heart-shaped pillow. A hot tear ran down my puffy face. "I can't even finish the movie if that poor, little animal has to live like that." Taking the remote, I stopped the movie and tossed the remote to the other side of the room. "That poor little deer lost his mom and had to go live with his *really* serious dad. I am so *not* finishing that."

He looked waaaay too grumpy for that movie to have a happy ending, and I am all about happy endings.

Sliding off the bed in my white nightgown, I glanced at the clock to see if I could leave my room. Mom and Dad have been waiting on the stork for a new baby brother. They said I wasn't allowed to come downstairs all night long—*the stork works the night shift, apparently.*

That was so hard, too, because I liked my midnight sneaky-snacks. I had a fun little hiding spot, right in the kitchen that Mom doesn't even know about. The best part of all, it keeps popping up with new candy all the time.

It's like magic, and magic is really awesome. Especially when Dad shows me his armor, he just wills it out—just like I do with my wings—and, BOOM, right on his body. He has this amazing sword, but it's so sharp that I'm not allowed to touch it.

Mom gets super cranky when he shows me his battle armor. *She gets cranky, like, a lot.*

Dad likes to watch me when I'm in the kitchen. He has this little smile on his face when I get near my hiding spot, so I can't go near it when he is awake.

He knows I have a secret stash, but I would never tell him where it is. In fact, I might have to change it really soon, so he doesn't steal it.

I pranced downstairs, not taking notice of my wings banging the stairwell all the way down. I squeaked, covering my mouth with both my hands. Mom hated it when I didn't put my wings away in the house.

It wasn't my fault they had a mind of their own. They just flutter when I get really happy, and then when I get all sad, they droop like those cute little killer whales' fins when they're kept in captivity.

Those poor whales.

Willing my wings back into my body, I tiptoed down the stairs. My parents' room was on the main level of the house because Dad has to leave suddenly sometimes. He's an archangel—*the coolest job*—and he has to listen to whatever his boss, Zeus, says.

Tiptoeing by my parents' room, I scooted into the large kitchen. Mom had all the best cooking equipment. She loved to cook and her favorite thing to make was double-chocolate cake with strawberry drizzle. It's my favorite, and she makes it when I argue too much about wanting to go outside.

Rubbing my hands together, I did a little booty shake before I opened the big box of prunes that secretly held my stash. The doorbell chimed, and my box of not-prunes went flying in the air before landing in the sink.

Gasping, I shrunk down to the floor, which was pristine white, just like everything else in this house—except all the greenery Mom kept everywhere.

Do you know how long it takes to water all the plants in the morning? It takes forever!

The doorbell rang again, but I stayed silent. Those were the rules: I could not leave the house without Mom or Dad, I couldn't answer the door, and I couldn't have friends, which made me sad. They said the world out there was crazy, with so much evil that I couldn't even imagine. They said it was worse than when Hans tricked Anna, but now, I'm thinking, *maybe it was worse than that little deer who just lost his mom.*

That poor baby deer!

But I had a wish, and that wish was for me to step out of here—*alone.* Mom always made me wear these itchy cloaks over my face, and no one ever noticed me! I didn't like wearing a cloak. I wanted to feel the sunshine on my face, but she said I could get skin cancer.

I didn't know gods got skin cancer, but apparently, they do.

When I first learned how to fly, she made me go out at night with Dad. It was so dark that I kept flying into poles, and I had a black eye for an entire hour! I cried and cried until Dad argued with Mom about how silly it was for me to fly at night, especially when it was so hard to see.

For a moment, Mom's eyes filled with regret, until her irrational feelings flooded over her again.

'There are too many dangers. Better a black eye than some demon taking her down to the pits of Tartarus.'

I didn't know what any of that was, but if it was worse than a black eye, I didn't want it 'cause it really hurt.

The doorbell chimed again, shaking me from my thoughts. Finally, a letter toppled through the slot. It was slightly aflame, but the paper had yet to burn.

Oh goodie, more magic!

I crawled over, peeking through the mail slot to make sure the mailman was gone. He doesn't know me, but I know him. The neighbor's pegasus begs him for sugar cubes every day, and when he forgets, the pegasus bites him right on the tushie! I snorted back a laugh.

It was a funny animal. When Mom and Dad aren't looking, I throw my carrots and celery out the window and it neighs happily.

I'm glad someone liked vegetables because I certainly didn't. Yuck!

I really wanted a pet, just like a pegasus, but Mom said no, *'they will poop all over the house.'*

Returning to the letter—still aflame—and touching it a few times to make sure it wouldn't burn my freshly painted pearl nails, I flipped it over.

To the soul-bonded couple, Goddess Hera and Archangel Michael

It was written in beautiful calligraphy lettering that shone when the light hit it at a certain angle. Mom and Dad always let me open the mail.

It was like opening presents on Christmas... except this was just a letter, so there weren't fun presents inside.

Ripping it open, the flaming envelope fell to the floor, turning to a light powder of ash before finally disappearing. "That's amazing," I whispered, my foot swishing the floor to feel for remnants of the ash.

I read its contents, examining the black stenciled drawing of a massive palace, with a three-headed dog on the letterhead.

From the delighted parents, Hades, God of the Underworld, and Ember, Goddess of Empathy and Bonding.

"Whoooa!" I held up the letter to the light. The dog was simply adorable, and the palace was the darkest thing I had ever seen. Black wasn't anywhere around the Celestial Kingdom, so this was exciting. My finger traced the slightly raised lines.

"Ugh, focus." I finished reading it, and I found that it was an invitation to a baby announcement with a party.

They had a baby! Babies were so cute, but I have never seen one up close, and I have never been to a party! I wonder if Mom would let me go? If it was up to Dad, he would let me do lots of things, but Dad tells me a lot that he is 'whipped' or his 'balls are on the fridge.' I never found a whip in the house, and there were no balls on top of the fridge, so I don't know what he was talking about.

Anyway, I could do two fun things at once, if Mom was in a good enough mood to let me go. She was always in a good mood in the mornings. Maybe we can all go!

I ran to Mom and Dad's bedroom door—*which I am not allowed to open.*

I have to knock really loud so they can hear because sometimes, they wrestle. Mom is super loud when she wrestles. Sometimes I have to turn up a movie all the way.

Knocking three times, I heard Dad's voice, "What?"

He sounded out of breath.

"Sorry, did I wake you up?"

"No, I've been up.," He choked back a labored laugh.

"Oh, okay." I pulled at the hem of my short nightgown, fiddling with it, still holding the letter in my other hand. "I was wondering—" I started.

"Yes!" my mom squealed.

My eyes brightened. *Did she read my mind?*

"So can I just g—?"

"YES! YES!" she moaned loudly, and I heard a thud on the other side of the door.

It sounds like Mom is winning.

I jumped up and down squealing, and my wings flew out of my body too quickly, causing a small vase to crash to the floor.

Whoops! I'll clean that later.

"Yippee!" Running up the stairs, I changed into my prettiest, fingertip-length, white dress because Mom said I looked best in white. I found some baby's breath flowers and wove them into a small crown to put on my head. The white flowers popped against my dark hair. Dashing a bit of glitter around my cheeks and checking my face to make sure it was clean, I ran back down the stairs, leaving the mess I made on the floor.

Checking myself in the mirror one last time and fixing the crazy curl that liked to curve around my neck, I took a large breath. For the first time, I was going to feel the sun on my skin, *and not the rough texture of that stupid cape.*

Mom didn't bring it up, so neither would I!

My smile brightened as I opened the door to the clear, blue sky. "Yes!" I sighed heavily, shutting the door and taking flight to the nearest portal to the Underworld.

Lucifer

"Where in Tartarus have you been?" I shut the door to my bedroom where my father was sitting on the bed with a scowl on his face. "Do you know what time it is, Lucifer? It's six in the damn morning, and you were gone all night! Were you off screwing some slutty demon?"

I growled, my hands turning black with cracks of red magma between them. "Don't fucking start with me, old man." Large, purple flames engulfed my hands, ready to fight against my father. His face instantly fell as he sagged his shoulders and sat back down on the bed.

"I shouldn't have raised my voice." His hand rubbed his mouth. "Your mother is worried, and in turn, it makes me worry. Where have you been?"

Willing my hands clean, I walked to the wardrobe, stripping off my bloody clothes and wrapping a towel around my waist. Father patiently waited, knowing I was calming the fire inside.

My anger was only worsening as the days passed; my own father had to control his just to make sure I didn't lose control. If I did, who knows what would happen to my family? My father shouldn't have to do that. He shouldn't have to calm his son; he should be able to punish me, to teach me a lesson.

I rubbed my face with both hands, sitting in my desk chair. "Sorry, Father." Father turned to me, his eyes softening. The internal battle within me was a losing one, and we both knew it. He knew how serious this had become, and we had both started preparations.

"I won't be able to control the rage much longer. It's best if we implement the plan we discussed."

Father shook his head, pulling his freshly styled hair. "No, I refuse to believe it has come to that. You are still so young. You have to fight it."

Abruptly standing from my chair, my black wings flew out of my body; the fire tickling the tips of the feathers grew brighter. "You don't understand—I can't! I thirst for blood; I hunger to destroy everything in my path. Who knows when I will slip and hurt the innocent? What if I went to Earth? What if I started the Apocalypse?"

"That is a human fairy tale. It's not real," he calmly stated.

"Maybe it is!" I chuckled manically. "Maybe I am the one destined to start it, and that is why you *will* lock me in Tartarus, right next to your father!"

Chapter 3

Lucifer

My father couldn't look at me. His smoke tendrils wrapping around his body said it all. He was angry and unable to control the emotions floating through him.

I knew I struck a nerve. Father tried so hard to keep his cool. He shouldn't have to, not when I'm his son. He should be allowed to punish me, to beat me into obeying like the young god I was, but now my power was equal to his, something unfathomable to imagine for the God of Hell, especially as the first-born child of Kronos.

"Lucifer," my father said calmly, his eyes glowing red, "you still have time; I believe this. If I lock you up now, what am I supposed to tell your mother? She asks for you constantly. I already have to lie and tell her you are working somewhere other than that pit."

My wings retracted with a gust of wind, several feathers falling to the ground and turning to ash. "I'm sure you will think of something." I mindlessly turned my back, my hand now on the doorframe of the bathroom.

There was no hope left for me. Even now, I desired to rip off my own father's head. Who is it to say that one day, I wouldn't go through with it?

I killed three guards coming up the side entrance because I was angry that I had to return to face a bunch of celestial beings. They only wished to kiss my father's ass and please my mother, hoping she would reveal their mates. My rage was uncontrollable. Sometimes I wondered if there were demons, witches, or dark magic possessing me, fighting for dominance of the body I no longer controlled.

"After the baby announcement, then. There's no need to spoil your mother's little show."

I chuckled darkly. The door was about to close until my father caught it with his foot, exposing himself to the bright light of the bathroom. "When your mother finds your mate, we will release you, and you will be back with our family, Lucifer."

Shaking my head, I leaned back against the cold, tiled wall. "I'll be too far gone for that, and you know it."

No woman, even my mate, could come near me. I'd destroy her before she got close.

Pushing the door closed, my father's usually stoic face held discontent. I tried not to let it get to this point, but who was to say what I was doing was working? Ares had stopped by many times, trying to help. He could calm the beast within my father because he gained a wolf after he mated with my mother.

Unfortunately, there was no beast inside me; it was only myself that I could not control.

The steamy shower soothed the aches in my body. The blood ran down the drain, staining the pristine, white tiles a shade of rustic red. My hands continued to rub my face as if to wake me from this reoccurring nightmare, but it never did. I always awoke to the same nightmare, no matter how many calming techniques I utilized.

Candles, music, meditation—none of it worked, it all just made me more... angry. Everything about me was steeped in anger; I had the constant itch to spill blood from the next person I saw. I could barely stand to be in this palace, even though my mother did her best to sate me.

Switching off the shower, I wrapped the towel around my waist and stomped to the closet. Mother had already picked out the matching suit that all her boys would wear for the day's event—black on black with a red tie. Mother thought it was cute how we all looked like 'mafia men.'

I chuckled to myself. *We are far more dangerous than that.*

Straightening my tie, slicking back my usually unruly hair with one last run-through of the mirror to look presentable, I stepped back to open the door only to find Loki looking straight at me.

"I know," he whispered. Both of his eyes squinted towards me. I kept my hand tightened on the handle.

"Know what?" I growled. "That you were adopted?" His bright eyes widened, his lower lip wobbled, and he ran down the hallway screaming for Mother.

The poor kid can give it, but he sure can't take it.

Keeping my back straight and my body ridged, I headed down the hall, following my brother. The now lightened walls of the palace gave a faux image of the Golden Light Palace of Bergarian. Mother said the outside of the palace—the dark brick and stone—could stay the same, but if she was to live here, she needed some light.

Father always tended to Mother. Anything she wanted, desired, or even thought about getting, he would give it to her. He gave her the world. I couldn't imagine myself doing that for anyone. I was too concentrated on my own problems.

The clicking of my shoes landed right in front of the closed door of my parents' room. Loki was sniffing, pretending to cry to gain Mother's sympathy.

That wouldn't work. Mother was too smart to be conned by him.

"Loki, I won't hear any more of it," Mother scolded him. She was brushing her hair as Nora, our werewolf personal assistant who mated to my father's right-hand demon, Loukas, stood beside the vanity mirror, making faces at Loki. He quickly smiled, and Mother straightened his tie and suit.

"You look handsome, Loki. Now leave your brother alone." She winked at him. Loki walked out with a mischievous look on his face, his feet bringing him into a run. He must have come up with another wicked plan to terrorize the more of the palace's help. I scoffed, approaching my mother from behind as she finished her makeup, trying to hide the exhaustion under her eyes.

My mother was beautiful. Her long, blonde hair and her green eyes matched those of her mother, Charlotte, but the fierceness in her heart was matched only by my grandfather, Wesley, Alpha to the Black Claw Pack on Earth.

"Luci," my mother cooed.

She was the only one allowed to call me by that name. Not even Father could try. When Mother said it, it only reminded me of the times of my youth when I didn't worry about imploding.

"You look so handsome. Thank you for getting dressed up and being willing to make an appearance. It means the world to me."

Her hands cupped my cheeks, finally pulling one of my hands to her lips and kissing it gently.

How Mother was cursed with a son like me, I'll never know.

Father stood holding Lilith. He swayed her back and forth, singing the same human lullaby Mother used to sing to me, "Hush Little Baby."

"You look just like your father," Mother whispered, "so handsome and strong. I mean that: you are strong, and I know we will get through this. I'm going to try to—"

"Mother." I pulled one hand from my cheek. "It's alright; I've got everything taken care of."

Mother's brows knitted in confusion. "You-you do?" She leaned toward me. Mother's eyes were steady on my face while I felt my father's heated glare from the periphery.

"Yes. I won't be a danger to anyone anymore, starting tomorrow. Just trust me, alright?" I smiled at her as she embraced me. Her head barely reached the upper part of my chest when I held her close, kissing the top of her head.

"I've been so worried... so very worried." She buried herself further. "I don't know what I would do if you weren't in my life. My family means everything to me—*you* mean everything to me. Once I find your mate in the Sphere, I'll make sure to pair you together and quickly seek her out, even if it is against the rules. I'll do anything to save my son."

The Sphere was a dark-blue orb that Selene, the Moon Goddess, used to pair souls. Now that Selene had gone on her own quest to find her mate, living the life as a werewolf, Mother had assumed the position. Mother had become so powerful in a short amount of time that, if souls were in the same room, she could pair them by pulling on an invisible golden string, which none of us could see, and leading them to each other.

The ominous emotions rose within my body. I tried to pull them back, deep into my soul, where they belonged.

She would never find my mate, and even if she did, I was too far gone. I stepped back from Mother, trying not to get angry.

Father, sensing my tension, spoke to me through my mind, *"Deep breaths, son."*

"Thank you." I gave her a tight-lipped smile. That smile brightened my mother's face ten shades.

I would give her the world; I just couldn't give her me.

"Luuuuciiiii!" Loki sang as he ran back into the room with a handful of whipped cream.

My fist tightened again, turning black and red instantly. Embers seared into the carpet as I watched the menace approach me.

"Loki! You do not call him that! That is my name to use! Now get over here so we can make you look presentable again!" Loki stood still, except for the handful of cream he got from some dessert on the buffet table. "And where is your nanny? Where did she go? What am I even paying her for?" Mother scolded.

Father closed his eyes and held back a smile. "Looks like Loki got another one. What is that now, fifteen?" Father chuckled.

"Seventeen." Loki smiled proudly with s mouthful of cream.

Mother glowered at Loki with her hands on her hips. The red jewels sparkled around her black silk gown. Her body was perfectly shaped once again, even after having Lilith just yesterday. "Where did you get that whipped cream? You shouldn't eat that! It is for our guests!"

"But it's good! Nora might be mad though." He licked the last bit off his thumb. "The pink frosting is the best!"

Father, still holding baby Lilith, lifted Loki in the air with one wave of his hand. Loki squeaked as he hung in the air. "Do you need to visit Tartarus?" Father's eyebrow raised as he pointed at my troublemaker of a brother.

"N-no," Loki choked out with a look of pure horror on his face.

My brother, the God of Mischief, hated the thought of torture. He was in for the play. He only killed the demon nannies because it was funny, and they could respawn in Father's demon soul pool. The deaths he gave them were quick and merciful—if you could call it that.

"That's enough of that, then." Father put down Loki gently. "I expect the best behavior out of you while the Celestial Kingdom and your mother's pack are here to witness the naming of the baby." Hades wrapped Lilith tighter. She cooed, nuzzling her head right into the crook of Father's arm.

"What about Lucifer? Aren't you going to tell him not to kill anyone like he did last time?"

Counting to ten, I strode over to the window that overlooked the front palace gates, my hands blackening as I tried to calm the fire within me.

The years have become torturous trying to stay calm around Loki, his incessant jokes and prods only brought out the darkness.

"I've just about had it, Loki." Mother slapped her hands to her thighs. "I know you crave attention because of the baby's arrival, but this isn't the way to go about it," Mother snapped. "Now, I love you, and I will make sure we have a movie night, just the two of us really soon, okay?" Loki's sniffs filled the room, and the fire in my hands weakened.

Father walked up to me, still carrying baby Lilith, and looked out over the front lawn as a few stragglers walked past the guards. His hand landed on my shoulder with a tight squeeze. "We are going to work this out. Even if you feel that strongly about being put down there, I will find a way to calm you. I believe the Fates are at least that kind."

I continued to stare at the lawn; the hellhounds were nothing but overgrown puppies to our family but remained the most ferocious guard hounds any world has ever seen to everyone else. Several of them sat by the edge of the sidewalk, keeping the visitors off the grass. That was their territory: the beautiful landscape that Mother had loved since the first time Father granted her the beautiful gardens of the palace.

"I promise you this, Lucifer, and I have never broken a promise." Lilith blew a raspberry with her mouth, having woken from her small nap in his arms. My eyes glanced towards her as her little, uncontrollable hand waved in the air.

How a soul so large inhabited such a tiny baby, I'll never under-stand. However, there were many things the Fates allowed that no one, not even the gods, ever would.

"Let's go. Your mother loves to show off her family." Father smiled, thinking of his mate.

Turning to walk with him, I caught a glimpse of something pure white with hints of gold. By the time I had fully turned around, it was gone—in the blink of an eye.

"Coming, son?" My heart leaped in my chest. It had never done that before. Rubbing my chest thoroughly, I walked with Father down the lit hallway. The lights became brighter and brighter as we approached the now, heavily pink, decorated ballroom. The balcony that we had arrived at had two winding staircases that met the guests below, both adorned in white marble, gold trimmings, and hints of red and black to maintain Father's traditional colors.

Mother stood at the forefront, smiling gratefully at the guests below. Loki stood under Mother's right hand, which lay on his shoulder. Father was beside her as he wrapped one hand around her waist and the other around his daughter.

"You speak." My father nudged her.

"This is the Underworld. Aren't you in charge?" She giggled, holding in her laughter.

"Not since you have arrived, my love. Now, do the honors." Father rolled his eyes. "We can always have them come another day. I know you are tired. They wouldn't be disappointed," he grumbled.

Father hated the spectacle, but with Mother having grown up in a werewolf pack, it was tradition to present the baby for all the wolves to admire.

"I'll make it through." Her sigh was heavy. The bags under her eyes were still visible, even the heavy amount of concealer could not hide her fatigue.

"A nap afterward, then?" Father said hopefully, raising a brow.

"Only if you mean one with sleeping, and not your type of 'nap.'" Mother playfully tapped his forearm.

"Gross, Mom." Loki rolled his eyes. "You just pooped out a baby and you are already thinking about—" Father slapped Loki on the back of the head.

"Respect your mother! Now you get to clean out the hell-hounds' bedding after the party."

Loki groaned, slapping his forehead with his palm. He then leaned against the banister with his elbow, his head resting heavily on his hand. "Are we done yet? Can I have dessert?"

Chapter 4

Uriel

It didn't take long for me to find the portal at the center of the Celestial Kingdom. Angels walked in and out of it like it was nothing. The large, stone archway was decorated with lightly colored granite. It looked like a mirror that was twenty feet wide!

I stood behind the corner of the bakery Mom likes to visit on Sunday mornings to plan my studies for the week. It was small with only a few tables, and Mom said their carrot cake was delicious. I licked my lips, peeking inside, wanting to taste something sweet and savory.

The itch in my wings made me flutter as I remembered the real reason I was out here: *to go to a party! A party that will have a lot of free snacks!*

My wings fluttered again, and I noticed they didn't look at all like the other angels' wings. Many female angels displayed large white and ivory wings, while mine held a hint of gold at the tips. I inched forward, only to garner a few stares before they continued along like there wasn't a care in the world. I let out a sigh.

No one was out to get me. There was no evil out here in the open, not with so many angels around.

I was just ordinary, which was fine with me. The cloak that would normally hide me from prying eyes was heavy and cumbersome.

Having people react when I smiled at them was so much better than them not seeing me at all.

Once I reached the portal, I watched how people walked in and out. They stepped through so effortlessly, and those exiting didn't even blink.

"Need some help?" a smooth voice spoke from beside me. She wasn't dressed in the normal robes or wraps made of fine linen that everyone else was wearing. She had on a light-tan pantsuit with silver trimmings, and her hair was cut short in a cute, pixie cut.

"Hello!" My eyes widened. I had never talked to anyone other than my mom and dad, but the excitement of meeting someone new overshadowed my shyness.

"Are you trying to go through the portal?" The glint in her eye and the smirk on her face seemed friendly enough. I nodded, giving her a bright smile.

"I would love to help you." Her tall form bent over. Her beautiful face was blemish-free, and her movements were so eloquent and fluid. The reading glasses perched atop her head gave her a studious look as she continued to scrutinize me.

"Can you please tell me who your parents are?" Her smile brightened causing mine to follow suit.

"Of course! My parents are Goddess Hera and Archangel Michael." I beamed proudly at my parents' titles.

The beautiful woman's eyes widened slightly, licking her lips while rubbing her pointed chin. "I see," she chuckled. "I knew it! Those sneaky little bastards," she whispered to herself.

Oopsie, she said a bad word.

"May I ask your name?" I picked at my fingers, waiting for her reply.

"Of course, dear, if you can tell me yours?"

"I'm Uriel!"

"Good girl. Now let's get you closer to the portal, and I can show you how to get where you want to go."

Before I could remind her that she was supposed to tell me her name, she placed me in front of the reflective portal. The mirror waved slightly as bodies moved through, but mostly, it stood still.

"In your mind, visualize your destination... may I ask where you are going?" Her eyebrow raised.

"To the Underworld, there's a party!"

Letting out a soft laugh, she covered her mouth. "Oh, this is going to be interesting. I wouldn't want to miss it! My name is Athena, and you, child, can accompany me. I will help escort you there so that you arrive on time."

I clapped my hands excitedly, prancing right up to the portal's shimmery surface. "You will? That would be so great! I don't get out much, and I was so worried I would get lost!"

Athena's eyes squinted, looking around us. "I'm sure you don't, and I think today might rectify that, hmm?"

I nodded quickly, sticking my finger to the mirror's shimmery surface. *Squishy*

Grabbing my hand and placing it in the crook of her arm, we walked through the portal together. I didn't even have to think before we immediately came out on the other side.

"You might feel light-headed your first time." My hand went to my forehead to slow down the spinny feeling.

As my eyes fluttered open, I found that we had arrived in the Underworld! It was significantly darker with a red light source instead of the bright, yellow one that lit the sky in the Celestial Kingdom. The ground was mostly deep-red dirt until a cement pathway came into view. Small deep-green bushes with beautiful red roses outlined the path, covered with tiny fireflies.

"It's a different kind of pretty." I leaned down, pressing my finger to the flower. It wasn't real; it was fake, but it was the realest, fake plant ever.

Athena observed my behavior, clearly amused by me sniffing the fake flowers. "You said that you have never left your home before. Would your mother and father not let you out?"

I shook my head. "Mom said it was too dangerous outside, but I got an invitation in the mail today while they were waiting for the stork in their room. When I asked, Mom screamed, 'yes, yes!' I was so excited because I never even dreamed that she would let me go! I got dressed right away, and then I left as soon as I could before she changed her mind."

"Holy shit," Athena whispered. She paused in the middle of the path, placing her hands on her knees as she caught her breath. "What are you, the goddess of, little one?"

"Innocence and Grace," I hummed, watching these gigantic dogs run around the gated palace. Their bodies were as big as mine!

"The Fates clearly want to watch the realms burn," Athena chuckled nervously.

"What about after the party? Have you thought about what will happen then?" Athena had my arm held in the crook of her arm again—*probably to keep me from stopping every five seconds, but I haven't been outside this long before, especially in such a different place.*

"I don't know, but I would love to travel. I've read all about Earth and Bergarian, but I haven't read about this place," I hummed, slightly annoyed. "It's probably because it's dark. I used to be afraid of the dark, so I guess Mom was just looking out for me."

Athena stopped in her tracks. Her tall form leaned over as my head fell back to meet her gaze. "And do you think your mother was doing you a favor by confining you inside the house rather than showing you how to maneuver around the worlds?"

My open mouth closed sharply, and my eyes shifted to the dark path in front of us. The dogs lined up in rows along the path, hiding the pretty grass and flowers on the other side.

Mom had taught me a lot during the time I spent locked in the house. I itched to go outside, and there were days I would cry on the floor like a child because I couldn't go out. Then I learned that even if I threw a tantrum, I still wouldn't get my way, so I just complied. I stopped fighting. I stopped asking permission to explore the outside world; instead, I did what Mom asked because it made her happy.

She was happy and I enjoyed seeing it. I really did. But did it only hurt me?

"You are a smart girl, Uriel; I can sense it. Did she teach you anything about the gods?"

I bit my lip, pulling at the now faded lip-gloss that I had applied earlier. "She did." I rubbed my ballet-toed flat into the textured cement. "She taught me all about the powers the gods had, but she never told me their names."

Athena exhaled harshly, "And you did not question her?"

I shrugged my shoulders. "It wouldn't have made a difference. She refused to tell me."

"I am the Goddess of Wisdom and War," I gasped loudly.

She was my favorite! She was so smart, and she was a woman! She could go into battle and beat up all sorts of people. My eyes felt like they would fall out of my head and land at my feet from my elation.

"Athena, you're the Goddess of Wisdom and War?" She nodded, smiling at me. "You were my favorite! You are so smart! You also specialize in practical reasoning and looking at things from every angle, even in everyday speech!"

Athena smiled, her hand petting my head. "That's right, and I already know that your mind is special. Did you know that?"

I tilted my head to the side, rubbing my itchy nose. "I-I don't know about that. Mom says I still have a lot to learn before I can ever be on my own."

Athena chuckled. "You are not a child," she insisted, crossing her arms. "You are smart, and you are most certainly old enough to walk around all the realms if you desire. In fact, when we return to the Celestial Kingdom, I will demand that you spend some time with me."

"You will?" I clapped my hands excitedly.

Athena only nodded her head before grabbing my arm and pulling me to the massive, dark palace. As we neared, my thoughts trailed deeper than I ever thought they could.

Did my mother play with my mind to make me feel inadequate all these years, to believe I couldn't linger in any of the realms? Such little faith she had in me. She tutored me herself. I graduated from the equivalent of a human high school at the age of eleven. I even did all Mother's budgeting for our house and her job because I get bored idling at home all day.

Did she think I would make a mistake outside? Away from her? I didn't typically make mistakes; I always did everything perfectly, thoroughly, and neatly. How was I to know whether I could succeed if I never tried? In the movies I watched, so many children made mistakes regularly, and they figured things out on their own. Now, at the age of twenty-five, I don't think I've ever been given the chance to navigate life on my terms.

My bottom lip stuck out, prompting Athena to squeeze my hand. "Don't think about it too much right now, Uriel. It will work itself out by the end of the day." She chuckled again like she was keeping a secret hidden.

The dogs stood up, backs straight with large, sharp teeth protruding from their maws. Some growled while others barked at the angels, gods, and supernaturals passing by. Many flinched away, but when I came close, the aggressive noises stopped. Expecting them to bark, I braced myself against Athena, but they didn't. Instead, they merely gazed at me, like overgrown puppies.

"Hi, puppies!" I whisper-yelled to them as Athena led me inside.

Large, red men with horns popping out of their heads looked down at me, carrying long, sharp obsidian spears. They were so tall and seemed intimidating as they stared down at me.

"Hi!" I waved as we walked past.

"Who are they?" I whispered to Athena, becoming utterly aware of the large room full of people and species that I had only ever read about.

"Those are demons. They reside here in the Underworld to serve their king, the father of the baby we're celebrating, Hades."

My mouth opened to ask another question, but was silenced by the presence of a woman, who I assumed was the baby's mother, Ember, at the top of a grand staircase. The staircase was gold and silver, and it was adorned with hints of red and black. My hand tightened around Athena's arm as Ember stood by the intimidating, slightly scary-looking King of the Underworld who was cradling a teeny, tiny baby.

"The baby!" I cooed, a little too loudly. Stares were cast my way. Looking around, I just waved, smiled, and whispered, "Sorry," before my eyes caught hold of another man standing on the balcony.

He was the same height as Hades with cold eyes; his fists gripped the balcony railing so hard it looked as if it would break. My heart fluttered at the sight of him. I couldn't pull my eyes away from him as he stood with a stiff back and clenched jaw.

He looked so pretty.

Like, really pretty.

Maybe he needs a friend.

Chapter 5

Uriel

I continued to squeeze through the crowd, practically disregarding Queen Ember standing on the balcony.

The cake on the table looked too delicious to be ignored, and no one even noticed it—except that boy on the balcony.

My wings were tucked in close to my body, but I still bumped someone gently on their shoulder.

"I'm so sorry," I whispered. My wings shuddered, I was too nervous to pull them inside my body, but the large man in front of me appeared unfazed as he looked down at me with bright, blue, brilliant eyes.

"It's quite alright. Are you okay?"

This man was really muscular, wearing a light tan suit, and had flowing, white hair that graced his shoulders. The white stubble on his face was a shade darker than the hair on his head. His hands steadied my shoulders, looking me in the eye.

"You look familiar." He tilted his head. "Yet, I have never seen you before. I thought I knew all the angels and gods. What is your name?"

I bit my lip, trying to back away.

"It's alright, I won't hurt you." His eyes softened, retracting his hands from my shoulders. "You just remind me of someone, someone I used to care about." The white-haired man's shoulders slumped, wrinkling his nicely pressed suit.

"My name is Uriel." I extended my hand for him to shake. I saw the gesture many times before on human shows, and it was used to greet someone new.

He chuckled, engulfing my small hand with his large one. "Nice to meet you, my dear. I'm Zeus."

I smiled back at him, nodding my head. "Great to meet you, but I have to go now. That cake looks delicious!" I turned to leave, but his hand didn't release mine.

"Who are your parents?" he questioned before letting go.

"Hera and Michael," I chirped.

Zeus' face paled, and he immediately turned to walk away.

I bit my lip, thinking that I should go after him to make sure he was alright, but a new tray filled with sweet honeysuckles was calling my name.

I can check on him later.

I tiptoed around everyone, hovering close to the ground so my wings wouldn't graze anyone else. Once I reached the table, the speech ended, and people began to talk amongst themselves.

There were so many treats: sponge cakes, dark choco-late—*which is nasty because they don't put enough sugar in it*—honeysuckle flowers, cupcakes, and many other things I had never seen before. There were also many different kinds of meats and vegetables. I internally gagged at those.

I could bring a few carrots back with me, just to feed the pegasus at our neighbor's house.

As I glanced at the last table, I saw an entire roasted pig! I slapped my hand over my mouth to keep from screaming.

The head is still on it!

Turning to another table, the demon beside it was smiling with his fangs sticking out of his mouth. I turned my whole body away, holding my plate of honeysuckles with extra honey. Now, I was face-to-face with Queen Ember.

She was the same size as me! So far, everyone else here was so much taller, but we almost matched! I giggled.

"Hello, I'm Ember; I don't think we've met," she greeted, offering her hand.

The Queen was dressed in a beautiful, black gown with shimmering gems woven into the bodice. They were so sparkly it took everything I had not to touch them. Her hand was still outstretched, and my mind quickly zoomed back to the present as I extended my hand to meet hers.

"Hi, I'm Uriel." My voice came out sweetly.

I wanted to make friends, so I had to make a perfect impression.

"I've never been to one of these functions before, so I don't really know anyone here." My voice and head dipped low.

It was rather embarrassing, really. I didn't know anyone other than Athena, and she was talking to her other friends across the room. Everyone had friends here, and I was here all by myself.

I gripped the plate tighter, wrapping my other arm around my waist for comfort. "But I'm here now, and I can honestly say, this is the best party I have ever been to!"

That would make her feel happy because it really was the best party that I had ever been to—the only party, but she didn't know that.

"I'm glad to hear that." Ember beamed up at the King of the Underworld who was standing beside her. He had a concerned look on his face as he studied me, which made me shrink back a little.

He still held the baby, so he couldn't be all that bad, right?

The baby made a cooing noise, and his attention diverted back to the swaddle in his arms, giving me a moment of relief.

"Are you with your parents?" Ember pried. "I would love to meet them and demand to know why we haven't met such a lovely lady like yourself before!" She giggled, nudging King Hades.

I noticed a drop of honey falling off my plate. Grabbing it with my finger, I scooped it up and put it right in my mouth, scraping it clean with my teeth and creating a popping sound as my finger exited.

"Oh, they weren't able to come, so they said I could." I smiled back.

I recalled the big Zeus man and his reaction to hearing my parents' names. *Would they do the same?*

One way to find out.

"The Goddess Hera and Archangel Michael are my parents."

Hades pulled a bottle from his suit pocket and gave it to Lilith, the tiny little girl in his arms. I stood on my tiptoes trying to see her, but Ember's questions kept interrupting me.

"How old are you, dear?" Ember's voice wasn't quite as friendly now. Instead, it was more curious.

"Twenty-five," I hummed, still looking at the baby. "Mom and Dad are at home waiting for their baby," I said, offering more information than requested.

"Hera is pregnant? Again?" Ember said excitedly.

"Pregnant?" I questioned, tilting my head. "No, no, they are waiting for the stork to bring me a baby brother or sister. I have to wait in my room every night because they think that I will scare the stork off." I laughed, putting the honeysuckle in my mouth.

Hades' eyebrow raised, looking at Ember. I could tell they were having a silent conversation, but I wasn't sure how.

Maybe they could mind-link like wolves can.

"What are you the goddess of, exactly?" Hades spoke to me. The power oozed from his body, freezing me in place.

I bit my cheek, trying not to cry at his scowling face. "Innocence," I muttered.

Hades looked at me and raised his eyebrows again before pulling Ember aside for a private conversation. Hades whispered harshly to Ember, "Don't do this. It will only create problems right now!"

I shrugged my shoulders, not understanding the conversation and not wanting to engage in whatever they were talking about. I wasn't feeling very welcome anymore, anyway. My mind returned to the puppies outside.

Maybe there was a garden to go look at?

"This will be a shit show!" Hades hissed loudly.

Another bad word! Dad said that word before, and Mom threatened to wash his mouth out with soap. I would never say such a word because tasting soap would be disgusting.

"Mother." A deep voice whipped through the air to my ears. It was velvety smooth with a hint of roughness around the edges.

Lucifer

"*Come down here, please, Luci,*" my mother's voice traveled through the link. She was standing alone with Father and an angel whose back faced toward me.

I swear, if she is trying to introduce me to a girl, I might just throw flames across the room, breaking my promise of a smooth-sailing party.

Several wolves at the bottom of the landing watched every stride I took down the stairs. They started to giggle incessantly. I took deep breaths. Using the breathing exercises I learned, I continued to try to cool the boiling blood in my body. When I all seemed lost, I caught the sweet floral smell of gardenias.

I hadn't smelled gardenias since we visited the Black Claw Pack when I was a child. Mother had taken us to celebrate Christmas. Persephone's powers of spring growth willed the flowers around my grandmother's house to grow year-round, despite the cold winter temperatures. I had always been attracted to the smell. It reminded me of my youth and the innocence that I had lost so long ago.

My boiling blood dropped to a low simmer as the fresh, sweet smell calmed the beast inside my soul.

"Mother," I spoke to her. She stared up at me like I was a miracle to behold, but I was anything but that.

"Honey, I want to introduce you to someone."

Here it goes; she is going to try to force me to make a friend. She wouldn't dare introduce me to my mate in the state I was in, would she?

Then again, she didn't know how bad off I really was.

My jaw tightened; Father told me to remain calm through our link, "*Calm. Calm yourself. You are doing great.*" His encouraging words helped me stand up straight, loosening the grip on my tightened fists.

The girl in front of me was short, just like my mother. Something about that had me sigh with relief. I liked that look on a woman: someone shorter than me. She flung her dark hair across her shoulder, hitting me with a wave of that glorious, floral scent. It wasn't overpowering; it was just the right amount of her and gardenias.

"Hi!" she spoke happily. "I'm Uriel!" Her face was pale, with no hint of the sun's rays having touched her porcelain skin, while mine held a tan from the bright fires of Tartarus.

My parents were holding hands tightly beside me. I could feel my father's anxiety roll off him in waves.

My breath hitched at her beauty. No other woman has ever made an impression on me such as this. Her long hair tickled the tips of her hipbones and her wings sported beautiful golden tips. Her wings were not as large as an angel's but were still suitable for flying. Lost for words, I continued to stare into her enchanting, blue eyes.

I reached into her mind, trying to uncover any ill-intention or future sins. I could find none. She had no ill intent towards anyone and no sins or deeds to warrant punishing. She was purer than anyone in this entire room.

Her head tilted to the side, waiting for me to answer.

"*Fuck, son, give her your name,*" Father spoke to me.

I cleared my throat. "I'm Lucifer." Uriel sat the plate full of honey on the table and rubbed her bare arms together as if she was cold.

My body reacted in an instant, emitting my heat to warm the surrounding air. I wanted to warm her body; she looked so cold.

Fuck.

"I'm the Goddess of Innocence. Everyone has been asking me my title today, so I guess that I should ask you. What are you the god of?"

I was cursed with destruction, the drive to destroy everything in my path. Part of me liked it, but I did not like the lack of control that filled me in its wake.

My body stiffened, but the fire did not fill my fingers. I was embarrassed—for the first time in my life.

I didn't want to tell her.

"That's okay! You don't have to tell me!" she quickly spoke. "I'm going to go outside in the garden to see the puppies." Uriel's hand went to mine and shook it frantically.

"Whoa! You tickle!" She lightly snorted.

After she dropped my hand, I looked at it in shock. The warmth and the fire instantly left my hand at our broken contact. I already missed it.

Fuck. She was my damn mate.

Uriel waved to my parents and me, sashaying her hips through the crowd and out the door.

"That went well," Father grumbled, now burping Lilith on his shoulder. Mother was grinning and bouncing foot to foot. I didn't want to break my stare on the door where Uriel had just left.

My body was pulling me towards her, the strange girl that piqued my interest. I wanted to know more about her. Despite my decision to lock myself in Tartarus tomorrow, I wanted to know what she was like, and what I would miss.

Putting one foot in front of the other, I charged across the room as the crowd parted before me, not daring to touch the God of Destruction. Athena caught my eye. The pensive look on her face exposed her amusement while she rubbed her chin.

Her body turned abruptly, and she walked straight to my parents.

The clicks of my shoes echoed through the room. The she-wolves from my mother's pack watched me with steady eyes as I left through the garden door, following the white-dressed angel—*that was supposed to be mine.*

Chapter 6

Lucifer

S tepping out of the front palace doors, many of the guests continued to glare holes into my back. The heat of their stares only magnified my mission to find this girl and figure her out.

Surely, there was a spell cast on her; a spell that would use my emotions to cloud my judgment while they sought some sort of revenge against my family and me.

It was no secret that my father was, in fact, the God of Hell, but he wasn't evil like the souls he punished. After my mother was saved from a sex trafficking ring, Father sent his demonic soldiers to pose as humans to uncover several entire rings of darkened souls which they were allowed to feed upon. The soul eaters became Father's new favorite creation. They sucked the lives of corrupt humans and supernaturals, sending them straight to the doors of Hell for never-ending torture, bypassing the judgment table. Once in Hell, they received their very own private session with me.

Their lifeless bodies dropped to the floor with no detectable reason to explain their death to the humans. The demons then released the women and children held captive by these monsters and returned them to their homes. Mother helped with the entire operation when it first started. She and Father saved countless innocent lives.

Humans and supernaturals had become dauntless, no longer hiding in the dark, but operating in the open using simple code words and phrases. They believed that no one could uncover their heinous acts. It was a daily battle. The supernaturals knew my father was hunting them, but they did everything possible to continue their operations, selling and distributing sex slaves to buyers.

Could this Uriel be using her Innocence to make me believe she was my mate? It took my father years, thousands of years, to find my mother. Why would I find mine so quickly? Could I not see through her deception? Surely, my mother could discern the use of any sort of soul magic.

Uriel pranced down the cobblestone path, dancing with one foot on each rock. From afar, the hellhounds watched her skip down the trail, closer and closer to the sod. The thick grass was Mother's joy. She loved to walk through it barefoot in the morning, letting her wolf roam free and dancing in the garden.

Father had forbidden any demon, god, or goddess to walk on the grass. He only permitted his precious mate and her beloved hellhounds to feel the special grass under their paws.

The hellhounds encroached slowly. Being the silent predators they were, they pawed through the grass stealthily. Their mouths salivated, the drool visibly dripping from their teeth while I stood against the palace walls watching her. My soul called for me to grab her arm and rescue her from the impending danger, but that could be her plan. The clicking sounds of my thick rings knocking against each other sounded as my fingers tightened into a fist. I continued to fight my urge to protect her as three hellhounds approached the sidewalk where Uriel stood.

As the ferocious beasts neared her location, Uriel took notice of them and smiled before waving right in front of their deadly maws.

"Hi puppies!" she whispered enthusiastically.

Their growling ceased, and their large black heads tilted from one side to the other. One of their tongues lagged out of their mouth, licking their chops.

Reaching into her skirt pocket, she pulled out a piece of meat. "I brought you guys something," she whispered as if it was a big secret.

Their mouths watered even more as she broke it into three pieces.

"Here you go!" Tossing a piece up into the air for each hellhound, each one took a large chomp, catching it and licking their maws.

"What good boys you are!" As she began rubbing their heads, they all laid in the grass at her feet. Uriel hopped into the grass with them as they rolled onto their damn backs letting her rub their bellies.

I shook my head exasperatedly.

"You are such good little puppies! I wish I had a dog." Her lip pouted.

Loki walked up from behind, carrying a leg from the roasted pig. Taking a large bite, he smacked his lips as he spoke, "She's a genuine piece of work, huh?" Then he licked his fingers.

I stared down at him, curling my lip. I didn't like that he was making fun of her, but I didn't want him to know that. He might get the wrong idea. I was still figuring her out, making sure she wasn't some fraud.

"I mean, she just walked right up in here, not paying any attention to the evil glances all the hellhounds were making at her." He waved his hands around. "And she didn't even notice the supposedly, two hottest and highest-ranking wolf warriors, the twins Timmy and Tommy, who were staring her down like turkey on Thanksgiving Day. They were ready to lick her up from head to toe and stuff her with their—"

I grabbed Loki by the neck, tight enough to make him turn purple. Dropping the pig leg, his claws shot out of his nails and the horns on his head grew.

"Don't fucking talk about her like that!" I growled lowly so that she wouldn't hear. He smiled, trying to giggle.

"You are such a sick fuck!" I dropped him while he gasped for air.

"Didn't you know I like being choked?"

Groaning, I hit the back of my head on the wall. *Mother is going to have her hands full with him when his balls dropped.*

Uriel continued to rub on the hellhounds, not at all perturbed by their grotesque-looking form. Hellhounds could sense any sin, even the smallest ones. They fed off it before finally attacking the ones that fed them the sin.

She had none from the looks of it. Her white dress was now stained with deep-green patches from the lawn. She stood up, wiping her hands down her dress only to run across the lawn giggling moments later with her wings trailing behind her as she ran towards the garden.

"You gonna follow her?" Loki looked up at me, mischief in his eyes, digging in his pockets and finally putting a sucker in his mouth.

"Why don't you go say hello?" I muttered. "See what she's all about?"

Loki rubbed his hands together, rolling the sucker between his lips. "My pleasure." Rubbing his hands in mischief, he hopped off the stairs, sprinting towards the gardens after Uriel. Loki stepped only on the stoned path, careful not to fall into the grasses.

The hellhounds would never actually attack him, but they didn't like Loki either. There were too many times he had changed his body into that of an animal, such as a deer, tricking them into nearly attacking him. It scared the shit out of the hellhounds because they weren't allowed to harm so much as a hair on his head.

Father once saw a hellhound get too close and killed it on the spot.

Uriel found the center of the garden. It was stocked with tons of roses, daisies, tulips, and even a few gardenias. I found it funny that she gravitated towards those particular flowers, unwilling to pick the flower but smelling it enthusiastically. Stripping my dress shirt and throwing it to the ground, I willed my wings out and flew to the top of the gazebo where she sat playing with the petals. Loki shook his head, watching my shadow fly over his head.

Loki cleared his throat. "Hello." He tried to make his voice sound deeper.

Idiot.

Uriel's head sprung up excitedly. "Oh, hi!" Standing up, she brushed her short dress off—the green stains still discernible. "I'm Uriel! What's your name?"

Loki took out his hand for her to shake. She shook it playfully. "I'm Loki, Prince of Hell." He tugged on his suit jacket, flashing her a flirtatious smile.

"That's right! You were standing up there with your family. Sorry, I got so excited I must have forgotten! You looked very handsome up there."

Loki puffed out his chest. "You think so?"

"Yes, yes, I noticed you first. You kept looking at the gigantic cake. Once I saw what you were looking at, I went for it," she squealed excitedly.

She acted like a child that had never seen a four-tiered cake before.

"You like sweets, yeah?" Reaching in his pocket, he pulled out one of his suckers.

It wasn't just any sucker—it was one of his 'special' suckers. When you stuck it in your mouth, it tasted horrible and glued your mouth shut. Once, Father and Mother went away for several days, and the nanny at the time was dumb enough to put one in her mouth. I wasn't around at the time, and no one else knew how to break the spell, except for Loki, who wasn't telling a soul.

As Loki pulled out the bight-pink, wrapped sucker, Uriel's eyes grew wide. She bit her lip, clasping her hands together. "For me?"

Loki nodded. "I only carry the best; it tastes fantastic!"

Uriel started to reach for the sucker but rubbed her chest instead. "What did you say?" Uriel asked.

"Said it tastes fantastic."

Uriel rubbed her chest again before sitting down on the cement bench. "N-no, thank you. That was very sweet of you, but I think I'll have to wait for another time."

Loki's mischievous eyes softened, and he sat on the bench with her. "What's wrong? You keep rubbing your chest. Does it hurt?"

Why the hell does he care? He's never cared about anyone before.

"Yeah, it did." Her nose scrunched, her pouting lips almost touching the tip of her nose. "It was weird. But thank you, Loki! You are the second-nicest person I've ever met! Few people want to come to talk to me, but you did, which makes me delighted. I don't get out much. This was my very first party, and I'm sure my social skills are lacking."

Loki shook his head. "Nah, I'm not nice." He shoved the sucker back in his pants pocket.

Uriel shook her head, placing her hand on his. Loki's eyes brightened, a touch of pink sparkling on his cheeks.

"You are nice, Loki. I can tell you are a good person, too. You came all the way out here just to talk to me." He leaned his head back. "You didn't have to, but you did."

"Fuck," he whispered.

"Loki!" she scolded. "That's a bad word. You shouldn't say that!" she insisted, covering her ears while Loki smiled.

"Alright, I won't say it again... *if* you promise to give me something."

Uriel leaned forward. "I don't have anything." She patted her pockets.

"But you do," Loki smirked mischievously. "Give me a kiss on the cheek, and I won't say that word again."

My fists tightened, heat filling my veins. *The piece of shit was trying to rile me up.*

Uriel abruptly sat back with her back straight, the wind playing in her hair. "I-I can't do that," she muttered.

"Why not?" Loki questioned, sounding offended. "It's just a kiss on the cheek!"

"I have to give it to someone I love," she whispered.

Loki stared at her, dumbfounded. "You mean to tell me that you won't give me a kiss, on the cheek, because you want to give it to someone you love?"

Uriel fiddled with the hem of her dress, her pale cheeks brightening to a deep shade of red.

"Have you ever kissed anyone before, then?"

Uriel rocked her head. "Mom says you only do that to people you love."

Loki scoffed. "On the cheek? You can only kiss the people you love on the cheek? What about the lips?"

Uriel gasped, holding both hands to her mouth. "Noooo, you definitely can't do that! Only people wanting the stork to come can kiss on the lips!"

Hell has officially frozen over. Loki, for the first time in his life, was speechless. His brain was apparently trying to reboot after the information he received.

Oh, for fuck's sake. I didn't even know what to think! I rolled on my back with my wings spread across the gazebo roof; the white pillars contrasted against my blackened wings.

This girl was not cursed with some spell to lure me in. There was no ill will or sin in her heart and no damn bad intentions in her voice. Her intentions were nonexistent, other than trying to make a friend, get to know people, and live life around her.

"What damn cloud did you fall out of?" Loki whispered.

Uriel covered her ears again. "Does your mom know you curse this much?" Uriel huffed. "I can't hang out with you if you keep spilling out bad words; only the uneducated use words like that."

Loki stood up, offended. "So, you won't hang out with me because I use bad words, yet you believe kissing brings on babies?"

Loki's tone cracked, his hand slapping his chest, "Everyone wants to hang out with me! I kiss she-demons my age all the time! I'm the Prince of Hell. I'm popular!" Loki waved his hands in the air before sitting back down harshly onto the stone bench. He wouldn't look at her, crossing his arms and huffing silently to himself.

Uriel stood up, pushing her white dress down her thighs. "I'd like to be your friend, Loki, but if you talk like that, then I can't be your friend. I have standards. Continuing to use those bad words, when a friend asked you to stop, isn't being a good friend." Uriel's hips swayed as she stormed out of the gazebo.

I snorted quietly. I hadn't seen Loki this disturbed before in his entire life. Any other girl, or woman, would normally throw themselves at the Princes of Hell to get their attention, but she just walked away from him. My heart warmed to know that she would give up being friends with someone.

Maybe she had more brains than I thought.

Uriel continued to walk down the path before Loki screamed out her name. "Wait! Just wait!" Loki brushed back his hair. I listened intently as he rushed to her. Loki was only ten years old but was almost as tall as the little goddess.

Uriel picked at her nails, not wanting to look at him, and rubbed her toe on the stones beneath her feet.

"If it bothers you that much, then I won't curse anymore. Okay?"

My eyes widened. *The fuck? Loki just did something out of the kindness of his own heart.*

The gold of Uriel's wings glowed as she fluttered the feathers close to him. "Really?" Her eyes beamed.

Loki put out his hand for her to shake. "Yes. I will try my best, but it is a hard habit to break, you know."

Uriel nodded, shaking his hand.

"Where is Uriel?"

The loud shriek came from the front of the palace. Lightning flashed and the entire garden lit up as brightly as Earth. Several gods, including Mother and Father, raced around the house, every single one of them disregarding Father's rule about staying off the grass.

The hellhounds began to swarm from the stables, surrounding the now-massive crowd following behind the enraged goddess who was charging toward them.

"Uriel! There you are!" Hera's sandals slapped the stoned path. "We must go! Now!" she hissed with her face hardened in disgust.

"Uh oh," Uriel whimpered, retreating towards the gazebo.

Chapter 7

Uriel

Everything was going great. I made a new friend, even though he had a bit of a potty mouth. He even offered me candy! But of course, my stomach and chest had hurt when he said it would taste so good. I might have had too many honeysuckles and honey. I've never had a problem with too much sugar before.

Maybe I was just too excited to be here!

Yup, I was because I got to see some outstanding puppies and got to play in this exceptional garden, full of flowers that I had never seen before. The Underworld was an amazing place, for sure, and I didn't want the party to end. I wanted to explore more.

Things with Loki patched-up nicely. I was worried about giving up my first chance at a proper friend, but he changed really quickly. It made my wings warm at the promise he made me—a real promise. Now I would have someone to give me a tour around the entire estate!

The flutter in my wings made me giddy until a bright light flashed at the front of the palace. Most of the area was darker than the Celestial Kingdom, so when the bright light came from the sky, Loki and I shielded our eyes. We both stared until we heard screaming—*all too familiar screaming, to be exact.*

It was Mom.

I knew that huff and that sandal-slapping anywhere. She wasn't happy.

She does this as she stomps up the stairs at home when she finds me watching too many movies, and not getting the housework done. I tapped my lips a few times, humming in question of what I could have possibly done wrong until my wings perked up.

Loki stared at me questioningly.

"Uh, oh." I took a few steps back towards the gazebo.

It felt safer there. I enjoyed sitting under the shade of the red light source they had here, but that gazebo gave me a warm feeling that I really liked.

My tiny slippers began shuffling back, feeling the scuff of the rough rocks. "Uriel! There you are!" My mom's face hardened, and her brows knitted together tighter than Medusa's scales.

"We have to leave! Now! What were you thinking?" She grabbed my arm a little too roughly, and I whimpered.

Mom has never been physical with me, but the tightening of her grip had me at a loss for words.

"Do you know each other?" Loki pointed to both of us.

"Yeah, she's my mo—" Mom slapped her hand over my mouth.

"That's none of your concern! Let's go, Uriel."

I was dragged away from Loki; his face contorted to anger, and horns emerged from his head.

"Wait, Mom, I don't want to go! You said I could come!"

Mom's head whipped back quickly. "I never said such a thing! I would never let you leave the house on your own! Are you that dense?"

My heart stung at her words.

Dense was another word for stupid. I should know; I spent many, many hours studying, trying to be the good girl she wanted.

My wings drooped, the sting of her hostility causing my eyes to water. My lip wobbled. I could not cry in front of my new friend or the giant crowd that was coming toward us. The immense crowd had me cowering backward.

Mother glanced back at them, her huffing becoming louder.

A large, warm hand gripped my upper arm. The funny tingles that I felt earlier came back in full force. Instantly giggling and forgetting the fury behind my mom's eyes, I turned to find a shirtless Lucifer.

"Is there a problem?" Lucifer's deep voice silenced the entire entourage. Not even the puppies whined.

Mom stepped forward fearlessly, keeping a firm grip on my arm. "I'm taking her back home," she muttered. "She doesn't belong here." Mom turned to leave, pulling me, but Lucifer maintained his firm grip on my arm.

I leaned back into his chest.

Mom grunted, annoyed with my resistance. "I mean it, Lucifer!" Mom challenged.

Lucifer's lip curled. Smoke oozed from the base of his feet, and I swear, his face grew ten times darker.

"GET OFF MY LAWN!" Hades bellowed. The gigantic crowd scattered with the hellhounds herding the supernaturals like sheep.

I love sheep; they are so fluffy. I've got my own sheep, well, a little lamb that I sleep with every night, called Lambert.

Snorting, Loki nudged my arm before laughing along with me.

"This is why I don't enjoy having everyone over. No one respects my space," Hades spat.

Ember patted his arm, shaking her head. "It's fine. The grass will grow back," she whispered.

Lucifer's parents walked up the garden pathway. Ember's dress swayed as she cooed at the baby in her arms.

"Your sister is so cute," I cooed at Loki.

"Yeah, but I'm cuter," he huffed, crossing his arms.

"No, you're handsome."

Loki smiled as wide as his horns. "You think so?"

I nodded.

"Stop that," Mom hissed at me. "Hades, Ember, lovely seeing you, but we must go." Mom pulled me again until I ripped my arm away. Mom whipped around so fast that her toga blew up to her knees.

"Mom, you said I could come," I whispered. Dad came up behind her, rubbing his hands up and down her arms.

"My love, let's calm down." Dad's wings engulfed Mom like a big cocoon.

He does that a lot with her. It helps knock her out when she gets really 'pissy,' as Dad says. He says there is a reason she is so uptight, but I am not old enough to know why.

Lucifer pulled me back to his side, his left wing brushing my arm where my mom had grabbed me too tightly. The tingles made the sharp pain fall away.

"I can't relax! We have to leave," she whispered loudly to Dad. "You know why! Why am I the only one looking out for her well-being?"

Dad caressed her cheeks. Between his feathers, you could see the concern playing across the corners of his eyes. "We cannot keep her sheltered forever." He wiped away a tear from Mom's cheek with his thumb.

"The hell I can't!" Mom burst through his wings, a new fire blazing in her eyes.

I had never seen Mother so dead set on anything.

"D-did you find my stash?" Everyone's head perked up. I repeated my statement and still, everyone stared at me. "My stash of candy; did you find it? Is that why you are mad?"

Loki snorted, garnering an assortment of evil looks.

I saw nothing funny about it. My magical stash was awesome. If Mom knew I had it and ate candy whenever I wanted, she would definitely take it away.

"No, Uriel. You left the house without permission, and the first place you went was the Underworld!"

"But you said I could go!" I defended. "You kept saying, 'yes, yes, yes!' over and over while you guys were waiting for the stork!" I stomped my foot, putting my hands on my hips.

Mom's face reddened instantly as she slapped her hand over her mouth.

Lucifer made a noise behind me. I turned to look at him, and a little curl of the lip graced his otherwise grumpy face.

"Is she serious right now?" Loki spoke to Ember. "Like, she really doesn't know?" Ember hushed Loki.

My frustration made my wings shake.

"Sweet pea," Mom began.

I knew what 'sweet pea,' meant. She was going to offer me cake. Part of me was excited until Athena's pantsuit came into view.

I waved frantically. "Athena!" I squealed, running up to her.

I was glad she didn't run away from Hades and his implied death threats about the grass. Athena was going to be my new teacher, and I was worried I would never see her again!

"Hello there, Uriel." She patted my head affectionately. "I see your parents have graced us with their presence." Athena didn't smile. Her hand stopped petting my head, and she brought me back to the group of gods and angels standing around us.

"Sweet pea," Mom spoke again, her body slightly bending to speak to me face-to-face. "We need to go home. I'll make you your favorite treat, alright?" Mom's smile widened.

The thought of getting some chocolate lava cake had my wings shuddering.

"Then can we come back? I made a new friend!" I pointed to Loki, who was smiling devilishly at Mom.

"Sure. We will come another time." She smiled, her hand brushing my shoulder.

That funny twinge of pain came to my chest; it caused me to step back from her.

"Sorry, what did you say?" My head tilted to the side as my feet continued to ease backward, toward Lucifer.

"I said that I'll bring you back another time."

The pain started up again in my chest. I pouted, not wanting to go with Mom.

I always listened to her, but the pain in my chest told me not to.

"No," I whispered. Loki and Lucifer came forward to stand on either side of me.

Mom let out a flustered sigh. "I'm very disappointed in you, young lady," Mom chastised.

Ember stepped up to Mom. "I think we need to talk, Hera. Why haven't we seen Uriel until today?"

Mom shook her head. "I cannot discuss this here, Ember. I need to get her home." Mom took another step toward me, but Lucifer and Loki pulled me back. "That's enough," she hissed.

Mom was adamant about making me go home. With how mad she was, I was sure I would never be let out again. I enjoyed being outside and seeing new things. I didn't want to go back to my bedroom and watch the same old movies over and over. I always did everything she said. What if I didn't listen, just for today?

Athena winked at me, giving me a small thumbs-up.

Was the pain I felt in my chest because she lied?

"Mother, will you let me out of the house again if I come with you? I don't want to stay inside anymore. There are too many pretty things outside." My lip wanted to pout.

That worked on Dad so well; it never worked on Mom though.

"Of course, you can!"

Everyone looked to one another at her quick change in attitude, but the same pain pierced my chest.

My mouth dropped as I heard Athena's voice in my head. "She lied, sweet one." Athena's eyes filled with pity while looking away from me.

That was the pain in my chest? Someone lying to me?

Mom reached her hand out, but I pulled away. Hurt by my actions, she grabbed her robes. "I said I would take you out," Mom repeated.

I shook my head, leaning into Lucifer. He jumped, but his black wing came around to hide me, which I really liked.

"You're lying," I whispered. "You won't let me back out."

Dad grabbed Mom, pulling her back behind Hades and Ember.

"Uriel, you come home with us this instant! It is dangerous out here, especially around him!" Mom pointed to Lucifer.

A growl in his chest let me know that he didn't like her accusation.

The twinge in my chest came back. Lucifer wouldn't hurt me; he might be scary, but he wouldn't hurt me.

"He won't hurt me," I whispered.

Athena kept giving me encouraging glances, moving her hands forward to keep me talking.

"I think it hurts me more that you won't let me out or let me meet new people. The people I have met so far have been really nice." Loki reached up and grabbed my hand, squeezing it for comfort. Smiling back at him, I tried not to cry.

"So, what do you want to do, Uriel? Live here in the Underworld? I doubt that Hades would let you do that!"

"Oh, he will!" Ember jumped up, almost waking the baby.

Hades rolled his eyes, rubbing his forehead. "We would love to have her! In fact, we have been looking for a new nanny for Loki, and would you look at that, he takes to her so well!"

"Yeah!" Loki butted in. "I promise not to kill this one!"

Mom fell backward into Dad's arms, her eyes closing as she groaned. Gasping, I ran to her. She was sleeping peacefully in Dad's arms.

Dad looked at me, softly brushing my cheek. "She'll be alright; this is just a lot for her."

I nodded as Loki pulled me away from her.

"Here, let's bring her inside, and we can talk privately." Ember waved over several servants toting a small cot to carry her inside the palace.

I pranced as I walked with Loki back to his brother, Lucifer, my hair swaying side to side. I was worried about my mom, but the excitement I felt had me light on my feet. I felt like I could fly all over the palace.

"Excellent job, Uriel. I'm proud of you." Athena, who had been standing nearby, quietly joined our little group. "I'll talk to Ember and see if I can come to tutor you if you wish?"

I nodded frantically while clapping my hands. "Yes! I can't wait! Will we go on field trips and stuff, like the humans do? Can we go visit the Earth and Bergarian realms?"

Athena laughed as I got closer. "Yes, and so much more. Maybe we can find your mate along the way." Athena winked.

"A mate?" I whispered. "Like a best, best friend?" I asked excitedly.

"Shit," Loki cursed.

"Loki!" I squealed.

Chapter 8

Lucifer

Loki looked shamefully at the ground as he was scolded by Uriel. I kept my face disinterested, still not sure how to handle the situation.

Uriel was my mate; her mother had kept her from all the other gods, goddesses, and angels while she grew up. She knew nothing of the Underworld because it was deemed 'too evil.' The only reason I met my fated mate was through a simple misunderstanding.

Since the gods started claiming mates, just twenty-five years ago, with my mother's new gift, babies had been born left and right. The children took either their mother's or father's original form at birth, so there was no mixing of whatever species the parents were. My father was a god, therefore necessitating my mother's werewolf genes to morph to make her immortal. This not only gave her the power to bond souls to help Selene, the Moon Goddess, but made Mother a goddess herself.

Mother organized numerous gatherings so that the new gods, goddesses, angels, and demons could mingle with each other, allowing them to learn more about the opposing species and allow the children to interact with others of their species. I loathed those gatherings growing up. I never played with the other deities. I just stayed in my corner sulking because if I took part, I'd blow up in anger over something petty.

Mother had always wondered about Michael and Hera. Hera was paired with Michael after they had already spent many years together, long before soul-bonding was implemented for the gods. They were ecstatic to find out they were truly fated soulmates. The only problem was that they never conceived a child after Mother paired them together.

That proved wrong today.

Mother was beside herself, stealing glances at Father, trying to understand the situation. We all continued to walk inside the palace while I hovered over Uriel, watching as her hips swayed. The light grass stains on her dress prompted me to shake my head at her childlike actions earlier, but I also found it strangely endearing.

"Come with me, Uriel, let's go to my room." Loki grabbed her hand.

She almost stumbled over her own feet until I caught her. "Whoopsies!" she yelped as my arm snaked around her waist to steady her.

Her wings had willed back into her body as I turned her around. Now the front of her body was flush with mine; her hands landed on my bare shoulders to balance herself. Uriel shook her head. Her bright gold eyes blinked up at me through thick lashes.

"Thank you, Luci!" Her bright smile drew my gaze to her lips.

The entire entourage stopped, turned, and looked at both of us. I noticed my mother and father's eyes swell in my peripheral, their hands gripping each other tightly waiting for me to erupt from Uriel's use of the nickname I detested.

"*Easy, son,*" Father sent to me through our mind-link. "*Easy.*"

However, I didn't feel the intense anger building inside me, the fire flowing to my fingers, urging me to break every bone in the body of whoever dared call me, 'Luci.' My body relaxed slightly as I exhaled a heavy sigh, twirling Uriel back up to a standing position.

The demons carrying Hera on the cot looked at each other, muttering quietly. Their tails making signals so I wouldn't understand their entire conversation, but I knew what they were thinking.

'*Why wasn't I blowing up and killing the innocent woman in front of me?*'

My heart was beating quickly in my chest, clanging against my rib cage until I finally dropped her hand. Clearing my throat, I nodded my head in her direction and left the area before I could inflict any harm.

I couldn't be sure that I wouldn't have a delayed reaction where I blew up suddenly, and I didn't want to harm her. She was the first woman, excluding my mother, that didn't deserve it.

"*Meet us in the Smoke Room once you've dealt with your anger.*" Father put his hand on the small of Mother's back.

I could feel her stare upon me as I walked away, but I needed this. I needed to think through my concerns.

Just tomorrow, my life was set to end. I would spend my days locked deep within a dark abyss and would never see my family again. That was the plan until she showed up. Now, I am not so sure. The deep pit of black sludge that held onto my soul didn't surface. The voices in my head didn't whisper to me to destroy the innocent angel in front of me.

"She isn't an angel; she's a goddess," I muttered to myself, slamming the door to my chambers. Falling back against the door, I slid down, my dress pants now covered in dust from the top of the gazebo.

She's just too innocent, too innocent of the evil that flows through me.

My worn hands rubbed down my neatly shaven face.

What would she do if she knew what I did every night? If she saw what I could do to the dark souls that were once alive?

Gritting my teeth, I stood up, rubbing my face again with my beaten, bloodstained hands. I could almost smell the blood lingering on them from the night before.

Throwing on a black sweater, I left my room. I walked down the halls to the Smoking Room—otherwise known as a meeting or conference room. Father spent most of his time in there with black smoke pouring off him because he was pissed off about something during a meeting.

Father did not dare to spill his smoke in his office. Mother turned it into a relaxing space for both of their use. She filled it with small little fountains of water, lavender smells, and so much more. She even included a little corner that she would occupy while he worked. Mother would stay up well into the night with him if Father was working out a problem, and the last thing that she wanted was to smell his smoke stinking up the room.

As I entered the Smoking Room, it was no surprise that Father was radiating his power. Uriel and Loki, however, were nowhere to be found. My heart immediately pounded in my chest.

"Luci," Mother grabbed my hand, leading me to a seat beside her. She had me sit down, rubbing my hand with her palm.

Mother had small ways to help soothe me, but it was not enough when I was at my worst.

"Uriel is with Loki," she whispered. "We need to talk to Michael while Hera is still unconscious, and I needed Loki occupied. Besides, Michael doesn't want Uriel to know what we are about to hear."

"Seems like they don't want her to know anything," I muttered, shooting a menacing glance at Michael. He shifted in his seat uncomfortably, not daring to look me in the eye. I didn't care that he was my mate's father; he was part of whatever Hera had done to keep Uriel away from me.

We could have known each other much sooner, grown up together even. Who knows, maybe our souls would have recognized each other, and my anger would have never gotten as strong as it had.

"Michael, I think we need some answers here." Father pulled his chair back, sitting across from Michael.

Athena sat beside him, writing notes down in some notebook—*like she needed it. She was the damn Goddess of Knowledge.* Her gaze landed on me, a smirk playing on her lips.

"I know you can hear me, why play that?" I scoffed.

"Because it humanizes me, and I find humans fascinating. Have you ever wanted to be normal? To be plain?"

I hummed, leaning back in the chair.

I liked my power, just not when the power snuffed me out.

"It all started the day Uriel was born." Michael rubbed his forehead, a few feathers falling from his back.

Fuck, is he going to start molting?

"Her birth was flawless. Hera and I opted to have a home birth after spending the entire pregnancy on Earth. We didn't want a fuss; we wanted our family to start with just us. We lived in a cottage on a Caribbean Island. She drank nothing but virgin strawberry daiquiris the entire time we spent lying about on the beach, enjoying our 'honeymoon,' as the humans called it."

"The point?" I growled, crossing my arms.

His head darted back to me. "Should he even be in here?"

I slammed my hand on the table, breaking it in half as embers flew from the fire building in my palm. "I have every right! Now hurry up with your damn story!"

Mother grabbed my flaming hand, burning her. I instantly lurched my hand away, upset she would even try to touch me during my fit. Father pulled Mother away as I sat back down in the chair.

"Lucifer, please," Father scolded. "Please continue, Michael... and get to the point."

Michael's hand covered his heart; his eyes never left my body as it continued to tense.

Sparks from my hand crackled.

"Right, umm... so, we came home and had a home birth, just the two of us. Uriel came out healthy and screaming. Her dark hair was already long, and her wings were imprinted on her back, just like any other angel babe, but her skin glowed like that of a god. She had only been in our home for mere hours before we heard a knock at the door—the three Fates walked straight in without a word."

Athena's head whipped to Michael, clutching her pen. "The Fates visit no one!" Athena slammed her pen down. "You should have told someone they visited you! What they said could have given us a glimpse into the future, and you had the audacity to keep that from the rest of us? What were you thinking?" Athena slung her chair to the side of the room, pacing the floor behind Michael.

Ignoring her, he continued his story. "They walked straight into our room where Hera was feeding Uriel. They surrounded the bed, all three: Clotho, Lachesis, and Atropos. The white hoods over their heads kept their faces hidden, but just by the aura they leaked, we knew who they were. The one called Clotho spoke for the group." Michael set his elbows on the table, burying his forehead against his palms.

"Her words were simple, 'Uriel, the Goddess of Innocence, will die at the hands of evil. The humans of the Earth will know no balance between virtue and immorality, sparking the infamous prophecy created by the humans that indicates the onset of their destruction.'" Michael let out a harsh breath, tears in the corners of his eyes.

The entire table was mute. Athena stared at the back of Michael's head; she held her arms behind her while her brows came to a head. My fists burned, and the warmth of my hands on my thighs had me stand abruptly, knocking the room from its trance.

"There is a choice," Michael sniffed, ignoring my stance. "The Fates said that her future is still 'clouded.' Uriel could still live, but it all comes down to 'a choice!' A choice that 'someone' will make. The Fates wouldn't even tell us who would be the one to make that life-altering choice! What would you all have done?" Michael's voice rose. "You would have done the same! You too would have hidden her from the evil that threatens to destroy her! Hera loves our daughter; she has lived much longer than I have, and I trusted her judgment to save her—to save our daughter! We will continue to keep her away from harm!"

Mother's mouth hung open, unsure of what to say. It was the first time I did not hear reassuring words exit her mouth. Lilith cooed in Father's arms, and he swiftly handed her to Mother.

"No matter the situation, you should have told someone," Father growled. "This doesn't just affect your daughter; it affects the other gods as well. What happens when the humans all die? Who would be next? The supernaturals? Us? She may be the Goddess of Innocence, and I know that you are trying to keep her pure so that no evil can find her, but these things affect more than just your daughter, they affect entire races!" Father's words were anything but calm—they were filled with resentment. Mother didn't dare speak.

"And do what? Go to Zeus?" Michael snapped. "No one knows where his head is at! He still loves *my* Hera, *my mate*! They were together for centuries! I would never go to him, especially not when my daughter's life was at stake! For all we know, he could hand her over to whatever evil it is that we are hiding her from, just to get back at Hera!"

Mother's hand gripped Father's forearm, standing with him. "We will figure this out," Mother muttered under her breath. "But you cannot do it alone. The Fates are cryptic; the future is '*clouded*', as you said. Decisions have to be made, and I don't think hiding Uriel and trying to keep her from this 'evil' will help. You are just rendering her helpless! Uriel should stay here, away from Zeus, if you are so worried. Ares can teach her combat and Athena could tutor her. Her supervising Loki is the perfect way to strengthen her innocence gift. He's a little terror, and he hasn't behaved this well in ages." Mother smiled.

Thank the Fates that Mother has some sense, out of everyone here. I can see her smiling at me, hoping I would be pleased.

"What about him?" Michael nods at me.

What does that motherfucker mean?

"What about Lucifer?" Mother questioned harshly. "He would be perfect to watch over her."

Michael shook his head, standing up to leave. "I've heard the stories. He's killed plenty of your demons. He's ruthless, just like his gift. Hera won't approve."

I crossed my arms. "No harm will come to her under my watch."

I'd be damned if Uriel left to go back into hiding. She may be my mate, and as such, I should be the one to protect her. I didn't even have to stay close or complete the bond to do so. The real question was: was I protecting her from another evil? Or was I that evil?

Father peered at the both of us. Michael, still sighing heavily, rubbed his neck.

"Lucifer would never promise, unless he intended to keep it," Mother boasted.

"She's right. Lucifer may be the God of Destruction, but he has never broken his word. Michael, you should take the deal. Let Uriel stay here while you and Hera try to find out more. Zeus was here earlier, and he spoke with Uriel already. He knows where you and Hera live, and his warrior angels will likely be watching your home already."

Michael growled. "I really don't want to discuss this with Hera. She's going to be livid."

"Grow some damn balls." Ares walked in, bare-chested in his sparing regalia. "You guys sound like a bunch of squawking chickens."

Chapter 9

Lucifer

"Are you not Michael? What happened to the badass Archangel from twenty-five years ago? You gotta take your mate by her ass and tell her how it is! Chicks dig that kinda shit." Ares plopped down on the thick leather chair, unconcerned that sweat and blood dripped on the expensive upholstery.

"Can't act like that anymore!" Michael through his hands up in the air. "I've got a daughter now. I've got to be a bit more civilized than that."

Ares huffed, rubbing the sweat off his brow and slapping the table. Opening his mouth, he paused, whipping his head back to Michael. "You got a kid? Fuck man, congrats!" Ares stood to shake Michael's hand before my father exploded.

"If you were at the party, you would have known!"

Ares scratched his head. "Oh, that was today?"

Father rolled his eyes, falling back in the chair as Mariah, Ares' mate and the head warrior of Mother's pack, appeared in the doorway. She was sweaty and covered in dirt and sand from the sparring arena in the basement.

"Um, sorry, but whoever you guys have locked in the guest bedroom has been banging on the door." Mariah's thumb stuck out behind her with her other hand on her hip.

"Oh, there you are baby!" Mariah walked in, swiftly sitting her rear on Ares' lap.

"Yeah, here I am, baby!" I rolled my eyes at the two of them.

They had yet to have children, despite being together for all these years. They wanted their alone time for a while before they had children. When I say 'alone time,' I mean 'bang each other's brains out every five minutes.' Father had to erect a soundproof barrier in their room just so everyone could sleep.

"Not here," she whispered seductively. "I don't think Athena would appreciate it." Athena looked on in disgust, willing earplugs to her ears.

Michael straightened up, tightening his robe around his waist. "I'll talk to her." His voice now held confidence.

Ares gave him a thumbs up. "Show her whose dick is longer, yeah?" he said.

Michael, who was giving himself a pep talk, had his butt slapped by Ares as he charged out the door to face his mate. Ares leaned back in the chair, his mate promptly sitting back on his lap, stroking his cheek.

How my father saw him as one of his best friends, I'll never know.

Father rounded the desk, leaving Mother to feed the baby herself. He approached me, both hands landing on my shoulder, his face to mine. His hot breath fanned my face, his smell fanning all around me. He was letting his guard down, his power weakening by the second, something he never did, unless it was for Mother.

His emotional wall crumbled. I felt Father's love for me, for all his children, deep within me. I dropped my wall as well; he could see the blackness hovering over me and the pain I felt every day.

Eyes softening, he pulled me into a hug. "I don't remember the last time you let me hold you like this," he whispered in my ear. "She's already changing you, even if you don't fully realize it, she has." Father stood back, looking deep into my eyes.

I didn't want to believe that one simple, innocent girl could affect me as she had, but she already did. I didn't kill her when she said my nickname. I wasn't repulsed by her touch. I wanted her to stay, and I wanted to protect her.

"What have I missed, exactly?" Ares broke our moment, like usual.

"Uriel is Lucifer's mate," Athena said eloquently, taking a teacup from the cart. "I could see it in his eyes as soon as he saw her." She chuckled. "I am curious to know why you didn't tell her father though?" Athena looked at my mother, the Goddess of Empathy and Bonding.

"Well,"—she burped Lilith on her shoulder—"the timing never really seemed appropriate, and I think that is something that Luci should explain, when the time is right, of course. I mean, Uriel isn't quite prepared to complete a bond yet." Mother glanced to Father, who was shaking his head and pinching his nose.

"Why the hell not? Is she still a baby or something?" Ares wrapped his arms around Mariah.

"Sort of." Athena sat back down in the chair, sipping from her cup.

Father explained Uriel's home life, which consisted of nothing but waking up in the morning, studying, doing chores, and even doing her mother's accounting work. She was extremely sheltered, and Hera did an excellent job keeping her in her own bubble for years. No matter how much she and Michael tried to do the right thing, it burned me hotter than anything ever had before.

"That blows," Ares huffed. "Guess you get to play doctor with her then, huh?" He winked.

I threw a fireball at his chest. He quickly pushed Mariah out of the way, catching my fireball and slamming into the wall.

Uriel

"Whoa! Your room is huge!" My bare feet hit the lush, green carpet as I examined Loki's room which had golden walls with hints of forest green throughout. Posters of animals that I had never seen before were pinned to the walls, small knickknacks of human model cars sat on shelves, and a large desk filled with books occupied the corner. Along with all the neat stuff, there was tons of junk. It covered most of the carpet besides the two paths: one that led to the bed, and one that led to the bathroom.

"Yeah, not as big as Lucifer's," he huffed. "Mom says I gotta keep this room clean first." Loki picked up a ball, threw it across the room, and got it through a hoop on the wall. He squealed and began jumping on the bed.

"Come on, wanna jump? It's almost like the trampoline in the back of the palace." My wings fluttered from my excitement that they would have such a contraption. "'cept that one is broken."

My wings hung back, wilting slightly. "Why is it broken?"

Loki landed on the bed with a thud, not even trying to remake it. "Had a nanny that was annoying me; she told me how naughty I was, all the time, so I invited her to come jump with me." Loki smiled with his fangs hanging out of his mouth, almost salivating as he explained, "I might have used my powers a little too much. I pushed the springs down super low and catapulted her into the hellhound pin. They were getting washed that day so the whole lot was in there. They had a lot of fun ripping her apart."

I gasped, sitting on a chair covered in clothes. "You killed her?"

"Well, yeah, dollface; like I said, she was annoying, and she kept trying to get into Lucifer's pants."

I felt my lip poke out. *That poor woman died by having her body ripped to shreds.* The heat in my eyes gave me the sign that I was about to cry right here for a woman I never met. My wings sagged. Rubbing my nose with the back of my hand, I sniffed carefully, trying not to let him know I was really dying inside.

"Hey, hey, whatcha crying for?" Loki hopped off the bed, running through a mess of clothes to get to my side.

"That poor demon, she could have had a family!" I stood up, backing away from Loki. His big eyes searched mine. "She had her whole life to live, and you just took it?" The lights in the room faded in and out, finally stopping when my eyes set on Loki.

"No, no, listen, it isn't like humans or werewolves dying. Demons don't *actually* die around here."

Rubbing a tear away, I sat back down on the chair. "What do you mean then?"

"Demons can be respawned all the time. Dad has this pool of souls, and he just goes in there, touches his finger in it, and out pops a demon. They get their body back and go on their merry way." Loki smiled. "I would never kill someone, like a human or supernatural, just the demons."

I fiddled with my hands, glancing from Loki to my nail polish. "Alright." Loki sighed, his breath fanning my face. "You wouldn't do that to me, would you? If I got annoying? I'm supposed to be your nanny now, right?"

Loki shook his head, bringing me into a hug, surprising me. "I can't kill you! I may be a trickster, but I don't go around killing people all willy-nilly." He pulled away from me.

He didn't look like a hugger, yet here he was, hugging me. I smiled, my wings fluttering showing too much excitement.

"I'd never do that to you, Uriel! You're the first person I've met that tells it like it is. I like that." He put his hands on his hips. "You know, it's gonna be hard to keep you as a friend," he spoke almost mockingly.

I twisted my lips, lowering my head. *I've heard that kind of tone with Mom sometimes. It was done in a joking manner, but it still stung just the same.*

"But I like it! I like a good challenge. I never met someone that didn't care about my status or wasn't willing to be my friend right off the bat. So, you, Uriel, will not just be my nanny, but a great friend, too."

Perking up, I grabbed the closest piece of clothing, which was literally under my arm, stood up, and excitedly threw it into the hoop, letting it drop to the floor. Then, the idea sparked: how to get him to clean his room while still having fun.

I stepped over the massive amount of laundry and toys to an empty laundry basket that was laying on its side. Picking it up, I put it under the large hoop. "Want to play a game?" I asked excitedly.

Loki looked at the basket and the clothes on the floor. He huffed, wadding up a shirt. "Fine, but let's make it interesting. Let's ask each other questions to get to know each other."

I nodded frantically, liking the idea to get to know Loki. He was mysterious, mature, and immature all at the same time. I found him interesting for someone his age—*which I'm guessing is about ten; it's hard to tell when he is as tall as I am.*

"Okay! You first!" I clapped. "Age before beauty." He wiggled his brows, throwing the shirt at me.

Aww, he thinks he's pretty.

"Alright, where is your favorite place to be?" Loki asked.

"Right now? Probably here in the Underworld; I've never seen anything like it!"

"Really? That's sad." He shook his head, watching me shoot. He picked up a shirt, wadding it up. "Your question, dollface." I giggled at that.

"Hmm... what is your favorite trick to play on demons." Loki rubbed his chin, looking to the ceiling. "Probably taking hellhound shit and putting it in the servants' toilets. Their shits are huge, and they can't flush, so you have to get a stick to break it up first. It makes all the older demon women scream so loud Dad can hear it in Mom's garden when we are all having breakfast!" Loki rolled back on the couch laughing.

I laughed too. *Even though he said a bad word.*

It went on like this for an hour. We got to know each other's likes and dislikes—he hates too much meat but loves the taste of roasted vegetables and tofu, and he feels like he has become the forgotten child now that he has an older brother who has a temper and a younger sister who is too adorable for him to look at properly.

Toward the end of our game, the room was mostly cleared of all the laundry, and it looked so much better. We were down to one sock, and it was my turn to ask a question.

"Better be a good one; you know almost everything about me." Loki threw a smile at me.

"I don't think that's true. I bet there is more to you than trivial questions like these."

"Easy there, dollface, wouldn't want you to choke on that sentence."

"Choke? On words?" I tilted my head.

Sometimes I think Loki is smarter than me, and he is so much younger.

"Forget it. What's your question?"

"Oh, yes. I wanted to know, what did you mean when you said, 'that nanny wanted to get in Lucifer's pants?'"

Loki dropped the model car he was holding only to look up, not at me but Lucifer standing in the doorway.

"Oops!" I squeaked, realizing I just hit Luci with the dirty sock. Hi, Luci!" I waved.

Chapter 10

Lucifer

After ten minutes of Michael arguing with Hera—*which could be heard from down the hallway, mind you*—I left my seat, unable to tolerate hearing them and listen to the bickering between Athena and Ares too. They were at opposite ends of the spectrum, intelligence-wise, especially on the topic of relationships, and no one was getting anywhere with their discussions.

I followed my body. I didn't think of where to go or what to do; for the first time in my life, I let my body flow with its surroundings. I went down the hallway and noticed that the paintings on the walls were lighter. The servants were chuckling and nudging each other as I passed. The smiles I had never seen—*or maybe never paid attention to*—had me doing double-takes down the hall.

Of course, once they realized I was staring, they busied themselves with their work rather than provoke my heated gaze.

My feet landed right outside Loki's door. Giggling and slight taps on the door intrigued me.

What could the God of Mischief and the Goddess of Innocence be doing in there?

Deciding it could be nothing good, I opened the door without knocking, and the thick air of tension knocked me in the face, along with a crusty sock.

"Oops!" A squeak came from the corner.

Loki, half jumping on the bed, dropped one of his toys on the bedroom floor.

"Hi, Luci!" Uriel frantically waved as I pulled the dirty laundry from my face. Looking down at it and back to Uriel, her lips were parted wide, showing off her perfectly straight teeth.

Slapping her hands to her mouth, she looked at Loki, either for protection or for the reading of the room, because right now, my face had not changed in the slightest.

"Don't call him that," Loki hissed at her.

Her face filled with embarrassment, tinging her cheeks pink. "W-why not?" She whispered back. Her wings no longer fluttered around in excitement.

"He doesn't like it," he whispered back. "Only Mom can call him that."

Her mouth was in the shape of an 'O,' as she looked down at the floor, studying her toes. "I'm sor—" Clearing my throat, I stopped her from apologizing.

I felt the black sludge tearing up my insides; I wanted to cut the air off from Loki's lungs for upsetting Uriel.

She did not know, and hell, she wasn't doing it out of spite. It was her own nickname that she had given me, not one she heard before.

"It's alright, Uriel." Uriel stilled, her wings no longer drooping, but insanely still. Her heartbeat rose as I walked to her, my feet parting the junk, allowing the carpet to cushion my leather shoes. "You can call me that if you wish."

Loki's mouth bobbed like a fish, raising his hand to point at me, his pointy finger shaking with fright. "She's y-y-your—"

My glare shut him up, his hand dropping. If he was any other person, he would have fainted in fright. My eyes bore into him, so much so that he could see the pain I could do to his mind alone.

Uriel, oblivious to this stare, had her big, golden eyes twinkling between her lashes. "Oh, thank the Celestial Heavens! If you didn't like Luci, you definitely wouldn't have liked the other nickname I gave you."

Loki's head shot up, crawling to the end of his bed, yet remained far enough away so that I did not strangle the little prick. "What's the other nickname?" He giggled.

"Lurch." Loki and I looked at each other, not understanding the new name. "You know, from the Addams Family? 'They're creepy and they're kooky, mysterious, and spooky...'" Uriel continued to sing the theme song from the human television show while Loki rolled on the bed with his arms on his stomach.

Sighing, I pinched my nose with my thumb and index finger. Her little bounce with the song and dance routine had me staring at her far too hard as her skirt swished around. Chuckling, I sat in the chair that was typically covered in clothes and chuckled at the situation.

"Why Lurch though?" Loki grinned. "What makes you think of Lurch when you look at Lucifer?"

Uriel stuck out her hip, putting her hand on it. Her finger tapped her lips, something she liked to do. They were lush and shiny; the pink gloss she wore highlighted one of her best features.

"Because he is really tall, he walks around with a scowl on his face, and he barely talks. Except he isn't ugly like Lurch. No, he is better looking." Her face blushed. A curl of my lip had her eyeing me, intently waiting for the smile that I would never give. "A lot cuter," she mumbled again before turning away.

"Holy Mary-Fucking-Poppins! What the hell happened to your room, Prince of Pranks?" Ares strode through the door with Mariah's arm wrapped around his hip. "Did Tartarus freeze over?"

Loki rolled his eyes, waving Ares away. "Nah, just pickin' up a little," he mumbled.

"We played a game!" Uriel chirped. "We threw all his clothes through the hoop to pick up. It was a lot more fun that way." Uriel fluttered her wings wildly, staring up at the enormous giant of a god.

"Ahh. You must be Uriel." Ares' side glance provoked me to growl at him. His smirk indicated that he was planning something.

I will fucking kill him if he tries to fucking touch her.

"So, do you like to play doctor?"

"No, but it sounds like fun! How do you play?" Uriel leaned in to listen more.

"You should ask Lucifer over here, his tingly hands will—"

That's it.

"Out!" I yelled.

Mariah, half-frozen in fear, tried tugging Ares, who stood there until we met eye-to-eye.

"You cannot speak to her." I was nose-to-nose with him. My physique made me appear weak in the eyes of the War God, but I had much more power than he did.

Ares snorted, walking out the door. "Just playin' around, man." He threw out some gang signs to Loki.

I don't know why Father is friends with him.

Before he left, he popped his head back into the room. "When you are done playing doctor, dinner is ready."

I launched a small fireball at him. It grazed the door but chased him down the hall. When it scorched his ass, he screamed like a little girl.

Loki stood right next to Uriel. He continued to talk, chatting about everything and nothing. Uriel skipped along, trying to keep up with the three of us walking down the hall. She looked like she had two bodyguards escorting her as we entered the dining room.

Uriel's eyes lit up, clasping her hands together like it was the best damn room she ever saw. "Whoa," she spoke as she walked in. "I've only seen rooms like these in books."

"Probably 'cause most of the things you have seen are in books," Loki muttered under his breath.

Hera did not take the sentiment well, her hand gripped around a fork, causing it to bend at the neck. "Uriel, sweet pea, how about you come to sit next to me?"

I ground my jaw. *Her mother was the source of my anger. I wanted to have her sit next to me, but of course, the only open spot next to her mother was smashed between her parents.*

Uriel skipped over to her mother. Loki, groaning, pulled out a chair next to me. "I wanted to sit with her," he whined. Mother only laughed at Loki while they served us dinner.

Dinner with my parents was typically pleasant. Mother would talk about her day pairing souls. Meanwhile, Father would listen intently and try to feed her while she talked because she usually got carried away telling mating stories. However, today, the one mating story she wanted to tell, she couldn't even mention. Her body swayed with the restraint, looking at Father, then to me, and then back to Uriel, who was oblivious of everything.

Father chuckled, moving the meat on his plate. We could both hear Cerberus chomping down the food Uriel was sneaking under the table. She tried sticking a vegetable below, but Cerberus began choking, causing the entire table to jump in surprise. Uriel's face tinged pink, pretending to stick the dreadful piece of vegetable to her mouth, only to spit it out in a napkin when her mother wasn't looking. I rested my elbow on the table, rubbing my chin as I watched her.

Her delicate skin had hardly seen the sun; her feet barely touched the blades of grass. How long had it been since a raindrop has fallen on the smoothness of her breast?

My lip curled, watching the delicate thing grab the first slice of chocolate silk pie off the dessert cart. Her lips savored each bite, pulling the spoon slowly away from her mouth.

I grunted to myself. *It was a long way off before we could ever be mates.*

My heart stopped beating in my chest. *I just said it would be a while, meaning it could happen. This wasn't what I decided just an hour ago. An hour ago, I decided that I would protect her and keep her safe, but now my mind, no, my heart was already changing everything.*

"You gonna eat that?" Loki pointed to the coconut cream pie on my plate. I picked it up and placed it on Loki's plate. He glared at me suspiciously. "What did you do to it?" he hissed.

"Nothing," I whispered back.

"You just served me your damn piece of pie. You never do anything nice for anyone, 'cept for Mom and Dad."

I ignored him and looked back to Uriel, who was so happy about a piece of damn pie. I was feeling an emotion I never thought I could experience—contentment.

Fuck, I'm screwed.

Hera was tight-lipped throughout dinner as she stabbed her fork into each little pea. Finally, she spoke to Uriel, "Sweet pea, your dad and I have some business to attend to." Uriel's eyes widened, biting her lips from her smile being too big.

She must know this was a rarity.

"We are going to let you stay here in the Underworld for a while. You will have to remain here, in the palace with Hades, Ember, and their guards. You are expected to watch over Loki, too. It will be a great internship for you, maybe an opportunity to get a handle on some of your innocence powers. You may have noticed them surfacing."

Yeah, because you smothered her and never gave her a chance to try them. I glared at Hera across the table.

Father tapped into my head, causing me to look away. *"Don't let her know you are her mate, Lucifer. Then we will have a slew of other problems."* My eyes shot to my father. Shaking his head, he stuffed another piece of rare steak in his mouth.

Dinner wrapped up, finally. *Thank the Fates, I'd never have to sit through that dinner again. It was only bearable because she was there. It was the best damn dinner if only for the sake of my eyes because I got to memorize each line, each curve, and each tiny freckle that dusted her cheeks. I'd take everything I've memorized and think of her while I slept.*

Michael bid Uriel farewell. She gave him an enormous hug while his wings engulfed her, causing her to squeal happily. "Remember, if you are ever in trouble, pray to me with this." Michael plucked one of his white feathers from the top of his wing. "I'll fly to you wherever you are, quicker than a heartbeat."

"She will be here," Hera interjected. "Uriel is not to leave the grounds, understood?" Uriel nodded, hugging her mother.

"Thank you, Mom. I know this is hard for you, but I'm old enough now. I can take care of myself." Uriel's enormous eyes blinked happily. Hera's hugged her tighter, kissing the top of her head.

"I know, dear." She sniffed, petting back Uriel's hair softly. "Protect her, please." Hera's eyes landed on me and my father. "I'm begging you."

Gods don't beg. Hera, once the second-in-command under Zeus, was now begging for us to protect her only daughter. Not just her daughter, but the fate of humanity.

"With my life," I promised.

Chapter 11

Uriel

"They're gone," I whispered to myself. For the first time in my twenty-five years of living, they are gone. I wanted to scream in relief. Mom had been so stressed, constantly hovering over my head for so long. I was barely alone in our home, and when she wasn't there, I could finally relax. Now I was in someone else's home, but it still felt alright.

It felt great, actually.

"How about Lucifer shows you to the bedroom you'll use during your stay? Some of your things have already been sent down from your home through Hermes' messengers." I nodded, thanking her profusely for letting me stay.

Ember was so nice, so much more laid back than Mom. I think I am really going to like it here.

"Can I come too?" Loki crossed his arms. "I've hung out with her more. She likes me better. She thinks Lucifer looks like Lurch, anyway."

Giggling, I playfully pushed Loki. "Yes, please!" I chirped. Lucifer rolled his eyes. Glancing at him, I saw him clench his fists.

"Are you mad?" I questioned, picking at my fingers; I picked too hard, making a stupid hangnail bleed. I sighed, sucking on my finger to make the blood go away. Ember pushed her son, nodding over in my direction.

"No, I'm not mad," he spoke stiffly. He pulled my hand away, looking at where I picked too hard. "You shouldn't pick at your nails." He blew on my finger. The heat of his breath warmed my hand, dissolving the soft tingles left on my skin from his fingertips. The pain melted away, and the bleeding stopped. "Come on."

He dropped my hand, and I immediately disliked it. My hand felt all cold and clammy now, and I wanted to run up and grab his hand again.

Luci was already walking down the hallway while Loki waited for me to follow. "Go on, hun. He won't bite." Ember put her arm around my shoulder. "He's a good man. He'll take care of you. He cares more than you think."

"You sure? I don't think he likes me very much," I muttered.

"People's emotions don't always live on the outside, sometimes they hide deep inside. Luci just doesn't understand how to let them out. That's why he needs you to show him."

"Me?" I questioned.

Hades wrapped his arm around Ember. *No matter how nice he was trying to be, he still reeked of unbelievable power which was super scary.*

"Lucifer needs a friend." Hades bent down to my level. "Why don't you show him? Hmm?"

"H-he doesn't have any?"

How could he not have any friends? He's so pretty! He could get a lot of friends, who are girls, I'm sure. He could also get friends that were boys, too. Loki and Luci were princes. That meant they were automatically popular, but maybe that was why Loki liked me so much because I didn't care about him being a prince.

"Lucifer is a butthead," Loki spat. "He doesn't know how to be nice. I, however,"—Loki pretended to wipe off the imaginary dust on his shoulder—"know how to be friends with people. Everyone wants to be my friend, except you. I have to work for you." I laughed.

Loki pulled on my hand. We had to run to catch up to Lucifer. He was already halfway to the family's side of the palace, on the East side. The red sun that lit the sky was already to the West, so the palace lights had been dimmed, and only left the main pathways lit.

Luci didn't even look at us as we ran up to him, out of breath. Biting my lip, I thought of what Queen Ember told me—*Luci was just misunderstood and needed a friend.* Not having many friends myself, I needed to figure out how to be a good friend to him without saying too much, since he doesn't like to talk.

Feeling his hand earlier was really nice. I wonder if he thought the same?

I'm going for it.

Staring at my hand for a few seconds, I shoved it right into his. Alright, not shoved, I might have tickled my hand into his. Luci's body stopped right in the middle of the hallway. Loki kept walking, but I had to stop because I was like, stuck to grumpy Lurch.

"What's wrong, Luci?" My head tilted to the side, wondering why he kept staring at our hands.

Luci's face looked up at mine. I smiled, tugging at his hand. "Ready?" He took one slow step to meet up with me, and we continued down the hall.

One step closer to being friends, check!

We finally reached the family wing. These doors were huge and black with a hint of red; demons decorated each of the panels and the trim around each door was gold.

"You know my room." Loki pointed to his door. His door had a dark-green hue to it. "That's Lucifer's door." He pointed to the room beside his. His door was the same as most of the others, dark with a hint of red. No personality on the door like Loki's.

"And this is your room," Luci spoke lowly. It was right across the large hall from Luci's room. It held a white, cream-colored door instead of matching the darkened doors. Walking up to it, I rested one hand on either handle. Looking back, I waited for the boys behind me to prepare for the grand reveal.

Of course, they knew what it looked like, but I didn't!

I pulled, jumping as I did, to open the heavy doors until they were expanded for all to see. Gasping at the magnitude of the room, I stepped on the light hardwood floor. The bed was sur-rounded by a white, fluffy, fur rug. I couldn't wait to feel it with my bare feet! The walls were a dark mauve, and the beautiful, white bedspread was fit for a princess!

"It's so wonderful!" I squealed. Running to the bed, I jumped on it a few times.

It was way bouncier than Loki's.

"Did you look in the bathroom?" Loki ran to the door, only to be stopped by Luci.

"Let her look," he growled. I snorted, jumping off the bed and running to see what the fuss was about.

Once I reached the door, Luci held it shut with his hand above my head. "You can't run," he whispered.

I turned, my face meeting his. My heart raced, feeling the heat of his breath. My whole body tingled in his proximity. Hair standing on the back of my neck, I gulped silently, looking up at him.

"You'll get hurt."

My whole body shivered.

His jaw was so sharp that I swear, I could cut my poor, little finger on it. He was more handsome than Prince Philip from Sleeping Beauty and more rugged than Aladdin.

My wings shuddered; my whole body was going to collapse at these new feelings I had for this stoic god.

Why was he so pretty?

I wanted to touch him!

What are these feelings? I squeaked internally, opening the door, stepping inside, and shutting it quickly.

Stammering, slapping, and roughhousing sounded from the other side of the door. Loki was yelling at Luci, but all I heard were growls of irritation and hushed whispers.

Backing away from the door, my bum hit the counter. I turned to finally meet the place I would call home every morning and evening to style my ridiculously long hair. I stared at the magnificence: a crystal chandelier, long, beautiful, white marble counters, pink and purple soaps of every kind, and a steam shower with huge showerheads. My mouth gaped, then I squealed in excitement at the giant hot tub in the middle of the room.

Squinting my eyes, I ran to the other side of the wall, checking the toilet. Expecting it to be gold, I shrugged my shoulders, disappointed in how plain it was, and began stripping right then.

Hot tub, here I come!

It was already filled to the top with silently popping bubbles as I slid my dirty legs inside.

Playing with the puppies had gotten me way too dirty. I wonder if they could come inside? I'd love to cuddle one while I sleep! Maybe I could ask.

"Are you alright in there?" Loki banged on the door. "Aren't you coming back out to tell me good night?"

I snorted, blowing a gigantic pile of bubbles away from my face. "I'm in the tub. I'll come to tell you good night when I'm done!" Giggling, I stuck my head under the water, coming up with a massive bubble hairdo.

I should have left home a lot sooner! If only I had known the Underworld was so much fun.

Once bathed, I hopped out and quickly towel-dried my hair before putting it into a messy bun. Keeping the towel wrapped tightly around my body, I peeked out, checking to make sure that both the boys were gone. Seeing that the room was now empty with the door shut, I shuffled over to the dresser. All my clothes had been magically put away in the same order I usually put my clothes.

Mom must have had strict instructions for the messenger who brought all this stuff. I feel sorry for those guys. Mom can be a bit of a difficult person.

Slipping on a pair of silky shorts and a matching top, I grabbed my favorite knee-high socks. They were awesome! They had these cute, little, pink pom-poms on each side and a little cat's face near the toes.

Cracking the door open, I found the hallway was dark except for one lone candle that hung between Loki and Luci's bedrooms.

I hate the dark. It was just a void of emptiness unless something decided to hide in it, scare you, and eat your soul!

I was halfway to Loki's door when he swung it open and grabbed my hand. I squeaked, as the 'monster' pulled me inside Loki's room.

"You take forever," he huffed. He stood in his pajamas, filled with superheroes from human comics. "Come tuck me in."

Shrugging my shoulders, thankful I didn't get eaten, I watched him climb into the massive bed and pulled the covers over him. "Good night, Loki!" I waved to him, but he grabbed my hand again.

"You're s'posed to kiss me goodnight! A good nanny, who cared about the kid they were looking after, would do that."

I bit my finger. *I only wanted to kiss the person who I would love one day.*

"Not on the cheek."

Loki groaned, "What about my forehead? Does that work with your silly logic?"

"I-I guess not. And it isn't silly!" I stomped my foot.

Loki laughed, shooing me out the door. "I'm just kiddin' with ya, Uriel. You are fun to rile up."

Squinting my eyes at him, I turned to open the door. Loki had already rolled over in bed, shifting to get comfortable.

Loki was a nice boy, just misunderstood. He plays a lot of mean pranks, but I think it is just because he wants attention. It didn't matter if it was good or bad, he just wanted it.

"Loki?" I called to him. "Would you like me to read you a story?" Loki rolled over with his eyebrows arched. "You might be too old or just not interested, but my mom reads to me every night. Maybe I just want to share it with you, you know, with my first friend."

Loki's eyes held no emotion. He stared at me as blank as a canvas. As I turned to leave, he jumped from the bed, pulling me back to the empty chair next to the bed.

"I'd like that," he whispered. "I'd like that very much."

Loki pulled out a book from his pillow and handed it to me. The golden words at the top of the book were, *The Little Prince*. I smiled, touching each raised letter before opening the famous book by the French author.

Lucifer

I don't know how to act around her. Hell, I barely know how to be in my own skin. The itch that fills me, day after day, to spill the blood of the evil souls Father has confined in his special section of Hell, only worsens my wrath.

Coming here was supposed to help with the discomfort of my heart beating erratically in my chest. Her touch was doing things to me, and I couldn't be sure if it was for good or evil purposes. My arms wanted to move on their own, caging her around my body so no one could touch her or steal her away from me.

Slinging another whip at the fallen mafia leader before me did nothing to satisfy me anymore. It gave me no rush of adrenaline to rival the exhilaration I felt around Uriel.

The touch of her hand—the delicacy and the pallor against my sunburned and callous skin, held stark differences. She was the silky cloud while I was the raging lighting that could split her in two.

Staying away from her would be impossible now. The golden thread that tied us together was strung too tight already.

My body, my heart, and my soul urged me back to the confines of the palace walls to ensure she was safe, sleeping soundly in her bed.

Dropping the whip, I waved to the demons to discard the helpless sap in front of me. No pleasure came from his beating, no sense of accomplishment, and no dark sludge eased from enveloping my heart.

I found a new way to keep my monsters at bay, and it was the goddess who slept in the room next to mine.

Uriel was so close to me earlier; she was willing to approach me, and she didn't even know why. She doesn't know who I really am, what I am capable of, or what darkness I've been fighting for so long. Would she accept me?

Should I fight it?

"No, you shouldn't." Father's voice rang through the torture chamber.

Chapter 12

Lucifer

"You shouldn't fight it." Father's voice rang again in the now empty room. "I fought the bond before I met your mother. I was so angry with Selene that I insisted I never wanted a mate, just some other goddess." He scoffed, touching the various whips on the wall. The blood smeared onto his fingers. Wiping them away on his pant leg, he stared at the pool of blood on the floor.

"But once I saw her, it all changed. I'm sure it will take you some time to see that. Although, considering you decided to protect her instead of following through with your proclamation, maybe not as long as expected. This morning, you were adamant about locking yourself in Tartarus." I ground my jaw.

That is where I should go, but I needed to protect her. What if there was something else that she needed protection from, besides me?

"Uriel soothes your anger. Why are you resisting it?"

"I-I don't know how to act around her," I said, embarrassed. "I've pushed everyone away all these years. You know that better than anyone."

Father agreed, pulling me away from the empty cell. "Uriel needs time to grow, as do you. It's a perfect match for the both of you." Father chuckled. You are growing to be more innocent of your evil, and she'll grow to have a little more..." Father stopped his words, feeling my anger spike. "Well, you know." He laughed aloud.

My bare feet crossed the red carpet of our family wing. My mind reeled at my father's words: *'let things take over; let the bond work its magic; don't fight it.'*

Easier said than done. I could still hurt her. I could still hurt my family if I wasn't careful.

Stopping at her door, my hand reached for the cold, golden handle.

Could I just check on her? Just to ensure she was sleeping soundly in her bed?

My body tensed, concerned she was uncomfortable, restless, or maybe scared of being in a new room, away from the parents she always had nearby.

She seemed like a person who would have trouble being in a new place.

Taking a breath, I knocked. After a few repetitions, calling her name quietly, I cracked the door only to realize the lamp was still shining on her side table, with no Uriel to be found. The fire burned in my gut.

Where the fuck is she?

I stormed into her room. The door banged the wall, leaving behind a nice imprint of the door handle. Raging into the bathroom, she was not there nor under the bed. I stripped the sheets to be doubly sure and finally checked the window to verify she didn't sneak out. Growling, I hastened to Loki's room to wake him to help me find her. The door swung open, slamming the wall like the previous, only for me to pause when I heard a soft purring flowing from the oversized, plush rocking chair.

It was my mother's favorite. She moved it from my room to Loki's when he was small, obliging him to stay in his bed rather than roam the palace. Now it sat bare most nights, starting just over a month ago.

Closing the door halfway so that the light didn't disturb any sleeping bodies, I noticed Uriel curled into a ball with a book on the arm of the massive chair; the book, *The Little Prince*, still opened to page twenty. My heart softened, observing my mate rub her cheek on the velvet chair. Her neck was bent at an odd angle with her hair hanging off the arm, almost touching the floor. Loki's face was toward Uriel with his mouth distended, drooling on his pillow.

I chuckled, taking the book and placing it on the nightstand. With Uriel's legs tucked close to her chest, it was no problem slipping my arms under her knees and behind her back. Uriel didn't stir in the slightest. She purred again, like a little kitten, as I walked across the hall. Her breath tickled my chest, which was still bare from working. As she nuzzled closer, my body relaxed, no longer feeling the tightness in my chest from the worry of harming her.

She was like freaking Xanax.

My nose veered straight to her hair. I was no werewolf by any means, but I must have inherited some of my mother's genes because Uriel smelled delicious.

She smelled like a sunrise on Earth, just rising above the ocean waters. It must've been the oil that she used in her bath. Mother often commented how much she enjoyed the ocean when she and Father visited.

Maybe I could take her to the ocean, just her and me. We could bring some of the demon guards, in human form, and let her feel the waves washing over her feet. I could almost hear her squeals of excitement seeing a dolphin jumping through the waves.

The small things. I could see she would appreciate the small things.

Pulling the sheets back on the bed, I placed her gently on the mattress. Her body curled into a ball except for a lonely arm sticking out, searching. Surveying her bed, I found a stuffed sheep and settled it into her arms. She seized it, sighing contently.

We had a long way to go if we were to be mates, and it wasn't just her. She had to grow up, and I had to learn to be less... me. Getting my hopes up was wrong, begging her to fix me was, too. I had to fix myself before any progress on that front could be made.

My lovely mate curled her body around the stuffed animal, her eyelashes fluttering across her cheeks. Uriel dressed her body in small silk shorts with knee-high socks.

I would never admit this to anyone, but that was something I loved seeing on a woman. There was something about her white thighs peeking through the small gap between her shorts and their covered knees that I found erotic.

There was no question. I was insanely attracted to her. I wanted her in ways I never thought I would. My devilish mind wanted to wreck her innocence and claim it for my own. That's what I was, the Destroyer, and my cock wanted to do just that—destroy her innocence.

Fuck, these feelings.

I grabbed my painfully hard erection, pulling the covers over her body.

As much joy as I would get watching her sleep, I needed to leave because I had a growing problem. I've never had to deal with it this bad before.

The throbbing ache in my dick was giving me the worst jean burn. Turning off the light, I exited her room, closing the door quietly so I did not disturb her slumber. As soon as I turned, a little head popped out of a nearby room.

Normally, I would not startle, but that head belonged to the only woman that could manage that feat. "Mother." My voice rang higher than I intended. Her eyes widened, and she giggled silently, patting my arm.

"I scared you?" she whispered, astonished. "Why, how could I? Oh!" Her eyes diverted immediately as she tried to glance to the floor but instead glimpsed a situation any teenager, or hell, even a man of my age, would find completely embarrassing.

"Good night, Mother." I walked to my bedroom door, opening and closing it quickly. Leaning against the door, I sighed heavily.

Not once in my teenage years had I been caught with a woman. Now, my mother catches me leaving my mate's room with a raging erection.

Soft knocks drew me from my embarrassment to open the door; Mother was still there. "Yes?" I hissed, still pushing my erection down from my jeans, making sure it was completely covered by the door.

"Do you need help?" My eyebrows raised, questioning what she was asking. "You know, with that, does your father need to—?"

"Mother! I don't need any help!" I hissed.

"He might have some pointers on how he dealt with me while we courted," she said lovingly.

"Ember," Father's voice rang behind her.

"Fates, could this night get any worse?" I spat, trying to shut the door.

Father put his foot in the door, preventing me from closing it. "Everything alright?"

"Just leave me alone!" I growled out. His foot retracted, allowing the door to finally shut.

"He's hurting, babe. He's got *man trouble* downstairs," Mother whined.

"Love, just leave the man alone. He will figure it out." Father began pulling on her hand, her feet dragging on the carpet.

"Maybe you can talk to him?" she pleaded. Father grumbled some incoherent words, leading her down the hall.

Uriel

A growl sounded somewhere in the room. My eyes flipped open, and my head turned in all directions. I wasn't sitting in Loki's room anymore. I was lying down in my bed. The growl happened again, and I jumped up in attack position. My arms spread out like a karate master with my knees bent, ready to lunge to the door. Then I put my hand to my stomach, hearing the irritating groan again.

Aha! I was just hungry.

Giggling, I jumped, landed my booty on the bed, and hopped down. It was still early; at least it looked early by the way the red sun had yet to appear over the horizon. The puppies outside weren't even leaving their pens to come out to play.

Taking a quick shower, not even daring to wash my hair since I did it the night before, I pranced out in just my lacy bra and panties, trying to find something to wear. Mom always liked me to wear white, which was a nice color, but I wanted to wear something different.

Shuffling through the massive closet, I found clothes that weren't mine, but they looked too tempting not to wear.

I mean, they are in my room, so I guess they are alright to wear, right?

Flipping through each dress, I found one that suited my taste for the day—pale pink flowers with hints of blue and yellow were scattered throughout. It was thin-strapped, showing off my shoulders, and would easily accommodate my wings breaking through in the back. Gasping, I realized it was exactly my size.

It was destiny!

Staying barefooted, I peeked out the door. The hallway was lit, no longer dark and creepy. *No monsters here.* Everyone's door was shut, and the baby wasn't crying.

Maybe I could make breakfast before the demons even got up to help prepare it.

Shutting my door quietly, I skipped down the hall. The dining room was dark but the light in the kitchen had me bolting to the door so no monsters could get me.

Stumbling in, a woman with a white apron tied loosely around her back glanced at me. "Goddess! Are you alright, child?" Dropping the bowl on the counter, she came to see if I had any cuts or bruises.

"I'm fine," I brushed my knees away. "I, uh, was actually coming to make breakfast for everyone since they were so nice to let me stay." The woman's fanged smile helped my nervousness float away.

"I'm Nora. And you must be Uriel, right?" Nodding with a broad grin on my face, I watched as she pulled an apron from the wall behind me. "How about you put this on? I bet Lucifer and Loki would love it if you made them their favorites." Gasping, I walked over to the counter to see what she was making.

"Lucifer loves Belgian waffles with dark chocolate chips and fresh maple syrup. Loki prefers strawberry preserves with whipped cream."

Nora helped me every step of the way. She made sure I put in the exact ingredients and poured them into the waffle maker with precise measurements. I committed all of it to memory since I wasn't allowed to cook back home.

You burn down the kitchen one time, and Mom won't let you anywhere near a stove for the rest of your life.

While I paid extra close attention to Lucifer and Loki's waffles, Nora prepared Hades' and Ember's meals.

Nora was a wolf who lived in Ember's pack back on Earth. She was just a simple omega, meaning she wasn't the strongest, but she helped with important roles in the kitchen. Loukas was her mate. He was a demon who held the highest position possible for such a creature. As she reminisced on how they met, I couldn't help but think of that word again—*mate*.

Dad called Mom that, a lot. I thought it was a just friend or someone you felt really close to, but it seems so much more than that.

"Uriel."

My mind replayed the times when Dad would repeat it to Mom.

"Uriel."

Like right before they would kiss, hug one another, or stare into each other's eyes.

It was deeper than friendship or companionship. There was a spark between them I couldn't figure out. Mate, a mate is more than a friend. It's someone you love, but it is also something else... it's a... it's a.... a special connection.

"Uriel!"

The bowl I was stirring for the fresh batch of waffles toppled to the counter, causing some of the batter to splatter on my cheeks.

"Whoops!"

Nora laughed, grabbing the towel from her apron. "You were off in dreamland over there, are you alright?" Laughing, I licked the batter off my finger.

"Yes, sorry. Can I ask you a question, Nora?"

Nora removed the rag, checking to see if I had any more batter on my face. "Of course. What is it, child?"

And for the second time in 24 hours, I asked again, "What is a mate?"

Chapter 13

Uriel

Nora dropped the rag, clutching her hand to her chest. The beads of sweat pouring from her head were wiped away with her free palm. "Oh, dear." She retrieved the rag from the floor and frantically wiped the counter.

"Um," she hummed to herself, engaged with arranging the food on the serving cart. "I think that conversation would be best with Ember," her voice trailed from the conversation.

I picked at my fingernails again, watching the pale pink polish flick to the floor.

Stop that.

That isn't sanitary in the kitchen.

I sighed heavily. *Everyone was dead set on not telling me.*

Turning away from Nora, I picked up the two special plates I made for my two favorite boys and put a silver covering over the top of each.

"Okay, okay, wait." Nora patted me on the shoulder.

Was it that big of a secret what a mate was? Everyone else knew and threw out the word in everyday conversation. My parents used it, but I just thought it was a pet name.

"Mates are something special in the supernatural communities. Do you understand how marriages work in the human world?" I nodded, sniffing up the snot that trickled from my nose.

I knew a lot about human customs; I knew more about humans than I did about the people around me. I spent hours watching them in Mom's little pool in the living room, especially watching children in classrooms. A lot of the things I learned came from those schools. It was fun, it was different, and it made me feel like I was part of the classroom. The only thing was, that I couldn't interact with them, and Mom would pull me away as soon as the lessons were over.

"Mates are similar, except... well, they mean *more* than a simple marriage. Mates are essentially soulmates; they are another part of your soul that compliments you, completes you, and, most of all, loves you for who you are."

"Oh." I rubbed my nose. "T-thank you for telling me, Nora." Nora nodded, satisfied with her answer until another question popped up in my head. "But how do you know? How do you know if you have found your soulmate?"

Nora's body stiffened. "That's a discussion for another time, dear; you don't need to worry about that right now." Nora pushed the cart out into the dining room, it was already set with beautiful placemats, dishes, and glass goblets. Several people sauntered into the room, including Ares and his mate, Mariah.

"Look at you cooking," Ares cooed at me. "I bet Lucifer is going to throw a fit."

Mariah swatted him on the shoulder. "It's adorable. I think it's great you want to help Nora, too. I tried a couple of times, but Ares is a bit of a beast when he doesn't get his morning—"

Nora cleared her throat, setting the large mound of waffles and pancakes on the table. "I think we got it, Mariah." Nora smiled at her. Nora looked the same age as the rest of us, but she had a very cheerful, calm attitude that reminded me of how a loving grandmother would be for humans. She pointed to me to sit down at the table and served me some yogurt and granola.

"How did you know?" I smiled at her.

"It's my job to know." She winked. "Plus, your mom made a giant list of all the foods you will and will not eat and handed it off to Ember." Nora rolled her eyes while I giggled.

That sure sounds like Mom.

Taking the granola, I sprinkled it on top, making a giant heart shape in the middle. Wiggling my booty to get comfortable, I lifted my spoon to dig in.

"Mother!" An enormous roar echoed from the hallway leading to the family quarters, and fire blew outside the dining room entrance. I saw Loki running past, screaming for his mom.

"Where the fu—" Luci walked in wearing black joggers and a tight, black muscle tee.

That must be his favorite color.

His breath halted, looking over at the table.

My favorite color is pink, obviously.

"Hi, Luci! Hi, Loki! Look, I made you both breakfast!" I jumped out of my chair, waving them over. Loki ran to me, swiftly hiding behind me.

"He's still hot. Blow him to calm him down!" Loki peeked from behind me, using my dress as a shield.

Ares slammed his fist on the table, laughing and making the cutlery rattle.

I skipped over to Luci to blow on his face. "Better?" His eyebrows furrowed but he followed quickly behind me to his seat.

Hades and Ember entered shortly after, staring at the now charred rug on the floor as they walked across it. The rug crunched and crumbled to ash beneath their feet.

"What happened to my rug?" Ember whined. Her eyes glanced at Luci, and her shoulders sagged. "I'll get a new one, sweetheart, just go eat."

Luci walked back over, trying to pull out a chair for me. His eyes glanced at me and the seat.

"No, *you* have to sit, so I can show you!" I whispered. His stern face lightened, a curl of his lip revealing part of his teeth. Once Loki sat down, everyone stared at me waiting for the big reveal.

I picked at my fingers again, only for those little tingles to appear as Luci grabbed my hand.

"What's wrong? Are you upset?" His eyes bore into mine, triggering those crazy butterflies from last night.

"Umm, it's just that everyone is staring." My face turned red hot, and one of my hands covered my face.

One scowl from Luci spurred everyone to avert their eyes and dig into their meals.

"Better?" His thumb grazed my knuckles. I smiled at him.

He was actually talking to me.

Freeing my hand, I pulled the silver coverings from their plates, displaying their favorite foods. Loki laughed at the funny face I drew with his whipped cream, while Luci's smirk widened.

That's the most I've seen of his teeth!

I jumped up and down clapping softly. I started to my seat only to feel my hand caught by Luci's.

How did I know it was Luci? Because it was all tingly!

He pulled me closer. I thought he wanted more waffles, but he patted the seat beside him. Nora had already picked up my plate, setting it down carefully at the spot Luci indicated.

"I've got ya, dear." Nora winked at me again before returning to her seat at the table.

The table continued with idle chatter, discussing the tasks at hand. Hades was doing his kingly stuff, and Ember was working today while tending to Lilith—*I wasn't exactly sure what work though. It had something to do with a sphere and matching.*

Loki stuffed his face with another mouthful of waffles, the syrup dripping from his mouth.

"Oh, Uriel, Loki is going to the Celestial Kingdom for lessons today, so you won't have to watch him much."

Loki groaned, getting up from his chair. "Do I have to? I don't really want to go; it's Uriel's first day, and I want to show her around."

I giggled, watching Hades shake his head. "No, Lucifer will do that," he said off-handedly. "Besides, you're behind on your modern-day human history. Hera said that was Uriel's favorite subject. Maybe she can tutor you when you get home."

Loki groaned, walking to the entryway. "Can you at least zap me there, so I don't have to walk to the portal?"

Hades dropped his fork, rubbing his temples. "Would it kill you to get a little exercise?" Hades huffed, and Ares slammed the table again with his fists.

"See, isn't Hades fucking funny? You know, the Underworld, killing, death?" Mariah shook her head, her face flushed.

"Oh, do you kill people down here?" I shivered, not liking the sound of it.

"Nah, they are already dead when they get here, Uriel. So, Dad? Little zippy zappy zoo?" Hades waved his hand, and abruptly, Loki vanished.

I squealed, jumping from the table. "That was amazing! Can you do it again? Make me disappear!" Luci pulled my hand, sitting me back down and moving the chair closer to him.

Lucifer

"Hey, Lucifer can teach you a few tricks." Ares snickered, pulling Mariah to his lap. Mariah playfully hit his shoulder, again.

She secretly loved it when Ares acted like an ass. Stupid damn mate bond, and their crazy shit.

"He will?" Uriel's dewy eyes looked up at me, her deep lashes almost touching her eyebrows.

Those eyes, I could get lost in their light gold swirls.

Her dark, curled hair covered her chest in an unwelcome manner. My finger extended to rid the stray hair from her face until the obnoxious God of War howled.

"Rawwrr! Get 'er, tiger! It might help if you talked to her though!"

Our moment was ruined, or at least my moment.

I whipped my head around with fire in my eyes. Ares threw his hands up, scooting him and Mariah down the table.

Uriel, seemingly oblivious, touched my arm, rubbing it softly. "You didn't say 'yes' or 'no.'" She pouted her bottom lip. My eyes glanced from her lips back to her eyes.

The damn thing was wobbling. That wasn't the only thing that was going to be wobbling back to the room if I didn't get a hold of myself.

"Yes, Uriel, I'll show you." My voice came out deeper than I wanted, but that didn't bother her like it did the others in the palace.

Her arms wrapped around my neck, shifting her seat closer to mine as her bare thigh brushed my joggers. My parents clutched each other's hands waiting to see what I would do next.

I wouldn't hurt my mate. I couldn't even imagine doing that now.

The coolness of her skin sunk deep into my chest, instantly calming me from Ares' outburst. My hand moved to return the hug, but it was cut short when she pulled away. "Thank you, Luci! After breakfast?"

I nodded—*because that was all I could do without choking on my spit.*

When I woke up this morning, my goal was to get closer to her, and here I was, getting ready to spend the day with her.

Hell, spending the day with another being was going to be a feat within itself. I couldn't stand more than five minutes with anyone except my parents.

Usually, I labored out at the rim of Tartarus, feeling the heat tan my face and the sulfur fester in my nose. When my eyelids dared remove the darkness, my mind flipped to her.

Did she sleep well? Was she worried when she awoke and realized her body had been moved to her bed?

Loki was already in the hall, banging on the door to Uriel's room when I went to check on her. My fists tightened. I wanted to be the one to wake her, or at least know if she was still sleeping. Pushing Loki aside, he grunted but knew not to complain.

After I knocked on the door respectably, Loki rolled his eyes and crossed his arms. "She isn't in there. She would have woken up."

I ignored his commentary, only thinking of Uriel on the other side. After cracking the door, it was clear that she wasn't inside. The heat of her bed had faded, and her soothing aroma of the gardenias didn't rush to me. Gritting my teeth and growling, my eyes grew red. Loki took off down the hall, knowing I was about to explode.

Where the fuck could she have gone?

Dashing down the hall, my body erupted into flames. My hands continued to blaze until I saw her, her eyes full of excitement, as I walked into the dining room, barefooted.

Never in all my years had my body calmed so quickly. The fire was doused within seconds. Even my hands did not leave charred remnants on my fingers. She stood there, like the angelic goddess she was, a woman who could best the beauty of Aphrodite. The weirdest part of it all was she didn't even know it.

Mother was smiling like the sneaky Cheshire Cat with her hand constantly patting Father's "I told you so." He only grabbed her face, kissing her gently.

Spending the whole day with her without making a fool of myself. That was going to be my next challenge.

Chapter 14

Lucifer

Once she finished breakfast, Uriel excused herself to her room to get ready for the day. Going around barefoot in the Palace wouldn't be smart. You never knew if Loki left a tack in the hallway for some unknowing servant.

My hands twitched on my thigh before running my hand through my hair. A shaky sigh escaped my lips as my leg shook up and down.

"Relax." Ares scooted his chair over, poking my shoulder a few times before finally resting his hand on it.

He made the mistake of trying to pat my shoulder when I was angry and earned a nasty burn on his hand that took an hour to heal, much longer than the usual burn he incurred from my father.

"Just be yourself. I'm pretty sure she would like anyone pursuing her," Ares snickered as I gave him a fierce glare.

The worst part of it was, that it was true. She may very well fall for anyone showing her any sort of attention because of her innocence.

I rubbed my scruffy face with my palm as my mother nudged my father repeatedly. She was trying to provoke him to say something, any words of encouragement, but it obviously wasn't panning out. He scowled at her, but her big, green eyes only fluttered, impelling him to bend a knee and concede to her wishes.

Sighing thickly, his hands landed on the table gently. "Son," he cleared his throat, "I just want you to know that she is *your mate*, she *is* attracted to you, and she *will* be yours. Just don't blow it."

"Hades!" Ember hissed. "Honey, you are going to be fine. There is a reason your souls were paired. Now, I know you have a lot of soul-searching to do with yourself, to find out who you really are. After all those years spent wandering the palace halls alone, refusing to socialize with your peers, this will be good for you both."

I hummed, billowing my shirt away from my body. *Fates, I was sweating, me, the fucking son of Hades, sweating like a pig.*

"I'm going to shower," I grumbled, rising from the table. The sliding of the chair across the dining room floor rang in my ears like nails on a chalkboard. Everything seemed heightened, and I couldn't figure out why.

Proceeding down the hall, I could visualize the younger version of myself. Sulking, I passed by my childhood replica. He was dressed in a miniature Armani suit, his hair combed over. I was the perfect gentleman, and the young girls raved for me, but I disregarded them. My hands tightened and released repeatedly—*a terrible habit I picked up after watching my father get angry at a few demons. Now it indicated the onset of the fire that would be released.*

My miniature self vanished; my breath heaved in and out as I continued down the hall. Stopping outside my door, I could hear Uriel singing in her room, oblivious to what we were.

The first time she grabbed my hand, she said she felt tingles, but does she still? She hasn't mentioned them once since seeing me for the first time.

Once dressed, I opened my door to find Uriel patiently waiting outside her door. Her gold sandals, which my mother had picked out, complimented the dress she wore. My mother was obsessed with all things cute and girly, she said it made her feel young. By the looks of it, Uriel would be the same. My lip twitched, thinking how similar my mate was to my mother. Father was a brooding man like myself, so I guess it made sense.

Only the exact opposites attract, right?

Huffing, I strode over to her; her eyes brightened immediately. "Are you going to show me a magic trick now?"

As I opened my mouth to answer her, Blaze, another family pet, ran across the hallway. His small foxlike body, and the fire that replaced his tail, zoomed down the hallway into the grand foyer.

"Wait, what was that?" Uriel took off down the hallway, her hair flying behind her, touching the back of her heels.

"Wait!" I exclaimed, but her contagious laughter echoed down the halls utterly carefree. Smirking, I ran at a pace to catch up to her, but she was fast, faster than I ever thought she would be, especially for a woman who had been cooped up in a house most of her life.

"Here kitty, kitty!" Uriel cooed.

Mother rounded the corner, holding Lilith. Her broad grin could light up the entire darkened hallway. Mother watched me, intrigued that I was chasing my mate down the hall. "Have fun," she whispered to herself, but I heard it. There was a hint of mischief in her eye as I glanced behind me, while she skimmed down the hall.

Shaking my head, I followed Uriel's inane giggles until we arrived at the palace library. Her body abruptly halted, like there was a giant piece of cake waving in her face. Barely stopping in time, I landed just behind her, my arms grabbing her to prevent her from toppling over.

I have a feeling I well have to catch her all day long if she went to find Blaze every twenty minutes.

"This is the biggest library I have ever seen!"

I chuckled, loosening my grip on her. "Probably the only library you have ever seen in person," I muttered. Uriel playfully hit me, walking inside.

"I could spend all day in here."

My knees bent, my body slumping in exasperation. "Not you too," I spoke lowly.

My mother spent so much time here.

Uriel's hair flipped in my direction, and her sweet smell invaded my nose, chasing whatever thoughts I had about sealing the library forever out the window. Instead, my body ached to move her bed in here if that would make her happy.

Uriel's hand landed on her hip, eyes narrowing at me. "I'll have you know, I *have* been to a library!" She sassed. Biting my bottom lip, I crossed my arms, amused at this little woman's temper. "One night, Mom took me to her office."

Office? Scratching my head, I couldn't figure out what the hell she was talking about. There weren't any offices in the Celestial Kingdom. Uriel's head yawed, surveying the three stories of wall-to-wall shelves. Lines of ladders on rollers were pushed by several servants who were dusting.

"What 'office' does your mom work for?" I asked.

"Uh..." Uriel put a finger to her lips. "The Celestial Office..." her voice wavered. Her golden eyes sought mine, looking for truth. "There isn't a Celestial Office, is there?" My mate's joyful smile turned into a frown, suddenly twiddling her fingers and looking away in shame.

I wasn't sure where Hera worked, but obviously, she didn't visit the Celestial Palace. Their library was extensive.

"Hey," I walked to her, pulling her fingers away.

That was a nasty habit I was obliged to break: she couldn't pick at her precious fingers. They were already inflamed, and I wouldn't have my mate doing that to herself. Then I needed to help her overcome this nervousness. Sure, she was innocent, literally. She was deprived of the worlds around her and cooped up in a house barely suitable for the high-ranking goddess and angel. They lived humbly to maintain the innocence they thought would protect Uriel.

No. My mate was going to discover the truth about everything, and I was going to be the one to enlighten her.

"Listen here." She tried to pull her hands away from mine. I gripped them tighter. She gasped when I pulled her pained fingers to my lips. They healed instantaneously and her skin was no longer irritated. "As much as you love your mother and father, they kept things from you. There is nothing to be embarrassed about. It wasn't your fault."

Feeling the heat well in her eyes, I knew she was about to spill tears, and the mate bond pulled me like a dairy cow trying to evade its milking.

I wasn't in love with her, yet. I was fighting it, but the strength of my soul reaching for her had me trying to recede, to let us both find ourselves.

Uriel blinked away her tears before they fell.

Thank the Fates. I would have turned into a flaming torch if she dared release even one tear. I disliked the gut-wrenching feeling of seeing her upset.

Uriel beamed at me, a smile barely reaching her eyes. "Thank you," she whispered. Our hands were still entwined as we stared into each other's eyes.

Could my infatuation with her get any stronger?

My question was quickly answered as our gaze broke when Blaze pawed Uriel's foot. She loosed an excited squeal before quickly covering her mouth to muffle the sound. Blaze cocked his head to the side, studying her intently.

"Oh, you aren't a kitty! You're a cute little foxy thingy!" Clearing my throat, Blaze floated from the floor and landed in Uriel's hands—*like damn Tinkerbell.*

"This is Blaze, he's a phantom tail. They help bring werewolves' souls to the underworld when they get lost along the way to their human counterparts."

Uriel

If I could crawl back into my bed at home with Mom and Dad, I would. Hiding under the covers, smelling my mom's favorite fabric softener of lavender and vanilla on the fresh linen would ease the painful beating of my heart. Being utterly embarrassed was completely new to me, but I felt it right now.

I was seeing myself as something other than the 'smart girl' Mom always called me. I can't go back home. For as long as I can remember, my mother told me how smart I was, how

I surpassed the intellect of women my age, but here I was, befuddled and clumsy with my words.

I didn't even know where my mom worked.

Ask me what type of virus werewolves use to impair their enemies versus the venom they use to mark their mates. Ask me the differences between fae and fairy wings and to explain how each line interfaces with the season to give them optimal flight. I knew it; I knew it all by heart, reciting each book I read from memory. I have a photographic memory, and I was bottled up inside the home where I spent 99% of my time.

I checked my mother's accounting numbers for the department of whatever 'office' she worked for. She never told me, even when I asked. She would just go about her day like she didn't hear me. I was too eager to please, so I did it anyway.

I didn't even know exactly what powers my mom had. It was all cherry-picked. She perfectly selected each piece of information that was given to me. She had me memorize information that I would never use, just to keep my mind preoccupied, so I couldn't ask questions about the things that really mattered.

Internally, I screamed at the top of my lungs because people are seeing me as something I'm not.

I'm. Not. Stupid. I'm not.

I'm just seeing the world for the first time I can't help but find everything so fascinating. I've read everything I could get my hands on, and yet, never interacted with other women my age.

Was I even considered a woman? To Luci and everyone else, I was probably just a child.

Luci grabbed my fiddling fingers and put them to his lips. The tingles rushed down my arm and filtered into my heart, radiating nothing but understanding and compassion. It was like he recognized what I was going through.

Surely, he understood.

I saw anger in his eyes when he scrutinized my mom from head to toe upon her arrival in a fit of fury. He even dared to wrap his wings around me. That felt like protection. The first real protection I had felt, unlike anything my parents provided—which is sad to admit.

Luci was different; he was different like me. I could already tell.

He held pain behind those eyes, and he didn't let it show on the outside. He built a wall inside, withholding all his emotions from everyone else. I just hide mine with empty smiles and laughter.

Maybe, just maybe, if I tore some of his walls down, he could show me who he really is, because these tingles, these bolts to my soul, were something I wanted to understand. The magnetic pulse that reigned down my body had me gasping for air, in a way I couldn't comprehend.

The air that surrounded him suddenly made my mouth dry as his words rang through my ears, "... there is nothing to be embarrassed about."

I wanted to hug him; I wanted to squeeze the life out of this man who had taken me under his wing today. His body tensed constantly, his fists balling tightly every time he became angry.

It hadn't escaped my notice. I just didn't know what to do or say when the awkward situation arose as his temper spiked. I was unsure if I would make it worse, so pretending it wasn't there was the only logical choice.

It had to be hard for him, to stick around and be social with everyone. Heavens, I knew what that was like. Luci was trying though... for me.

That had to mean something.

He wanted to spend time with me, of all people.

As the phantom tail sat on my hands, I rubbed the cutest animal I had ever seen up close. I knew good and well that there would be other things in the worlds I would get to explore now that would continue to top the previous.

Chapter 15

Uriel

I continued to pet the phantom tail. He purred into the palm of my hand, still rubbing his teeny-weeny, little head against it. "You are so cute! Yes, you are!" Luci hummed, petting it as my hand fell away. Our fingers touched, shooting that fun spark through me again. This time we both stilled, his fingers centimeters from my flaking fingernail polish.

Luci's dark eyes flickered. I felt my heart pound in my chest as his hand dared to touch my fingertips again. Internally, I was screaming, jumping on the balls of my feet, ready to just shove my hand back into his.

That's when he did it: he grabbed my hand gently, all on his own, intertwining my fingers with his! I dared not cough, sneeze, or even wiggle my toes for fear the sensation would end.

He felt it too.

It was plastered on his face: the cute raise of the eyebrow and the curl of his lips. His thumb grazed over my knuckle; I wanted to speak, but I feared if I did, I would say something so utterly stupid that it would ruin the moment. So, I just stood beside him, scrunching my toes in the gold sandals, waiting for him to say something, anything.

Blaze, sensing the tension, jumped from my other hand. The movement caught my attention, my eyes trailing him briefly. As my eyes backtracked to the dark god before me, I found he was still staring.

Do I say something?

It would really help if I had someone to pray to right now.

Luci turned his body, adjusting his fingers to lead me further into the library, without uttering a word. Taking me up the first set of stairs, he peeked back at me, seeing the flustered look of a teenage girl crushing on the hottest guy in school. Clearing my throat awkwardly, he chuckled.

Fates that chuckle! It vibrated in the back of his throat, heavy and filled with such manliness.

The butterflies began to stir in my stomach, becoming way too much to bear. I almost wanted to burst. We stopped moving halfway up the stairs.

Luci turned to me, looking down from his vantage point that was two steps higher. "Are you alright, Uriel?"

Um, no. I'm not.

"Yes." My raspy voice left my lips before I could clear my throat. Rubbing it with my free hand, he tugged me forward again, leading me to the top floor.

"This is the fantasy section."

His voice had me slowly melting into a puddle. Each step was harder to take. My stomach's butterflies were now traveling lower. His touch was overwhelming. This was the longest we held hands besides the hallway, but the tingles became strong, too strong! I whimpered, covering my mouth.

"You do like it. Good," he sighed, rubbing his hand through his dark brown hair. "I was worried you'd prefer to read all those scientific books like you read at home."

I wanna put my fingers through your hair... let me play with it.
Oh, better yet, let me smell that shampoo you used this morning.
Holy phantom tail, what is happening to my body?

My eyes couldn't leave his perfectly chiseled face. It was too pretty. The stubble gave him a rugged look that I had never seen before. I began seeing him in a whole new light than when I first met him. My hand clamped over my mouth to keep my tongue from hanging out. The heat created an unbearable pressure between my thighs.

This feeling, what is it?

Ripping my hand away, Luci's head darted behind him, watching me intently.

"I-I'm not feeling well." I backed away, gripping the railing.

Luci advanced, and I feared what else would happen if he touched me again. Gripping the banister tightly, I lifted my free hand to stop him. His eyes looked so broken, softening considerably, but I couldn't let him touch me. Otherwise, my body might explode.

"I... I... I'm going to go lie down." My wings exploded. Gliding down the staircase, the rush of the wind cooled the heat at the surface of my skin.

Blaze, who was curled up on the corner of a desk, lifted his head, watching me leave the great double doors.

My feet pounded along the lush, red carpet. Each step further from Luci weighed in my chest, slowing its pounding as if I shouldn't have left. Disappointment radiated from my heart, a strong feeling that I didn't think was mine. Tears brimmed my eyes as I hit the white doors of my room, pushing and pulling on the door handle until the door finally unlocked. I saw Luci down the hall, poking his head from behind a door, watching me fall into my room.

Diving onto the freshly made bed, I climbed under the covers in utter embarrassment.

My body was doing strange things, right in-between my thighs, and I couldn't understand it. It started when I held his hand, and looking at him more closely, I found him insanely good-looking—too good-looking.

I mean, I always saw him as handsome, but now it radiated so much more. His silence contrasted my incessant chatter. I never shut up. Mom told me as much, thousands of times when I tried to tell her about my day.

Granted, I'm sure my theories explaining why supernaturals in the Bergarian Realm were leaving to go to the Earth Realm were quite boring, but I felt like I was missing something. I was missing a vital piece of information that was available to everyone but me.

Why could I not figure it out?

My legs ached. My mind trailed straight back to Luci. Rubbing my thighs together for some sort of friction helped the ache, but it wasn't enough. I poked my head out of the covers to check that the door was completely shut, then I hid back under the covers again.

I've cleaned myself in the shower; I've touched that area before, but the pounding, my heart beating between my thighs, was so new. Biting my bottom lip, I lifted my dress slowly. Every touch on my skin was heightened to unexplainable extremes. It felt like peanut butter spread all over my body, warmed to the touch, and was melting off of me.

What am I doing?

My white laced panties were wet.

Did I tinkle? Oh, I peed! How embarrassing!

Throwing the covers off to jump in the shower, I heard a steady knock at the door. I froze in the middle of my room, unsure what to do.

Should I answer?

It could be Luci, and he will see how upset I am. I didn't want him to get mad. Biting my fingernails, I took several steps to the bathroom until a friendly voice stopped me.

"Uriel, it's me, Ember." Her voice was soothing.

Huffing at almost making it to the shower, I crept to the door, still not willing to let her in. I cracked it slightly, and her eyes peered straight into mine.

"Is everything alright? Luci said you ran off because you weren't feeling well." I nodded, trying to shut the door. Ember's little foot was already there, however. "Uriel, gods don't get sick."

Biting my cheek, I felt the tears well in my eyes. Whimpering, I finally let her in, certain I would get scolded into telling her what I did.

Walking in with the baby in hand, Ember had me shut the door and sit on an elaborate white couch in the middle of the room. "What's wrong? Why did you run? Did Luci say something to upset you?"

Shaking my head, I looked away from her, crossing and un-crossing my legs while messing with the hem of my dress.

"You can talk to me, Uriel, I know you've lived a pretty sheltered life. I lived similarly when I was younger." A tear ran down my cheek, only for Ember to catch it. "You better not let Luci smell your sweet tears, or he will barge in this door."

As if on cue, loud banging resonated from the door as soon as the words left her mouth.

"See I told you." She laughed.

"Is she okay?" Luci yelled through the door, making me flinch.

"He's mad at me." I let a few more tears fall until Ember stomped to the door.

"You listen here, young man"—she opened the door only wide enough to speak to her son—"she is fine. We are going to talk girl stuff now, and I'll call you when she comes out."

Luci's head popped over his mother, looking at me. His eyes bore into me again as I wiggled deeper into my seat.

He's pretty when he's angry.

Mom looks like one of those demons outside when she's angry.

Luci looked at his mother and turned his body away from the door to go into his room. Ember gently shut the door and walked back to her seat on the couch. Her eyes were warm and ever so motherly.

"Now, Uriel,"—her free hand patted my hands—"I have a fairly good idea of what's going on, but I think it would be better if you explained it to me so that I can fully understand what you are going through."

How could she possibly know what I was going through? My princess parts are acting as if I had another heart inside them, and rubbing my thighs together only helped a little. On top of that, I swear I peed myself.

I whimpered, and she looped her arm around me, the other holding baby Lilith who nuzzled into her mother's chest.

"Uriel, you need not suffer alone. It's just us girls, alright?"

Nodding slowly, her warm arm slid from my back, and I sat up straight. "I- well... my body was doing things."

I'm going to die of shame. Send me to Earth and bury me six feet under the soil, so my body can come back as a beautiful tree. Then chop it down and make paper, so some toddler can draw a picture of a dog crapping on the tree I used to be and throw me into recycling.

"What kinds of things?" Ember pried, her smile too big for my comfort.

Wiggling in my seat, I scooted farther from her. "It tingled, like a lot when I touched Luci's hand. Not like the first time when it tickled. Now it goes down my body and makes me feel weird." Ember nodded her head, her grin widening.

"You are scaring me," I whispered. Ember only laughed.

"I'm so sorry! I'm just... it is completely normal. I'm so happy you told me."

My shoulders slumped, feeling relieved and somewhat confused. "It is?"

"Of course, it is!" Her enormous smile fell, watching my reaction.

"Even, like... I feel like I might have tinkled in my panties." I gritted my teeth, waiting for a scolding.

I still remembered wetting the bed clear up until I was seven years old because of my terrible nightmares. They scared the tinkles right out. Luckily, I stop drinking water three hours before bed now.

"That's normal too," Ember cooed, pulling me closer to her. "And you didn't pee yourself. It's your body getting excited."

"E-excited about what?" My eyes grew wide, not understanding.

Ember shook her head, pulling Lilith closer. "I think it's time we talked about women's bodies and what they can do." A smile crept up her lips. "I'll invite Athena."

Chapter 16

Lucifer

Pulling my hair out, I stormed into my room and slammed the door.

Uriel just left; she just fucking left. I thought I had everything planned out perfectly. She looked like she would be into fantasy books. She loved to read. What woman doesn't love a good romance or even a fantasy novel?

As we reached the top of the stairs, she was hesitant, until her eyes widened not at the books but me. I was relieved, thinking, '*hey, I did well for a first date,*' and '*Definitely a Beauty and the Beast moment,*' only for her to rip her hand away, looking at me in fear.

Patting myself down several times, confirming my body wasn't on fire, my wings burst from my back; I was completely fine.

The sparks that lingered on our hands the entire way up the staircase gave me a raging boner, but I did a great job hiding that!

She stared at me like I was a beast; like she could see the destroyer I was.

I pummeled the wall of my bedroom with my fist. The dark wall crumbled as I used my other hand to beat the weak plaster.

I am failing already, and I haven't even started. She flew like a dove to the bottom of the staircase, running away from me as if her wings were on fire.

I could only watch in disappointment, concern, and yearning as she slipped away, closing her bedroom door. My emotions of disappointment in myself quickly turned to anger. My hands blackened and the cracks of my knuckles turned bright red. Soon my entire arms were ablaze, ready to destroy my entire room. I had to leave. I had to go beat the ever-living shit out of something because the one thing that kept me calm was afraid of me.

"*Lucifer, come to my office,*" my father's voice rang through my mind.

"*Not now,*" I growled, opening the bay windows to the outside. Pulling my shirt from my body, my wings protruded from my back, feeling the heat of the day's red sun. Fire lit the tips of my wings, ready for me to take flight to find my only remaining place of solace.

My mate wouldn't have me. I will have to spend the rest of my days in Tartarus.

"*It's about Uriel. Get the fuck down from the balcony and get in here. Now.*"

Hearing her name calmed me enough to fold my wings away, the fire burning in my hands now just black embers, smoking with the residual anger inside me. Stomping from the windows, I turned to leave my room and thunder down the hallways.

Servants scattered in the opposite direction upon seeing my state. They hunkered in the corners, but my eyes never trailed to them. My eyes stayed on my father's office, the doors open, ready for my entrance.

"Thanks for listening before flying off." Father's face was buried in his laptop, twirling his pen around his finger like his son wasn't about to lay ruin to a city.

"What of Uriel? Is she alright?" My deep voice reverberated through the walls. Father took no notice and wrote on a piece of paper to his right.

"Yeah, you did a good job with her this morning. The bond is working faster than I expected." The heat in my hands chilled, returning to my normal tanned skin.

"Pardon?" I questioned, walking barefoot into the room. "It sounded like you said, 'good job,' when in fact, she ran away from me in terror." I threw my hands up, exhausted.

Before I went to sleep, I planned everything in my head. I was going to take her around the palace, show her a great time, and maybe make her laugh.

Rubbing my hands up and down my face, I groaned and sat down on the gigantic, black leather couch. As I sunk into the couch, Father didn't once divert his attention from the paper he held, giving me nothing to go on.

"Yeah, your touch got too strong for her," he chuckled, flipping through another stack of papers.

My head perked up, slapping my hands on either side of the couch. "It did what?" I blurted and jumped from the couch.

"Yeah, the bond caused her to feel things she's never experienced." He laid the stack of papers on the desk. I rushed around where his chair sat, staring him in the face. Panting, I put both hands on either arm of his chair, he leaned back, wide-eyed watching my gaze burn into him.

"What. Happened?" My voice was no longer my usual deep voice, but that of a high-pitch prepubescent teen whose balls had yet to drop.

"Son, I usually worry for you when you get angry, but..." He licked his lips, still trying to back his head away from mine, "you are downright terrifying me right now." Releasing the chair, it snapped back from the weight of my father leaning away from me, forcing his hands to slam on the desk to catch him.

"Fates," he sighed.

"What happened?" I asked again, pleading for answers.

"Your mother is talking to her right now. She let me hear part of the conversation, but I cut her off when it got too detailed." He cleared his throat, pulling on his collar.

Too detailed? What was Uriel talking about? Was the bond that strong already, where she felt something other than friendship for me?

"Tell me every word." My hands slammed on the desk. No more begging, the fire inside was raging. I needed to know every bit of information I could.

Father eyed me warily but nodded his head in agreement. "Uriel left because the bond effects hit her all at once. The way you both have interacted with each other before was harmless, but as you spend more time together, the bond grows. Uriel is feeling the effects now..." his voice trailed, lowering his head, urging me to catch on.

How would she feel the effects? Were the tickles or tingles becoming too strong? Could I not hold her hand? Kronos, I had to touch her sometimes. I'll go mad.

My silence drove my father to grunt in disapproval. "Lucifer, what have YOU been feeling when touching her and holding her hand?"

It was my turn to clear my throat. Straightening, I walked away from him, rubbing my mouth with my hand. "Things," I grumbled.

"That is what she is experiencing: *things.*"

Turning back quickly, I eyed my worried father. My heart leaped in my chest.

The desires I experienced were now being felt by Uriel too. She wasn't completely a child?

Granted, it was obvious she wasn't. She was twenty-five years old, but her parents treated her like a damn child. Her mind was brilliant; I knew it was. It was her social skills that were lacking. I felt guilty that these lustful stirrings were inside me.

No holding back now.

"I want every word." I leaped back to the desk. "What did Mother say to her? What did she say back?"

Father slumped back in his chair, pinching his nose. "Please don't make me do this," he groaned. "I really don't want to do this." I ran back around to his chair; he stood abruptly, straightening his jacket. "No, don't you pin me again! I'm going to have nightmares of those eyes." He shivered, walking away. "Here it is. It's all I'm giving you, so listen up."

I stood far away from him, gripping the desk in excitement. I couldn't recall the last time I felt so giddy, so wonderful.

"She ran away from you because her *stuff* tingled." Standing there, still gripping the desk, my eyes wandered around the room.

Her stuff tingled?

My eyes widened at the sudden realization: HER STUFF TIN-GLED!

"No shit?" I covered my mouth with my hand. I don't remember the last time I smiled, but I was close, and I only wanted to give that smile to Uriel. "It tingled?" I repeated again.

Father eyed me cautiously while clearing his throat.

"What else? What else did she say?"

Father groaned, dragging himself to the large, glass window overlooking the perfectly manicured lawn. "Please don't make me."

He couldn't stop now. If he said anymore, I would explode in happiness. *Uriel liked me and I needed to know more!*

"She... she thought she... 'tinkled.'"

I stopped mid-track as I was approaching my father.

What the hell? Think here... I backed away, trying to discern what that meant.

Father grunted, furiously turning around. "Did you not watch porn like a normal teenager? Hell, even now?" I shook my head.

I spent most of my time in Tartarus. He knew that.

"Did someone say porn?" Ares walked in, a beer in hand. His mate was absent.

Thank the Fates.

Ares chugged the rest of the beer and sauntered into the room, slamming himself on the couch. "Does the young Prince need help in finding some *documentaries*? I have a good stash, so you could learn how to pleasure your mate at all levels of intimacy." He wiggled his eyebrows.

"There are levels?" I questioned, eyeing my father. His head banged on the glass as I looked from my uncle to my father.

"Duh, there are levels. I'm guessing your pecker hasn't graced the inside of anything. Good for you, but that means you are going to be clumsy as fuck when it comes to mating. She needs it to be good. She's gonna want you to know all the right places."

Ares willed another can of beer, chugging it down. "And also, she's so damn submissive, you could play her like a damn fiddle and have her cum all over your—"

"That's enough!" I growled.

He didn't need to speak of her that way, not in front of me or anyone else.

Ares held his hands up in the air, offering a truce. "What started this porn-watching chat then? Hades, I thought you said they were far from doing any of that." Father shook his head, stepping away from the window.

"From the looks of it, Uriel is progressing faster than anticipated. She's smart, intellectually anyway. Hera sent her diplomas; she's a damn genius. It's just her social skills aren't great after being babied for so long. Uriel will figure things out quickly. She knows her parents sheltered her, and she's willing to learn. With that... the bond took over, and her body is in hyper-drive. She didn't get to experience her teenage years, so her body's sexual appetite may grow rapidly as she spends more time with her mate." Father and Ares looked at me.

Ares was grinning like an idiot at my predicament. "That means my favorite nephew needs some lessons, eh?" Ares clapped his hands and rubbed them together. "Lucky for you, I've recorded all the best stuff. Athena should even hire me to teach a sex education course up in the Celestial Kingdom because it is that good. You can ask Vulcan, he and his wife are still banging it out on their weekend vacation that should have ended three years ago."

Too much information.

I groaned, but I didn't need Ares teaching me shit. "Just hand over the videos. I'll teach myself. I can't tolerate you providing commentary when I'm trying to concentrate."

"You mean, you don't want me in there when you rub one out?"

I willed a fireball to my hand, and Ares screamed like a girl and ran out of the room.

Chapter 17

Uriel

After a long, cold shower, I felt so much better. My hair was a tangly mess, so I spent a good portion of my morning brushing and detangling it with my favorite pink brush. Being in no rush to walk outside and face Luci, I played with the stuffed animals my mom so graciously had the messengers bring.

They were my only comfort while I hugged them tightly, pulling at their ears to make the little fuzzy hair go in the right direction.

If my body acted that way towards Luci, does his body do the same thing? It must not be, because he didn't look petrified like I was. Maybe he already knew all about what a body does, and he just ignored it.

My body reacting to him means that it likes him, so does that mean that I like him too?

Rolling on my stomach, I waved my legs behind me, swinging them back and forth in the air.

I wish I had some gum. I think better when smacking on gum.

"The tingles mean you like someone," I whispered to myself, fixing the bowtie on my stuffed unicorn. Stopping suddenly, I pushed Mr. Rainbow Farts away from me.

It's actually quite funny how he got his name. Dad was putting me to bed one night. He leaned over, and, BAM, he just let one fly. Giggling hysterically, I called him out and told him he was a 'Mr. McFarty Pants.' He didn't like that, so he blamed it on one of my stuffed animals. Of course, I asked which one, because I knew my stuffed animals, and none of them had a loose bum like him.

Then he pulled out a pretty rainbow unicorn! He had big, fluffy hair on top of his head, a colored horn, and a long bright tail. 'This is Mr. Rainbow Farts,' he snorted. 'He did it.' Dad pointed to the stuffy. I knew he was lying, but for the sake of getting the stuffed animal, I agreed to blame it on Mr. Rainbow Farts.

"Oh, I like him!" I whispered again, putting my hand to my mouth. "Like, I *like* him, like him."

Throwing my face into the pillow, I let out a gigantic scream. *I had my first crush! And I didn't even know it!* Releasing another scream, my legs kicked frantically while the excitement rushed over me.

Stopping suddenly, I stared back at Mr. Farts, pulling him up and staring into his eyes. "Mom is going to kill me."

I wasn't allowed to have a crush on a boy. Mom said they would steal my innocence, which was hard to believe because I'm the Goddess of Innocence. How could they steal my power away? I didn't even know how to use it properly. I shrugged my shoulders and heard a knock on the door.

"Are you ready for your lesson?" Ember peeked inside. Her eyes were the only thing I could see, but the pitter-patter of her feet echoed against the carpet.

I've got really good ears.

"T-today?" I questioned. "You set it up for today?"

How did Athena work so fast? She's such a smart lady and very important, and yet she came all the way back to the Underworld to teach me!

"Oh, yes. She does this lesson regularly with those going through..." Ember's voice trailed off until she came back with a new thought, "with those who are first realizing all their body's functions." She smiled, now approaching the bed. Picking up Mr. Rainbow Farts, she looked at him and set him back on the bed—like he was a living being. It made me smile.

Mom just tossed my stuffed animals around the room, completely apathetic to their feelings.

"Come on, I tasked Lucifer with watching Lilith. I don't want to miss the lesson." Grabbing her hand, we hurried to the conference room, or 'smoking room,' as Ember called it.

Apparently, Hades gets mad a lot when he is in the conference room talking to people. So, they could call it the 'God of the Underworld's Anger room,' but I guess, 'Smoking Room' was much shorter.

Athena had a projector set up at the far end of the room. The wall had a screen that was easily pulled up and down. Her eyes didn't lift to register our arrival. Instead, she just mumbled incoherently as she stacked her papers.

Plopping myself into the leather chair, I swirled it around to be extra sure it was a good twirling chair until I was stopped my third time around by Athena.

"Welcome, Uriel." Her voice emanated smoothly.

She is such a nice goddess! I am so happy I met her on my first day out in the 'real world.'

"Hi, Athena!" I chirped and put my hands on the table like a responsible student. According to the lessons I watched through

Mom's mirror, students should raise their hands in class, sit up straight, and pay super close attention. I was ready for this.

"We are going to start from the beginning." Athena picked up a clicker and pressed it with her thumb. The room went dark, and a bright light shone on the screen. Clicking it again, an image of a giant tadpole appeared.

"Aww, it's a tadpole!" I cooed.

It looked a little different, but I would not point that out because that would be rude. Maybe he or she had a problem that they didn't want to talk about.

"No, this isn't a tadpole, Uriel. This is a sperm."

I narrowed my eyes at her. "Should I take notes? This might be difficult because that looks like a tadpole." I pointed to the screen. Athena centered her nose between her finger and her thumb and pinched.

"It does look like a tadpole, Athena," Ember added.

"Did you not get a *proper* education on the miracle of life?" Athena snapped back.

"I just know what makes me feel good, and that sometimes it produces a baby." Ember shrugged her shoulders. "The whole nitty-gritty of why and how never really came up."

Athena threw her head back on the wall, clicking the remote in her hand again. "This is an egg." Athena looked both of us in the eyes, waiting for a response.

It looks more like a tiny, cute, little pink ball. I think I am already on her bad side, so I better stay really quiet.

"You aren't on my bad side," Athena muttered and clicked the remote again.

For the next ten minutes, she explained how this tadpole gets into an egg, but she never mentioned how said tadpole finds the egg. She just said that the sperm penetrates the egg and cells begin to divide. I got really excited when she brought up the cellular structure and processes, explaining how the mitochondria go into overdrive as the cell divides repeatedly to create more and more cells until, finally, they form muscles, organs, and a whole baby!

Wait. I sat back in my seat.

This isn't at all what my parents told me. The stork is supposed to bring the baby in the middle of the night. The little baby comes all swaddled and then you get to sit in bed all day and rock the baby to sleep.

My parents lied.

A sting in my chest confirmed I was right. It was the same sting as when Mom lied to me about going home and letting me come back.

They withheld information from me; they told me things that were untrue. Why couldn't I tell they were lying when I was at home? Why do I only feel those lies now?

"That was so dry," Ember groaned. "Get to the good stuff." She waved her hands in a shooing motion. "Maybe Ares should teach the lesson. I bet he would be hilarious." She snickered.

"Talking about sexual positions is *not* teaching a lesson." Athena clicked to the next slide.

I raised my hand. "What is a sexual position?"

Mariah poked her head into the room. The door was still open just in case Lilith screamed for Ember. "Did you say sexual position?"

Ember's eyes lit up, waving frantically for Mariah to come in. "Why yes, we did. We are having the '*birds and the bees*' talk with Uriel and explaining why she gets all tingly in her '*princess parts*.'" Ember informed.

Mariah made a big 'O' shape with her mouth. "Her mother didn't—?" Mariah made an O.K. symbol with her fingers and stuck her finger through. Ember laughed audibly, but Athena rolled her eyes and rubbed her forehead.

"No, she didn't." Ember snorted a laugh.

"Fates, what about... does she know about..." Mariah looked at me and whispered, "periods?"

"I know about periods." I folded my arms. "They go at the end of a sentence." Everyone in the room stared at me like my head fell off. "Right?"

"Do you bleed?" Athena approached me. "Every month do you bleed, between your legs?" I shook my head, and my eyes watered.

That sounds horrible. Why in the fluffy balls would I bleed, willingly, through my legs once a month?

"Don't make her cry! Luci will come in here!" Ember darted to my side, rubbing my arms up and down. "It's alright. You just don't know what is going on sweetheart."

Sucking my tears back up into my eyes, I gripped my dress. I *already wasn't normal, and now I was really weird.*

"D-does everyone do that? Bleed near their—between their...?"

Athena clicked through to another slide that showed what a uterus was. She explained that the egg is fertilized inside our fallopian tube, where the 'tadpole' swims around to find it. Then it travels to our 'womb' where the baby grows. But if a 'tadpole' doesn't come to visit the egg... then the uterus strips its lining causing a 'period' of bleeding.

I bit my lip while everyone continued to wait for me to say something. *I've never had any of that, and Athena said it begins at puberty which happens around 11 to 13. I am way past that.*

Swirls of information had already clogged my head. I couldn't tell my parents were lying to me when I lived at home. Now I was absent of a period which every girl gets. I balled my fists, trying not to cry. I was frustrated and feeling an emotion I haven't felt in a long time: anger.

Small whispers around me were drowned out by the beating of my heart. Blood rushed through my head and back down to my legs. I thought of guess after guess of why they would keep these things from me, but none made any sense.

Why keep me from everyone? Surely it wasn't because there is evil. There is evil everywhere, and everyone else just continues with their daily lives.

Athena's eyebrows narrowed looking at me, the pencil that was in her other hand broke in an instant. "Just take a few slow, deep breaths, Uriel." My breath evened out as they watched me.

"Let's get back to the lesson, shall we? We will figure this out together. Alright, Uriel?" Encouraging words surrounded me as Ember and Mariah sat on either side of me.

"To be honest, you aren't missing much. Periods suck," Mariah droned on. "Sometimes there is so much blood it leaks right out of your tampon and ruins your perfectly nice sparring pants and everything. Others think you are dying and run screaming because Ares would kill them for touching his wanker cleaner's junk."

Gasping, I fanned myself.

"I forgot to mention," I gulped audibly. "I'm scared of blood."

Chapter 18

Uriel

Athena cleared her throat, placing the clicker on the ledge by the screen. Her hands clasped together, and her eyes closed while taking a deep breath. "I will have Ember take care of that when the time comes."

Ember's cheery face turned to me. "No worries, it will be fine." She patted my hand. "I'll be there every step of the way!"

I let out a breath I never knew I was holding. Athena rubbed her nose. Her stoic features faltered, her feet shuffled, and the usual perfect bun that sat on her head was unraveling.

"Are you feeling alright?" I questioned as another pin fell out of her hair.

"Yes, quite," she replied curtly, adjusting the glasses she obviously didn't need. "In the next segment of the lecture, I will introduce you to the scientific anatomy of a female." Clearing her throat, she picked up the clicker again and revealed a completely naked woman.

With a loud gasp, I snapped my hands over my eyes.

Ember and Mariah laughed, trying to pull my hands down. "It's fine! It's just a naked girl. We all have the same parts in here, don't we? Some might have some bigger parts, though."

Having pried my hands from my face, Mariah poked Ember's chest, continually watching her boobies bounce. Laughing hysterically, Ember swatted Mariah's hand away.

"Shh, you will get us in trouble," Ember snorted.

Athena was unamused. Her laser pointer now circled the chest area. "These are the breasts," Athena said plainly.

"Or tits," Mariah blurted. "Boobs, jugs, mangos, the globes, hooters, and so many other names your man can call them."

As the other girls giggled, I continued to write vigorously on a small notepad that sat in the middle of the table. This was all valuable information, and I would need to study it later.

"Mariah, they cannot be called 'tits' because that word specifically references these, the nipples." Ember and Mariah still held each other's hands while struggling to keep a straight face.

"Nipples!" I blurted. "That sounds like a fun word."

"It's even better when your mate sucks on them." Mariah burst into laughter.

"Mates are supposed to suck on nipples?" I questioned.

"Grab 'em, suck 'em, 'pinch 'em, you name it! Anything they want to do with their hands or mouth playing with this whole chest area right here!" Mariah stood up from the table, snatching the laser pointer from Athena who stood in shock at the lack of respect. Her mouth hung open, and her hair had toppled down to her shoulders.

"This area"—Mariah circled the chest area—"and this area"—Mariah circled the lower half—"are crucial for interactions with your mate. Down here is where they can put their—"

Athena grabbed the laser pointer and waved her hand in the air. Mariah stood quietly, her face looking off into the distance.

"What was I saying?" she uttered to herself.

"You were going to sit down," Athena spoke calmly, "and remain silent for the remainder of the lesson." Mariah obediently sat in her chair, folding her hands neatly on her lap.

"What did you just do?" Ember waved her hand up and down in front of Mariah's face to see if she would blink.

"I made her lose her train of thought, sort of like a brain reboot. By the time she registers what happened, we will have finished the lesson." Huffing, she turned her back to us, now showing a woman with her legs wide open for all the Underworld to see.

"Sugar, honey, iced tea! What is all that?" Ember put her hands over my eyes and uttered a stream of unintelligible noises.

"Athena! We don't need to see a real one! A cartoon picture with a couple of lines pointing to the parts would suffice. Not an actual one!" Ember's voice turned into a growl as Athena clicked off the slide. When Ember's hand fell from my face, I stared at the picture.

"So much hair..." I muttered. *I don't have any right there!*

"Thank you, Athena, but I think we are done now." Ember began to stand until Mariah pulled on her arm to sit back down.

"We were talking about BOOBS! I remember!" she shouted playfully.

A knock on the door alerted us to a new visitor, Ares. "Did I hear someone say boobs?"

"Leave!" Athena shouted. Her blouse was now untucked from her pantsuit and her glasses were askew. "This is proper education. It is *not* the place for your crude tactics. I need you gone."

Ares stormed into the room anyways, polishing his nails on his white muscle shirt. "Listen here, sweetheart. I know my way around some things. I think I could help little Uriel understand what a man has and what he should do with it." Ares strode up to Athena, who backed away and grabbed the clicker.

Ares had a wicked grin on his face. His eye twitched as he looked at Mariah, winking at her while she blew him some air kisses. Looking at both of them, I saw there was an undeniable connection. As soon as they were in the same room, they were fawning over each other, looking deeply into each other's eyes.

"Now! I mean it, Ares, you cannot do this. Neither Lucifer nor Hades will condone your presence here." She attempted to retrieve the clicker, but the War God lifted it above her reach.

"Now listen, *Professor*, why don't you sit down, and I'll show you how to remove that pencil up your ass so you can put something nicer up there instead?"

Mariah giggled, pointing to Ares. "Yes, he means that. Much nicer."

"Gods," Ember gasped. "Ares, this needs to be PG-13—no triple X stuff allowed! Do you understand?" Ares only chuckled, not even answering her.

"I don't see how this is supposed to help me," I spoke up.

"How does this help explain the tingles I had?" I whispered to Ember. I looked down into my lap, where my legs continued to cross and uncross of their own accord. I wanted the tingles to go away, but by the way everyone acted, it sounded like someone else had to take the tingles away—*like a mate.*

I don't even know where to find a mate or how to know if I have one?

Ares' eyes glistened with excitement, covering his mouth, rubbing frantically over the scruff on his chin. "Okay, wait—back this shit up!" He clicked backward, showing the lower half of a woman. "Holy crap! Now that's a bush!" He roared with laughter before he looked at me, "Just so you know, you don't need to grow it like this." The laser pointer swirled all around the area.

I gasped again, closing my eyes.

"Hey, pay attention! I'm the teacher now, and I'm gonna teach!"

"Since when do you know a female's anatomy?" Mariah joked, fiddling with her fingernail.

"Take last night for one: I had you singing two octaves higher than that singer, Mariah Carey." Mariah gasped, throwing a ball of paper at Ares' head.

Ember leaned towards me, nudging my shoulder. "I'll teach you what you need to know. Come on."

We both stood from our chairs, at which Ares' head whipped around quickly. "Aye! Where you goin'! I haven't even shown you what a cock is!"

Ember and I were halfway out of the room, but my curiosity got the best of me. Athena sat, passed out in the chair with her mouth hanging open. I could definitely see why. There was a picture of a large male body part on the screen.

"This is a male's dick!"

I saw similar pictures of that part on animals because that was the only way to tell if an animal was a boy or a girl, but I had never in my life seen a picture of one on a man!

It was scary.

"Ares!" Ember growled deep within her body like there was an animal inside her. "That's enough!" She widened her stance with her fists clenched together.

"How is that"—I pointed my finger shakily—"supposed to make me, um...?" My question was directed to Ember, but Ares, giving a dangerous smirk, had the laser pointer point to the... *thing.*

"This..." he laughed circling the image of the male part. Ember growled again in warning.

My body shook, not understanding the emotions radiating in the room—heat, tension, anger, and excitement all rolled into one. I could feel it all.

Ember's hand grabbed mine, rubbing her thumb along my hand. "I will call my mate," she warned.

"Goes into"—Ares continued unperturbed by Ember's warning. His thumb clicked back to the woman's lady parts—"here!"

I stared, wide-eyed with a slack jaw. Ember's eyes were closed, breathing deeply.

Hopefully, she is counting to ten. Luci's whole family has some anger issues.

Ember's grip became tighter until she calmed, and the growl subsided. "How dare you." Her tiny feet padded three steps away from me before she turned to face my horrified expression. "It isn't just doing that." Ember's hands reached for mine, cupping them in hers. "It's about love and trust. You can show love by doing special things to one another. Not just by doing what Ares said."

"You mean sex! This is sex! Intercourse!" Ares interjected.

Ember rolled her eyes, continuing with her speech, "When two people love each other, this is the next step: physically showing them how much you care. You and your mate can do many other things besides that." Her eyes narrowed at Ares. "The tingles that you feel are your body's reaction to someone you find attractive. Your body wants to feel good; it wants more of the tingles. You can try to take care of the tingles yourself, too," Ember continued with her speech.

Ares pulled Mariah from her chair by his fingertips, her red face holding back the laughter. Dropping his playful demeanor,

Ares kissed Mariah gently on the lips. Slowly kissing her cheek and down her neck.

Ember was still explaining... something. I couldn't concentrate as I looked over her shoulder at the pair behind her. My head tilted to get a better look. Ares's mouth was grazing her collarbone, leaving little trails of his kisses. Mariah's head leaned back. Ares assaulted her neck, biting it with his teeth. His hips pressed closer to hers, rubbing the front of his body against hers. His hand grabbed Mariah's breast and gripped it tightly.

I closely studied how he moved, and how she reacted. They were actions I would have never thought of myself doing with anyone. Something that should have repulsed me, had my heart racing. Ares' hand trailed further, closer to the seam of the leather pants she wore. My eyes drifted away, feeling too guilty to watch. Instead, I thought about what it would feel like if Luci was doing that to me.

His dark eyes, devilish good looks, and powerful body leaned right against me. His large hands touched me in forbidden places. Luci's finger touched my lips, trailing down my neck and to the valley of my chest, pulling my dress to the side to put his lips on—

My breathing changed at the thoughts of his hot breath near my neck, those thin lips barely touching me while his hands wrapped around my waist. Tingles erupted over my body, imagining everything we could do.

It was like he was right here.

Shivers ran up my spine; I closed my eyes only to feel someone shake my shoulders.

Ember waved a hand in my face. "Are you alright?"

Nutter Butters!

I was not alright. I was tingling all over again. The tingling had come back at full force. If I wasn't careful, I would leak down my leg and people would think I peed!

"She's horny!" Ares laughed. "She's thinking about someone special right now, aren't you?"

My face turned red; the heat of my cheeks now covered by my trembling hands.

How embarrassing could this possibly be? Hot, salty tears filled my tear ducts as I backed away.

Ember growled, white hair spreading throughout her body. The room darkened as the lights flickered slowly. The glasses filled with water on the table toppled over, spilling all over Athena's files. When the darkness lifted, I saw that Ember had shifted into a gigantic wolf. She was so fluffy, but I resisted the urge to pet her because she was growling and not looking cute like I thought Queen Ember would. Saliva pooled in her mouth.

My hands were thrown out as I tried to protect myself from the upcoming scene. So much violence was about to appear, and my body trembled, urging me to flee from the room. "I need to leave," I muttered. Turning my body, I bumped into the one man I was thinking delicious things about—Luci.

Hades and Luci were standing in the doorway; both with furious, glowing, red eyes, and fists clenched tightly together. Luci's black wings flew from his body, encircling me, hiding me from the utter embarrassment I was feeling. As embarrassed as I was, I was excited to be blanketed with his wings.

"What's going on here?" Hades' dominating voice shook the room.

Ares quickly pulled Mariah away and shoved her behind him, ending their romantic embrace.

Chapter 19

Lucifer

My mother's growls seeped out of the room. It wasn't long after Ares left my father's office that he found a way to cause more trouble.

Ares was a mess. I told Father he should go back to the Celestial Kingdom. However, Ares supported my father during his darkest times, and Father could never toss his brother out.

Still, some shit was going on with him, and Father needed to figure out what was wrong.

Father and I sat in silence after he left. I kept my head buried in my hands, absentmindedly sitting on the worn leather couch.

What have I gotten myself into?

Do I know nothing of the female body? I never planned for an event such as this, especially since I had given up hope and even considered rejecting my mate because I was too far gone. Uriel proved that impulse wrong, the moment she stepped into my life. My thick skull was now melting into an enormous pile of mush.

What would I learn about myself now that I have sustained more control of my anger? What would become of Uriel? Learning to be around each other with both sides of the bond pushing us closer together, took a toll on both of us. I could feel her now; her worry and curiosity seeped into me from the room down the hall.

Father sighed deeply, sitting on the couch next to me. This was the first time in years that he has approached me in an unwary manner. Before I met Uriel, my body would have burst into flames in proximity to any other soul, but at this moment, his presence was comforting.

"Just one step at a time, Lucifer." His jaw ticked, cracking his neck. "The bond Selene created will pull you both together, but you still have the choice. You are compelled to unite by a strong, unbreakable force unless one of you rejects the bond." He eyed me warily. "Try to repress the urge and take it slow. It's new to both of you, but you understand more of it than her. I think it is time to enlighten her, especially with this new onset of feelings that have surfaced." I hummed in agreement.

She needed to know. She deserved to know.

"Ares, that damn idiot!" Father growled out, balling his fists and hitting the couch.

Snarls from down the hall had me gawking at the opened door that Ares had just left. Father stood, straightened out his suit jacket, and stormed out the door, away from me.

"Come. It involves your mate."

Shadowing him out the door and down the hall to the Smoking Room, I noticed Mother's wolf had surfaced.

There were only a handful of times had I seen her release her wolf unintentionally. Once was when a maid got too close to Father after ordering him to let females back into the palace to work. I didn't know Mother had it in her to kill a demon, but with one fatal swipe, that demon was reduced to dust in seconds. The second time was when a nanny tried to walk into my bathroom half-ass naked. She killed that one too. It was years before I was told what happened. Mother was half-werewolf, so her parental instincts were strong, and she was just as possessive of Father as he is of her. However, she maintained her stance of allowing females in the castle, saying, 'not all females are like the whores that tried to get the men in her life.'

Rushing through the door, the growls and snarls intensified. Uriel was retreating with her hands over her mouth and tears brimming in her eyes, shaking her head in disbelief. My wings automatically ripped my shirt from my body as they flew out in a gust of wind. The bond pulled me to her as I draped my wings around her waist. "I've got you," I muttered.

Her head buried into my chest, and I felt the brush of heat from her cheek. As much as it should excite me, my body was in overdrive to protect her, to stop her from being upset.

"What the hell is going on in here?" my father roared. A yell that was commonly used when dealing with unruly demons.

Ares stepped back, pushing Mariah to the other side of the room, motioning for her to leave. He stood tall, clearing his throat, and waving his hands in submission. "Hey now, buddy, we were just having some fun—a lesson, just a lesson." He chuckled, trying to force a more authentic laugh through his mouth.

"A lesson?" Father growled. "Are you serious? What the hell is that on my wall?"

A picture of a *very real* feminine body part sat in all its glory. I suppressed a budding growl in protest. I wanted to fucking kick Ares' ass for being in the same room as a damn sex-ed. lesson with my mate. Lucky for him, Uriel's trembling prompted my wings to grasp her tighter.

"Just showing her how things work." Ares lowered his hands. Uriel cleared her throat, her big golden eyes glancing up at me.

"He was telling me what goes in there." She pointed meekly.

My body shook with irritation, my hands smoldering. Soon fire would ooze through my fingertips, but Uriel, to my surprise, grabbed my hand. Worried I would burn her, I pulled away, only for her to scramble and renew her hold on them.

"Wait!"

But it was too late. Her hand touched mine. The blackened hands that could burn even the God of the Underworld, didn't even eke out a flinch from Uriel. Instead, the blackness faded from my hands turning back into my tanned, calloused fingers. Uriel's fingers rubbed over them with her thumb, staring at our hands caressing beneath my wings.

"Does it hurt when it does that?"

Every single time it hurts. It's like my skin coming ablaze, the effects singe my nerves until I feel no pain.

"No, it doesn't." I tried to soothe her.

Her hand went to her chest, scratching it. "Don't lie, Luci," she whispered.

Father was laying into Ares, his smoke oozing all over the floor which would infuriate Mother later. Gritting my teeth, I decided not to beat the hell out of Ares, and instead, I would take my mate elsewhere—out of here, far from the chaos. As much as my mother tried to help, this whole situation had derailed.

If Uriel and I were to be mates, I had to be honest and tell her things independently, without the interference of others. It was my job to protect her and keep her safe. All this shit was making compounding the issue by encouraging my crazy family's intervention. It was all blowing up in my face.

"Let's get out of here," I whispered. Retracting my wings from around her body, my hand grabbed hers instinctively, and I dragged her down the hall. Halfway out the door, I remembered that our touch had bothered her earlier—the 'tingles' were too much.

"Are you alright with this?" I muttered, holding up our hands. She beamed. "Yes, I am."

Nodding, I smashed my hand to the wall near my father's office. Pounding on it once, it cracked just enough for me to slip my fingers through and push the wall inwards.

"Oh! A secret passage, how neat!" Uriel whispered in excitement. My smirk widened, pulling her in behind me. "I can't see." Pulling my hand from the hallway, I hauled her closer to me and shut the wall. "I'm scared of the dark." Uriel's hand moved, latching onto my arm as if afraid that I would let her go.

"I've lived my life in the darkness. I'll show you the way." Her heartbeat raced, hugging my arm tighter. Taking the short walk down the hallway, I found the door I was looking for; it led right outside to the garden.

Mother takes this passage when she doesn't want Father to see her go outside alone. He still had a problem with her being out of his sight for too long and would monitor her in the mirrors of the palace all too often.

Humans believed mirrors to be one-way, only reflecting their outward appearance at them. This was not the case in the supernatural world. To supernaturals, they are portals to other mirrors and once you unlock the secrets of the mirror, you can speak to someone on the other side. Supernaturals had only figured this out within the past fifty years, and they have been most helpful to those who rebuked the technological advances humans utilize.

Uriel shielded her eyes as we entered the back of the garden. The gazebo, where I watched her yesterday, still carried her scent in the air.

"Does all the Underworld look like this?" Uriel wondered aloud while staring at the fountains that adorned the pond. "Because I would think a place that held immoral souls would be so much darker, especially considering how some of the demons look. Oh, but I guess I shouldn't assume that though," she stammered, waving her hand. "That was awful of me to assume." She continued to ramble until I placed a finger over her mouth.

"You are right, Uriel. The Underworld is a dark place." Her eyes widened, feeling the heat between my finger and her lips. "The area surrounding the palace is altered with magic. The grass, trees, and flowers are all lightened with Father's abilities. He does it for Mother; she is very connected to nature because of her wolf."

"Oh," she spoke as I liberated her lips. "Sorry. I was just curious." Her toe kicked an invisible rock. "I just know so little about this place."

"Because your mother wouldn't let you know," I stated, grunting in disapproval. My mind turned over in my head, certain I was going to piss off Hera, but I didn't care. "That changes today," I mentioned, pulling Uriel with me.

The back of the palace had various small labyrinths of bushes, shrubs, and strategically placed swings. As we continued to meander through, trying to lead her where I wanted to go, she pulled my arm to stop among the statues. Petals began falling from flowers, and the wind picked them up, laying them on the path in front of us.

Statues of the twelve original gods stood here along with some depicting the second and third generations. One caught her eye the most, the same one that caught my mother's eye many years ago—Selene. She was depicted with her long hair swirling down her back, cloth fabric wrapping around her, modestly covering all her private places. A blue sapphire moon donned her forehead and a gigantic wolf leaned into her body.

"Who is that?" Uriel pointed. "She's the only one with a decorated forehead."

Uriel may have been socially awkward, but she was smart. She knew more than she let on, and I beamed at her ability to pick up on the most minuscule details.

Walking back towards the statue, I placed my hand on the exposed foot. "This is the Moon Goddess, Selene."

Uriel leaned into me. The warmth of her body encouraged me to say more, to tell her who she was, and what she meant to us. I wanted to tell her it all so we could work this through together. Uriel had sustained enough withholding of vital information.

"I didn't see her at the party," she said. "I thought everyone was at the baby announcement." Shaking my head, my hand circled her shoulder, gathering her closer. Her gardenia scent relaxed me into a meditative state.

If I could stand just by her, and remain close to her, I wouldn't have to contemplate going to Tartarus for the rest of my life.

"She wasn't there," I muttered into her hair. "Selene is on a mission of her own now. Most gods don't know where she is, but I'll tell you if you promise to keep it secret."

Uriel jumped in surprise, clasping her hands together. "You will?" Her smile reached ear to ear. "Tell me, tell me!" Uriel's hands pulled on my arm excitedly, causing me to laugh. She gasped, covering her pretty little mouth. "You laughed! I have never heard you laugh! AND! You smiled!"

My smile dipped from a toothy grin to a mere smirk. *There, she won my first laugh.*

"Yeah. Only you can make me laugh, Uriel." Her heart raced. I could hear it from here. It was so loud. "Now, calm down, little bunny, and I'll tell you her story if you follow me. I held out my hand, but she just squinted her eyes.

"Did you just call me 'little bunny?'" Her nose wiggled.

Exactly what reminded me of a rabbit.

"And what if I did?" I stepped closer to her.

Her eyes widened, and her breath hitched, but her little mouth didn't falter. "Because bunnies are cute. Does that mean you think I'm cute?"

Chapter 20

Lucifer

Well, that was quite the turn of events.

"Luci," she whined, standing on her toes with her face unbelievably close to me. I could smell the hint of vanilla yogurt on her breath. "Do you think I'm cute?"

Uriel's nose wiggled again, and my fist constricted, not from anger but her proximity. Her hot breath rolling across my bare chest from when my wings had ripped through my shirt, sent uncontrollable chills down my body.

"Come with me." I broke the trance, grabbing her hand and walking beside her.

She pulled my hand again, trying to pull me back. "But you didn't answer; that isn't fair." Her lip pouted.

Fuck, that damn lip.

Her begging and whining had me burning to do unspeakable things to her. *I will have to figure out what was normal because I want to slap her ass until she obeys me.*

"If you are a good girl..." Her eyes widened, and her arms dropped to her sides. Her heart immediately picked up in her chest, and her breath hitched in the back of her throat.

Bing-fucking-o. She definitely liked that.

"If you're a good girl, I'll tell you everything you want to know and then some," I purred, extending my hand again. Uriel's hand shook as she finally let the smoothness of her palm hit my rough one. Pulling her to me, I put my hand around her waist.

Fates. I craved her body.

"Are you going to behave now?" I hummed in her ear. "Or do I have to punish you, little bunny?" The heat of my breath tickled her ear as she giggled.

Either she doesn't think I'm serious, or the tingles are becoming too much for her little body.

As I smiled at her, she cupped her mouth with her hand, giggling silently to herself. I cocked my head in confusion, and she pointed to my mouth. "You look great when you smile. You should do it more often." She blushed.

I elongated my fangs before smiling again to see if it disturbed her. Something about the hint of fear in her eyes excited me. Gasping, she jumped up and down like it was some miracle that I could change my appearance so easily.

"Oh my! Grandma, what big teeth you have!" A snort left her nose.

Biting my lip to restrain a smirk, I returned the timeless story with a reply, "All the better to eat you with, my dear." I snarled a primal growl at her.

"Oh no! Don't eat me!" she playfully screamed. Reluctantly, she escaped my arms and ran towards the stables. She didn't even let her wings explode from her body. Instead, her dainty ballet flats hit the grass, parting each blade with the softness of her shoes. I laughed, shaking my head as I chased after her.

Seeing as how I was exceedingly fit, I could catch up to her easily, but taking my time was more fun. I couldn't remember the last time I ran out of pure joy or playfulness. The only time I ran was to extricate some dirty soul from the pits to release my fury upon them. This was different; it caused my heart to beat in ways it never had before. It flipped in my chest, rising in my throat as her laughter permeated the entire palace grounds.

Demon servants who tended the garden rose their heads, wiping the sweat from their brows. They watched the girl who was screaming in laughter intently. Her dress whipped around her legs, and Uriel's body continued to sway in slow motion as she ran from me. I feasted upon every inch of her body as it bounced with each passing foot into the grass.

As I followed her intoxicating gardenia scent trailing from her hair brushing into the wind she created, I glimpsed Ares hanging outside the palace walls by a rope. His legs were bound by my father's thick trails of smoke, hanging upside down and bleeding from his head.

Watching me chase after my mate, Ares' hands cupped together before he screamed, "Yeah, man! Gobble her up you big, bad wolf!"

Groaning, I didn't let his rude comments deter me in my fervor to catch my new, little bunny. I would not permit her to evade me for long.

The stables were immense, several stories high, housing the most exotic of animals. They quickly came into view as I trailed my mate. The dark, wooden doors of the stable were open, revealing Father's most prized horses from battles fought long ago. Before Uriel reached the entrance, I grabbed her from behind. Her breath was heaving as I wrapped my arms securely around her body.

"I caught my little, white rabbit," I whispered in her ear. Instead of tensing at my touch, she relaxed and pooled into my arms.

"Now, will you tell me everything I want to know?" Her head twisted, permitting me to stare into those golden eyes.

"Soon," I whispered, grabbing her hand.

I led her along over fifty stalls holding horses. Today, I would take her on my finest horse, one I was gifted when I was ten years old. I had spent little time with my capricious stallion. His spirit was wild and volatile with any other handler, so he spent most of his days in the field corralling the mares for his harem. I couldn't recall how many demons refused to tend to him, but the number continued to grow, so he remained wild unless I took care of him. I groomed him weekly and tended to his needs since I was the only one able to touch him.

Uriel continued to inspect each stall, eyes filled with wonder and innocence. Stallions, mares, and the few pegasi that were being groomed put their heads through the windows, watching Uriel with curious eyes. Uriel was a wonder, her spirit like a child who craved the world before her.

As we approached my stallion's stall, you could hear his cries, begging to be released for the day. His hooves banged furiously against the stall doors, leaving deep impressions of his fury at being kept from his daily schedule.

"Absalom," I called. The neighing and grunting ceased abruptly as his head poked through the window of his stall.

Uriel gasped, watching his red eyes peer at her with curiosity. "He's so pretty," she cooed, walking towards him.

"Careful!" I pulled her back. "He's not exactly tame. He's only amicable with me, but I wanted you to meet him."

As much as I wanted Uriel to ride Absalom with me, it was likely that it wouldn't happen, but one had to try. She was my mate, and surely the animal I regarded dearly would take a liking to her. Absalom stilled, his head lowered, and his snout reached for Uriel. A flick of his head beckoned her closer. My hand still clung to hers as she tentatively reached for the top of his forehead. Absalom's eyes blinked closed, feeling the touch of Uriel's hand in his forelock.

My only childhood friend, whom I sought for comfort before my anger became too great had accepted Uriel.

"Do you want to go for a ride?" I unlocked the gate, feeling more comfortable with Absalom after he was so gentle toward her.

"Really?" Her eyes fluttered between my horse and me. "Do you think he would let me?"

Chuckling, I grabbed the bridle from the hook next to his stall. Fitting the bit into his mouth, I decided we would ride bareback. We wouldn't travel too far and would remain within the palace grounds.

Helping her mount Absalom as her fists grabbed his mane, she held on tightly until I could position myself in front of her. I wanted her to hold on to me, and part of me knew if I sat behind her, my dick would rub on that glorious ass of hers. Her arms wrapped around my waist as I kicked Absalom into a canter. Uriel squealed in excitement, feeling the large hooves beneath us hit the grass below. The wind created by our speed had Uriel's dress riding up her thighs, her milky skin showing in my peripheral.

Fuck, this was going to be hard.

The bond pulling me to her, wanting to complete the sacred ritual of binding our souls, made my body frantic. We both still had much to learn about ourselves before we achieved such a bond and learning about each other in the process would be difficult.

Absalom cantered towards the vast lake that Father created only ten years ago. As a family, we rode our horses here, carrying picnic baskets and swimming clothes, to relax on the weekends. Loki was only a baby, but Father did his best to help with my anger and my fury as a child. Both of my parents did. Who knows what I would have become if they hadn't tried to help me.

As Absalom drew closer, he grew excited recognizing our old refuge. For a horse, he sure loved the water and would wade into the lake until the water reached the underside of his body, relishing the coolness. Speeding to a gallop, Uriel's body pressed flush with my back. Her breasts rubbed on my bare skin as the motion of the horse rubbed her nipples to a peak. I groaned, feeling her nipples harden. If the wind was not blowing her scent away from me, I'm not sure what I would have done.

Once we arrived, I jumped off of my stallion before helping Uriel to the ground. She landed in the grass, light as a feather, her feet barely parting the grass. "Come with me," I led her to a bench overlooking the lake while Absalom took it upon himself to trod into the lake, drinking the cool water as he did so.

"This is so peaceful and beautiful," Uriel said as she looked over the lake. The red sun was setting in the distance; steam rose above the water as the warmth of the red sun no longer heated the air. Pulling Uriel close, I noted the chill on her arms and rubbed them as she surveilled the surrounding nature.

If she loved the simplicity of nature, from the grass to the hellhounds, horses, and flowers, I'd give it to her, all of it. The one thing I wanted to share with her was more beautiful than any of it, and yet, she did not know it existed. Pinching her chin, pulling her towards me, I exhaled a stuttering breath.

This is it. This was what I brought her here for, to tell her what we are to each other, what bound us together, and why she felt the sparks between our touches. No longer will Uriel be left in the dark. My mate would know everything.

The question is, will she accept it? Will she accept that we will be lovers, friends, and mates with bounded souls?

"I think I owe you some explanations," I muttered. Uriel's eyes lowered to my lips before darting back to my eyes, breaking my concentration. I couldn't keep my head straight. Closing my eyes, I tightened them, shaking my head to rid myself of the thoughts of kissing her with all my might.

"Is it about the bunny thing?" She giggled, breaking the tension.

Chuckling, I pushed a piece of her dark hair behind her ear until my fingers trailed lower, tracing her jaw and neck. Her eyes closed, feeling the sparks follow down her delectable body.

"Yes, it is about 'the bunny thing.'" My fingers traced her lips. Uriel sat perfectly still, leaning into my touch. "I don't think you are cute," I muttered. Her head pulled back, only for me to take my other hand, cupping it behind her head.

"I think you are fucking beautiful. So beautiful that no sunrise can compare to the glow you radiate in my heart."

Uriel's eyes blinked, her thick lashes tickling her brow. "You said a bad word," she whispered as her body leaned toward me, following the bond.

No longer able to resist the urge, my head dipped down, placing a chaste kiss on her lips. As she returned the kiss, the palm of my hand cupped her face, pulling her deeper into my body.

Chapter 21

Uriel

"You said a bad word," I whispered close to his lips. My body was pulling me closer, trying to melt into the heat of his body. Luci was insanely handsome; his hair brushed his forehead as the gentle breeze pushed it across his brow.

My eyes fluttered from his eyes to his lips. I thought I would save my kiss for someone I loved or deeply cared for but this pull, this longing, just felt so strong. Kissing him like I've seen my parents do was something I craved, and my thoughts have been thrown out of the window of my mind.

So, I leaned closer, following what my body desired. And then he touched my lips with his own.

The tingles I felt on our fingers from our touches were nothing compared to this. The heat of his softer-than-I-imagined lips sunk into me, rubbing my now swelling lips with his rough ones. Luci was gentle as he pecked them, but soon he pulled me closer until I became flush with his body. I whimpered, putting my hands on his chest only for both of his hands to cup my face.

Luci pulled back, allowing me to take a breath only to force his lips on mine again. He was being greedy, but I didn't mind. Having no shirt to grip onto, my fingers trailed up his chest to land on his shoulders, my head now leaning back from the fervor of his kiss.

"Luci," I breathed.

He hummed, still planting kisses on my lips. One hand snaked around my waist, causing a tickle on my skin making me gasp. He took that moment to slip his tongue into my mouth. The warmth and sucking from his lips had me pooling into a big pile of slime—*with sparkles.*

I always need the sparkles when playing with slime.

But as his fingers grazed the lower part of my back, my body arched pushing my chest straight into his. My girly parts screamed at me to do something, but I didn't know what. I grunted, trying to pull away—*it's too much again.*

I don't know what to do or how to fix it, but I can't ask Luci to help. No way.

Pushing away abruptly, I stood up, leaving him sitting on the bench. His eyes widened with his hand running through his hair as I looked down on his oh-so-pretty face.

"I'm sorry, bunny. I got carried away."

His haggard breath only made me squeal internally at the pet name. My hand covered my mouth, still processing what I had just done.

I have a mate; he has a mate, somewhere out there. What happens if they catch us? They wouldn't want us anymore.

I began shaking. Luci stood up to walk towards me only for me to hold out my arm to stop him.

"Uriel," he growled again. "Don't push me away." His wings flew from his body, and the fire in his eyes I had only seen directed towards his brother and Ares came to light.

It didn't scare me, not in the slightest. In fact, it made the butterflies in my tummy roar like mighty eagle wings.

"W-we have mates though, don't we?" I sputtered. "I-I promised I would save my kisses for someone I loved, and—and I-I feel like I've already messed up." The warmth in my eyes let me know tears were going to fall. They were threatening, impeding, but Luci stepped forward, moving my hand down and wrapping his arms around my waist. My hands pulled my hair to one side, pulling on it as I tried to explain.

"Shh," Luci's finger came to my lips, hushing the rambling words that protruded from my mouth.

The heavy breathing of my panic slowed as Luci continued to coo, the soft sounds of air rushing through his teeth melted me into his arms. An arm wrapped around my body, his hand reaching up petting the back of my head.

"You are such a good girl, little bunny," he whispered to the top of my head. My heart raced, hearing such praise.

I thought I was being bad—a bad girl that wasn't listening. I already disobeyed my mom by not wanting to go home with her, and so far, I had embarrassed myself in front of Luci and his family with my ignorance.

Even after all of that, Luci still thinks I'm a good girl?

My body wanted Luci, and part of my heart did too, but I was still so hung up on the words Nora had spoken previously, 'Mates are our special someone.'

"The reason I brought you out here is to explain everything. Everything you want to know." Luci pulled away from me, tilting my chin up with his rough fingers. "Will you come to sit with me now?" I nodded my head silently, and he gripped my waist tighter. "Words. I need to hear your beautiful mouth speak to me."

My face flushed bright pink, rolling my lips into my mouth. "Yes," I finally whispered back as he led me to the bench.

Absalom trudged out of the lake, shaking the water from himself as he went to find a patch of sweet grass near the base of a large willow tree. The leaves brushed the top of his back, shooting a shiver down his back and flank. Luci's hand never released mine as he saw me watch his beautiful horse pawing at the grass to release its sweet scent.

"Remember the statue that you pointed out in the garden?" Luci began as his eyes stared into the distance of the palace. A haze had gathered around it, giving it a darkened, mysterious vibe.

I nodded my head again only to correct myself and whisper, "Yes."

"My good, little bunny." His hand rubbed the top of my head, making me smile brightly as his teeth glistened in the red sun.

Clearing his throat, he pointed to the moon that hung on the opposite side of the sky. "Selene is who you saw. She is the Moon Goddess, which is why she has a crescent moon on her forehead." My eyes trailed to the blue moon, cocking my head to the side in wonder.

"Thousands of years ago," Luci began, "when the world was still young with human life, Gods and Goddesses enjoyed observing their small creations. It took all of their power, working together to create a species that they could watch flourish—the humans."

I scooted closer to Luci, laying my head on his shoulder. His gentle squeeze let me know it was okay as I listened.

"They wished to create creatures that looked like themselves, but a simplified version. They wanted them devoid of powers, with no strength beyond that of their own bodies. Gods wanted to see if, without powers, they would be more loving creatures than themselves."

I shook my head, giggling. *I know humans can be bad. I've seen it plenty of times when studying their wars.*

"Gods have always wanted power; they fight amongst themselves and bicker relentlessly. They wanted to know if there was a creature that they could create with its own agency that would choose love over hate?" I pulled on my hair gently braiding a small section. "Unfortunately, humans were created with all of the gods' personalities, and many were ripe with hate, selfishness, and greed. Some gods wished to destroy humans, deeming them a failure. However, many refused this notion questioning, 'how could they destroy all the creatures when only a few were evil?'" Luci shifted in his seat, so I draped my legs over his.

"As time went on, many gods took small groups of humans and experimented with them. Many suffered and even died, but that did not deter them from them trying to create a being that would ultimately destroy the human race. With this experimentation, vampires, fae, witches, and warlocks were created, as well as many others. Just like humans, these new species also held good and evil within them. Humans realized that their existence was in jeopardy, so the strongest warriors gathered and began training to fight. These human warriors took many years to train themselves and helped countless humans in villages across the land. The warrior numbers never dwindled, but the human race was on the brink of extinction." I gasped; I couldn't help but be engrossed with the story.

"The God of War, Ares"—Luci winked at me as I squealed. *I knew him!*—"took notice of these large human warriors. He appreciated how fearlessly they fought." Luci held up his arm to flex. Feeling brave I reached out to poke his muscle only to have my finger bounce back in protest.

Luci is so strong!

"He wanted to protect the innocent too, so Ares took flight and landed in the middle of their training field." My eyes still hovered over Luci's strong arm that flexed every time he tried to explain the story.

"Are you paying attention?" Luci's chest growled inside him.

My head perked up and I nodded fervently. "Yes," I whispered, remembering Luci likes it when I talk. He hummed and played with my hair. I waited patiently for him to tell me that I was a good girl.

"Ares decided to bless the warriors with a gift," Luci continued. I pouted my lips, a little mad he didn't call me 'his good girl.' Shaking his head with a smirk he continued his story, "His favorite animal is the mighty wolf, so he gifted the warriors the ability to shift into their own wolf."

I pulled on his arm, wanting him to tell me that I was good. He shook his head again, tapping my nose. "Pay attention," he whispered.

"The warriors could feel the strength in their bones; their eyesight was magnified, and their sense of smell was heightened—the ultimate warrior. Many battles were fought, and soon, these beasts became known as *werewolves*. Once the battles waned, the human race flourished again. Soon, forgetting the werewolves saved them, the humans grew to fear the supernaturals that had protected them. Fearing they would be overpowered one day, the Werewolves went into hiding. After all, Earth was created for humans, not the supernatural." Luci willed a rock into his hand, throwing it into the lake.

"With no wars to fight, werewolves became restless. Their inner wolves craved blood. At times the race could not control their wolves and lost control, feasting on the innocent animals of the forest. Seeing that Ares created werewolves, Selene descended into their pack. She presented them with the ultimate gift for protecting humans, one that would soothe their beasts." My eyes widened hearing about Selene.

"Selene gifted each of the werewolves a *soulmate*. Each werewolf would be blessed with a *mate*—the second half of their soul—to help alleviate their ferocity. Once together, they would balance each other, and their infatuation would ease the war cries of their bloodthirsty wolves. With each mate comes a balance, moderating both personalities." My mouth widened hearing the blessing that the goddess had given to the wolves that deserved it. "Selene specifically picks each werewolf's mate. Nothing is left to chance, and it is always done purposefully." Luci paused, now pulling me into his lap. My arms wrapped around his neck, feeling the heat of his breath on my neck.

"But Luci," I prompted, nudging him, "that is for werewolves. How does that help everyone else?" Luci chuckled, tickling my neck with his nose. My legs squeezed together trying to keep the tingles from creeping into my belly.

"Selene, seeing that the wolves became so happy, decided to bless all supernaturals with a mate. As this progressed, she saw the blessing in calming those beasts. One day, an idea smacked her right in the face as she looked on at her fellow gods and goddess." My eyes blinked, seeing where this was going. "She now also blesses gods and goddesses with a soulmate, calming the evil nature of the power many gods and goddesses possess.

My father, Hades, was the first of the twelve original gods to be blessed. Once he mated to my mother, she became a goddess herself. Her abilities gave her the ability to help Selene with the overwhelming task of pairing gods and supernaturals," Luci mumbled, his lips kissing my neck.

"Goodie gumdrops," I moaned, feeling Luci taking over my neck.

"Then, your mother and father were paired." He kissed my neck closer to my ear as my fingers twisted in his hair and my back arched. "And now me"—He kissed my earlobe—"and you" —he pulled on my ear with his sharp teeth, having me seriously about to wet myself—"have been paired, my little bunny."

Chapter 22

Lucifer

S wiftly pulling Uriel's legs apart, I had her straddle me on the wooden bench. The bench groaned at the sudden movement of weight shifting. Uriel's hands slinked up to my hair as my hands landed on her waist. I had just dropped a sizable piece of news on her, and she was sitting here, still sucking on my bottom lip—not that I was complaining.

One of my hands traced lower, feeling the warmth of her outer thigh. The damn dress she was wearing was doing something to me. Feeling the coolness of the thin fabric and the small breeze brushing past, my hand slinked further up her thigh, now bordering the crease of her ass cheeks. My rough fingers wanted to graze just part of her underwear, the forbidden area I have yet to ever reach, but I felt no line as I inched further to her voluptuous ass.

Fuck.

I growled as my tongue continued to wrestle with hers. Uriel's lips were now puffy and swollen, and her eyes were held tightly shut with those thick lashes. Feeling brave, my hand traveled farther until I was clearly past where her underwear should be. My hands continued until I felt a thin, lacy strip.

Fuck, she was wearing some undergarment that let her cheeks bounce freely as she walked.

I groaned, imagining what color they could be. *What a naughty little bunny she was to wear such a scandalous piece of clothing with her short sundress.*

Her body leaned into me again, aligning her core next to my cock. I groaned, feeling the heat of her pussy so close to my dick.

I need to stop. If I don't stop this now, who knows how far this will go. She still needs to understand what we are.

"Bunny," I groaned again as she pulled my hair. "Fates, curse me," I whispered into her mouth. Uriel ground her sweet pussy into my groin again.

I'm going to fuck her on this bench.

"Bunny." I grabbed her shoulders to separate her from my mouth. Her hair billowed in the wind; her lips were swollen and red, and even the area around her mouth looked like it took a hit from the scruff of my beard. Eyes hooded, her panting breath had me look on with such joy.

For once, I believed I could be happy, and it was all because of this woman.

"Did you hear what I said?" My thumb grazed her lower lip, as I watched her pouty mouth spring back.

"Hear what?" her raspy voice replied. Uriel's breasts had been pushed to the top of her dress, her cleavage damn near in my face.

How the hell am I supposed to concentrate with this?

Clearing my throat, I grabbed both her hands, kissing the top of her knuckles. "Repeat what you remember," I ordered.

Uriel's eyes widened, her face turning a beautiful shade of pink. "Umm..." She bit her bottom lip. Taking my thumb, I pulled it from her assaulting teeth.

I will be the only one to bite that damn lip.

As I pulled her lip away from her teeth, her tongue licked the top of my thumb.

Fuuuuuuuuck.

"Uriel," I growled. She squeaked in her seat as her ass jumped slightly. Her head lowered before she took both of her hands and fiddled with them. "Answer me," I growled.

"Y-you said your mom helped pair my mom and dad," she began, looking between her lashes to my stern face, "and then you got paired with" —Uriel's eyes widened—"Me?" Her finger oscillated between the two of us while her face lit up cheerfully.

"We are mates?" Her voice rose in excitement. She put her arms around my neck, and I laughed. I smelled her sweet scent of gardenias, burying my nose into her neck. "Does that mean you can take these tingles away?" she whispered in my ear.

Fuck! If there was a God of Cursing, I would take home that title today.

My eyes rolled back in my head as her hips pushed back into my dick. "Uriel," I groaned, pushing her back.

"Sorry," she whispered again.

Once we both calmed ourselves enough, her head tilted to the side, eyes wandering everywhere but my face. "Wait... How long have you known?"

My hands landed back on her bare thighs, her dress only covering the one spot I wanted. "When you touched me at the baby announcement. The tingles"—I laced my fingers between hers—"let me—let *us* know we are soulmates." Uriel hummed, processing this new information.

"Why didn't you tell me then? I thought it was just me." She hung her head low.

Letting out a heavy sigh, I pulled her chin back up to meet my face. "Your parents"—I reigned in my anger—"kept you hidden. You didn't, and still don't, really understand a lot about these things. I didn't want to push too much on you when we first met."

Uriel shook her head. "I thought you didn't like me. You had a grumpy face. You always had a grumpy face, until today." Uriel stared me down.

For the first time in my life, I was damn scared, scared of what she would think when I told her I wasn't sure if I was going to claim her.

"Uriel, before you came that day, I was planning on doing something." Uriel sniffed, listening. "I was going to lock myself away. I can be scary sometimes. I get angry, so angry." Gripping my hand, she pulled it to her chest and loved on it, like one of those stupid stuffed animals in her room.

"I didn't want you to..." I trailed off, my mind reeling, deciding if I wanted to tell her everything. "I didn't want to scare you." I stopped. "You are the Goddess of Innocence. What if you weren't supposed to see me... angry."

Uriel dropped her mouth. "That's kind of stupid." She put her hands to her hips and my jaw dropped.

Did she just talk back to me?

"I see Mom angry all the time. Just because I'm supposed to be some Goddess of Innocence, doesn't mean I need to be hidden from *everything*. You, my mom, my dad, and everyone else know nothing about me." Uriel stood up. Her weight leaving my body had me jolting toward her. "I don't even know anything about me." Her head looked to the palace as I entrapped her in my arms.

"You are so smart, Uriel."

Her head whipped back, this time a hint of fire in her eyes as they landed on me. "If I'm so smart, then don't keep things from me." Her lip wobbled. "If I'm so smart, then tell me why you didn't embrace me immediately if you knew what a mate is? If they are really so special? If you had let me walk out those palace doors, I would have never known! I could have been alone forever and not known any differently!"

My anger erupted. I didn't want to tell her what I was. I wanted her to see me how I am now—*different*. I am different with her, and I'll revert to what I was before her.

"Uriel, I am the God of Destruction," I whispered in her ear. Her body stilled as I held her close. "My powers were out of control. My anger and my ability to hurt others have grown stronger with each passing day. I didn't want to hurt you," I growled, pushing her back gently to look at her. Her eyes looked up at me, brimming with tears.

"I had to be sure that I wouldn't hurt you, but the pull we have is strong, Uriel. It is so strong that in the *one* day you have been here, you have changed me." My thumb grazed her cheek. "The bond is complicated. At one time, I didn't even believe it could help me." My voice softened. "But with you being here, I can see that it has." Putting my hand on her lower back, I pulled her towards me. "It really has, and I don't ever want to let you go."

Uriel glared at my bare chest, still not looking up at me on her own.

Smelling the salty tears in her eyes, I sighed. "I'm sorry you have been left in the dark," I grumbled, still pissed off at her parents. "If there is something you want to know, just ask, and I'll tell you. I won't keep anything from you ever again."

"You better not," she whispered, "because I can tell when people lie." My body shivered at how she said it so cryptically. "You haven't told me a lie that would hurt me, just Mom," she muttered.

"I'll never lie to you, bunny."

Uriel whined. "You promise?" she asked innocently.

"I promise." My head dipped lower to meet Uriel's lips. Her head leaned back, accepting my offer. "You are my girl, you understand? I'm your mate, and I'm going to take care of you." She hummed, no longer paying attention as our small kisses intensified again.

Before my hand could slip down to her ass, I felt my father trying to communicate with me. Uriel moaned right as Father broke through.

"*Lucifer, where are you?*"

Pulling Uriel's lip with my teeth, I replied sourly, "*I'm busy.*" I grumbled bitterly when he continued blathering on as my hand finally reached my mate's ass.

"*I need you back here. Immediately. We have a situation.*"

Parting my lips from Uriel's, she pouted. "*I hope it's good because I'm fucking busy.*" I barked.

"*Zeus is here, about Uriel.*"

I growled out loud, causing Uriel to jump. *I haven't even told Uriel everything, yet. I guess now was better than ever.*

"*We're coming.*"

"So…" Uriel spoke as we continued to ride Absalom back to the palace. I had just finished explaining the entirety of the situation with the prophecy to her. "I'm in danger? Humanity is in danger?" Uriel sat behind me with her arms fastened around my waist as we rode.

I don't think my poor dick could handle her ass right now. I was about to damn near explode.

"No, you're not in danger," I said flatly. "Not with me, or my father, here. You must never go outside the palace without me, or him, present. Do you understand?" I felt Uriel nod on my back as she lay against it. "Uriel? What did I say?"

Clearing her throat, her whisper of a 'yes' filled my ears.

"Will you ever leave the palace by yourself?"

"No. I won't," she replied.

"Good girl," I smirked while feeling the wide smile on her face. She squeezed me tighter in her delight.

Doesn't look like I'm going to need much of Ares' videos. I think the bond will direct us just fine.

Dismounting and patting Absalom on the back, I grabbed her hand, and we walked to the palace. Uriel understood that Zeus and her mother were an item long before mates were thought of for gods and deities. My little mate was nervous about why the High God was requesting to see her. She mentioned briefly talking to him at the party the day before.

Hera must not know that Zeus is here. Maintaining Uriel's distance from Zeus was the only reason she was allowed to stay here, in the Underworld. If Father is allowing Zeus to see Uriel, there was surely a reason. Mother's empathy powers could sense people's intentions, and Zeus must have an emotion that merits his presence in the Underworld and it must be vital to Uriel.

As we entered, a servant handed me a shirt to put on before we proceeded to the throne room.

Uriel made a face as I pulled it over my body. "Aw," she muttered, disappointed, before grabbing my hand and lacing our fingers together.

"What's wrong, little bunny?" I teased as she skipped down the hall with me.

"Nuffin." She covered her mouth to giggle.

Several large hickeys adorned her neck, at least one on each side. I smirked.

She has no damn idea and now everyone is going to stare at her as soon as we walked in. Mother did always tell me the bond is marvelous, so she, of course, won't be surprised. If only I had listened to her sooner.

The double doors opened to the dark throne room, which Mother left 'as is' when she first moved into the palace to allow Father to emit his whole 'King of the Underworld' persona. Red candles lit the way to where Father sat on his throne with Mother in his lap. Zeus watched my father as Father's hand beckoned us closer.

Chapter 23

Lucifer

The room brightened as Uriel and I walked up from behind Zeus. I haven't had the pleasure of being this close to him in person, but that was for his own safety.

My father was the firstborn of the gods, swallowed up by Kronos himself. It was only because Zeus was hidden by Rhea, their mother, that Zeus became strong enough to battle Kronos, once his powers had fully emerged.

Father, being the firstborn, was, in fact, stronger than Zeus, but sitting in the stomach of Kronos for many years had soiled him. He didn't want to deal with his depression and rule over the gods. Zeus willingly took the position, saying 'he was the one who started it all,' thus giving him the power of the High God.

Most of the gods hated him and just tolerated his antics.

Zeus had been quiet for many years, especially since Hera found her mate, Michael. It broke him. He was trying to win Hera back after his many infidelities while they were together, but Hera was no fool. She fell in love with Michael even before a bond united them, and she left Zeus in the dust to settle for the Celestial fairies in his bed. Of course, it did not soothe Zeus' depression, but he hid it well.

Zeus gracing us with his presence at my sister's baby announcement was a shock within itself. Many kept their distance, but a few hungry she-wolves and fairies dared to talk to him. He snubbed them, drinking his ambrosia as if he didn't care for the female species. After my own isolation, being quiet for many years and merely observing those around me, I could see a change in Zeus. He was unlike the cocky, arrogant god that Father described many times. He was lonely and changing.

Hermes, the Messenger of the Gods, often graced the palace when he wasn't with his mate, whom he lived with in Bergarian. Notes upon notes of inquiries whether Ember had even an inclining of the whereabouts of his mate. Hermes, sworn to secrecy, could not elaborate to anyone other than my mother. Father was enraged, but Hermes' powers prevented him from defying the directives he was given when delivering secret messages amongst the gods.

Did Mother eventually tell Father? Of course, she did, and she told me as well.

Father hated Zeus. They fought often regarding the treatment of gods and demi-gods inflicting their evil tendencies upon the Earth. Zeus had tired of supervising them from his throne on the clouds above; he even let his angels slack, recalling the demi-gods from Earth and confining them to Father's prison for their transgressions.

"She's here," Father growled while holding Mother.

He often did that. When he was angry, and nothing could sate his anger, he grabbed onto Mother like a lifeline. Something that I would have to do now that Uriel had somewhat accepted me.

Zeus turned around. His shoulder-length white hair swayed, and his short beard was ungroomed. His white designer suit, tight to show his muscles, nearly burst at the seams as he turned. Deep bags darkened his bloodshot eyes.

"Uriel," he muttered. Uriel hid behind me, holding onto the back of my shirt. Her head peeked out from behind my arm. I couldn't help but chuckle as her body leaned in close.

"It's rude to not return a greeting," I warned, pulling her arm with my hand. My fingers could wrap around her dainty arm twice if I wanted. Hesitating, she inched forward, her dress swinging around my leg as she clenched onto my arm.

"Hi, Mr. Zeus," she mumbled, giving a small wave. I smiled down at my mate, who had already captured my heart.

"They?" Zeus pointed back and forth between the two of us.

My mother sat up proudly, nodding her head. She leaned over Father's lap looking at me for confirmation that it was alright to proceed. I smiled at her, at which she grabbed Father's hand, kissing his cheek.

"Yes, they are mates." My mother beamed. "We are not announcing it to everyone because..." she trailed her voice, looking at me again for permission.

"She knows," I exclaimed. "Uriel knows everything: the Fates visiting her parents, the prophecy—it has all been explained. She knows it all." Uriel squeezed my hand, beaming with pride. The twitch in her chest that did not surface filled her cheeks with a bright pink glow, registering the honesty I exuded.

"That's why I'm here." Zeus turned to Father.

Father's eyes narrowed, his fingers of one hand gripping his skull throne. "How do you know about the prophecy?" Father's sharp nails slid across the skull.

"I'm the High God. Why would I not know?" he said cockily.

There it was, the little tick in his words towards Father, touting that Father couldn't do a damn thing about it. Father could overthrow him easily, but not without a mess to deal with later.

"I knew the Fates visited someone, some goddess who was hidden from me for all these years and believe me, I have searched. I just couldn't fathom that the one woman I trusted, who has worked under me all these years, would be the one who hid her." Mother's head leaned forward, undoubtedly trying to read Zeus's aura. "Once I decided to give up on finding the mysterious goddess, there she was, in the most obscure place, alone." Zeus trailed Uriel from head to toe, ogling my beautiful mate like she was a prize to be won.

I growled loudly as my wings erupted, ruining the second shirt of the day. The tips of my wings blazed as my hands were charred with soot. Uriel stepped back, gasping, but I felt no fear in her. She clasped her legs tightly, sending the faint hint of arousal floating to my nose.

Fates.

"Hold on there." Zeus raised his hands in surrender. "I'm here to explain myself, not to start a fight."

My wings stiffened, trying to hide Uriel from his wandering eyes, but of course, she had to touch them. The brush of her fingertips triggered a shiver to jolt through my body as her finger grazed the fire at the tip of my wing. It never burned her; surprisingly, she played with it like it was a string to wrap around her finger.

"When I first met Uriel, I recognized Hera and Michael's auras surrounding her. The innocent golden eyes that bore into my soul at Lilith's party assured me that I had found the elusive goddess." Zeus backed away, walking towards the golden candelabra that held red-flamed candles. His fingers trailed over each flame, crushing them between his fingers one by one.

"Hera lied to me all these years." He hissed as he felt the burn. "I thought we were closer than that. I even told her about the Fates visit, informing me of this goddess that would be in danger. I told her that we needed to protect this child, but... I guess she didn't trust me." His hand coiled around one candle, squeezing it and breaking it in half.

"And that pisses me off," he growled, throwing the candelabra to the ground. Mother sat back into Father, watching Zeus throw his tantrum. Father sat stoic, acting like nothing was bothering him in the slightest. "Then she thinks she can hide you here? Thought I wouldn't figure it out eventually? I know she thinks I'm an idiot. I've always listened to what she said. I still do. We have ruled together for millennia, and I put my complete trust in her! Yet, she cannot do the same?" Uriel grabbed the back of my shirt, fisting it tightly.

"Look at it from her perspective, Zeus." Mother got up from Father's lap who only grabbed her hand so she could not descend the throne steps. "Hera has found her mate. You both share a history. She has agreed to work with you for the sake of the Celestial Kingdom. She knows you still love her..." Mother's voice trailed. Zeus stepped back, his hair no longer neatly groomed. "Think how hard it would have been if you knew she was pregnant. She told me how much you loved her being pregnant when you and she had Vulcan." Zeus' face fell, no longer looking at anyone but the darkened room.

Zeus had his affairs, but once Hera stepped away, no longer putting up with shit, he knew he fucked up. Being High God didn't preclude your sins.

"When Uriel wandered down here, I felt Hera's emotion, Zeus." Zeus' head perked up. "She was afraid you were the evil threatening her."

Zeus gasped. He sat on the floor with his face in his hands. "I would never!" he yelled. "I would never harm something she had created!" His face reddened with anger. Uriel stepped up beside me, holding onto my torso while I wrapped her in my wings.

"I trust her more than any other being or creature in the three realms," he sighed. "I still see her as a close friend, I still even love her."

Uriel pushed my shoulders, having my wings retract as she stepped through. My hand caught hers, not wanting her to leave, but her eyes held determination and warmth as she tried to step toward Zeus.

I followed close behind as she knelt to put her hand on his back. She rubbed his back while his head hung between his legs. "It's okay," Uriel cooed. "I'm sorry you are hurting." Looking back to Mother, she only stared and watched the interaction. "If it makes you feel better, Mom lied to me too." Zeus' head slowly rose from between his legs.

"Yeah. She kept me hidden away and didn't tell me anything. It wasn't until I met all my new friends here that I was told what I've been missing." She smiled at him. "You were innocent in it all, just like me. We just have to learn to let it go." Uriel's hand glowed; a light from her palm lit Zeus' back. The dark circles from under his eyes brightened, and the angry scowl departed from his face.

Zeus' eyes softened, looking at Uriel. "Thank you, Uriel." He grinned softly. The rest of the room sat silently, watching their interaction. Uriel didn't question the light flowing from her hand, and Zeus didn't notice it either.

"*Did you see that?*" Father asked.

"*The light? Yeah, I saw it. Did neither of them see it?*" I questioned.

Uriel stood up, holding out her hand for Zeus to take. His hair resumed its normal groomed look and his clothes were unwrinkled. "You are a kind soul," Zeus said, patting her hand. "Uriel is not only the Goddess of Innocence but of Grace as well. You should continue to strengthen that power. You will be a wonderful goddess to have around once we find this darkness that threatens you." Uriel hummed, her mood dampening at the words.

"Would you like angels sent to assist your demons? I could send Gabriel." Mother shook her head.

"Can we leave Gabriel and his mate out of this? I love Persephone and all, but I prefer Hades' former flame to remain out of it." Zeus laughed, a sound that I had never heard.

Zeus waved his hand around. "Only joking." Father didn't like the joke and shook his head, rubbing his hand down his face.

"Let's not bring too much attention to the Underworld. My demons will be fine, and we have Ares." Father said without emotion. "Just find this darkness. I've tasked demons with checking Tartarus daily for anyone trying to escape, and we have no leads as to what this thing is that we are fighting against." Zeus nodded, walking out the door.

"Oh, Uriel," Zeus shot back over his shoulder. "I very much like your father. He was the perfect angel to be paired with your mother." Uriel grinned, renewing her hold on my torso. "Just don't tell your mother about Lucifer yet. I think she might shit her robes," he snorted as he walked out the door.

Chapter 24

Uriel

Mr. Zeus was nice.

I squeezed Luci a little tighter as his large hand caressed the top of my head. *Mr. Zeus had a big potty mouth, but I tried my best not to say anything. When people get mad, it is best to let them get their anger out until they sit down in the corner somewhere to breathe. That was what Mom taught me when I was younger, and I figure it is an excellent piece of advice to heed.*

Eventually, Mr. Zeus sat down with his legs set apart and his head hung low. *He reminds me of me when I was little. I would throw my words out in frustration because my parents didn't understand what I wanted. It was exhausting. Mom would just watch from afar with her arms crossed until I finally put myself to sleep, exhausted from the tantrum.*

I don't think Mr. Zeus is going to fall asleep anytime soon though. He just sat there with his head hung so low that no one could see his eyes. He could have been crying or been utterly embarrassed about knocking over the fancy candle stand.

I mean, he broke it. Tiny metal pieces peppered the floor.

I hugged Luci tighter when I saw Mr. Zeus motionless, then stepped away to talk to Zeus. *It's always nice to have someone comfort you when you are sad and feel like no one understood you.* Luci reluctantly unclasped his hold on me and followed until I sat on my knees with my hand barely touching Mr. Zeus' back.

His body was warm and made my hand tremble from the emotions rippling through him. The hotness in my hand never wavered as I spoke to Mr. Zeus, assuring him everything would be alright.

He wanted a mate too, and maybe when he gets one, he will feel so much better, just like Luci!

My hand heated, yet again, as I encouraged him to let it go. *He just needed to forgive my mom, like I had.*

Could I still be angry with her for keeping so many things from me? Sure, I could, but festering over what cannot be changed only makes you feel gross and icky inside.

Mr. Zeus' head perked up, his blue eyes rimmed with red. "Just let it go," I whispered to him, hoping the others couldn't hear. His body no longer hunched, and his posture straightened as my hand remained close to his back.

People, even gods, need touch to feel better. It lets you know someone is there watching you, helping you, and assures you that you are not alone.

Mr. Zeus' face brightened drastically in just a few seconds; it was like he was another person. My eyes widened, shocked by how much lighter he looked, I even felt better for him. My wings, folded inside me, tingled, wanting to spring free, but I had to compose myself.

Mom said it wasn't good for my wings to just fly out randomly, it might scare people. I didn't want to upset Mr. Zeus now that he seemed so much better.

His smile stretched, showing his white teeth. Finally rising from the floor, I felt a tickle in my ear. It felt like the wind was whispering into the depths of my brain.

"*Thank you.*" I touched my ear, thinking it was my imagination. "*You have shown me grace,*" it whispered again.

Blinking my eyes back at Mr. Zeus, his hand rested on my shoulder. The wind gathered again, tickling my ears.

"*Keep using your powers of grace to help others. It will help you grow.*" My eyes didn't leave his until Luci pulled me away.

I may be the Goddess of Innocence and Grace, but Mother concentrated on the innocence all my life. Isolating me from the worlds, keeping me in my tiny room with limited activities, and exposing me to humanity and the gods' way of life through heavily filtered lenses. The gift of grace was barely an afterthought.

"I showed grace," I whispered to myself. *Showing grace could be used in many ways. Using words to comfort, being there for someone, having gratitude, and teaching forgiveness.* My hand clutched around Luci's torso as Mr. Zeus began to leave.

Did I just help someone forgive? Using my words and my touch to comfort those who were the most conflicted?

As Mr. Zeus exited the front doors, my head tilted back to look up at Luci. He was staring down at me with one eyebrow raised in question.

"What did you do, Uriel?"

Luci called me by my real name.

I stuck my lip out, disappointed he wasn't using my new name. *I like the new name, bunny. They were cute and fluffy. I just helped*

Mr. Zeus not be sad anymore, and he called me Uriel. I was being good!

Luci gripped my waist with his fingers, pulling me closer. "What is that lip for?" he whispered huskily in my ear.

I grunted, still unsatisfied that he didn't understand what I wanted. "You called me 'Uriel,' instead of 'bunny.'" I pouted again, folding my arms against my chest.

"Are you going to be bratty right now, *bunny*?" The hint of a growl in his throat had me grinning wildly.

He called me 'bunny.'

"Not anymore," I hummed, rubbing my head on his chest. Luci sighed, shaking his head while Hades and Ember walked down the steps of their throne. Ember continued to watch us, smiling as her hand wrapped around Hades' arm.

"So, what did you do?" Luci questioned again, staring at the spot where I had helped Zeus get up.

I tilted my head in question—*I wasn't really sure what I did, I just comforted him.*

"I just told him it was alright," I spoke innocently, "that we sometimes just need to let it go. Then my hand felt all warm, and I felt so relieved once Mr. Zeus got up looking so much better!" I smiled, holding onto Luci's hand again.

"Did you see anything?" I shook my head, with one finger covering my lips.

"See anything? No. Should I have?" Luci shook his head, his eyes drifting to Hades.

"Zeus has been here a while," Hades mentioned. "He arrived, unannounced, demanding if I knew all along that Uriel was, in fact, Hera's daughter. Zeus thinks the entire Celestial Kingdom is out to get him, trying to undermine him. Of course, he thought I had something to do with it." Hades' smoke creeped out from underneath his royal robes. Ember pulled on his arm, pointing to the mess he was making on the ground.

"Sorry, my love." Hades kissed her lips.

"Aww!" I cooed, watching the two so deeply in love with each other. Luci chuckled, and both his parents whipped their heads toward him in bewilderment.

"You laughed." Ember's eyes glistened with tears. "You actually showed an emotion, other than anger."

"Because I'm his mate," I chirped. "Luci said I help him, and he helps me. That's what a bond is for, right?" Ember took me by the arm, pulling me into a hug.

"That is so right, I'm so happy this didn't have to be prolonged. You both deserve each other; it's why you found each other so quickly." Luci pulled me back from Ember, encircling me with his wings.

"Excellent job, Lucifer." Hades slapped Luci's back. "I hope we won't have to have any more conversations like earlier." He stared at Luci pointedly. Ember and I popped our heads back and forth between the two like we were watching a ping-pong match. "Right?"

Lucifer shook his head, his arms wrapping around me tightly. "Nor with Ares, we will be just fine."

Hades visibly sighed, wiping the invisible sweat from his forehead. "Oh, and Ares has been handled. He is confined to his room with Mariah until further notice," he said flatly.

"Did I get them in trouble?" I whispered up to Luci.

I didn't want to get anyone in trouble. I just wanted him to stop talking about all that stuff. It was too much, and my poor little head was still getting over the fact that the other poor, little tadpoles die once the biggest and strongest one reaches the pink egg.

"Ares is going through some difficulties right now," Hades sighed, pulling Ember to his side, rubbing his temple with his other hand.

Before I could ask if there was something I could do to help, a shrill scream resonated from outside the throne room doors. Loki dashed in, straight to me, hiding behind my legs, but Luci picked me up and wrapped my legs around his waist.

"Luci, my bum!" I squealed, worried my cheekies would fall out of my dress.

"I got you, bunny." His arms pulled my dress down, folding them so that I was sitting on his arms, keeping my bum covered.

"Bunny?" Loki questioned as a pretty demon with bright red skin, black horns, and a really low-cut top sauntered in.

"Loki, you cannot treat me that way!" Her voice came out smoother than the screech we just heard. She tossed her long, black hair over her shoulder while sashaying up the aisle in black high heels.

It had to hurt wearing those all day long. How could she possibly run and play with Loki like that?

"Your Majesties." She bowed slightly.

I think if she curtsied, her lady parts would fall out. Then again, her... bosoms were about to fall out too. I covered Luci's eyes. It would be a shame if those came out while we were all staring.

"Alana," Hades' tone soured, "I respawned you, but you know the rules. If Loki somehow manages to kill you, you forfeit the position. I need someone competent, and wasting my time respawning demons, I find annoying." Alana stood, her once pretty, straight shoulders drooped.

"I apologize," she muttered. "I would love another chance if you would permit me. I enjoy hanging out with..." she hesitated, noticing Lucifer, "Loki." She gritted her teeth.

Maybe she has a toothache.

"No. Uriel is my new nanny." Loki tugged on my arm trying to pull me down, but Luci growled at him. Giggling, I put my head on his shoulder, and he grabbed my butt.

"Not in front of your parents," I muttered into his shoulder

"Uriel is not your nanny anymore," Luci spoke harshly to Loki.

Loki groaned, rolling his head back in annoyance. "You told her?" he whined. "Can she at least still look after me? I only want her."

I gleamed. *Loki liked me so much that he wanted me to hang out with him, to take care of him.*

"Can I?" I fluttered my lashes at Luci. "I really like Loki."

Luci growled, his teeth grazing my shoulder. "We only asked you to be his nanny to convince your mother to let you stay." He nipped me. "Now that we don't have to withhold information from you, I want you with me."

I squeezed his neck, loving how possessive he was of me. *I really liked it. He wanted to be with me all the time.*

"But Loki is lonely too," I pressed.

"Excuse me?" Alana interjected. "Is there any way I could still work in the palace? My parents were quite proud I made it here. I don't want to disappoint them." Alana's head dropped in defeat.

I took her job, even if I didn't mean to.

"Could I possibly be this woman's assistant or attendant?"

Before I could concede, to ease my guilt of taking her job, Luci and Hades both let out a firm, 'no.' Alana turned to sulk back down the aisle.

My lip wobbled. I felt so bad. She was so sad.

"Luci, what if—" his mouth met my lips, forcing his tongue into my mouth. He squeezed my bum, and I let out a sigh while my hips pushed further into his groin.

"Eww, that's fucking gross."

I pulled my lips away from Luci to correct Loki, but Luci forced my head back to him with his fingers to finish kissing me. When Luci's assault finished, he pushed me to his shoulder.

"Don't say bad words," I whispered to Loki, who only snickered.

Chapter 25

Uriel

Dinner with Luci's whole family was uneventful. Luci caught me several times trying to feed my vegetables to Cerberus. *Cerberus doesn't like vegetables any more than I do.* He snubbed his nose after the second bite and began gagging with the next, which only got me caught again. My bright red face gave me away, and Luci scowled at me.

Even the lip wobble didn't work.

"Don't be naughty, bunny." He told me.

I feel utterly terrible for even trying, but those veggies looked so gross. They looked like tiny trees cut down from some miniature forest. How can I eat a veggie that looks like that?

The disappointment on Luci's face when he found out I was trying to feed Cerberus made me feel so utterly guilty. I wasn't his good girl right now, and that made my heart tighten in my chest.

I have to get back in his good graces.

Luci and Hades continued to speak about Mr. Zeus and whether his intentions were true. Ember repeatedly insisted they were. Mr. Zeus became a new person and was trying to be the best leader he could be after all these years.

Mr. Zeus was just having a hard time accepting that not everyone liked him after so many years of his 'whoring' around. Whatever that means. I'm guessing it meant he wasn't paying attention to his duties very much.

I played with my food, twirling the silver fork around my plate to make it look like I was eating. I liked a little meat, so I had my fill until three-quarters of a steak still sat on my plate along with those icky trees called broccoli and mashed potatoes.

I wonder, what's for dessert?

My elbow sat on the white linen tablecloth, supporting my head as I continued to move food around. Luci had one hand holding my leg, squeezing it from time to time. It gave me those funny feelings again in my stomach that I like so much. Sometimes the feeling made my girl parts tingle and made me think back to all the kissing we did earlier, which made me come to one very important conclusion.

I really like kissing.

Not just like, I love kissing. It was so much fun; it made your body warm, melting into the other person, and with Luci being my mate, it made it all the better. Technically, he is my first and last kiss, and I will never have to worry about finding my soulmate because he is sitting right beside me.

I wiggled in my seat, causing Luci to squeeze my leg to be still. His side-eye, as much as he wanted it to be scary, wasn't scary to me. It made me grin at how beautiful his eyes were, those dark brown eyes that I could dip my soul into and come right back out. He curled his lip in amusement as he inched up my thigh with his really big hand.

Oh, geez. Here come the tingles.

We have a bond, sure, and we are supposed to be together. The bond pulls us and makes us want to stay in each other's presence, but each day I am with him, it gets stronger, and I wanted more of him.

After my lesson-gone-bad with Ares today, a lot of the things we discussed had me squirming in my seat. Now that I knew Luci was my mate, he can help me with the tingles. His fiery touches that went around my bum had me really, really excited. So much so, that I wonder what other parts he could touch to make them feel better.

The tingles between my legs were the worst they've ever been after he pulled on my hair to keep my mouth open, but I persevered, ready for him to push me the way he liked. I figured that out about him after he said he was the God of Destruction: he likes to be in control. I like to follow.

He must know all about the bond since his mom is such a good person and helps pair souls together. Those tingles between my thighs will be taken care of soon, and hopefully not the way Ares talked about.

It's like shoving a sausage into a donut hole.

I crossed my legs, picking at the mashed potatoes on my plate. Luci lifted his hand to situate it and put it back on top of my leg. I squirmed again. Luci looked at me, his nose flaring as he squeezed my leg harder.

"What are you thinking about, bunny?" His lips brushed my ear.

"Um, nothing," I muttered, stabbing a piece of broccoli with my fork.

"So, as the Goddess of Innocence, you can lie, yet others can't lie to you?" His lip curled while his finger ran circles on my inner thigh.

"I..." I stuttered, not wanting to tell him I wanted him to get rid of the tingles.

I wasn't ready for his sausage to go in the donut.

Luci let out a deep chuckle at the table, causing everyone to glance at us. Ember smiled, all too knowingly of what was probably going on.

"Luci, leave her alone," she chided, putting another piece of bloody steak in her mouth. "She's had a strenuous day with those lessons and then hearing you are her mate. You still need to take it slow with each other as you control your emotions. You are both all over the place." She laid her head on Hades' shoulder, who only looked at her adoringly.

"Leave them be," Hades muttered to Ember, drinking some of the red drink on the table. "Everything will work out in their favor. I'm sure of it." He winked at me, and I looked away, biting my lip.

I kept my thoughts away from any more kissing and wonderful thoughts of Luci helping me with my problem. The other question I had was, does Luci ever have a problem?

His sausage was huge in his pants when I straddled him earlier. Does he get tingles there too?

Loki grabbed my hand as soon as he saw Luci finished dinner, begging me to tuck him in and finish reading our story, *the Little Prince.* I smiled cheerfully, telling him, "I would love to help." But Luci growled at him.

"She's my mate, not your nanny," Luci hissed. My arms wrapped behind his back as he stared down at Loki. Loki's mischievous spirit completely died, and he looked to the floor in defeat.

"Luci?" I pulled on the sleeve of his third shirt of the day. His mother made him wear it at dinner.

I didn't like it when Luci wore a shirt.

"Can I please read him a story? You can come too," I fluttered my lashes, tenting my hands together like a brief prayer.

"Actually," Hades interrupted, "I need to see you, Lucifer, in my office." Both of their eyes glazed over, until Luci sighed, exasperated, shaking his head.

"Fine," he grunted before turning to me. "You do not leave Loki's room until I come to fetch you. Do you understand?" I hummed in response. Luci's hand tightened on my chin. The slight pressure had me feeling the burn down to my toes.

"Yes, sir," I joked until he let go, groaning with a twinkle in his eye.

"From now on, respond with that," his lips hovered over mine. He stayed there, waiting for a response.

Eager to please him, I smiled and whispered, "Yes, sir."

Luci hummed, petting my cheek with his other hand. "What a good girl, bunny. You make me so proud." The tingles rushed through my chin and straight between my lady parts. I balled my fists up by my side trying to calm my excitement.

I'm his good girl again!

He placed a quick peck on my lips and walked away, only to look back before he rounded the corner with his dad. I turned back around to Loki, whose mouth hung open with his head tilted like a puppy.

"Uriel, what the he—I mean heck has happened in the twelve hours I was gone?"

"What do you mean?" I asked innocently.

Loki shook his head, running his hand down his face. "Sure, you found out you are mates but... the way you... it's just..." His hands pointed in various directions: one at me and the other at an invisible Luci by my side. "Just keep it down when you guys start doing 'stuff.' I am literally right next door." He turned his back, waving me to follow him down the hallway.

Doing what stuff?

We trailed to Loki's room. He went to the bathroom to shower, and I continued to tidy his room.

Even if I was Luci's mate and, technically, not the nanny anymore, I was going to still help and do my part. I liked Loki. I enjoyed hanging out with him. Maybe Luci would be more amenable if we all hung out together, and I did not split my time with each of them individually.

Loki, even if he is the God of Mischief, was hurting on the inside. He needed a friend, a close friend, and he technically is my first friend since leaving Mom and Dad's. I couldn't just abandon him like that. Picking up the remaining clothing from the floor, a knock on the bedroom door caught my attention. It was already open, ready for anyone to walk in.

"Uriel," the demon Alana spoke as she entered. The click of her shoes on the dark wood floors had me aching to cover my ears.

Since when did walking have to become so loud?

"Hi, Alana!" I gave her a small wave. I felt guilty taking her job, and now she had to leave the palace because of me. Being friendly was the nice thing to do.

"I'm very sorry—" I began, only for her to have her hand raised.

"Don't worry about it, I understand.," She clasped her hands together.

When Mom does that, it usually means I'm about to get scolded for having too many sweets.

"I just worry for you, Uriel." Alana went to the nightstand table, picking up Loki's book. She chuckled and put it down with a slam. "You haven't been down here long, but woman-to-woman, I figured I should let you know some things before you make it official with your mate, Lucifer."

I tilted my head in confusion. *He was my mate, and I was his. How much more official can you be?*

"I don't understand," I whispered.

Alana only chuckled, swiping her claw down Loki's bed. "Oh, you wouldn't, dear, since you have been kept in the dark for so long. But that isn't what I am here to talk to you about." Shaking her head, she took a seat beside Loki's bed—the same chair I used when I read to Loki.

I didn't like it, that was *my* new chair. Folding my arms, I let out a heated breath as I waited for Alana to continue.

I have to be nice. I did take her job. She is only trying to help.

"I need to tell you about Lucifer's ways, woman-to-woman," she cooed. "I would hope someone would show me the same favor with my mate."

"Lucifer's ways?" I questioned. "I know he is the God of Destruction, and he has"—I gulped, trying not to think of the terrible things he could have possibly done—"done things." Alana sat back in the seat, her long black nails scratching the fabric. I gritted my teeth, resenting her messing up my new chair.

"I mean, his ways with women he's had." My head perked up.

Did Luci have a girl that was his friend before me?

"What do you mean?" I whimpered at that thought.

"You see, he has had many conquests before you. He has had many women in his bed."

Luci shares his bed with other women? Like a sleepover?

My chest began to hurt; I rubbed it as she spoke. She continued to tell elaborate stories: of women sneaking into his bedroom, how he kissed and touched other women before me, how he didn't care about the bond. My chest heated, my fingers almost piercing into my skin, trying to relieve the pain.

Lies. She's lying.

"You lie." I interrupted her as she was talking about the supposed concubines that warmed his bed.

Apparently, warming a bed was a lot of work because he supposedly had three or four at a time, but my chest hurt at that too. They didn't warm his bed. Maybe I can get him a heated blanket for Christmas so I can warm his bed.

"Excuse me?" She raised a brow, sitting up in her seat.

"You're lying." I stepped forward, no longer clutching my chest. "Lying is a bad thing. You are not an innocent person, Alana. You are a really evil demon." My eyes bore into her chest—not to look at the large cleavage from her super tight undergarments, but to look at her heart.

There was no remorse in her like there was in Zeus, and I felt no warmth as my hand reached out to touch the top of hers.

For a demon with red skin, who was able to withstand the fiery atmosphere of the Underworld, I expected her skin to feel warm, but it wasn't. It was icy, like her heart.

She was a really bad person.

I stepped away, taking my hand away from her. Black dust soiled my fingers where I touched her with my fingertips.

Then that was when I realized: I didn't get my dessert.

Chapter 26

Uriel

I gasped as I watched the black dust on my fingers crumble. The opening of the bathroom door broke me out of my stupor as the ash fell from my fingers and landed on Alana. She sat there, still in the chair wide-eyed, grasping her chest.

"I did... lie." She lingered with her words, staring now into her lap. "I lied," Alana said again, glancing at the door.

Loki, wearing only a towel, stomped up to Alana, seething. He grabbed my hand, now unsoiled from the blackened dust. It had all disappeared, not a piece of blackness remained on my hand like it was never there. Even the remnants that had fallen on Alana's lap were now gone.

"What are you doing in here?" Loki snapped. "Trying to get Uriel to leave so you can come back and try to get in my brother's pants again?" My head snapped to Loki, not used to the harshness in his voice, which was usually playful with me.

Alana can't get in Luci's pants. What was in Luci's pants was mine. I'm his mate!

"Yeah, that's right: you sluts are all the same." Loki shook his head in disgust, pulling me away. Alana sat quietly, her eyes glancing from her hand to mine, rubbing at her chest thought-fully.

What did I do?

"What's the meaning of this?" Luci walked in the door. His dark attire of just black dress pants and a tight black shirt made him look so attractive. Internally swooning, I smiled at him.

Again, I remembered—I did NOT get dessert!

"Luci!" I squealed, running to him playfully. He grabbed me in his arms, wrapping around me and putting his nose to my ear.

"Why are you here Alana?" Luci redirected his attention to the 'slut' in the room, as Loki called her.

"Oh," I fluttered my lashes, trying to regain Luci's attention. "The 'slut...'" I tasted the word on my tongue as Luci stared at me wide-eyed. Loki shrugged in the corner, snickering to himself. "Yeah, the 'slut,' told a fib, and I told her she was fibbing," I spoke proudly, waiting for Luci to tell me I was *awesome*.

Because I am. I used my powers. Luci would never have to use some girl to warm his bed. I was going to get him some heated blankets, so no one will have to do that.

"She lied?" Luci questioned, his face darkening. "What did she lie to you about, bunny?" Alana started to stand up, but Loki willed a large stuffed animal to crush the poor demon, trapping her to the seat. Tape was planted across her mouth in a matter of seconds.

Loki is so prepared.

"She said you had a lot of women warming your bed," I began. "Then she said a lot of girls wanted to kiss you and do things to you that"—I lowered my voice to a whisper—"only mates should do." I winked. "I knew she lied right away though. My heart told me so." I pointed to my chest, tracing over my breasts. Luci stared down at them, slipping his hand just below where my bra met my ribs.

Growling ensued from under the gigantic panda, only for Loki to jump up and down on it, still in just his towel.

"Get down," Luci snapped to Loki. "Mother will be upset if you kill her again."

Loki scowled, his arms resting around his chest. "She's a lying bitch. I think I'm in the right."

I gasped. "Loki," I hissed. *Another bad word!*

"No. I'm going to do it," Luci snapped.

Loki rubbed his hands together, jumping from the fluffy animal. "Oh goodie, I wanna watch!"

Shaking my head quickly, I pulled on Luci's sleeve. "Don't do it. I think she's sorry."

Luci pulled me by my waist, his lips grazing my ear. "Anyone that talks against the God of Destruction has to pay." His hot breath melted into my ear. My knees gave way while his dark chuckle had my nipples in my dress perk against his chest.

"Oh," I whimpered. "That's unfortunate," I said breathlessly while his tongue licked the curve of my ear.

"Later. She will be put in the dungeon for now." His teeth nicked my earlobe.

"That's enough!" Loki shouted, finally dressed in his pajamas. "Uriel still owes me a story. You take that *thing* out to the trash while Uriel finishes reading me a story." Luci stood stoic in warning, but it didn't deter Loki from grabbing my hand.

My little legs felt like putty when he sat me down in my favorite chair where the 'slut' stayed until she was willed to the dungeon.

"I think she's sorry," I repeated to Luci as he headed to the door. "I touched her when she was telling her lies... and I think my fingers sucked up the bad stuff." Luci turned, resting his hand on the door frame. His thoughtful look had me wiggle in my seat. His eyebrows furrowed, stepping back in with the click of his fancy shoes.

He's cute when he thinks.

"When I touched her, my fingers turned black. It didn't hurt my hand, just maybe I felt a little weak. Then as I remembered that I didn't get dessert"—I narrowed my eyes at Luci—"the black stuff on my fingers flaked off and blew away into nothing. Alana looked weirded out." I sat back further into the chair, causing my feet to no longer meet the floor. "So, I think she's sorry," I stated again as I opened Loki's book.

Luci's hand reached out, examining each finger that touched Alana. Nothing was to be seen except for a hint of pink on each nail. "Thank you, bunny," Luci kissed the back of my hand.

I leaned closer, ready for him to say it, to tell me those few little words.

Luci chuckled, winking at me with those dark eyes, only for him to walk out the door.

Meanie.

"And I didn't get dessert earlier!" I yelled as he walked away.

Loki didn't take that long to fall asleep—which I find surprising because he was a ball of energy when I was around him. I tucked him in with his blankets, careful to turn out the lights and shut the door really quietly behind me. The soft click had me blow out a breath I didn't realize I was holding.

Suddenly, I backed into a giant wall—it was Luci!

"Hi!" I whispered, trying not to rouse Loki. Luci said nothing as he grabbed my hand and pulled me to the doors just down the hall. It was Luci's room with the big black doors and hints of red in the wood. Opening his door, he pulled me into the dimly lit room of soft reds as the door clicked behind us, locking us in. He stalked towards me and pulled me flush against his body.

"Luci?" I whispered, grabbing onto his shirt. He pressed me backward, and my feet stumbled a few times before climbing two stairs upward to reach his bed that lay on a raised floor. Landing on the cushy bed, a black, fur throw lay behind me as my hair cascaded onto the red velvet comforter.

Luci hovered over me, his eyes no longer dark but ablaze with a fire I had yet to see. Both hands landed beside my head. My chest rose with the excitement I felt. My fingers tickled up his clothed chest, wishing I could feel his skin and the beating of his heart better.

"Are you scared?" Luci's voice sounded deeper than I remembered. His fingers entangled in my hair, pulling it up to his lips and inhaling my scent deeply.

I shook my head silently. One of his hands reached down to my thigh, slapping it lightly to catch my attention. Deep guttural growls hammered through his throat, instigating me to clench my thighs together.

"N-no, sir." I tried to redeem myself.

Luci's eyes widened, his hand palming his man parts. The deep chuckle reverberated into his chest and turned into a heated kiss when his lips slammed into mine. Luci's hands roamed my body, touching everything on the outside of my clothing. He had me craving more, and the tingles grew stronger with every moment of his touch.

"You drive me crazy," he growled in my mouth. "Those little innocent things you do, what you wear—you do not know how much I want it." His mouth sucked my lips, piercing my bottom lip with a fang.

My tongue darted from my mouth, tasting the blood.

"Sweet, isn't it?" Luci's lips traveled lower, kissing the side of my neck. Leaning in the opposite direction, his kisses pulled on my skin.

"What do you mean by you 'want it?'" I barely uttered the words. Luci's hand was now on top of my thigh, scooting it towards my hip where my panties lay. I forgot my question.

"Bunny, I want all of you."

I hissed as he pulled the tiny string that held the front and back of my panties together and let go. It slapped, giving me a rush of tingles.

"Did you think of me when you put these on this morning? Are you really *that* innocent?" The tension in my panties gave, and I felt both sides fall away from my skin.

"Luci! My—" Luci's eyes darted to me, his devilish smile had me gripping the blankets below.

"I want you to call me sir." Luci's tongue licked his bottom lip. My head cocked in confusion.

But his name is Luci?

"It would make me really happy," he purred, his lips kissing up my thighs. My body going into putty mode, I melted back into the bed.

I can get new panties.

Luci's fingers trailed up my torso, so painstakingly slow. The little scrapes of his nails gave me the same fun goosebumps I got when I ate too much ice cream.

"Sir?" I rasped. He seemed satisfied with my reaction.

"Is this alright, bunny?" he questioned. "I can stop."

Honestly, I doubt he is going to stop, but I didn't want him to either.

"More." I pulled on his hand to touch my chest.

His guttural growl rumbled as he kneaded my mound with one hand and pulled my dress up with the other. The lower part of my body was bare, and now my chest was available to him.

I whimpered as his mouth clamped on my nipple. He took my loud moans as a good sign and sucked tirelessly. My hands wrapped around his head, relishing the heat of his mouth.

Too many tingles.

"Sir?" I pulled his hair again to get his attention. He freed my chest with a pop. "Tingles... but... I don't want to..." I trailed my words.

Luci's eyes softened, and his hand cupped my cheek. "We don't have to do anything you don't want, Uriel."

"Bunny," I pouted.

"Right." He nipped my neck. "I can make it better," he whispered into my neck.

His fingers tickled down the side of my hip while his lips met mine again, distracting me from what he was going to do. But I felt it. Oh, I really felt it as his hand finally met the parts that make me a lady.

His fingers parted my tiny lips, his finger pulling up and down in a spot I never noticed. Tingles erupted with a flick of his finger.

"Fuck, you are so wet."

I grimaced. *Did I pee?*

As I tried to push him away, his lips became hungrier. "I like you wet," he growled, hovering over my mouth. "The wetter you are, the more I want. Feel how much I like it." Luci's crotch pushed into my thigh. I gasped at the feeling.

Did he grow a third leg?

"It's my cock, and it wants you, Uriel." His husky breath warmed my ear. His finger flicked on the outside of my body, causing me to spasm. My arms wrapped around his neck, needing something to hold on to. His body continued to hover over me while his 'cock' rubbed against me.

My body spasmed, pushing my hips rhythmically against his hand. I moaned, the tingles now pushing me higher.

"What a good little bunny, taking my fingers." Luci dipped his finger inside my body. I winced at the intrusion, but the coos from his lips, telling me how wonderful I am, eased my urge to resist—it had me yearning for more.

I wanted it faster too.

"So, so wet," he groaned again. "I want you to fall. I want you to come all over my fingers, bunny." Gripping his hair, I pulled until I reached the top of a mountain, and I fell. I fell so freely down trying to head back to Earth.

"My good girl," he purred. Luci continued to push his large finger in and out of my body, leaving the sounds of wetness on his hand as he continued to push it into me.

Chapter 27

Lucifer

Her body—I craved it.

I craved the sweet sounds coming from her mouth, and how her body withered beneath me as she grasped my hair. My lips—the fire burned in them as I sucked her tits until they puckered in my mouth. My hands couldn't stop massaging her supple skin, the gentle curves of her body, as she pulled me closer to her.

I was losing control. I misplaced all my inhibition, the ability to fight this feeling inside me. Praying it was the bond, I followed it. I followed her until my hands ignited, and the fire rolled through them. Her skin was the only way I could quell the heat. It sated my flesh but only for a moment until her sugary smell of arousal sweetened the air.

Her pussy was wet, so wet I could imagine slinking my body into her slit and not having any trouble. It was then I realized, as I dipped my finger into her cavern, that it would be a tight fit.

Puffy lips wrapped around my finger. Greed consumed me as I felt the walls of her pussy.

Fates, I want it so badly; I want to destroy what is rightfully mine.

Uriel's head flipped back, her body shaking.

"What a good girl," I cooed, tracing my nose to her ear. "Such a good girl, taking my finger." I rubbed vigorously at the same pace. She took it gladly, her secretions coating my finger with the ambrosia she released while moaning my name.

Fuck, it was glorious.

My cock strained against my pants, pushing up hard against her thighs as she gripped my hair. Feeling the tug on my scalp and inhaling the scent of her arousal, my cock rubbed against her leg, causing me to release far too quickly.

"Shit, bunny," I growled into her shoulder as her body sunk into the mattress. My hips continued to push into the heat of her leg. Still, too many clothes covered my body to feel her soft, glowing skin.

I would be utterly embarrassed right now, but lucky for me, she does not know what just happened. Her body stilled with her fingers still entangled in my hair until her eyes fluttered shut. Panting, my fingers touched my lips, smelling her sweet desire, that I created. My mouth couldn't resist it any longer; I sucked them into my mouth, moaning at the sweet honey she expelled.

She tasted as good as she felt.

Thinking she would rest for a moment, I grabbed the furs on the bed, covering us both. My eyes continued to wander her body as I traced my fingers over the soft lines of her skin: from the valley of her breasts, down to the dip of her stomach, to her hip, and down to the puffy pubic bone that I will eventually taste with my tongue.

"So good," I whispered. Glancing up, I noticed Uriel's breathing slowed and her thick eyelashes touched her flushed cheeks.

"Bunny?" I sat up, but she didn't stir.

"Uriel?" I gently shook her, but she still didn't wake.

Did I do something wrong?

What if it was true? What if her body needed to remain sexually innocent, and I was the evil that killed her?

"Uriel!" I pleaded, but she didn't wake.

My head darted to each side of the room, half-expecting a random deity would appear to let me know that I screwed the world over, but it never came.

Taking the next step, worried for my mate, I decided to mind-link, "*Father?*"

Groaning came from the other side. "*What?*" he snapped.

"*I think I did something wrong. Uriel, she isn't waking up!*"

Father was silent as he cleared his throat. "*What happened? Is she safe?*" I could hear my father rising from the bed, throwing the covers from his bed, and stomping closer to the door.

"*We were doing...*" I paused, "*things.*"

Father's stomping ceased in the mind link. In fact, the door never opened, and I could hear the rustle of sheets again.

"*Father?*"

"*I thought we agreed we would not talk about this?*" he grumbled. "*You were going to figure this stuff out on your own?*" I scoffed at his lack of empathy for the situation. "*Son, you made her orgasm. Sometimes it can put them to sleep if you do it... right. You did fine, maybe better than fine.*"

Cutting the mind link, I looked back down at Uriel to see her big, gold eyes staring back at me. I jerked back, not ready for her to wake so quickly.

"Hi.," She blushed, pulling up the soft furs.

"I thought you were sleeping." I ran my hands through my hair.

No, actually I thought you were dead because I finger-fucked you into oblivion.

"I was sleeping, for a moment. I felt so relaxed." Her nose emerged from under the furs, and she fluttered her lashes. "That was fun," she whispered again.

I agreed with a kiss on her nose. "It was." I kissed her lips. "Was it too much? I got carried away," I mumbled, not wanting to look her in the eye.

Carried away? I had more than just got carried away. I let my body take over.

What if the evil that lurked inside of me came out and took hold of her, choked her, hurt her, forced her? What kind of person would I be? I'm supposed to protect her, to love her, and here I am trying to ruin her, and way too quickly might I add.

Then using her innocence and her love of praise, telling her what a good girl she was... it was like I was manipulating her.

Fuck, now I feel awful.

I rose from the bed, sitting up and putting my hands to my face. *I used my mate to fulfill my own selfish desires. I am the Monster of Destruction.*

"Hey?" Uriel's dress, which was raised to her neck, had been pulled down softly. Sitting up on her knees, she put her arms around my neck behind my body. Her head rested gently against my shoulder, the soft pants of her breath running down my collar bone.

"Luci? What's wrong?" Her lips kissed my ear, causing tingles to go straight to my dick.

Fates, she makes it hard.

"I used you, Uriel. I let my primal urge take over, let the bond carry me into doing things I had only thought of in my"—I cleared my throat—"alone time." I pulled the collar of my shirt, fidgeting now with my own hands.

Even Uriel's mannerisms were rubbing off on me.

"You didn't use me," she muttered, her finger grazing my cheek. "You got the tingles to go away, and it was so much fun. We are mates. Only mates do that, right?"

I hummed, kissing her cheek. "That's right, only me."

Giggling, she made me sit up so she could sit on my lap.

"But I took it too far, Uriel. You are unaware of the things that I did to you." I looked away. I couldn't look into those innocent eyes of hers, it only furthered my guilt.

My hands blackened, burning from the fire until her hands cupped one of them. The fire didn't burn her delicate hands as she blew the embers that tried to spark away. Uriel's face softened—if that was even possible—taking her fingers and interlacing them with mine until the ash fell and dissolved before us.

"How am I to know these things if you won't teach me? How am I to feel these wonderful sensations without you showing me, telling me? I know how to say no, Luci." Her eyes narrowed. "If I don't like something or don't want something, I would let you know."

Wiggling her fingers between mine, her eyebrows let go of the tension inside her until she whispered, "I'm not stupid, remember?"

"Bunny, no." I wrapped my arms around her. "I don't think you are stupid. It's just that, I took advantage of the moment. You look so good, all the time," I growled in her ear.

"Well, I have felt nothing like that before. You can do it again! I already feel the tingles coming back!" Her mood quickly brightened, compelling me to follow suit.

I groaned, feeling her tight, little ass on my dick. *Oh, she has no idea.*

"Bunny, easy." I wrapped my arms around her. "I think that is enough for the night. It's late." The sky had darkened quickly, and the storm clouds were rolling in.

Father must be flustered if he isn't keeping the rain at bay for Mother.

"But... I wanna do it again," she pouted.

"Oh, I can do it myself, right?" Uriel's enormous eyes widened, but my wings exploded from my back to hold her tighter.

"No," I growled, my lips capturing hers for a hard kiss. "It's mine, and only I can touch it. You tell me when you can't handle it, and I'll take care of you." Uriel nodded her head, making me raise an eyebrow in question.

"Yes, sir!"

Pushing her down into my cock, I reconsidered the possibility of doing more. But I had almost crossed a line.

"Whatcha thinkin'?" her voice said cheerfully.

The brightness of her face and her laughter as she stared at me like I was everything, had me not wanting to ever let her go.

Is this what everyone feels with a bond? To crave someone so much they don't want to have anyone else look at their mate the same way?

"Nothing, bunny. Nothing."

Coaxing her into the shower, leaving her a shirt and a pair of my joggers to step into, I sat back on the bed to wait for her. My hand rubbed over the stubble of my beard, catching the hint of her essence on my fingers. Sighing heavily, I kept it near my nose.

This was going to be damn near impossible to go slow now that I have gotten a taste.

Changing my thoughts back to Alana, my mood shifted completely. After leaving Uriel with Loki to check that Alana was indeed in a prison cell—she was. In fact, she was bound in chains with two guards on either side of her. I wrapped my fingers around the iron bars. Not once did she fight her restraints—or so the guards said. Alana's head remained low as she knelt to the dark floor, letting herself sit in filth, succumbing to her future punishment.

Her eyes were dazed as she looked into her lap. My lip curled in the satisfaction that she was beaten so quickly, but how?

How could she be so broken, before I could even touch her? Did it have to do with Uriel and her touch? Surely, she could not wield my powers before our bond had been solidified. That was damn near impossible.

It is quite probable that her personality could mirror my own in some way, but mirroring my powers? Looking at my hands, I willed the hot ash to surround them, making them dark. Bits of ash crumbled as I willed them clean. *This was something I would have to investigate further.*

Hearing the click of the door, I stood up ready to take my shower until my angel came walking out of the steamy bathroom. Uriel's hair was wet, cascading down the darkened t-shirt that reached her mid-thigh as she held up the pair of joggers I gave her.

"Um, they don't fit." Her small set of pale legs walked towards me. "And you kind of ripped off my panties," she giggled, handing me the joggers.

Fuck.

Chapter 28

Uriel

Luci wouldn't let me go back to my room. He said that since we are mates, we have to be close to each other now, especially after doing all that fun stuff we just did. Not that I minded, I liked being close to Luci. He was all warm because, I guess, he has fire in him. He is supposed to be some destroyer, and he is part of Hades.

My own little furnace.

Then, why the flowers would he need someone to warm his bed? Why does he need the heated blankets at all?

I shrugged my shoulders and climbed under the sheets with him. He made me scoot my booty right up next to him, and he wrapped his arms around me.

This was better than when Dad would come into my room and wrap me up like a burrito and call me his little enchilada. I snorted, thinking about that.

I hope I don't snore in my sleep.

Luci's arms were wrapped around me tightly. His heart finally slowed, and his breaths evened out; I figured he was asleep. Especially since, when I whispered his name, he didn't respond. I pouted my lip because I wasn't tired at all. After what we just did, I was ready for more of that fun stuff.

But he denied me.

That was frustrating.

The wind howled outside; soft rumble noises reminded me of the videos I watched of Earth going through storms. We were safe inside this massive palace, but I knew one person that would be so scared right now: Mr. Rainbow Farts. He was probably really scared. There weren't any thunderstorms in the Celestial Kingdom. It was bright and happy and had none of this grumbling from the sky. Luci rubbed his cheek against my neck, causing me to sigh happily.

But I knew what I had to do.

Slowly wiggling free from his tight hold, I grabbed the pillow I was laying on. It still held my warmth, and I hope, that nice perfume that I found in the bathroom. It was like Luci knew I would be in his bathroom one day because he had everything for me!

Internally squealing, I tucked him in with the covers, careful not to make a sound.

Luci was so pretty as he slept—his angry lines faded, and he held a faint smile on his lips. The first day I met him, he was anything but happy. I am so glad he decided to tell me who he was to me. The tickles and tingles were awesome! Maybe in my heart, I would have found out on my own, but it was so much better that Luci was honest with me.

Sliding off the bed, my feet finally hit the floor as I pattered across the room. Every few steps I looked back to make sure he didn't move. Giggling softly, I opened the door and dashed across through my bedroom doors.

You never know when a monster is hiding in the dark around here. Especially since we are in the underworld.

Grabbing Mr. Rainbow Farts, I scooted out of the room, gently closing my bedroom door. It was do-or-die now. The halls flickered with only a few torched candles, keeping the light way too dim for my liking.

Taking a step, my stomach loosed a battle cry that could be heard out to the stables. "Oops," I whispered, pulling out my rainbow unicorn. I spoke softly to him, even though I knew he couldn't hear me.

Sometimes it's nice to have someone to talk to.

"I'm hungry," I whispered, holding him tight. My eyes darted to Luci's room and down the hall. The kitchen wasn't too terribly far. I never got my dessert earlier after I told Luci, specifically, that I didn't get my dessert.

Oh.

Maybe he thought playtime was dessert. It was awesome, but that is not dessert. That is playtime. I will have to tell him this next time.

Turning away from Luci's door I tiptoed down the hall and slowly crept down the stairs. Cerberus was walking down another hallway with Blaze. They looked like great friends, but the sudden whack in the head that Cerberus just took, told me otherwise. He growled, nipping at his back to get Blaze off. I giggled watching the two, only to have them dart their head back at me.

Whoops.

"Hi!" I waved quietly, stepping up to them. "Do you guys want a treat? I'm going to the kitchen! But you have to be quiet."

Cerberus and Blaze glanced at each other, having some sort of conversation.

Probably mind-linking of some sort, I heard some animals can do that through my reading.

Both nodding, I grabbed my stuffy and headed right to the kitchen. I kept the light off so as to not disturb anyone. *Nora could come in at any moment since she and her mate had a room so close.*

I began opening each cupboard. It was nothing but canned goods, fresh veggies, and fruits. Nothing I wanted—I wanted dessert! With lots of sugar... and maybe some chocolate!

I gasped, thinking of the magic that lived in one of the cabinets at home. Candy would appear every day and there was always something new to try. I bit my lip looking at the cupboards above the counters. It was a long way up, but I think I could do it.

Curses for being too short.

Pushing the kitchen island chair over, I climbed up, making sure that Mr. Rainbow Farts was close. He was going to get a treat too. Cerberus whined, sitting on the floor with his cute puppy dog eyes. appearance

"I'm trying to get us some treats. Hang on," I pressed, reaching higher. Opening one cupboard, I found nothing but baking supplies, but no sugar. I couldn't just eat raw sugar, that would be gross. I needed sustenance to get me through the night.

Dinner was yucky, but I couldn't tell Nora that. She was too nice.

My knees scooted down the counter, looking in each cupboard. My shirt continued to rise further and further up my body. I could feel the cold breeze on my tushie when I heard a small whisper of a bad word. My body stiffened and I glanced behind my shoulder to see Luci in his joggers with his arms folded over his bare chest.

"Uh oh," I whispered.

"Uh oh is right, bunny." He sauntered over and picked me up by my waist to put me down. "Your butt was hanging out of your shirt! Someone could have walked in here and saw what was mine." Luci growled in my ear, and that only made me clamp my legs shut.

I sort of forgot I wasn't wearing panties, but that was Luci's fault.

Luci sat me on the counter as I held my legs together. "Now what are you doing in here? Cerberus linked me and said you were in here, getting into trouble."

I gasped and darted my head to the guilty puppy. "Oh, you are mean!" I pointed my finger at him. "I was going to give you treats too!"

Luci chuckled as I wrapped my arms around my body. "I thought you got your dessert earlier?" His nose ran up my neck. Leaning in, I smelled the spicy cologne he sprayed on. It was making me melt.

"T-that was p-play time," I stuttered. "I need something in my t-tummy." Luci chuckled again, gripping my bum.

"Then next time I can show you how you can have a snack *during* play time." His voice rumbled in his chest. The growling in his throat had me forgetting my snacks and wanting to make Luci my new snack.

I wonder what he tastes like?

"Give me a kiss," he ordered. His head pulled back, his eyes full of fire. Leaning closer my lips lined up with his, it was slow until he pulled his body close to the counter and placed my bum on the edge. I felt the heat between his legs too; it rubbed me as my shirt rode up higher on my thighs.

"Oh," I whispered in his mouth.

The guttural growl in his throat had me push harder into him. My fingers laced in his hair while he pulled my bottom lip and released it with a pop.

"Maybe you should be my snack," Luci whispered, still kissing my lips until he broke away from me suddenly.

Luci's eyes darted downward, and that was when I realized, his sweatpants were completely off, and his sausage was staring at my donut! I squeaked, covering my eyes quickly. It was there, it was real, and it was much bigger than the picture Athena showed me. Luci's hands heated as he turned around to pull up his pants.

But then I saw his bum, and boy, it was a nice bum. *He must work out.* It was all firm and stuff. I covered Mr. Rainbow Farts' eyes, hoping he didn't see anything.

He doesn't have anything like that because, well, he's a stuffy.

Cackling came from the other side of the island, far away from Luci and me as we stared at Loki in disbelief.

"That was so awesome! Uriel, your eyes got so big!" Loki snorted as he fell to the floor. Luci's angry face came back, but I pulled him back by his shoulders. His posture relaxed and turned back to me.

"I'm sorry," he whispered, putting his nose into my neck. "I didn't mean for you to..."

I giggled, laughing at how ridiculous he sounded. *He saw my lady parts; it was my turn to see his... god parts.*

"It's okay, I just wasn't ready," I blushed, holding my stuffy up to my face. "Loki was being naughty, not your fault."

Loki finally stood up, now the kitchen held Nora and, I'm guessing, her mate. His skin was red, and he had small horns on his head, very different from the rest of the demons I've seen. Nora mentioned he was different, that he was like, Hades' right-hand demon.

"What are you doing, child?" Nora fussed as she walked in. Luci was trying to hide his god part by pushing it down, and then he shoved my legs together with his other hand.

Oh right, no panties.

"I was hungry," I guiltily said. "I didn't get dessert." Nora's heavy sigh left her lips as she went to a cupboard on the other side of the kitchen.

That would have taken me ages to get over there.

"I'm sorry. Your mother said you couldn't sleep without dessert, and I totally forgot. Here are some homemade cowboy cookies for you."

I squealed, taking three, four, then five before Luci grabbed my hand.

"I think three will do, you don't need to get a tummy ache." He took several cookies back and returned them to the bag.

I pouted—I wanted more. I didn't eat dinner.

"Please, one more." I held up my finger in protest.

"Aw, give her the cookie," the demon chided as he held onto Nora. "She came all this way from her room."

Nora shook her head, patting his hand. "When we have children, Loukas, you shouldn't give in so easily."

The demon, now dubbed Loukas, rubbed his nose on Nora's neck. "But she looks so helpless with that pouty lip," Loukas whined for me.

"Please, Luci," I pleaded.

Giving me a narrowed look, he gave me one more.

Ha! Now I can always negotiate!

Loki must have known what I was thinking because he snickered behind Luci, who grabbed him by the neck.

"Gotcha," he laughed, pushing him to the floor.

"Hey!" Loki replied, rubbing his neck. "Uriel, did you see what he did to me?"

I shook my head putting another cookie in my mouth. "No," I said honestly. Because I didn't *see* him get thrown to the floor. I just heard the loud smacking noise his tooshie made.

Chapter 29

Lucifer

After coaxing my mate back to bed, she threw her stuffed animal on the other side of the mattress. Her body curled up next to me, nuzzling into my neck. For a minute, I was worried I would have to fight a damn stuffed animal for the affection of my mate.

The whole way back to bed, she said she just went to get him because he was 'scared of thunderstorms.' I shook my head at that.

How can she be so intelligent one moment and so childish the next?

My chest heaved in a breath, smelling the rich smell of her shampoo. I became so obsessed with her in such a short amount of time. I don't know what I was going to do to hold myself back. My cock was already strained against my joggers, and she kept rubbing her body closer to get warmer.

Uriel's eyes twitched, making her eyelashes rub against her cheeks. My finger trailed down her nose, gently tickling her lips as I stared at her. Uriel was some other kind of beautiful, and even with her childish ways, I sort of liked it.

I liked taking control of her, and she didn't mind submitting. She always came when I told her; she wanted to please me as much as I wanted to please her. My demands didn't scare her, they only excited her, filling her room with her arousal. Was it her mother that made her so submissive? Or was she born like this because of her goddess attributes? Maybe it was a combination of the two, but still, I wanted to know more about what her powers had to offer.

Pulling the blankets over her, having sensed the chill running over her arms, I pulled her closer still. Tomorrow, I had big plans for my mate, and part of those plans included getting away from this palace. Her mother may have demanded that she did not leave the palace grounds, but damn, she was my mate, and I'd fucking destroy anything that got too close to her.

Where we were going had close to no evil, just a few small siren children that liked to grace the shores of the hidden island. I had already ensured that no other beings—besides the dragons—would be there, and I knew Uriel would be excited to see more of Father's creations.

After confirming Uriel was indeed asleep, one of my wings engulfed us both, protecting and shielding her from any threat, or maybe to make sure she couldn't sneak away from me again.

I'll have to show her what happens when she runs from me.

"Where are we going?" Uriel skipped down the hall as I held her hand.

Two of her skips equaled one of my steps, and it made me smile at how completely reliant she will be on me. My urge to protect her and keep her safe doubled over the night. Especially now that I realized she was going to be challenging when trying to sneak sweets.

Maybe I should put a snack bar in my room for her.

"It's a surprise," I smiled down at her.

Her golden eyes brightened while pulling on my sleeve. "Please tell me!" she squealed again, echoing through the dining hall.

Nora had just situated the last serving tray in the middle of the table when Loukas helped her to her seat and wrapped his tail lovingly around her waist. Now that I understood the bond, it no longer sickened me to see my family so enamored with each other.

"Morning Uriel!" Loki poked his head out from under the table. He scrambled to his seat, right next to Uriel's, and patted it excitedly. Uriel gave Loki a hug—which I hated, but allowed, since he was in fact, my brother.

"Plans for the day?" My father cradled Lilith in his arms as he unbuttoned his suit jacket and sat down. Mother handed him a bottle. Each morning, Father liked to hear all of our plans for the day; he didn't like it when we all sat idle. Loki was the worst one to leave unoccupied because he would cause mischief, far worse than normal.

"School," Loki slouched in his seat.

Ares, who sat on the other side of Loki, nudged Loki to sit up. Ares hated slouchers; he expected his nephews to hold themselves with pride as he did.

"Can I stay home with Uriel today?"

Mother shook her head, placing a napkin in her lap. "No, not today."

Loki whined more until Uriel poked his cheek with her finger. "When you get home, we can hang out." Uriel's voice lightened the tables' mood considerably as the tension left Father's heavy scowl.

"We can go swimming in the pool," Uriel whispered, and Loki nodded quickly.

"No," I spoke deeply as I put a piece of sausage in my mouth. Uriel's eyes dilated, looking at the meat on my plate.

What was she thinking?

"Why not?" Loki whined again, pushing his eggs to the side.

"I'm taking my mate somewhere; we won't be back until late." As I popped the sausage in my mouth, Uriel gasped. "What?" I whispered, trying to cover my mouthful of food.

"Nothing," she whispered, giggling to herself. I squeezed her thigh, expressing that I would want to know later.

Ares didn't say a word this morning. Surely, Loki had spoken to Ares about the prank he pulled last night: scaring Uriel. Ares and Loki both had a sick sense of humor when it came to pranking people or nudity. Ares just sat quietly, continuing to hold Mariah, who was petting his cheek lovingly.

Those two were never quiet, so it only piqued my interest more.

"*Not now,*" Father linked me. "*He will talk when he is ready.*"

Sighing, Uriel patted her face with the napkin delicately and pulled on my arm. "Can we go?" she whispered.

They all heard her trying to be sneaky, making everyone chuckle. Excited about her surprise, I excused us from the table only for Mother to stop us.

"Can we at least know where you are going? Just in case you-know-who decides to stop by demanding to see someone?"

"Who would want to see Luci?" Uriel cocked her head to the side.

I chuckled, patting her head. "Isle of Dragons."

Mother scooted her chair back, running to Uriel. "Oh, that is wonderful!" She winked, clearly thinking that I was going to seal the deal today.

"Quick, let's pack a bag," Mother grabbed Uriel's hand, trying to pull her away, but I stopped them, jumping in front.

"I've got it taken care of, Mother. Don't worry about us." Mother pouted but gently took her hand away from Uriel.

"Okay," she sighed. "I don't get to help with the fun part, only the important stringing people together," she huffed, walking back to Father, who was now scowling at me. Rolling my eyes, I pulled Uriel along, watching Loki's gloomy face.

"He's so sad," she whispered, her lip wobbling at me.

I dared not look her in the eyes. This was our time—mate time. She can spend time with my brother later.

"Tomorrow," I gruffed. "You can both hang out all day tomorrow." Loki's head perked up at the comment, and he scarfed down the rest of his eggs.

Taking Uriel outside, I led her to a clear patch of grass on the lawn. The hellhounds were running and playing tag with each other. Uriel watched them intently.

"Are you ready, bunny?" I pulled her close to me.

Her wings pounced from her body as she jumped happily. Glitter shone in her eyes as she squealed an overwhelming, yes! Her wings filled with golden tendrils that intertwined with the feathers. It had me watching in awe. She sparkled all over, not just her beautiful personality.

"I'm going to transport us," I whispered, holding her close. "Let me know if you get too hot." Uriel pressed close, her wings quivering at the sudden wind surrounding us. Smoke circled us as bursts of flames swirled like a tornado. The lightning flashed inside, finally engulfing us until we reached our destination, and it began to fade away.

As the smoke began to dissipate, Uriel's wings meshed back into her body. Her head immediately looked down at the feeling of thick, warm sand between her toes. Out of all the beaches in both realms, Isle of Dragons had the best sand. It was thick like porridge, yet soft on the most sensitive feet. Uriel gasped, rubbing her feet into the new material.

"Sand?" she whispered, now bending and combing through it with her fingers. She darted her head to the ocean as a wave crashed into the shoreline.

"The beach!" she yelled, grabbing my hand and pulling me into the surf. Her laughter filled the air as she pulled me until we were both knee-deep in the ocean.

"It's so blue!" she whispered, now cupping her hands beneath the water. Fish—of several vibrant colors that were indescribable on Earth—swam towards her as if she was a siren. "So pretty," she muttered.

"Not as pretty as you," I whispered.

Her body stiffened, straightening to look into the darkness before her. My dark attire was completely out of place in this world. She laced her fingers with mine, glancing up at me with glitter falling from her cheeks—her tears.

"Thank you for bringing me here," she uttered. "I've always wanted to see the ocean." Pulling her close to me, she sighed, putting her head on my chest.

I don't know why her mother had to be so adamant about keeping her hidden. She lost out on a childhood, a real one, with people and friends, and now she is crying because she had never seen such beautiful colors. My fists tightened, trying not to let my hands blacken around her beautiful body. I'd show her anything she wanted, and I would never deny her.

"Kiss me," I ordered her, my voice emitting harsher than intended. Her thick lashes parted, showing the beautiful sparkle of her wet face. Pulling her face closer, I planted an innocent kiss on her lips. She hummed, pulling on my shirt.

Parting from her lips, she groaned until I pulled her up into my arms. "Let's get you dressed for a beach day, huh?" The kiss forgotten, she beamed as I pulled her from the ocean's waves. Both of us were now drenched from the waist down, but that didn't stop me from taking her to the tent just outside the forest edge. It looked rather worn and dirty from the outside.

Uriel's questioning eyes looked to me for answers. I only pulled her by the hand, wanting to get her inside. The tent opened into a large room filled with pillows, snacks, candles, and—best of all—the swimsuits we were going to wear. Having picked the skimpiest outfit I could find in her drawer earlier this morning, I pulled her to the small changing room so that she could change into it.

"Dress in this." The golden sparkles of the tiny, white bikini caught the light. Uriel's pretty little mouth gaped into the shape of an 'o.'

That's exactly what I want to see when she screams my name later.

"I-it's so small!" She held the top to her chest.

Fuck yeah, it was small. Because I wanted it to be small.

"You'll look great. It will fit perfectly."

The bottoms—looking even smaller—would definitely have her sweet cheeks sticking out for me to stare at all day.

"It looks like my undergarments," she giggled.

"Yeah, but this is a swimsuit. I have others if you don't like it." I tried to hide my disappointment.

She swung it around until it landed on her shoulder. "I got this." She strutted into the small changing room.

"Good fucking girl."

Chapter 30

Lucifer

Alright, the bikini was a bad idea. Uriel just pranced out of the tent—like she was a damn pixie.

Her perky little ass jiggled as she opened the flap and let the golden hue of the sun trickle on her skin. She sighed heavily as I carried our towels, chairs, icebox of food, and yes, even some damn sandcastle molds.

If she didn't get the proper childhood, I'd give it to her now because I was damn well falling in love with her.

Her toes hit the surf as I laid out our chairs and blanket. She bent her ass right over, her swimsuit hitting the crevice of her cheeks which I hope to hit later in the day.

She was fucking gorgeous. I hope Aphrodite doesn't come down here to curse my mate for showing her up.

Uriel stooped down and let the sand run between her fingers, just like a child would do the first time touching a new substance. Small crabs and birds approached her, inspecting the innocent woman. Uriel's eyes darted up, watching the animals as they came closer.

Surely these animals would find anyone a threat, even if this is the purest of beaches in all Bergarian.

But they didn't.

They came right up to her, even as her tiny finger rubbed each one on the head. Their eyes closed, enjoying the warmth of her touch.

I was getting damn jealous over fowl and crustaceans.

I wanted to be the only animal she touched. Taking a deep breath, I walked over to her to bring her a bucket and a shovel. My swimsuit, which already sat at mid-thigh, was hiking up from the tent in my trunks.

Yeah, beach day before claiming my mate was a bad idea.

"Uriel." I reached down, rubbing her back. Sitting beside her, I handed her a bucket and a shovel. Her bright eyes looked at the bucket, and she began to just watch the sand pour inside. She concentrated, watching it drip with the salty water.

I cleared my throat; I wanted to know more about my bunny. *Even if she was just sitting in her home all day, what exactly did she do besides studying?*

The most cliché questions came to mind as she spouted off answers one by one.

"Bunny, what's your favorite color?"

Of course. It was a rainbow, because 'she loved every color.'

Uriel's goal in life was to teach. She loved learning, and she loved books. Teaching other children what she knew seemed like the most logical thing for her.

The questions became deeper, and the few things she wanted in her life were so simple, that they were almost boring. One might think she was crazy.

She always wanted to feel the grass between her toes, have the sunlight warm her chocolate locks, and have time to sit and paint a pretty sunrise or play with other children. Her golden eyes warmed as she professed her wants and desires, and my heart only ached for her to attain what she has always wanted.

It wasn't until the last desire she recited, that she struck me in the darkest places of my soul.

"I always wanted what my parents have." She looked out over the ocean. "How they look at each other; how they touch one another." Uriel's head turned back to me as our thighs touched, and the heat of the Bergarian light sources hit our backs. "Kinda like what I see with you," she said bashfully, looking away.

Pulling her chin back to me, I dipped my head lower, unable to speak the words that circled in my head. Unable to tell her, I fucking loved her.

Barely touching her lips as her nose tickled the side of mine, I pressed my lips firmly to hers. "That's what I've always wanted too," I confessed, "and now I've got you."

Uriel, unable to keep a serious face, giggled, wrapping her arms around my neck. Her body swiftly sat on my lap, causing me to groan at the position of my dick.

"Easy, bunny," I groaned as she planted kisses on my cheek.

"You think we have that too?" she cooed at me.

"We share a bond Uriel, but even without it, I would have made you mine." Squeezing her hips tighter, I sensed a new presence behind me. They were in the tree line.

My opposing hand heated, forming a bright flame in my palm. "This better be good," I growled into Uriel's mouth making her shiver. Her legs tightened, causing the bottoms of her suit to lower.

Fates help me. I'm horny and ready for battle at the same time.

"Athena!" Uriel squealed, jumping from my lap.

Willing the fire to vanish, I stood up to watch my mate run into Athena's arms. Athena was wearing the same pantsuit she always wore, and her hair was in a tidy bun.

Much better than the last time I saw her with Uriel and Ares.

"I'm glad you are okay." Uriel's voice was laced with concern. Athena patted her head and let her know she was just fine. I growled, interrupting the interaction.

The whole reason we came here was to get away from prying eyes and interruptions. I'm supposed to help Uriel and get us closer to completing the bond.

"Something we can help you with, Athena?" I gritted my teeth.

Unfortunately, my body had other plans and my hands charred within an instant. Uriel rushed back to me, holding my steaming hand like it was nothing.

Athena chuckled, looking down at her fingertips. "I needed to speak with you, Lucifer. It's rather important, but I would like to do so privately."

Uriel's eyes had already looked down the beach. Beautiful shells had washed up on shore looking like the conch shells of Earth.

"Do you want to go gather those shells and bring them back?" Uriel pulled on my arm to make my body bend, kissing me on the cheek before gathering her bucket.

Watching her every step, Athena came forward and watched our interaction. "You are doing well," she mused. "I hope I don't have to teach her anything else?" Her eyebrow lifted in question.

"Of course not, because what you all did was a disaster," I heaved out a breath. "Utter disaster," I reiterated.

Humming, she crossed her arms as we watched my frantic mate gather shells from the surf.

"What do you want, Athena? This is my day with my mate."

Scratching her nose, pushing her glasses up, she put a hand on my shoulder. "Zeus has summoned Hera and Michael for trial."

My mouth opened, stepping away from her.

"It's true." She nodded her head. "Zeus wants to assert his power over the gods. He wants to make Hera and Michael pay for their crimes."

"The hell for? Sure, Hera shouldn't have kept things from her daughter all these years, and she should have come forward about the threat, but there is no law regarding this. It's never happened in anyone's lifetime." Athena shifted her feet from side to side, still not letting go of her arms.

"I believe it is my fault," she whispered. "I traveled to your mate's home and found the most disturbing thing..." Athena's eyes met mine, her brows furrowed in anger. "Hera has been keeping an assortment of plants in her house. While each plant has its use when the leaves, roots, or flowers have been crushed, keeping these plants alive and in proximity to gods or supernaturals..." Athena paused, "can stunt their growth and development."

Dark clouds loomed on the horizon, and the waves crashing into the shore were now breaking well before they should. The sea's whitecaps over the darkened water crashed in on themselves.

"Athena," I growled. She backed away as my tanned skin grew even darker. "Are you telling me that her parents poisoned her for most of her life?"

She continued to back away, holding her hands away from her in surrender. "I don't know the real reason they were there, Lucifer. I walked in knowing some botany, but Persephone confirmed that the combined secretions of the plants created a toxic poison."

"Fates!" I cursed to the sky as lightning hit over the water.

Uriel came running back, hanging onto my torso. "C-can we go inside?"

Uriel's touch calmed me, but not enough for the storm clouds to completely roll away. "It's alright, bunny." I smelled her hair. "The lightning won't touch you; I won't let it."

Uriel relaxed, scratching her arms lightly down my bare back.

"And you reported this to Zeus?" I snapped. Athena's slow nod had me grip Uriel tighter.

Once a goddess or god was summoned by Zeus, they would automatically be held in the Celestial Prison and could not roam until a trial was conducted.

"Alright." My lips pursed into a thin line. "Anything else?"

Athena uttered, "no," and stepped away from us. "I will send Hermes to let you know what else I hear. They have forty-eight hours to report to Zeus, or there will be genuine problems."

Zeus seemed fine just yesterday. Why was he now out for vengeance? He seemed lighter, happier that he no longer felt the burden after Uriel blessed him. Something must have changed. Perhaps, Uriel's power doesn't last very long. Poisoning a god is a major offense, especially when dealing with minors. Not that she is any longer, but the plants still live there, cursing her body. The growth of my mate's body was stunted, and her child-like attitude could likely be attributed to this as well.

"*She's coming down from the effects,*" Athena spoke into my head. "*Uriel should have the poison out of her system soon, but with her being kept away from people for so long, I'm not sure how long it will take for her to overcome her childlike nature.*"

"*I don't want it gone.*" I smiled at my mate. "*I love her how she is.*" Petting Uriel's cheek, she nuzzled against me.

My mate is the Goddess of Innocence. I would expect her to have a lighthearted nature and be aloof to danger. Isn't that where the 'child-like innocence' expression came from?

Athena smiled, waving her hand before the wind surrounded her, sand picking up as it engulfed her until she was gone.

My mate was going through changes in her body to help it mature, experiencing feelings she may not understand, and the bond was pulling us closer. This is when she will need me the most. I will need her as well. My anger flares when I am apart from her—even if she is just down the beach.

Letting her go when the storm clouds faded, she held up her bucket. "Check these out!" She pulled one out. "We should keep them and put them in our room."

"Our room?" I chuckled.

Her face turned deep red, putting the beautiful shells back into the bucket.

"I think that sounds like a great idea."

Pulling out each one, we sat them on the enormous blanket I had prepared for us. Her body glistened as the saltwater dripped from her suit. One drop trailed down between her small breasts. My tongue darted between my lips, wishing I could lick it straight off her body.

"This one is awesome!" She pulled out a large clam, still intact, flipping it from side to side. I chuckled as she studied it.

"Do you want to look inside?"

We both laid on our stomachs as the sun dried our backs. Uriel's legs swung in the air in curiosity as I pulled out a pocket knife from the beach bag, gently slicing it open. Her eyes widened as I prodded the meat and revealed a beautiful black pearl.

"Wow!" Her body sat upright next to me. "It's so pretty." Staring at it in wonder, she prodded it with her finger.

Chuckling, I pulled it from the clam, handing it to her. "Not as pretty as you, bunny." I kissed her temple.

I couldn't wait to play with her little pearl.

Chapter 31

Uriel

"Here."

Luci put the pearl in his palm with one hand, cupping the other over to hide the pearl. Light shone between the crevices of his fingers, so brightly it almost blinded me. Smiling, he lifted his hand to reveal the pearl now entangled by a dark, delicate chain. It wove in so many different directions, you couldn't understand the pattern, just that it was one piece.

"Turn around," he ordered.

I did as requested, feeling him move my hair to the side and winding the chain with the darkened pearl around my neck. Fiddling with the chain, his fingers touched my upper back ever so softly, shooting those familiar tingles down my spine. He chuckled as he finished and turned me back around.

"Now you have a piece of me with you always." He smiled, picking up the pearl centered on my chest.

"Thank you," I whispered. This was a beautiful gift and the first piece of jewelry I had ever owned. I looked down at it, playing with the little bead until Luci cleared his throat.

"I think it's time to go inside." He held out his hand. "You were up late searching for cookies; I think a nap is in order." I pouted my lips only to have a tiny yawn escape.

"Mhmm," Luci hummed, pulling me back up to standing.

Luci continued to console me as he pulled me along, letting me know we would come back outside after we rested. I still had so much to see and so many things I wanted to do before the day was done but that stupid yawn ruined everything.

Fixing my eyes to the ground, we trudged to the cabin. Luci stopped us once we reached it, pushing me towards the back of the tent. He pushed back a flap to reveal a small shower to rinse off.

"How does that even work?" I stood with amazement. Luci patted my bum to get me inside.

"Magic, sweetheart." I gaped at him until he pushed the flap downward.

By the time I was done, Luci was already in a pair of shorts and cleaned from all the sticky sand. As much as I liked the beach, I wasn't a fan of how it stuck to every part of your body, and I'm talking about every part. I had to clean my girly parts, and I knew Luci didn't want me starting anything there.

It was super tempting though.

I giggled as I walked out and sat on the fluffy pillows laying on the floor. Luci, standing with all his tanned muscles on display. He was still slightly damp when the candles in the room dimmed lower as he lowered his palm.

Right, he controls fire stuff.

As I was getting comfortable on the pillows, he pulled me to his chest, stroking my hair. "Sleep and we can go back out, I don't need you getting crabby later," he laughed.

"I will not get crabby!" I threw a leg over him, cuddling up to his chest. His body heat warmed me in no time, and the crazy tingles returned as he pulled the pretty blanket over us.

Having my leg wrapped around one of his seemed like a good idea at the time, but now, my lady parts were right next to his hip. Every time he or I moved it rubbed my clit in ways I really liked. Moving every thirty seconds to elicit the sensation made Luci growl.

"What are you doing, bunny?" His voice whispered.

I shrugged my shoulders as his hand gripped my thigh to stop my movements. A deep chuckle reverberated in his throat, making me whimper.

"Are you not tired?" he taunted.

Biting my lip harshly, I hummed a good no, only to feel a swat land on my thigh.

"Owie!"

"What did I say about answering, Uriel."

Oh, bananas! He said my name and not bunny.

"I'm not tired, sir."

Luci groaned, pushing me to my back. His six-pack of muscles strained, giving them a wonderful definition.

I could run my tongue all over them.

"Is that right?" Luci's nose came down, tracing mine until his lips kissed the length of my neck. My thighs rubbed together, yearning for more, but Luci's hip stayed well above where I wanted him to.

"Do you want to play?" His growl hit my ears, causing my fingers to probe his abdomen.

"Y-yes sir," I said shakily. Luci's hand trailed down below my tank top, where I didn't have any undergarments, and he cupped my breast, warming me with the heat of his hand.

"You feel so good, bunny." His lips finally kissed me.

My hands pulled at his hair as he folded each strap of my top down my body. Luci's sausage was straining against my hips which caused me to push my hips up to feel him more. In the brief moment that I saw it, I knew it was huge. At first, I was scared, but the more I thought about it, the more I wanted to see it.

"Luci?" I whispered into his lips; he paused as my chest stood bare to him. "Can I see it?" I whispered, blushing fiercely.

A curl formed on his lips. "See what bunny?"

Boo, he was going to make me say it. Pulling my hands to my lips to cover the big, embarrassing smile, I shook my head.

"Bunny, I want to hear you say it," he teased. Pulling my hands down, he kissed my lips.

"Your... thing." I pointed lower to his pants. Lifting his hips, he displayed the massive tent pointing straight to my donut.

"Oh dear," I giggled.

"You really want to see it?" He mused, waiting for an answer.

I didn't pause but nodded eagerly with his favorite phrase, "Yes, sir." I pulled eagerly on his shorts only for him to groan.

He rolled on his back, making sure a pillow was behind him. One arm laid behind his head until he tugged one side. "Are you sure?" he repeated.

Getting frustrated with him asking me over and over, I reached for his shorts and tugged them down, causing his thingy to hit his stomach. It stood straight up—-way bigger than the sausage he ate for breakfast this morning. The tip was wet and leaking.

"It's precum, bunny. It helps get you ready for me." He groaned as one of his hands gripped the shaft, stroking it up and down.

I stared at it longingly, wondering what I should do. *Luci made me feel so good yesterday, I wanted to make him feel good too.*

Sitting on my knees, I looked to Luci for confirmation that I could touch it. He hissed as I grabbed hold of it just above his hand.

"Good girl," he groaned, throwing his head back.

The sparkly liquid at the tip was about to pool over until my thumb came to the top and rubbed it. He seemed to like that, a lot, and bucked his hips.

"Do you want to make me feel good, bunny?"

I smiled eagerly. *I would love to make my mate feel good.*

Luci showed me how to put my hands on him. Gripping him tightly, my hand slid up and down his shaft. Luci's eyes didn't leave me, watching me as I straddled his legs and pumped him. It didn't just make Luci feel good, it made me feel good too. My heartbeat pounded between my legs, and my urge to touch myself grew stronger and stronger. I whimpered, watching more of the liquid spill from his sausage.

"You can touch yourself, Uriel." He groaned, sitting up. "Let me see you touch your pussy."

My face reddened. *He told me not to touch it before.*

"Touch it," he ordered. "I want to watch you."

Taking one hand from him, I trailed down until my finger met my thighs. Luci stared into me, watching my every move. I jerked at the sensation, but quickly recovered, remembering how Luci stroked it last night.

Luci stopped my hand, having me lay on my back. "I love watching you," he huffed, spreading my legs. "Keep touching yourself. Let me see you play with your pussy."

My finger continued to rub my clit back and forth; my breath hitched as I climbed. Luci's tongue darted from his mouth, his hand running up my leg.

"Stick a finger inside, bunny," he rasped. "I want you to finger-fuck yourself."

I groaned, losing the climb, but I wanted my mate to be happy. Sticking my finger far into my hole, I watched as Luci grabbed himself, rubbing his shaft up and down.

"What a good girl you are, bunny. Taking your fingers like that."

My chest heaved at the foreign intrusion. It felt so good, but I wanted Luci to do the rest.

"Sir?" My voice trembled.

"What does my bunny want?" Luci's head dipped lower, so close to my little lips. "Does my bunny want me to take care of her?"

I whined, unable to form words. Waiting for a slap to remind me, instead he only chuckled, gently removing my hand from my wetness. His face was right between my thighs, and my face turned red.

What is he going to do?

"You smell so good, my beautiful mate. I just want to taste you."

Luci's hand trailed between my thighs; his eyes never left me as his tongue descended from his mouth. "Watch me eat you up, my prey." His tongue disappeared, touching my clit.

I melted into his mouth, closing my eyes. He stopped until I looked back up to see why he would do such a thing.

"Watch me, or I won't make it feel good," he commanded.

Why was that such a turn-on?

His tongue circled, his hot breath fanning the rest of me. Gripping the sheets, I moaned how good it felt.

So much better than the finger.

I moaned again when his lips attached to that fun little spot while a finger prodded the opening to my wet hole. He sucked hard. I gasped and pulled on his hair tightly with my hand. I didn't know if I wanted him to stop or keep going, and my eyes rolled to the back of my head. He tugged on the area between my legs.

My slow climb to ecstasy rose faster and faster while his finger pumped into me, pulling and stretching. My breath ragged from the overwhelming pleasure rolling through my body. Luci's head lifted from between my thighs, his mouth glistening with moisture.

"Like I said, I could eat you up," he growled, hovering over me. His mouth descended, tongue entering my mouth, making me taste myself.

"See how good you taste?" he said between kisses, pulling at my lip. "My sweet little bunny," he cooed. "You are such a good girl."

The ache between my legs recurred, but this time, I wanted to pleasure him.

"Can I taste you?" I asked boldly.

His head reared back, studying my face. "You want to taste me?"

Nodding shyly, I traced my hand down his six-pack and to that delicious V that pointed straight to my new desire—*His thing.*

Luci kissed my forehead, sitting with his back against the pillows. I pushed his legs apart so I could get a good seat on my knees. His hand rubbed himself, and that alone, had me panting.

"You don't have to," he growled with a strained voice. "I don't want to hurt you."

"But I want to please you, sir." I glanced at the throbbing head, which was leaking profusely.

"Bunny," he whined as he squeezed himself.

I removed his hand, just as he did mine before he bestowed me with those wonderful feelings. His hands clenched the pillows beside me as my bum went right in the air, and I lowered my lips to his tip. I licked it slowly, watching Luci lull his head back.

I stopped licking until his eyes met mine again. "You are supposed to watch," I whispered.

Luci heaved a breath, growling in his chest. "You're right." His hand went to my face, cupping it. "Make me proud, bunny."

My heart soared, ready to do what I needed to do. Licking the tip again, I ignored the hisses and swirled my tongue around the head.

"That's it," he cooed. "Go lower for me, bunny." My head dipped lower, feeling the velvet smoothness of his shaft along my tongue. The ridges from the head down his shaft had me arching my back.

If his tongue and fingers felt so good, I wonder how this would feel?

My throat widened, trying to go as low as I could. "Fuck yes, Uriel. Fucking so good!"

I pulled my mouth back up, making sure my teeth didn't hurt him as I sucked his length, feeling the warmth of his hand behind my head. He pushed me back down, I followed where he wanted me, matching the rhythm from the pull of my hair—even when he pushed me so low that I felt the tears pool in my eyes. I didn't want to stop, no matter how much he had.

"So good, bunny. So good. That's it," he growled.

My hand cupped his underside. They were large and heavy, and I enjoyed the texture that filled my hand. Hissing again, he grumbled some pretty bad words and grunted.

"You can get up, bunny. I'm going to come."

I didn't want to stop, I wanted to taste him too. I only got a little bit earlier.

"Bunny," he rasped with his hand now gripping the pillow beside him. Luci's balls tightened and loads of hot liquid pooled into my mouth. I sucked and swallowed him down just like he drank me.

"Uriel! Fucking hell!" His hand reached back to my head, pulling my hair as he finished.

Once he was done, I made sure to lick him clean, like he did me. Staring at me in awe, he pulled me to his chest so I straddled him with his thing laying right next to my backside.

"Open your mouth," he ordered. I did so gladly, and the biggest smile decorated his handsome face.

"My good girl," he cooed, kissing me. Pushing the pillows away from him, he had me lay on top of his chest, running a hand through my hair, caressing the, now tangled, mess. His grip tightened, and his lips caressed my forehead as I nuzzled into his neck.

"I love you, Uriel," Luci said, as plain as day, as if he had been saying it all his life.

I sat up, my hair covering us, while his dark eyes begged for me to return the simple phrase.

It was a no-brainer.

"I love you too, Luci."

Chapter 32

Uriel

Snuggling further into the sheets, the faint rumble of thunder reverberated through the tent. A breeze blew the flap open, causing a steady wind to hit my bare legs. Snuggling even further, I hoped that Luci would pull the flap shut when another angry gust pushed the blanket off me. I wanted to growl, wondering where Luci was.

He wasn't near me at all, and the pillows were scattered across the room.

Where could he have gone?

I was dressed in a small, black, silky nightdress. The straps fell repeatedly as I slowly stood, and the candles around the room blinked out. The gusts continued to batter the flap so hard it made the sound of a whip.

"Luci?" I called, but his calming voice and muscular body were nowhere to be found.

Despite being on a beach, and it being so warm just hours ago, the breeze was cold as I gripped my arms. Walking barefoot across the scattered bedding on the floor of the tent, I glanced outside to see dark clouds approaching on the horizon. These looked angrier than the almost-storm just hours ago. Red and blue lightning replaced the white lightning from before, and the whitecaps of the ocean grew larger.

Is there a hurricane coming?

I yelled for Luci again, but he was nowhere to be found. Stepping out onto the sand, I noticed it did not hold the warm, playful feel as my feet sunk into it. Our chairs and the blanket we laid on were picked up and hastily thrown down the beach. The cooler overturned, spilling the contents from within.

"Luci!" I called out again, stepping completely out of the tent. The palm trees swayed low, nearly touching my shoulders. I ran toward the middle of the beach as the clouds rolled in, and the lightning quickly followed. Trees on the shoreline cracked, falling into the sand.

"Luci!" I screamed one more time. My voice was lost in the storm. Red lightning struck the broken tree limbs. It was just enough to heat the wood, igniting a fire.

The red flames consumed the broken branches, quickly spreading to the rest of the trees. My nightgown clung to my body for dear life while another lightning bolt struck the tent I had just exited. It burst into flames immediately, and I let out a whimper, holding my hands to my ears. The wind became too much as a tear tried to roll down my face before it was scooped up by the wind. I watched the tiny drop of tear get sucked into the swirling gusts.

Deep, echoing laughter replaced the sounds of rolling thunder as I pulled my hands away from my ears. It grew louder and louder as the dark clouds hovered overhead. Deep black smoke swirled like a tornado, descending to the beach just ten feet away. I tried to retreat, but the wind pushed me where it wanted. It was far too strong for me to resist it.

The deep chuckles stopped as the black swirls of smoke encroached. I saw nothing but a shadow since the wind did not disperse the smoke in front of me. Continuing to struggle against the wind, I was forced closer.

A hand emerged from the smoke, reaching to touch me, holding out my lost sparkling tear on just one finger. The shadow growled before letting it drop to the sand. Screams of children caught my ear. Looking away, I saw several tiny little children, varying in age, drowning in the surf. I screamed, watching the innocent children struggle against the violent waves.

My body turned, no longer protecting my ears from the deafening wind and thunder. I cried out, trying to exude the same bravery Luci emits, pushing against the wind until I finally managed a step.

The smoke stepped in front of me, now holding the shape of a person. It chuckled menacingly, throwing its head back in laughter. The screams of the children in the surf lessened as the waves continued to crash down on them. I tangled with the wind, as the invisible wall squeezed me tighter. The blackened clouds cracked, and deep red hues filling the cracks in the sky had me shaking my head in disbelief.

Where is Luci?

Animals from the forest scattered on the beach, each one pummeled to the ground by an invisible force. They cried in pain as they tried to flee the invisible entity holding them hostage.

"Stop!" I screamed, feeling the heat of ash falling around the beach, covering the beautiful porridge-colored sand that now looked like a dusty gray.

"What do you want?" I screamed. The smoke formed into a perfect, tall shadow. Deep red eyes bore into me as it crept closer.

"This!" Its thunderous voice echoed in the wind. The black hand pointed to a fuzzy scene of Earth: millions of screams, flashes of countless buildings toppling to the ground, people—men, women, and children—running for their lives. Mothers held their babies to their chests as they begged for mercy. The entire Earth realm was collapsing before my eyes.

"Make it stop!" I sobbed. My tears were sucked in by the smoke as it chuckled darkly. "How can I make it stop?" It drew closer to my face. The heat of the entity and its sulfurous breath made me gag.

"You can't," it taunted. "It will happen and once it does..." it paused as the wind let go of my arms.

I stared at my fingers; the scorching heat turned them black as it crept up my arm, slowly engulfing me up to my elbows. The wind pushed my fingers fiercely, catching the ash on them in its wake. The further the black soot covered me, the more my body disappeared.

"Stop!" My hands waving into the air only made them disappear faster. I was wasting away.

"No more innocence on Earth, therefore no need for a goddess," it growled again. Lightning flashed, revealing my feet disappearing into the ash below me. I continued creeping up my body until only my head remained visible.

"Luci!" I screamed until it all faded to blackness.

Lucifer

Holding onto Uriel as she slept, I kept one eye open. Even if we were on an island with only the two of us, I continued to keep guard, never knowing if the evil after her would come. My nose went to her neck, tickling her, remembering her smell as her curves melted into me.

She was so perfect, such a wonderful surprise that I never thought I would encounter. My heart did not beat heavily with guilt and shame as it did before. Uriel accepted me for who I am, and she loved me.

I thought I would only ever know a parent's love, more specifically my mother's. She saw me for who I was. She saw how much I fought the darkness inside, and I never wanted to disappoint her. My finger brushed Uriel's dark hair from her face. We both still lay naked in the mountains of pillows and blankets.

Her body stirred, and her brows furrowed as she gripped my waist. The hums exiting her were discontent as she began moving her body away from me—I wouldn't let her. Being a selfish bastard, I held her tighter.

Can't let her go now. Not ever.

She continued to wrestle, calling out my name several times before I decided to wake her. A bad dream must have infiltrated her mind, and I, being an idiot, did not realize it.

"Uriel," I shook her, kissing her cheek to wake her, but her eyes stayed closed tight.

"Uriel!" I shouted again until those golden eyes looked back at me.

"Luci," she breathed, putting her arms around my neck. Her heart pounded and beads of sweat now formed on her head. "I couldn't find you!"

"Find me?" I questioned, pulling her away to study her beautiful face. "I've been here the whole time."

Biting her lip, her head leaned back into my shoulder. "I must have had a bad dream," she whispered, pulling me tighter. "A terrible nightmare. I woke up, and you were gone, and there was a storm over the ocean. Some black shadow-man made me disappear into the wind." Her voice came out rushed as she gripped me even tighter.

"What happened? Tell me everything!"

Her words had my body constrict as she explained the nightmare down to the very last detail. My fists tightened, furious that I could not even protect her from a dream. Dreams are held in high regard in the supernatural and Celestial realms; they can predict the future, have deeper meanings, or could be used by a god to send a message—even to other gods.

"We're going home," I growled. "We need to stay within the confines of the palace until we can figure this out."

Uriel didn't complain. She didn't mind that we were leaving the place that she had wanted to visit for so long. Now her view of the ocean, the beach, the sand, and the time spent together was tainted by that damn nightmare.

This being, this shadow that loomed over her, it was the evil threatening her. It had to be. It was an obvious message announcing that it was coming for her. To destroy her. Along with it, humanity would be destroyed as well.

I knew I would not bring this destruction. *I am not the impending evil, because my heart could never bear to hurt my Uriel.*

Getting her dressed promptly, I pulled her hand to take her out of the tent.

Shaking her head, she stepped backward. "What if he is still out there?" Tears welled in her eyes.

Grabbing both of her hands, I kissed her knuckles. "He won't be. I am here, and I'm not leaving your side, my beautiful mate. I will fight until all the realms are defeated to make you safe." The shaky sigh she held gave some comfort, but not enough to sate me.

Whatever evil was coming for her was doing so quickly, or it would not have sent such a horrid dream for her.

Once we stepped out of the tent, squeals of laughter could be heard from the shore. Brief bursts of giggles and splashing had Uriel let go of my hand.

"The children," she whispered. "They have to get out!" She ran toward the shoreline.

I called for her to wait, but her steps hurried and her wings flew from her body. Some of her beautiful golden feathers fell from her wings as she flew into the air to check on the children.

The children's laughter died as Uriel hovered over them and shouted. "Get out! Or you will drown!" Her hand went down to grab one of the child's hands, but they thought it was a game.

"We can't drown, we breathe water," one snipped as the four stood up. "Come on, guys."

Uriel, happy with their choice to leave the surf, landed with her feet in the water and her wings gently parted by her side. Grabbing her hand, I pulled her from the surf.

"You can't do that, Uriel!" I chastised. "It could have been a trap! Someone could have taken you!" I growled. Her head lowered, wobbling her lip. I pulled her flush to my body, and she cried.

Feeling like a complete idiot, I rubbed her head, kissing it softly. "I'm sorry, bunny. I was worried for you."

Humming and wiping away her tears, she gripped my shirt. "I was just trying to help them. You didn't see what I saw."

The children, most likely sirens who are allowed on the beach, glared at me. Their bodies were covered in a net-like garb.

"You made the pretty angel cry!" A girl with long pink and yellow hair called out to me.

"She didn't know we could breathe under water. Lighten up!"

I growled at the boy with blue and green hair.

He hissed, flashing his fangs.

My brows furrowed in anger, gripping Uriel tighter. Hands blackening and willing fire in one hand. They all stood back.

"Thaaaaat's a god! You just screwed up, Thalamere!"

Another girl with similarly colored hair approached, pulling on his arm. "Please forgive him. He's got a big mouth!"

Uriel giggled at the young girl. "Don't hurt them, Luci. They didn't know." Growling vibrated in my throat until Uriel kissed my chest, causing me to relax.

"I'm sorry, I thought you were going to drown," Uriel said sheepishly. They all shook their heads.

"We are sirens. We can breathe underwater," Thalamere spoke. "I'm Thalamere Jr., son of King Thalamere and Queen Scorpia, and this is my sister, Alyssa." Alyssa curtsied, and Uriel cooed at them.

"These are our friends," Alyssa spoke as her hand pointed to the two others with pink and yellow hair, "Manta and Scurry," The boy, Scurry, bowed low, and his sister curtsied but toppled over into the sand.

"Stupid legs," she muttered in frustration.

Chapter 33

Lucifer

"You guys are from Atlantis?" Uriel's eyes widened. Thalamere and Alyssa nodded in unison.

"Yup, we wanted to walk on land to practice using our legs. We're supposed to visit the Golden Light Kingdom in a few weeks. We don't want to look silly when we walk out of the water to meet Aunt Melina."

I held Uriel close, not daring to let go of her again. She was far too slippery for my liking, and with her dream, I wouldn't let her slip away again.

"It was nice to meet you, but we must get going." I pulled Uriel with me, out of the surf. I didn't want to burn the siren children when we were transported back to the Underworld—water dwellers don't do well with fire.

"Will you come to visit again sometime?" Manta spoke up, her tiny arms in a praying motion.

"We want the angel to visit with us again. Maybe we can teach her to swim too!" Scurry ran towards us to hear her reply.

Pulling Uriel away from them, I growled in warning. *Even if they were children, I would not let my mate be susceptible to their greedy little hands.*

"I'd love to!" Uriel peeped from behind me. "I'm Uriel by the way." She reached her hand out, but I pulled her closer to me.

"That's enough," I growled, glaring at the children.

Uriel's golden eyes blinked at me. "Luci," she whined.

Pulling her closer, I whispered in her ear, "May I remind you of the dream you just had? We need to get home."

Uriel's eyes went from filled with excitement to sorrow. Looking away from me, she slowly waved at the children and pulled me back to the dried sands. "Maybe some other time." Her voice was now sad.

Shit. Now I'm the bad guy.

The children looked at me in disgust, since I chastised her. I growled again, pulling Uriel back to me.

"Listen," I said, loud enough for everyone to hear, "as soon as we figure some things out"—the children's heads whipped to listen to my voice—"I will take you to Atlantis so you may visit your new friends."

Uriel's eyes widened. The warmth of her tears washed away. "You would do that? Take me to Atlantis?"

I chuckled, rubbing her cheek with the pad of my thumb. "If it would please you, then yes. Of course, I will."

Even if it means being buried under millions of gallons of water. It was already giving me an extreme case of claustrophobia.

"Anything you want."

The children beamed before running back into the water.

"Come soon! We will tell Mother and Father! They will be so happy!" Their hands waved excitedly until we saw their fins retreat into the water.

"They won't even believe you," I muttered.

The surrounding sand swirled, and the black smoke buried us as we were transported back to the dark palace.

As soon as we arrived, we found the palace bustling with servants and warriors. Father's warrior demons stood in every corner and looked at us warily while passing. Uriel held tightly to me, not liking the warriors who didn't generally roam the palace. These warriors were beasts. Ares himself helped train these demons. Their black horns were as large as a ram's, and their tails swayed as they trotted down the hall with a heavy gate. The loud, clopping noises of their hooves made Uriel wince each time their feet hit the marbled floor.

"What's going on?" she inquired with her arms wrapped tightly around mine. I soothed her with my other hand, keeping her close to comfort her.

"Father knows about your dream," I mumbled, heading straight for his office.

I would never leave Uriel alone. Not now that the darkness was evidently progressing far faster than I would have liked.

The office doors stood agape. Mother was inside, sitting on Father's lap while looking into the Sphere of Souls, which Selene left for her.

"Luci!" Mother went to leave Father's lap, but was quickly pulled back down. Father's smoke smothered the entire floor; the dark wood floors and red carpet were now stained permanently.

"Lucifer, come in."

An old friend, Hermes, sat on the couch holding parchment and a quill, taking notes.

"We are being questioned by Hermes to make this trial a quicker process for Zeus," Father explained as I sat, pulling Uriel onto my lap. She yawned before putting her head just under my neck.

She clearly didn't rest while she dreamt. Instead, she was running for her life and fighting the darkness that tried to eat her alive.

"Have either of you seen Hera or Michael recently?"

Uriel's eyebrow raised, but she swiftly shook her head.

"Why? Are they not at home?"

Hermes sighed, pinching his nose. He was typically a playful god. There were too many stories I heard of him playing tricks on Father and Mother, especially one involving a red bathing suit. That one had Father cursing him for months afterward.

"Uriel, they are missing," I whispered. "Zeus has summoned them for a trial for..." I paused, unsure how to explain that she was drugged most of her life. My mate was unfortunately still in the dark on that note. If she was told at the same time as I was, we both would have been too upset to console one another.

"Your parents have been using the plants in the house to keep your powers hidden, and they stunted your growth." Pushing her hair behind her ear, she stared across the room at the bookcase.

"She wouldn't," she whispered. "Mom and Dad wouldn't do that." Standing up, she escaped my embrace, but I didn't release her hand.

"You know I'm not lying, bunny. That's why Athena came to the beach, to tell me."

Uriel's mind had to be running a mile a minute. She had a look of anguish on her beautiful face and had a firm grip on her dress.

"No." She shook her head again. "Mom has only lied once." Uriel held up her index finger in emphasis.

Standing up and pulling her to my chest, I rocked her gently. The room stood still—Hermes went back to writing on the parchment, and my parents observed our interaction.

"Those plants," I whispered, "held your power inside you. You wouldn't have known if she was lying or not."

"But why would she do that?" Her head brushed my chest, pulling at my shirt.

"To keep you safe, Uriel." I gritted my teeth.

Hera was a bitch for doing it this way. In her own sick and twisted mind, she thought she was helping, even though it was in the worst way possible.

"Your parents thought they could hide you from the evil threatening you all on their own. She took things into her own hands, trying to help you." Uriel gripped me tighter, her tears wetting my shirt. "Now that he knows, Zeus is furious."

"Your parents broke laws, Uriel." Hermes stood up, straightening his tan suit jacket. "First, they kept you hidden from all the other gods. Zeus is supposed to be presented with each new god or goddess' birth to put it on record. You were never brought before him to be blessed. Your parents also poisoned you, well until you were twenty-five years old. Poisoning a god is prohibited. They have committed serious crimes." Hermes came closer, too close for my liking.

Glaring at him in warning, he stepped away, putting his hands up.

"And now they are missing," I uttered to her. "If they do not report to Zeus in"—I checked the time—"twenty hours, they will never leave the Celestial Prison. In fact, they may even have to be held in Tartarus." Uriel gasped, holding her hand over her mouth.

"No, that can't happen. I disagree. I don't want to press charges!" Uriel's voice echoed in Father's study.

Hermes shook his head, capping his quill. "Doesn't work like that with the gods, Little One. These laws are put in place for a reason. After the Demeter fiasco, I thought your mother would be smarter than that."

Uriel continued to shake her head in disbelief. She backed away from me, her glittered tears pouring down her cheeks.

"Bunny, it's alright."

Her head whipped back to my parents and then to Hermes. "I wish to be alone right now."

My mate ran to the door. I went to follow, only for Mother to grab my hand to pull me back.

"Let her be, Lucifer. She needs time."

My heart broke for my mate. She was feeling an overwhelming collection of emotions. I felt her sadness and her distress; I could feel her crying on the other side of the bond, and there was nothing I could do to make things better.

"This is her parents' fault," I growled, looking at Hermes. "What is the plan once they arrive for trial?"

Hermes shook his head, sitting back down on the couch. "Zeus is furious. He is tired of the gods thinking of him as nothing but a joke. He plans to carry this trial out seriously, and with the overwhelming evidence, there is a great chance both of them will be locked up in Tartarus."

My hands blackened, feeling my mate's sorrow. *Her parents might be complete idiots, but this would devastate my mate, and I could not have her unhappy.*

"What are our plans?" I directed my question to Father.

He leaned back in his chair, the smoke still pouring from his body. Mother continued to console him, sitting on his lap, and kissing his cheek. Still, the smoke flowed out the office doors and into the hallway.

"I am not High God. I have no say," he spoke to himself. "Uriel will have to speak at the trial, but I'm sure Zeus will consider her wishes."

Hermes laughed, picking up the glass of whisky on the table. "Zeus hasn't exactly been the same since he returned from the Underworld," Hermes mused.

Father's head picked up in question.

"Yeah, he came back with this devilish smirk and uttered something like, 'what a show this is going to be.' I don't think he will consider Uriel's feelings."

"But Uriel helped him," I spoke. "She helped him forgive himself using her grace." Sitting back down, I rested my elbows on my legs, burying my face in my hands—things were falling apart quickly.

Zeus could forgive himself with Uriel's powers. He should have felt his burden lighten, not the desire to see a 'show,' whatever that meant. Surely, Zeus couldn't be the evil that was supposed to take my Uriel.

Uriel

Letting go of Luci's hand, I raced down the hall. The big, angry, warrior demons followed me slowly, watching me run to my pretty, white door. Pushing on the handles, the warriors chuckled as I growled angrily before finally pulling the door outward. I grunted, falling on my bum before pushing off the floor, clambering into the room, and slamming the door.

I hardly even got up off the floor. I just sat there, curled up against it while the tears filled my eyes. I hated crying. When I cried, glitter got everywhere, and it made such a mess. Wiping them away with the back of my hand, I sniffed trying to keep the snot out of my mouth.

I was such an ugly crier, big fat tears with a red face and snotty nose. There was nothing pretty about it, and I didn't want Luci to see me like this. I heaved again, processing the revelation that my mom and dad would do something like this to me.

How dare they! I listened to everything they said; I obeyed like a good girl, and they hid me and kept the powers I was supposed to have away from me.

Slamming my fists on the carpet, a heavenly breeze brushed my hair away from my face. For a minute, it smelled like my mother: light vanilla with a hint of coconut.

About to sob again, I felt a gentle touch land on my chin. My glittered eyes glanced up and saw, none other than, the woman I had so many questions for.

Chapter 34

Uriel

The gentle touch on my chin lifted my head slightly. My eyelids widened at the woman before me. Mom stood there in her pretty white sundress with her favorite gold laurel crown on her head. Her eyes held that same warmth I witnessed every morning when I woke, her cheeks were rosy like she had been smiling too much.

"Mom?" I questioned.

Did I fall asleep again? I wouldn't doubt it because sometimes a great long sleep followed after a good cry.

"Hello, Uriel," her knees bent down to meet me on the floor. "Your father and I wanted to check on you." Her voice held the softness she had when she put me to bed before reading to me every night. I had a whole mess of information to sort out, and she was the first person I needed to talk to. I bit my inner cheek, trying not to remember the happy times when I was utterly ignorant.

"You've kept secrets from me," I whispered, turning my head and standing. Walking towards the bed, I picked up Mr. Rainbow Farts and clenched him to my chest. Mom only sighed, walking towards the bed. The apparition she cast was translucent in appearance and didn't disturb the bed when she sat beside me.

Picking at my unicorn's hair, the room became deathly quiet. My mom took ragged breaths. "I had to," she whispered. "I had to, to keep you safe." My heart didn't ache or feel the pinprick of a lie. She honestly believed she had to keep it a secret from me to keep it safe.

"You should have told me when I was older," I murmured as I braided the unicorn's hair.

"Being a child, I would understand you keeping things from me, but I'm twenty-five years old!" my voice rose. "You kept me as a child, so innocent and locked away from the world. I trusted you! You and Dad were all I had!" I threw the unicorn to the ground, and hearing the flop of him hitting the floor; I winced.

Sorry, Mr. Rainbow Farts.

"You are a part of a prophecy—" I cut her off, growling at her. Mom's eyes widened at my outburst. She was trying to explain, and I almost snarled at her.

"I know what I am a part of, Mom." I hissed. "I know all of it, every bit, and those plants you kept in the house, which you made me water every day, kept me from growing up!"

Mom shook her head, dumbfounded. "What?"

"Yeah, those plants stunted my growth. For flower's sake, I couldn't even get something as normal as a period!" Mom sat back down, her hand coming to her mouth.

"How do you know this?"

"Athena went to our home and saw the plants! She's pretty smart, you know? Oh wait, I guess you do know because you know everything and kept it hidden from me!" I hissed.

There were scratching sounds at the door. More than likely, it was Cerberus. I could hear his grunts and growls from the other side.

"I didn't know about the plants," she whispered. "They stunted your growth?" Mom's voice whispered. My chest didn't feel the pain.

Did she not know?

"How can you be blind to that? I didn't grow normally, I didn't get as tall as you and Dad, and I never came to you when I started bleeding?" Mom shook her head, her hand over her forehead.

"I thought it was your innocence, Uriel. I swear it. I wasn't even sure you would get a mate..." she paused, covering her mouth.

"Oh, I know everything, Mom." I narrowed my eyes at her. "I've learned more in the past two days than in the twenty-five years I've been with you!" Mom had her hand to her heart.

"What do you mean, you know?" She growled out. "Who told you these things? I'm gone for a few days, and you come back with an attitude, thinking you know it all?" Mom's teeth ground into each other. She tried to pick up a book to throw, but it only slipped through her fingers.

"Someone who cares about me deeply enough not to hide things from me." I stood on my own two feet, my wings sprouting from my body. They didn't tremble like they usually did. They were displayed outward in a defensive position, ready to charge whatever offense may ensue.

"Who told you?" Her fists balled at her sides, and her tiny vein that liked to poke out when she was angry pulsated.

"Luci," I whispered. Mom lost all control, growling until she buried her face in a pillow she had on the other side of the apparition. Once she finished, her eyes were red with anger as she lunged toward me. Her hands tried to grip my shoulders to shake me.

"Did he taint you? Say that he loves you? Uriel, you can't be that naïve? He is the God of Destruction! It is his job to destroy things! He will use you and throw you away!" My breath hitched in my throat, and the pain could be felt throughout my chest and body.

Lies.

"Luci loves me, and I love him! He would never!" I growled back. The golden tips of my wing's feathers glowed around me, brightening the room until it burned.

Mom scoffed, "what do you know of 'love'?"

My eyes burned, feeling it deep within my heart. I could see their reflective glow on my mom's face. Her mouth dropped, watching the majestic glow of my body come to light.

"More than you! I would have at least told my child the prophecy and let them decide what to do once they were old enough! You kept me from all the gods who could have helped me from the beginning! You hid me in shame, expecting that your daughter would bring destruction to the humans and the gods. You dared not ask for help because your pride made you think you would do a better job," I hissed. "It wasn't about protecting me; it was about protecting yourself because if it all failed, you would have been the goddess who produced the destruction of all the realms."

Mother sat back on the bed, her mouth agape. Her face reddened and sweat started beading on her brows.

It was all true, every bit. Did she even love me, or did she love her reputation? Surely the gods thought highly of her since she helped Zeus rule?

"My, you've grown," she chuckled, hiding her bewilderment. "Honestly, I didn't know the plants would stunt your growth," she uttered. "I just thought they would hide your aura and your powers, not do anything to harm you. I never wanted to hurt you." She shook her head, her hands cradling each side.

"Uriel, I'm sorry," she heaved a breath. Silent tears ran down her face. I couldn't remember the last time I saw my mom cry. I don't think I'd ever seen it. She was always the strong, regal one in the family.

I could detect lies, but that doesn't mean I would forgive her so easily. What if I never came to the baby announcement? I would still be sitting in her home living in ignorance. Even if she did it to protect me, she poisoned me and she hid things from me.

She thought I was nothing but a child; in her eyes, I was. If there was anything that I learned in the past few days, it was that I am not a child. I am a woman, and Luci helped me realize that fact. I am stronger now.

"I did it to protect you!" Mom stated louder. "I would do it again to keep you safe because I love you; we love you!" Her hands went to mine but fell right through, the apparition unable to hold on to objects.

"Dad was in on this too, then?" I questioned. Mom's face fell.

"He didn't want to do it. He spoke against it." I hummed, anger boiling inside.

At least she wasn't lying. Not this time.

"You've lied to me all my life." I turned my back to her. Not one word left her lips as a sniff reached my ears. "Do you know how hard that will be to rectify? You've ruined our relationship!"

"To protect you!" she yelled. "All of it was just to protect you!"

A sting in my heart: lie. What was she hiding?

"And your reputation!" I snapped as the thought came to me. "Everyone knows you work alongside Zeus, and you practically run the show! Now Zeus is angry that you went behind his back and didn't tell him about me!" I screamed. "You will go to prison, and you aren't even sorry for what you did!"

"To protect you!" she yelled again.

Another sting.

"I can detect lies, Mother," I whispered. Mother shook her head in disbelief.

Was she lying to herself this whole time? Claiming she was protecting me, when deep in her heart, she wanted to protect herself, too?

Guilt—I could feel the guilt radiating off her, but that didn't calm me.

Heat flushed through my body. It only reminded me of when Luci would get angry. I was experiencing what he feels all too well. My wings flapped harshly, the wind pushed the covers off the bed. Mother's teary eyes looked at me; it didn't faze me.

She kept me from my mate. We could have met so much sooner; we could have helped each other grow.

"Those plants..." I spoke again. "You've tried so hard to have another baby, but those plants kept you infertile." Mom's face paled. "Or were you too busy to think about that when you made me water them every day? The properties of those plants not only stunted my growth and power but also made those who live in the same home unable to grow theirs. A child could not grow within your womb."

A silent tear ran down my face. As much as I wanted my mom to suffer for what she did—keeping from my mate, the lies, the ulterior motives she wasn't aware of—I could see her heart break, and it broke mine. My hand went to her shoulder, resting on the partially visible form she had. I could feel her guilt just as I did Zeus. She was sorry.

I felt the warmth build in my hand as I pulled the guilt from my mom's body until she slumped over on the bed, now lying across from me. Looking at my hand, it felt heavy, just as it did with Zeus until it disappeared entirely.

Her eyes looked heavy as they blinked slowly, staring out the window that she could now see.

"I think there is a phrase that humans like to say..." I muttered so she could hear. "It goes: 'Karma is a bitch.'" I bit my tongue at the foul word. Mom winced, holding her stomach as she cried.

"I forgive you. I don't think I can stomach holding onto anger." A tear left my cheek. Sitting next to the bed, Mom sat up trying to hold me. My head leaned to her shoulder, feeling the gentle breeze the apparition left on my skin. I may forgive her, but I will never forget. Our relationship was now tainted. It will never be what it was ever again.

"I'm going to find the evil hunting you, Uriel. I came here to see if it was Lucifer. He is the only god with whom I am not familiar." The breeze became tighter as I shook my head.

"Luci isn't the evil." I leaned away from her.

"How can you be so sure? He is the God of Destruction; he could destroy all the worlds in an instant. He is just trying to get close to you!" I giggled, holding my hand to my mouth.

Luci could never do that, not with me by his side.

"Lucifer is my mate, Mom."

Chapter 35

Uriel

"Your... What?" Mom's deathly silence after each separated word made me cower. I had some courage before, but this was another side of Mom I had not seen. Her eyes darkened as she tried to grip the sheets beside me. "How do you know this? He's lying!" she spat.

"He is my mate!" I sat back up angrily to defend him. "I feel the tingles when we touch. I'm drawn to him. I love him. He is everything to me that Dad is to you" Mom sighed, slouching over herself.

"This day keeps getting better and better," she uttered. I knew that was a lie without having to feel it through my chest.

Was she that upset that I found my mate? How rude of her to think such a thing: to try to be angry about something so special that she and Dad had together and want to deny me it. My heart twisted in my chest. Did she not care for me or my feelings on any matter whatsoever?

Harsh banging at the door had us both whip our heads at an ungodly speed. "Uriel!" It was Luci and Cerberus was scratching at the door, again. "Open up, Sweetheart, or I will break it down!"

Luci was not kidding. I didn't feel one twitch of pain on that statement.

"Mom, turn yourself in. It will only make things worse if you run away," I whispered to her. The banging continued, now echoing through the room.

If Luci found out my mom was in here, she would be in a heap of trouble. It was like I was harboring a fugitive, but kind of not. She wasn't really here, it was just her apparition.

"Not until I find that evil, Uriel!" Mom stood up, determined, as she slid across the room. Her bare feet didn't even sink into the carpet as her translucent form stopped. "I will even find out if your supposed 'mate' is to blame as well. I still don't trust him. Do not let him mark you!" I stood up on the bed, pointing my finger at her.

How dare she tell me what to do after lying to me for all these years!

"I will do as I wish!" I snapped. "You have no control over me anymore!" shaking my head in disbelief. To think I felt sorry for her earlier.

The loud banging now pushed the large white doors until they bowed. Luci's smoke and fire could be seen through the cracks of the door.

"I mean it, Uriel! Be a good girl and listen to your mother!"

I shook my head again defiantly. Stomping my foot on the ground, I yelled out for Luci.

No way! No way can she tell me what to do anymore!

"She's in here! My mom is in here!" I shouted, half crying. I couldn't believe it came down to this; I thought she could change after I took away the guilt, but it looks like it just fed the fire inside her. Mom was bent on trying to protect me, even when I knew my mate would help.

Mom's face softened from her angry scowl to disappointment, thinking I sided with my mate instead of her. She has taken care of me all these years. She did it in her own way, but still, it was wrong the way she did it. Mom couldn't let go; she couldn't trust her daughter; she couldn't trust the way I felt about things. Luci would never, ever hurt me and I am stronger than what she makes me out to be. She understood nothing about me, just her perception of me: the innocent little Uriel who still loved bubble baths and was ignorant of the realms.

Ok, I still loved bubble baths.

"We will figure this out, Uriel," Mom spoke before the white double doors of my room blasted open. They fell to the floor; the once pristine white doors now charred black with flames on the corners. Luci's black wings held fire at the tips, and his eyes glowed red.

"You!" Luci growled.

Luci lunged to capture Mom's apparition. His flapping wings nearly engulfed the entire room. Ash flew from his wings as Mom took one last glance and disappeared entirely.

I gripped a pillow next to me and silently cried.

Could she not see that Luci was trying to protect me? Now she looked like the evil one in all this mess: she kept me from my mate, she hid me all these years, and she lied to me. The only evil I see is her. Mom was going about it all wrong. She loved me, but why did it hurt that she wouldn't listen to me?

I heaved in deep breaths until Luci's warm arms engulfed me. His wings shielded us both by wrapping them around me. He whispered in my ear while petting my hair, kissing my cheek, and giving me all the love that I had craved since learning we were mates.

Luci comforted me. He loved me, and I loved him fiercely even though such a short amount of time transpired. Mom should have been happy for me. She got her mate and loved my dad deeply. Now I sit here with my mate, and she tells me not to let my mate mark me as his?

What does marking even mean?

"Luci?" I sniffed, drying my tears on his now tattered shirt. His eyes were no longer the red that stared down at my mother. "What does it mean to mark your mate?" My head tilted to the side, gripping onto the rags of his shirt.

"Oh, bunny..." he whispered, brushing my sparkly tears away. "What did she say to you? Did she hurt you?" I shook my head, leaning into Luci. His wings held us in the dark with only a tiny bit of light emanating from the fire on the tips of his wings. It lit just enough so I could see his face.

"She didn't hurt me," I sniffed. "She is very confused. She thinks she is helping me, but she isn't. Mom thinks you might be the evil that is after me, and when I told her we were mates, she kind of lost it. She told me not to let you 'mark me,' but I don't understand that." Luci held me tighter, the growling in his chest became louder as he kissed the top of my head.

"To complete the mating bond," he muttered, "we have to actually mate. As we both come close to feeling that wonderful pleasure we like to give each other," I blushed, covering my face as I giggled. Luci chuckled, kissing my temple, "our souls will disconnect from our bodies and merge. We are then one in body, mind, and spirit." My eyes widened. It sounded so beautiful to be connected to him. I felt so in sync with him already. How was I to feel once we completed this?

"I want to do it," I whispered. "I want to be mated to you." Luci's eyebrows furrowed, his fingers tracing my lips.

"I do too, more than anything." His lips touched me, my hands reaching to cup his face.

"But I don't want you to do it because your mother forbids it. You have a lot of emotions running through your body, bunny. I want you to have a clear head because I know," he tapped my nose, "you fear my cock destroying your precious, little flower." I giggled, knowing that was precisely how I felt.

"How do you know so much?" I mused, tracing the tattoo on his shoulder.

"I can feel your emotions. We have become close in a short amount of time, but I can sense what you feel. You are an open book, my innocent, little goddess." Luci's breath was warm as it fanned my neck. Straddling him, I put my head on his shoulder as he rocked us back and forth.

"Is that why you came in here? Because you felt me?" I kissed the base of his neck. My tingles returned as I sat straddling him. Rocking against him, he groaned, putting his hands on my bum.

We didn't have to mate now, but we could do playtime stuff, right?

"Uriel..." he kissed my shoulder. "Yes, I felt you. I felt your distress and your sadness, and it made me hurt for you. I don't want my precious mate hurting over stupid things," he whispered huskily. "I want my bunny happy, prancing around the palace in her beautiful dresses and laughing at the silliest things." Luci's hand went up my dress, feeling my bare bum. "You are not wearing any underwear." I felt his sausage twitch.

"I-I thought we could do something when we got home," I blushed. I really wanted playtime, all the time, especially when he licked my tingly spot. That was the best. "I didn't want you to rip my panties again," I rubbed my donut against Luci's sausage again.

"Is that so?" his hand gripped my bum. "I'll try my best to get you more underwear so I can do it whenever I want. I enjoy ripping clothes off of you," a smirk played on his lips before he kissed me. Humming into his mouth, I could taste a hint of smoke. It reminded me of a burnt marshmallow.

Luci's wings came down from their defensive hold and folded into his body. My, much smaller, wings retracted as well as his hands trailed up my back. Luci groaned into the kiss, his hand now cupping my breast. His sharp claw thrummed my nipple, causing me to break the kiss to throw my head back.

"Ew, gross!" Loki's voice exclaimed from the doorway. Luci grabbed me, his wings flying back out instantly to cover me. "I just got the perfect view of your mate's ass, Luci! You've got to learn to not blow down doors with your temper tantrums."

"Loki! Bad word!" I scolded. Luci's grip became unbearably tight before I gasped. Feeling a blanket thrown on me in an instant, Luci flew off the bed to chase a screaming Loki down the hall.

Now I was all tingly and wet. I huffed in annoyance.

As I was making the bed and cleaning the room, Luci walked back in with his hands in his pockets muttering out an apology before pulling me to him.

"I'm hungry," I pouted, wrapping my arms around his waist. Luci only smiled before biting his bottom lip and then rolling his tongue across it. As delicious as he looked, I needed actual sustenance, not *that* snack.

"Like actual food," I poked his chest. Again, he pushed his hips into me.

Narrowing my eyes at him, he laughed joyously before picking me up and wrapping my legs around him. Kissing me on the lips and diving his tongue into me, he lets them go with a smack. "Fates, you taste like apple pie," he growled playfully. I shook my head, not liking the sound of tasting like pie.

That wasn't the best dessert.

"Oh?" he raised a brow. "Then what do you taste like?" I hummed, thinking as he walked over the flaming bedroom doors with his bare feet. The doors began to crumble beneath him.

My mate is so strong.

"A cupcake!" I quipped until I leaned in closer to tell him a secret. "A danger cupcake!" I giggled.

Danger cupcakes were special. Sometimes they had cinnamon or were topped with peppermint, giving them a little kick in the patootie for your mouth.

"I see," Luci pulled my lips from his ear. "That's great because I love danger cupcakes." Luci's mouth descended on my lips as I squealed in laughter.

Wiggling down, I pranced away from him, turning back to see if he would follow. His feet led him to me faster until I turned and flashed him my butt—*that didn't have any panties covering it.*

"That is one scrumptious-looking cupcake," he warned. "Think I need to take a bite out of it!" I squealed again, running down the hallway.

Now my bum was no longer my bum but a big cupcake for Luci.

Chapter 36

Hera

Lucifer lunged towards me, his eyes were red with black seeping down his eyes like cobwebs. Looking at my beloved daughter one more time, I covered myself with my arm, blinking twice to end the apparition. I fell from the table I stood on, my loving mate, Michael, catching me in his arms.

Falling lifelessly, being cradled into his chest, I pulled at his loose tunic as he carried me to the couch. It was a simple living accommodation that we had acquired on Earth in one of the many hotels that Zeus owned. He would never know we were here, in this apartment building, because I oversaw the real estate properties on Earth.

This typical apartment was a basic one-bedroom. It had beautiful granite countertops in the kitchen and large, bay windows in the living room overlooking the New York skyline. The square footage was incomparably more petite than our home back in the Celestial Kingdom, but this was all we needed. A place to sleep, hide, and confide in each other as we searched for the lurking evil.

"Did you hear it all?" I whimpered into Michael's chest. He pushed back my laurel crown, setting it on the table before us. Humming to my forehead, he graced it with a gentle kiss.

"I did, my love." His voice was filled with disappointment. I could feel the pity emanating from him as I stared up at the ceiling, unable to look him in the eyes.

He told me countless times not to bring those forbidden plants into our home, but I did so carelessly. They had been known to weaken powers, especially those of young gods, and I had to do everything I could to protect my daughter. I just didn't know the mixture of the various plants would stunt her growth.

The night we were told she would die and soon all life with it, I had to do something. We did not know what evil was coming for her and, who knows, it could have been Zeus. I couldn't ask for help from him. He was still upset that I had found a mate, while he had not. I left him in the blink of an eye to be with Michael, whom I had already fallen in love with long before Ember found our souls to be bonded.

Zeus was the number one suspect. I had to hide Uriel's powers, so he could not detect them in the Celestial Kingdom. I couldn't just stop my job as his assistant; it would bring too much attention. We had to make do, so I had to hide her. Surely Uriel could see that?

Then again, I never gave her the chance to actually see it.

A ragged breath left my body, my eyes heating with tears. I have not cried in decades, not since the day I found out about Zeus' many affairs. *What kind of Goddess of Women and Marriage was I if I couldn't even maintain a monogamous relationship with Zeus?* He paraded his dick around the whole Celestial

Kingdom and Earth and look where it got me: a laughingstock for centuries. I saw the stares and the pity in their eyes.

'The poor goddess of marriage couldn't even keep her partner around.'

I could see those thoughts running through their minds. Never again. I promised myself that I would never be looked down upon again. I would prove to be a better goddess and hold my bonding together. Now that I had Michael, I knew he would be faithful. The bond is so powerful that I can feel what he feels and know if he ever tried to stray. His love has outshone all the love Zeus ever had for me, and it warmed my heart to feel his overwhelming emotions.

Since Uriel has been born, his love has stayed true. Michael could feel the tension in my body, and all the worry I had over our child's safety. Our beautiful daughter, created with our love, drove my motherly instincts into hyper-drive. She wasn't my first child, but she was the first child with my mate. The bond we had connecting us was strong, and maybe I did want to keep her locked up. The prophecy gave me an extra reason to keep her with me always. That was my subconscious talking: to keep her and never let her go. I never wanted to hear those words leave my lips, so there they stayed deep within me. Unfortunately, my brilliant Uriel found those thoughts and quickly called me out.

I love her. She represented everything that I cared about. I knew she was the Goddess of Innocence, but of which innocence, I wasn't sure. What if the evil was actually her mate, and destroyed... THAT innocence? My heart twisted: thinking she would do those things. She acted so childish, but was that all my doing?

It appeared to be so, since those infernal plants, which I insisted upon keeping, stunted her growth. When she never asked why blood stained her underwear, I never questioned it. Not once did she come to me asking why she had sexual feelings in parts of her body. Not once did I question any of it because I thought she was the Goddess of Innocence—*of sexual purity.*

Obviously, this was not the case.

It was my fault.

It was my actions that ruined her and prevented her body from growing. I had poisoned her—*her whole life.* I had not only hidden her power but prevented her from becoming her true self. All over my selfish desires to keep her with me forever, to always have our family bond, and to restore my reputation so no god or goddess could laugh at me again.

Gripping my white dress, I felt unbearably hot. Uriel had stripped me of my guilt only for it to come back tenfold as I pondered these things. Twenty-five years of caring for her, and the Fates laugh at me, in my face. Maybe this was some sort of trick to get me to realize what a failure I am as a goddess. The evil will come to take her from us and along with it, my own power, because I was obviously a terrible goddess.

"My sweet goddess," Michael interrupted me from my thoughts. His hand stroked my hair as he sat with me on the couch cradling me with his wings touching the floor. His clean-shaven face rubbed my forehead while he kissed me gently. How is it that a bond can make one relax so readily?

"Will you now let me take this burden from you?" Michael hummed into my forehead. His deep voice soothed me down to my stomach. Sighing deeply, I leaned into him. Maybe I needed him; I couldn't be strong all on my own. I had been stern about being in charge of our family and our bonding/marriage. As the Goddess of Partnerships, I didn't think to accept his help.

Was I that obtuse? I've had millennia to fully understand my powers and learn to let my mate in, to have him help me. It takes two to create such a strong bond. Why did I not let him in sooner?

"Uriel will forgive you. I am sure she already has, just like she said." I gripped Michael tighter. "I know you do not trust Lucifer. You seem to think you are the only one able to protect her, but I promise you, if Ember thought her son was a danger, she never would have paired them. She has never been wrong, now has she?" I shook my head in agreement.

"Will you let them be then?" I hummed, letting him know I heard him. *If Lucifer is meant to be Uriel's mate, then there must be a reason. I knew nothing about Lucifer since he hid as much as I hid my Uriel. With my daughter's defiance against me, she must care for him, and he must have treated her properly.*

In just the few days I have been away from her, she has done fine on her own. I'd like to think we both had something to do with that. Her playful nature was calming to the God of Destruction, just like Ember was calming to the ever-brooding Hades.

"Mate, what are you thinking?" Michael tilted my chin up to look into his eyes. *He has weathered every storm that we have ever encountered and told me he would love me regardless of our bond. He has been my rock, my everlasting anchor to this mess of a storm we were in.*

"I love you," I sniffed, letting a tear fall. "And I'm sorry for how I have acted since Uriel was born," I cried into his chest. Letting the walls crumble around me and the fortress I tried to build for this family, I wailed into his chest. "I wanted to protect her, protect us, and also not look like the fool I was with Zeus. I wanted to show everyone I was strong, and that I could do it all."

Michael continued to stroke my arms, planting kisses on my face as I cried. "I don't want my baby to leave. I don't want anything to happen to her. I can't let whatever evil is trying to take her from me succeed. If I lose her, I lose everything. I still remember it like it was yesterday when I nursed her to sleep, played with her in her room, taught her how to walk, and you taught her to fly. I just cannot lose those precious moments."

"You won't," Michael made me look at his face. "You will never lose those moments, but you need to realize she is grown now. I will not fight you, Hera. You are a strong woman and this fear you have of not being strong enough has to stop. You are only hurting your family when you try to do everything yourself. A family involves more than one person, even a marriage involves more than one. You needed to see what you were doing, other- wise, you would have never listened to me." I bit my lip, knowing he was correct. Michael had been more than accommodating of my tantrums. He knew I had to face the truth myself before I could crawl out of this deep hole I dug for myself.

My relationship with Uriel was hanging by a thread. The evil still coming for her and now being summoned by Zeus for trial had me falling into a pit I could not escape.

"What do we do, Michael? I don't know what to do now."

Michael picked me up, carrying me to the bedroom. I don't remember the last time I just laid limp in his arms while he carried me. My mind was spent, my body ached, and I just needed his touch.

"Let me figure some things out." His thumb rubbed my cheek as he laid with me while his large wings encased our bodies. "Right now, I want you to sleep. Think of Uriel and give her sweet dreams when she sleeps. Tell her you care, you love her, and you bless and accept Lucifer as her mate." I blinked, letting the rest of the water flee my lashes. "It's the right thing to do, Hera."

Nodding silently, I buried my head into Michael's shoulder, closing my eyes so I could give my baby girl the messages she needed.

Chapter 37

Lucifer

U riel flashed her bare ass in front of me! I took my thumb and wiped it across my lips, smiling as she giggled while trotting down the hall. My heart leaped in my chest at how she could be such a tease. My little bunny was more than willing to show herself to me fearlessly. She was the only woman alive that showed such innocence and purity; it immediately made me think of awful things to do to her, pleasantly awful things.

She pranced down the hall with her dress swaying side to side and half her hair pinned up by a neat little bow, the rest falling down her back. The bow was completely oversized and gave her a rather youthful appearance for a twenty-five-year-old.

My steps widened to catch up, causing her to squeal in excitement before running down the hall in flight. My heart lightened, enjoying this new game.

She would not win.

It was hard for me to understand how, just fifteen minutes ago, my heart's desire was devastatingly troubled. I felt her distress from within my father's office, and soon after, I felt her emotions shift from sorrowful to stunned and, eventually, to anger. I didn't think that Uriel was capable of that emotion, but there it was, nearly matching my own.

The bond had already begun weaving the threads of our souls together, so quickly that she pulled part of the fire from me. My wings shot from my body, and, before I even realized what was happening, ash fell from my wings onto the carpet beneath my father's smoke. Mother growled from her seat in his lap.

"You guys are ruining all my carpets," she huffed. Father simply kissed her forehead, but my mind had been taken somewhere dark. Uriel's emotions flashed through my body again, unsure which emotion dominated. I darted down the hall, but before I could even step out the door, Cerberus linked me: there was trouble.

Thank the Fates I had him. He was always in the shadows guarding what was mine.

"*Another voice,*" he grumbled. "*Another voice other than Uriel's is beyond the door.*" Cerberus' usual playfulness turned protective, frantically scratching the door. Banging on the whitened doors, which now donned black scorch marks from my burning fists, hushed whispers echoed through to my ears. I growled, hating that my mate's door was locked.

"Uriel!" I banged on the door again, while Cerberus linked my father. His eyes glazed over, permitting Father to watch the scene unfold. Father loved to take control of Cerberus and watch through his eyes. "Uriel, be a sweetheart and open the door." My loving voice began wavering.

Hearing my love screaming that it was her mother, my patience dissipated. I blasted the door with both hands. The once pristine, white doors were now charred black from flames. It was indeed Hera. I stepped inside, and my glowing eyes illuminated the room with a deep shade of red.

This woman brought my mate to tears. Uriel stood on the bed pointing accusingly at her mother. Hera was merely an apparition, but my body wanted only to destroy it. She could have taken my mate, stolen her from me, and caused even more damage than she had already.

I could never let Hera take her. I was lucky that Uriel called for me, letting me know she was there. My mate cried in my arms, battling her overwhelming emotions and the torn alliances with her mother and father. Even though her mother was wrong, she was still her mother.

My heart swelled; I could hardly believe she would choose me and only me. After kissing her head gently and comforting her, I knew I had to find her family. I had to bring Uriel justice. Even if my mate became angry with me, Hera had to be reprimanded.

Uriel continued to giggle as she rounded a corner, now out of my sight. I picked up the pace, not wanting to lose sight of her, but her head popped back around the corner. Her dark hair cascaded down wistfully, her face bearing a bright smile as she checked to see if I was still following. Chuckling, I attempted to grab her hand, only for her to slip away before I made contact. She was damn fast for a little thing.

Continuing down the darkened hall, she didn't look back. Using my wings as levitation devices, I hovered over her, close to the ceiling, so she couldn't detect me. I watched through the dim lights as her playful prances became slow and steady steps.

"Luci?" she called out, her warm breath panting softly. "Luci?" she called out again, now seeing only the darkness of the hallway. The fire in the torches barely illuminated the darkened hallways, there was just enough light to see in front of your face.

Uriel looked down the hall, rising on her tiptoes as if to improve her view.

"Luci?" her voice softened to a whisper. She played with her fingers as her heart raced. I bit my bottom lip, trying to contain a chuckle. Uriel's heart pounded rapidly in her chest, now fully panicking. I lowered myself behind her, blowing softly into her ear as my hands wrapped around her arms. She immediately calmed, feeling the tingles we shared diffuse along her arms.

Feeling her body relax, I pushed her against the wall in the darkened hallway. Luckily, this hallway was rarely used, because it was perfect for what I wanted to do to her. My little bunny showed me her damn cupcake, and I was going to get my taste.

"What are you doing, Luci?" I lifted her sundress by her sides, exposing her perfectly white skin as it rose above her hips.

"Luci?" she questioned as my lips pressed to her right shoulder, kissing it delicately.

"You were teasing me," I growled into her skin. She shivered before her fingers climbed up my chest and gripped my shoulders. "What do you think happens when you tease a beast like me?" I teased before biting her bottom lip.

Her golden eyes stared up at me with curiosity. "W-what happens, Luci?"

Placing my large hands against her tiny thigh, I lifted one leg and planted it above my hip, leaving her standing there, exposed to me. The breeze lifted her beautifully pink pussy's aroma to my nostrils. Taking a deep breath, my guttural growl made Uriel stiffen while I gripped her leg tighter around my body, pulling her closer.

I chuckled, moving my hand near her core, leaning to her ear, "you get to deal with the primal urge it elicits."

Uriel's breath hitched, at the sensation of my warm fingers sliding into her beautiful lips. She was already wet, her gentle pants and the movement of her hips grinding closer to my finger. Dipping inside her core, I groaned, feeling warmth engulf me.

"You are always so wet, bunny. Are you needy for me?" She whimpered, unable to respond. "Give me words, bunny," I gripped her thigh firmly with my other hand. My wings engulfed us, pinning us together as I slid my finger deeper inside her.

"Yes, Sir, I need you."

Humming, I curled my finger, hitting a spot that caused my mate to tighten her grip on me. My cock strained against my jeans, making me regret not wearing boxers. My hips pressed closer, pushing her against the wall.

"How needy are you?" I pulled my finger away as she whined.

Gripping her thigh tighter, she moaned, "so needy, Sir. I'm really, really, needy."

My lips captured hers, sucking her lips until they were as dark as a blooming red rose. Dominating her was so easy, so sinful, and she loved every minute.

Was this what sated my dark desires to destroy the universe: The ability to control every aspect of this goddess before me?

I loved her, but I wanted to destroy her innocence at the same time. I needed to feel my cock glide into her, to mold our souls together, to become one so no one could ever take her from me. She would let me conquer her every night until the light from all three realms ceased to exist.

"You're mine, Uriel," I growled in her ear. My finger picked up the pace, my hips rubbing against her body. My mouth reached her neck, sucking and leaving an obvious bruise. Fingers tangled into my hair before her hands reached for my feathers to steady herself. Leaning my head back, I felt the ultimate pleasure as her hands gripped my wings.

Holy Fates.

Her hands pulling on my wings made my cock burn with desire. Planting my seed in her womb was now my ultimate dream. "Fates! Yes, bunny!"

Sliding another finger into her core, her back arched. Her trembling legs were unable to hold her weight. I would support us both until we reached the summit of our pleasure.

"Legs around me, bunny," I gritted my teeth. She obeyed, like the good girl she was. "Excellent, bunny, such a pretty little bunny," I whispered huskily into her ear.

"More, please," she begged. My teeth sunk into her shoulder, and she cried out while her hips thrust into my fingers.

"I love your manners," I mumbled into her neck. Her hands reached out, now able to wrap her arms around my head, only this time she didn't grab my neck but the base of my wings.

"Fuck!" I growled into her ear.

Uriel moaned, kissing my neck. Feeling her tongue against me, I pushed my fingers harder into her core. Her ambrosia leaked down my fingers, the soft sounds of moisture echoing in my ears.

"Luci, please!" I pushed one more finger into her. She moaned, despite smelling the hint of blood, I continued.

"Tell me if I need to stop, bunny." Using my arm, I thrust into her aggressively, but her needy core continued to suck me in. Her hands gripped the base of my wings tighter until I finally spilled. The euphoric feeling of her gripping my wings jolted straight to my cock, my head buried into her neck until I heard her moan my name as if I was the god she prayed to.

Hell, I hope I was.

Our heavy pants and the sweat dripping between us left me kissing her salty shoulder. I didn't want to let her go. I wanted to stand like this forever until the skies fell upon us.

Uriel's head lifted slightly, her heavy eyelashes fluttering. "I'm a little sore," she blushed, covering her mouth. I hummed, pulling my fingers from her. Tints of her blood stained them until I licked them clean while staring into her eyes.

My mate's head fell straight to my shoulder as I chuckled, "you aren't embarrassed, are you?"

She shook her head and muttered 'no' into my shoulder.

"I might have taken part of your innocence with my fingers, but later I'll stick my cock in you to finish the job," I promised

A soft gasp escaped her lips, and she held onto me tighter by the base of my wings.

"Easy!" I grunted, feeling my cock raise back to life.

Fuck, I was going to have to be more careful leaving my wings out around her.

Gently putting her down, I straightened her dress and smoothed the wrinkles. I trailed kisses up her stomach to her neck before planting one long, soft kiss on her lips.

"Someone could have seen," she hissed at me, her face still flushed.

I laced my fingers with hers, pulling her back to my room. "Doesn't that make it exciting?" I nipped her ear. She pushed me playfully and gleamed.

"M-maybe," she stuttered before she pulled on me to stop. "But I want dessert still," she pouted.

My mind went elsewhere, but of course, my little one was hungry. I had denied her food for a second time today. "They will send dinner to our room." I pulled her down the hallway.

"Like dinner with sugar, right?" she raised a brow. Even if I wanted her to eat healthily, one meal of nothing but sweets would be fine.

"Of course, bunny," I winked. Pulling her down the hallway, my mind reeled back to her mother.

Once I have my bunny's tummy full and she is sleeping peacefully, I will speak to my father to capture my mate's mother and make her pay.

Chapter 38

Uriel

I groaned into the sheets, my fists twisting the bedding as I tried to get up. The last thing I remembered was eating an enormous German chocolate cake with vanilla icing on the side. It was so good, I swear I could still taste it on my lips. My belly was completely full, full of all the sugary things I had been wanting since arriving here.

Luci's family ate way too much meat and veggies, it was beyond disgusting. I still haven't found the magic cabinet in their kitchen, not that Luci would let me slip away. He told me if I ever left our room again without telling him I'd get my 'cupcake' spanked.

I giggled aloud. *He would never do that. He is my Luci and he wouldn't dare try.* I bit my lip looking around the room. *Well, maybe he would, he did do some naughty things in the hallway.*

Sitting up and wiping the sleep from my eyes, I find myself in my old bedroom. The white and baby pink the room even brighter than I remembered because the large plant that covered the window wasn't there. I tugged the duvet closer until Mom came into the room holding a large tray of chocolate chip cookies.

My mouth watered until I realized I shouldn't be here. I should be with Luci, and I was still mad at Mom!

"What's going on?" I muttered as Mom sat down in her favorite chair. Every night she read me a story, but I'm twenty-five years old now and don't need such a thing; I just needed Luci.

"Where is Luci?" Mom sighed, trying to ignore me as she turned on the lamp. The cookies looked warm and gooey, I could almost see the steam rise above the melted chocolate chips, and the milk to the side had a thin layer of condensation coating the glass.

"This is a dream, Uriel. I did not take you from your mate." My head shot up to see if I misunderstood something. She chuckled, picking up a cookie and putting it to her lips. "Yes, Uriel. I accept him as your mate; your father practically demanded it." A sigh of relief left me as I reached for a cookie.

"I know you will never understand the things I did: the plants, the secrets, keeping you hidden. I thought what I was doing was for the best—for you and me. If I failed to raise my daughter, I failed to uphold my title as the Goddess of Marriage and Family." Swallowing the cookie heavily, she looked away.

"You found that in me, Uriel. Your power is growing stronger and faster since the poison is now leaving your body. You give comfort; it's part of your grace." Mom's eyes began to water. "I failed you as a mother, my sweet one. I hope one day I'll be able to forgive myself. Your father and I love you very much, and we want to stop whatever evil is coming. I can't see you hurt." Shaking her head, she stood up and sat on the bed beside me, petting my hair.

"My sweet Uriel, I love you to the moon and back. I hope you can understand. When you have children of your own, one day, maybe you will—or maybe I am just really messed up." Mom sniffed, holding back her tears. "That is probably why I was unable to have more children, because of what I did to you. The fates' retribution for going about this the wrong way."

Putting back the unbitten cookie, I held onto mom. The words I said earlier were a punch in the gut to her. Mom had always wanted more children, especially someone for me to play with. I stabbed her and twisted the knife so she could feel how I felt.

That wasn't very nice of me.

"I—" Mom put her finger to my lips.

"I am not mad at you," she sighed. "I never was, and I deserved it."

"Uriel!" I could hear Luci's voice ring through the dream. I clutched my mom tighter: I didn't want her to go now. She just said it was okay to be with Luci.

"I bless your union with Lucifer, son of Hades and Ember." Mom's hand glowed as she touched the top of my head. "May your bonding and life together be fruitful." I felt the warmth spread from my head to my toes as Mom rose from the bed.

"It isn't often that I bless supernatural couples anymore, not since Selene began mating their souls. I try to concentrate on pure, loving humans," Mom chuckled. "But this pairing with my own daughter, I believe it is deserving."

"Mom?" I reached out to touch her again, but her back turned to head towards my old bedroom door.

"I love you, Uriel, no matter what happens." Before I could watch her walk out the door, I was shaken until I awoke in Lucifer's arms.

"Uriel!" Luci pulled me to him as my eyes opened. My eyes scanned the room, everywhere but Luci's eyes, until he moved my chin to look at him. "You kept saying, 'Mom,' over and over. I thought she had come to you in a dream to try to take you." Luci gripped me tighter, afraid I was leaving.

"I'm not leaving you," I giggled. "Mom did visit me. She blessed our mating and union." Luci's eyes raised in skepticism, but I continued to nod my head gingerly. "Yes! She did!" Luci shook his head before gently letting me go.

"She wouldn't change her mind that fast; it's surely a trick," Luci growled. I bit my lip, not wanting to argue back, but I needed to be heard.

"Mom didn't lie," I growled out. "I would have felt it! She was telling the truth! I even felt the warmth from the blessing she gave us." Luci's naked back faced me as he hung his legs off the bed, his hand repeatedly running through his dark brown hair.

"I want to believe you," Luci shook his head. "I do, but we still need to be cautious." I hummed, not wanting to fight anymore.

Mom was telling the truth, not unless I can't feel lies in a dream. I don't understand my powers well enough to know if that was true.

Luci stood from the bed; his gray joggers hung low on his hips while walking across the room. Putting on a black shirt, he opened the bathroom door and waved for me to follow. "I need to speak with my father. He's cast a spell so that no apparitions can appear. Don't go to sleep because it doesn't work for dreams. She can't take you from me—no one can," Luci growled. His black fists touched the door marring its surface with burn prints.

How many doors do they have to replace around here?

"I'm not going anywhere," I pushed up onto my tiptoes to kiss him. Instead of the peck I intended, he pulled my waist to him, taking more like the greedy god he was.

"I mean it: you're mine! No one will have you but me!" I giggled, listening to his temper tantrum. Patting his cheek, I walked into the bathroom and shut the door.

After a wonderfully steaming shower, I leaned my body against the counter, using my hand to wipe away the steam-covered mirror. All things considered, in the past few days, I have done well. I winked at myself in the mirror, before hearing Cerberus scratch at the door.

I bet Luci sent him in here to check on me.

"Hi, Puppy!" I cracked the door to let him in. "Whatcha doing in here, huh? Did you come to visit me?"

Cerberus wagged his tail while his three heads looked up at me adoringly. I patted each head but took extra time for the third head, scratching firmly under his chin.

"Such a good boy you are!" He groaned, finally sitting on the floor and rolling to expose his belly. I giggled, rubbing his tummy as his leg began to shake. I must have hit the right spot because his groaning became louder.

"Yes! Such a good boy!" I snorted, laughing to myself, finally standing up.

Still holding the towel tightly around my body, I looked at myself in the mirror.

Yes, I have done well the past few days. Smiling brightly, I drew little happy faces on the mirror and some hearts with mine and Luci's names inside them.

Inspecting my work, my tummy twinged. I rubbed it with the palm of my hand and went to sit down on the side of the massive tub. Cerberus, watching my distress, came over and laid his head on my knees. "My tummy hurts," I grumbled.

Maybe too much cake last night really messed me up.

"Uriel?" Mariah's voice caught me by surprise as she knocked on the bedroom door.

"I'm in here," I whined, shifting myself on the tub. My tummy was hurting worse, and now Cerberus started to whine.

"I came to see if you wanted me to walk you down to breakfast?" Mariah poked her head in. Her bright smile faded once she noticed the frown on my face. "What's wrong?"

"Luci told you to come to take me, didn't he?" I grumbled.

He won't let me do anything on my own right now. I liked it, but at the same time, I didn't. Right now, I didn't know what I wanted. I thought I was happy, but now I wasn't so sure. This pain in my tummy made me feel crabby.

"Honey, what's wrong?" I stood up, only to have Cerberus yip and nudge my ankle with his nose. I grunted, not sure what the big puppy wanted. Mariah's nose flared.

"Uriel," she whispered, putting both hands on my shoulders and sitting me down gently back on the tub. "I want you to sit here, alright? I'm going to go get your clothes. Don't move from this spot until I come back, alright? I want you to pet Cerberus while I'm in your room." Mariah's voice was calm but laced with a twinge of panic.

The last time I heard that tone was when I cut my knee, and blood seeped onto Mom's brand-new, white carpet. There was so much red against my white skin it dripped over my knee and fell onto the floor. I panicked and ended up passing out.

"Did you hear me, Uriel?" I hummed, holding the towel tight around me. Cerberus put one of his heads underneath my hand,

and I pet him lovingly. Another cramp; I rubbed my tummy with my other hand.

Why does my tummy hurt so bad?

Not listening like a good girl, I stood up and walked to the cabinet that held medicine. Sometimes, gods drank too much alcoholic ambrosia and would get tummy aches. Mom said the roots of the Nafaro plant were good for sating the knots in your stomach. As I reached up, putting my fingers on every bottle of medicine, a drip tickled between my legs. I was mostly dry, the only reason I was still holding the towel was to hide my nakedness.

Lifting the towel—so the puppy couldn't see me naked—I noticed a dark red line that went from my lady parts down to the floor. I clutched my towel, my breath picking up. "Fates! No," I whispered before Mariah stood at the door. She held a pair of black leggings and an oversized t-shirt with a cute little cartoon bunny on it.

"Uriel," Mariah placed the clothes on the counter, "I want you to breathe. Everything is fine."

Shaking my head, I backed up, and my bum landed on the toilet. "Blood!" My voice quaked after looking at the mess I was making.

I just got something I should have gotten over ten years ago, and it has come forth with a vengeance! You know what? I don't forgive Mom because this is the worst! She should have been here for me when this happened!

"It's alright," Mariah chuckled as she knelt on the floor. Grabbing my hand, she stroked it lovingly. This was the softest I had ever seen Mariah. She was the God of War's mate, the ultimate female warrior companion. Now she sat at my feet.

"It is blood, honey. But you are a strong one, aren't you?" Gripping her hand, I didn't say a word. I didn't know whether I was strong or not. "You are strong," Mariah said with more conviction. "Women—humans, supernaturals, goddesses—we all deal with this because men wouldn't be able to." A tear tried to escape, but my questioning look gave Mariah a chuckle that made me laugh.

"Men are a bunch of pussies! Women can take more of a beating when it comes to our bodies." Mariah pulled a kit from under the counter filled with small, decorated square packets. "If a man had to deal with this, they would huddle in bed for days until it was over. Not us though, not us women," she hummed, helping me get dressed.

"Just because you got your cycles a little later, it doesn't mean anything. You have been through the wringer. You may be a little sheltered, but you are stronger than anyone thinks. Luci may baby you," she giggled, "but you can hold your own." I sniffed, comforted by her words.

"You are going to be just fine, Little Goddess." Mariah kissed me on my head. "And if you ever need anything, you can always come to me—even when Ares is around. I'll always come to help you, no matter what." Mariah pulled me up from the toilet, now completely changed into comfortable clothes.

"We, strong women, need to help each other out. What do you say?" I nodded into her embrace, relaxing. I was okay; everything was going to be okay.

Chapter 39

Uriel

Mariah moved to wash her hands in the sink. I stood, holding my arms around my stomach. My tummy continued to have those funny 'cramps,' as Mariah called them.

"You need to stay close to Lucifer, okay?" Mariah's smile didn't stretch as it had earlier. "Being near your mate lessens the pain. You can even have him lay his hand on your stomach; that makes it much better." Mariah turned back to the sink, pretending to concentrate on her hands, but I knew better.

Call it my gut instinct, but something was bothering her, and I had to know what. It was the same funny feeling I felt when my mom got really sad before I touched her.

"What's wrong?" My head leaned over the sink to look her in the eyes.

'Eyes were the windows of the soul,' they say. It's hard for someone to look you in the eye and lie—they could dilate, twitch, or look away. I noticed these things since coming into my power to sense lies.

"I can't lie to you, can I?" Mariah chuckled, drying her hands with Luci's fluffy, black towel. I shook my head, glad that she knew.

Every time someone told me a lie, it made my chest hurt. I don't think I could handle my chest hurting while my tummy was cramping.

Mariah leaned both hands on the sink, her body sagging while staring at her beautiful face in the mirror. Her dark-brown eyes and her delicate facial features were a stark contrast to her muscular body.

Ares was really lucky. She was fierce and muscular but still had that beautiful feminine look that would make the perfect mom one day. Those soft eyes held such warmth for the God of War, who slaughtered thousands, maybe millions, of lives.

"It's just that talking about Lucifer comforting you when you have your monthly—it just reminded me of some things." Mariah turned her back to walk out of the bathroom, but I quickly followed, grabbing her hand.

The warmth from our hands, which I felt before with Zeus and my mom, burned brightly. Only this time, I didn't just feel warmth, I saw her despair. My eyes widened. Mariah's eyes did the same until they calmed to a half-hooded state. Her rigid body slumped before taking a step closer so that I didn't have to stretch to keep her close.

The glow lasted a few moments before finally disappearing, entirely. I felt more this time: her worry; her love, and her concern for Ares.

Wait, Mariah was concerned for Ares? Why would she be concerned about him? He was strong and unstoppable; he was such a great god possessing all things strength related.

"You helped me, Mariah. Let me help you?" I looked up at her tall stature. She towered over me, much like most of the male gods, but she was something else; she stood at least six feet tall with beautiful, muscular shoulders. Shockingly, the warmth in her eyes held unshed tears. I never imagined her crying, not when she always appeared to be so happy with her mate. But now that she was away from him, I could see her walls crumbling.

"Please," I begged her. Now my body. and this power inside me wanted to know her worries and to help calm her. It was my duty, but, most of all, I just *wanted* to help.

Mariah sighed deeply, sitting right there, in the middle of the carpeted floor. Her hands went to hide her face. "I'm strong. I'm a warrior," she whispered as I sat in front of her. Her hands were now only covering her mouth. She sighed heavily again. "I worry for my mate," she whispered, barely audible.

"He is strong physically, but I worry about his mentality. He puts on a strong front, but, on the inside, he is crumbling, and I'm not sure why." The crack in her voice caused her to sit up straight, trying not to cry in front of me.

"But do have an idea," she sniffed. "I fear it might be me." Mariah was too proud to let a tear fall. I grabbed her hand again, pulling the freezing darkness from her body into mine. The glow flashed again, taking more of the burden that burned inside her. "That feels—that makes me feel better; like a cool cloth to my body." I hummed, concentrating on her feelings.

She worried for Ares. It was deep. I could feel it in her soul.

"What is wrong with Ares?" I muttered, still holding her hand. Mariah tried to retract her hand, but I didn't relent. I held her hand tightly, the feeling of worry was too strong to let go. I couldn't let her go, not now.

"I can't give him children," she muttered. "We have tried since the first day we mated. I cannot conceive, and I don't know why." Mariah choked, still trying to pull away.

"What else?" I pressed.

There was something more, something she wasn't telling me.

"You're a warrior, Mariah," I looked up at her. "A warrior." A flash of determination in her face let me pull more of the deep sorrow from within her.

I could now feel the guilt. She felt it was her fault—her fault she couldn't give him a child.

"He's wanted to plant his seed in me, to have children of his own, for the past twenty-five years, and I cannot give it to him. Ares puts on a strong front, a funny one, and yet I know it worries him, even if he hasn't talked to me about it." Mariah leaned closer to me, finally spilling her secrets.

"I visited Aphrodite. Her sub-power is fertility, but she says nothing is wrong with me! It has to be, though! It has to be!" Mariah choked. Letting go of her hand as her tears fell. She collapsed to the side, her head dropping into my lap. The gentle movement of my fingers playing with her hair calmed her. Mariah's sobs lightened, her walls restoring to the stronghold they were earlier.

This power inside me was overwhelming. It was like I unlocked a whole new world. I could not only feel lies and take away guilt, but I could look inside and extract the deepest and darkest secrets.

Letting out a breath through my lips, when Mariah sat up, I muttered, "Let's go see Ares."

Mariah shook her head, her palm wiping away the leftover tears. "He's sleeping. He isn't having a good day." I bit my lip.

This can't last much longer. Mariah felt that it was her fault she couldn't bear a child, but obviously, that wasn't the case.

It all lay with Ares and some secret he was keeping from his mate. She was suffering. The constant doting upon him—making his plate, petting his hair and cheek—was taking its toll upon her. They obviously loved each other, but now, thinking back to the times they sat together, there was always worry in her eyes. Why didn't I notice it sooner?

"Then we visit while he sleeps." Leaving no room for argument, I stood up and walked to the door.

Ares was strong, no doubt about that. It was clear from the way he walked and the way he carried himself that he had a cocky attitude about him. He displayed his strength and trained warriors with his mate constantly. Everything he did was to display his manliness. What if he was hiding something else? What if there was something deeper inside that prevented them from bearing children?

The warmth in my body led me to Mariah's room, without her guidance. The pull to find him was much stronger than I ever thought.

"How do you know where to go?" The warmth radiated from Mariah, it felt the same as her glow.

"I honestly don't know," I whispered. "I'm just following the pull of my powers."

Just to the edge of the wing that housed the King of the Underworld's family, there stood a dark wooden door. It was more rustic than the other doors in the house. It had enormous hinges and a big handle, and everything inside screamed 'power' when it opened. Mariah stood at my side, grabbing my hand.

"He's over here," Mariah whispered, pulling me to the enormous bed. It was the size of three king-sized beds and adorned with large pillows and animal furs. A single torch lit the room, just enough to register the outline of a sleeping Ares. His breaths were low and steady, but there was a hint of twitching in his sleep. I knew it was disturbed. His head faced the opposite direction, preventing me from studying his expression.

Mariah hovered over me, watching as my hand covered Ares' hand which lay against his chest. The light of my power glowed brighter than with anyone else I had touched. I winced at the scorching sensation it left in my hand, but I dared not recoil.

Worry, pain, suffering, and regret all swirled together inside my mind as I forced myself to delve deeper. My eyes closed, really concentrating my power for the first time. Urging my power to search within him, I could see the darkness that loomed inside. Inadequacy, lack of worth, and fear swirled inside him. Judging from the exterior, someone would be crazy to describe Ares, the God of War, with these words. These feelings were ingrained so deeply, that they entwined with his soul, forming evil black tendrils that encompassed his heart.

I could visualize my hand as it pushed the tendrils away, keeping the darkness from seeping into his heart. Mariah's hand touched my shoulder, squeezing it tightly. It gave me a jolt of power as I untangled the surrounding darkness, pulling it all away until Ares woke from his slumber.

Ares grabbed my hand, but I continued to let the golden light pull the negativity from him, sucking up every bit of guilt, worry, and doubt until I felt those feelings that were buried deep within him come with it. The feelings of being inadequate and unworthy were all right there, but I couldn't pull them out. I couldn't take them from him before I lost the grasp of the light and dropped to the floor.

"Uriel!" Mariah lifted me to my knees, Ares' hand still wrapped around my wrist. Shaking himself from his sleep, he finally let go. Mariah pulled me up to the overly gigantic bed and sat me softly on the mattress. Unable to sit up, I laid at Ares' feet while he rested his back on the headboard.

"What happened?" His voice was softer than I had ever heard it. Mariah gasped before running to him and burying her face into the crook of his broad neck.

"Baby, what's wrong? Why do you cry?" The funny, playful god's eyes now brimmed with tears as his mate cried. I laid and watched, too drained to get up to get a better look.

"Uriel was comforting you." Mariah put both hands to his face. "She was trying to make you feel better." Mariah sniffed, her thumbs brushing away Ares' tears. His fingers went to his face, feeling the wetness.

"What is this?" he continued to let the water flow.

"Tears, baby, they're tears," Mariah cooed. "You have been keeping something from me for so long, haven't you?" Ares shook his head, shaking the wetness away.

"Lie," I whispered, smirking as he looked down at me.

"Right," he chuckled. "You brought the lie detector." Mariah hummed, kissing his lips.

"It's about me not being with child, isn't it?" Ares bit his lip, rubbing his mate's thighs as she now straddled him. She nodded, urging him to continue.

"It's my fault," he breathed in heavily. "I can't get you pregnant, and Kronos, I want to get you pregnant. I want you to be swollen with our child." Ares rubbed Mariah's stomach, lovingly kissing her cheek.

"Why do you think it is your fault? Maybe it is me?"

Ares shook his head. "I know you went to Aphrodite," he muttered. "I can't leave you the fuck alone for five minutes, and you suddenly wanted to go hang out with Ember for the entire afternoon one day. I followed you, and I heard everything."

Mariah sighed heavily. "Nothing gets by you, does it, Baby?" Ares chuckled.

"Nothing." He growled, squeezing her close.

Both sat in silence for the longest time as I lay there watching. I wasn't sure if they could talk to each other through a mind-link, but the silence was deafening. Looking at my hand, it glowed as I felt the warmth.

"Ares," I muttered, still laying on the bed, "why do you not feel worthy?" Mariah's head jerked back to Ares so fast, that the wind in the room shifted.

"W-what?" He choked back a laugh.

"You don't feel worthy to be a father," I muttered again. "You feel that you will not be good enough; you feel inadequate to be one. Your mind is holding you back." I whispered.

Ares' head hit the headboard. Closing his eyes as he gripped Mariah's waist tighter.

"Don't lie," I whispered, smiling at Mariah. Mariah's wet lashes fluttered again, realizing what was happening.

"Why would you feel that way, my love?" Mariah's fingers traced his jaw. "You are my strong mate, my love. With our love, we would create beautiful children. You would protect us, see our children grow, and teach them so many wonderful things," Mariah cooed.

"I am not smart, not like Hades." He whispered like it was a prayer. "I am not worthy. I've slaughtered, fucked up. and made terrible decisions in my life. How am I to raise a child? As much as I want one, I am just me." Mariah shook her head.

"You have me. That was a good decision, right?" Mariah leaned in, her nose nuzzling his neck.

"Of course, it was an excellent decision, but we both know I am unworthy of you."

"You are worthy," Mariah snapped. "You waited to mark your mate, me! Since then, you have been the most upstanding god. Look at Zeus! He's seriously fucked up, and you have turned out so much better than him!" Mariah laughed. Ares couldn't help but laugh along with her.

"See, baby? You waited for me, you marked me as your mate, and you have helped Hades through his dark times. Your humor has made the palace a lighter place. Together, we will raise our children and I pray to the Fates that they turn out just like you."

"Mariah," his voice grumbled. His arms surrounded her, peppering kisses on her neck, "you are too good to me." Ares shoved his tongue down Mariah's throat. It was all I could do not to gag.

"We are good for each other, my big, powerful warrior. I just wish you could see that." Ares pulled Mariah around his waist, causing a big problem to pop up.

Gracious.

I sniffed, breaking them from their trance.

They had a long way to go before babies would come into the picture with all the pent-up tension Ares had. Who knew that the God of War had self-confidence issues? I'm glad that they both could work on it together now.

"I'm... gonna go..." I muttered awkwardly, sliding off the furs.

As soon as my feet hit the floor, Luci picked me up and slung me over his shoulder.

Chapter 40

Lucifer

Not one damn moment of peace. Hera had another thing coming. She was playing with her daughter's emotional strings, pulling her up and down like a damned yo-yo, and I was damn near sick of it.

'You can't be with him,' she says.

'He isn't good for you. I'm trying to save you.' She blubbers.

'Oh, never mind, I thought about it. Now I will let him be your mate, and I'll even bless you on top of it.'

Lies. All of it.

Could Uriel not see the endless string of lies? Could she not feel them in her dream? It was possible; she was still growing, and she didn't fully understand her emerging powers yet. Remnants of the poison, which her own mother gave her, still lingered in her body.

Standing outside the bedroom door, I waited until I heard the water from our shower turn on.

She would stay awake; she would be safe. There was no alternative.

I gripped my fist, the ash already crumbling to the ground as I vanished, only to reappear in my parents' room. Mother sat on the pale-yellow rocking chair she loved so much. A stark contrast to the rest of the room, my father liked to keep the room darkened to help him sleep better.

A white crib sat beside Mother as she fed my sister, humming quietly. Her smile brightened as she noticed my sudden appearance. "Luci," she called, waiving me over. I leaned over, letting her kiss my cheek.

"Oh, Luci," she cooed, seeing my hands blackened. "What's wrong? Did you and Uriel fight?" Steam escaped from their adjoining bathroom as Father exited it, wearing nothing but a towel. His appearance was that of his natural form with bright blonde hair, instead of the darkened skin and hair he preferred when dealing with matters of the Underworld.

"Son, what's wrong?" His face softened. The sight was uncommon for anyone but Mother, however when he suspected one of his children was in disarray, he dropped his defenses.

"Hera," I growled. "She visited Uriel in a dream. She won't leave my mate alone." My wings flew from my back, making Mother jump and Lillian hiccup in surprise.

"Lucifer, let's take a breath." Father willed his darkened suit with his preferred, King of the Underworld, appearance.

"I will not stand for this!" I growled. Black, laden chains suddenly appeared around my neck in my anger, crossing over my chest. They heated to unbearable temperatures, searing my skin and making the room smell of burned flesh. My anger radiated so vividly that I barely felt them settling on my skin.

"Luci! Breathe!" Mother stood, covering Lillian and stepping away, ensuring that I didn't inadvertently hurt my sister.

More fury bubbled within me. I couldn't control it; I couldn't hold it in. The blackness in my soul consumed me, feeding every emotion I felt.

Father stepped forward with his eyes furrowed, his hand landing on my shoulder fearlessly as I stood panting. Smoke spilled from the flames on my wings, the embers of my feathers floating around the room. The fire that attempted to light the carpet crawled back to my bare feet which had become covered in black tar.

"What do you want to do?" Father stood, unwavering.

"Eliminate her! I could do it," I growled. "I could destroy her in the blink of an eye." The red glow of my eyes lit the room as the lights dimmed in each of the torches. Father looked to Mother, who was clutching Lillian.

It would be so easy: to seek her out, to find her. Once I did, I would grab her by the neck. Even if she was thousands of years older than me, I would end the light in her eyes. I would end the evil that she dared to impose upon my mate. I'm certain Uriel's mother was the evil that tried to destroy her own daughter by hiding her from me and keeping her away from her mate.

My teeth elongated, forming into sharpened fangs. Mother's gasp didn't deter the deadly stare I held with Father. If he nodded, I would be gone and back before Uriel's dainty feet left the shower. He knew what it felt like to have someone or something after his mate. He knew the fear of losing something so precious.

Protecting Uriel was my priority. I would make sure nothing touched her, that nothing would come near her beautiful skin.

"Lucifer," Father's voice hung heavily, "would Uriel want that?" My head jerked back, his words shaking me from my vengeful thoughts. "Would Uriel want you to destroy her mother? What kind of mate would you be to induce that kind of torment upon her?"

My breath hitched, thinking back to my sweet mate's face.

Heartbroken, she would be heartbroken if I did these things, especially if I didn't consult her. But she didn't know the truth, she thought her mother was being honest. Uriel didn't understand the ways of the world.

"I'll do it to protect my mate!" I growled, hardening my face. Father stood with his hand on my shoulder, squeezing, even as my skin burned his hand.

"Then what? Would you then force her to complete the bond with you, after the heartache you would cause? Then who is the real evil?" My face softened, the fire easing, but it was still not enough to will my body back to its normal state.

"You are still young, Lucifer." He squeezed my shoulder. "If your future daughter was given the same prophecy, you would do anything in your power to prevent it. Stupid decisions were made in haste, and we don't yet know where the evil truly lies." Father pulled me closer, my wings drooping.

I didn't want to lose Uriel because of my anger. I couldn't. If I did, then I would let my desire for destruction consume me. Without Uriel, life wouldn't matter.

Father lifted the chains around my neck, easing the burden. "You need not try to protect her alone, son. Your family is here. As long as we all fight for her, we will succeed. That's what the family of the Underworld does." Father chuckled.

"Come," he held out his hand for me to grasp. Taking it, he willed us to Tartarus.

Since Uriel came into my life, I hadn't been back to my usual stomping grounds. The sulfur filled my lungs, the smell of burning flesh wafting through the air as we walked over the burning coals. Demons ran as they saw Father and me approaching the rim of the pit. The pit inside imprisoned the Titans, Kronos, and the vilest creatures in existence. Those who abused other men, women, and children in any manner—sexually, physically, or mentally—all resided in this area. Since Father's mating to Mother, he changed the rulings about who could stay: no longer reserved for the dangerous titans and gods, but evil supernaturals and humans too.

No longer would those who lived in Tartarus be tortured just by Father's demons, but us as well. Circling the pit, Father snapped his fingers again, willing the top half of his body bare and his staff into his right hand. My wings picked up in excitement upon hearing the screams of the unruly demons that escaped the Underworld two decades ago. Those demons were feisty, always putting up a fight. I grinned as we passed them, chained to the coals.

Maybe later.

Father didn't get as much pleasure as I did tormenting the sinners of Earth, Bergarian, and the other realms, but when he did, it was brutal. I learned most of what I know from him, especially when it came to a particular human, Teddy Johnson.

Teddy Johnson tortured Mother and several other women for years at the strip club he owned. He beat them, starved them, and kept them in cages when they weren't working in the clubs for his profits. Now, he remains bound to a stripper pole as demons beat him with whips and paddles and maybe cut off his dick a time or two.

Father motioned for the demons to step away. They kissed his feet as he approached Teddy. He leaned against the pole, naked with his protruding belly hanging over his revoltingly pungent genitals. Endless humiliation was part of his punishment.

"It's been a while," Father's smirk didn't go unnoticed by the man's bloody eyes. His head rolled back, hitting the pole. Trying to stand, he slipped in his own urine, giving up and waiting for a blow from my father. Father chuckled, watching him struggle before he willed him to stand, strapping him tighter to the pole with iron chains.

"You see, son," Father walked around the shaken form. "When I found out your mother suffered for so many years because of this man, I made sure he received the proper care." Snapping his fingers again, another pole appeared beside him, this one holding Malachi, a fallen angel that helped conspire against him and my mother, intending to keep them apart. Malachi's once white wings were now charred, and his face was blackened with soot. "And this angel," he chuckled darkly, "will never see the light of day again," his fingers gripped Malachi's throat, watching him sputter, "will you?" He patted his cheek, smiling.

"You may be wondering why I brought these two here," Father directed me to stand beside Malachi, who hung his head in defeat. "It is because they weren't the ones who first conspired to hurt your mother." He hissed, waving his hands. "No, it was someone else," his eyes darkened at the thought, "but I ensure they all suffer equally."

Snapping his fingers, another pole appeared that held, none other than, the woman who made the God of the Underworld's mate suffer. Her name had been stripped from her, she no longer retained her god-like qualities and was nothing but a pitiful soul. Her eyes were sunken, and a crown of thorns lay upon her head. Her lips parted to spit at Father, but he was quicker and bound her mouth with chains.

"You see, Lucifer…" Father went to whisper in the nameless, once ethereal deity, "we find the evil," he chuckled, making her wince, "and we stomp it out like an ember in dry leaves."

The woman leaned her head back as Father choked her and the rest without touching their vile skin. All three struggled, trying to escape the hold only to slump over once Father released them.

"I hope this visual has shown you what you and our family will do once we find the evil threatening Uriel."

I smirked, enjoying the lesson Father provided. It will be one that I always remember.

"But until we know who all is involved, we take it one step at a time. It makes vengeance so much sweeter." A demon walked towards Father, holding a mallet with long needles on one side.

Looking at my blackened fingers, my long claws extended. This new rage surged within me, whether it was strengthening from being around my mate or from the sheer, overpowering drive to protect her, it unlocked a new set of skills I was ready to try.

"Father-Son bonding time?" I chuckled, standing before Teddy Johnson. He shook his head, his once blue eyes now fading into darkness as my claw scraped slowly down his cheek. I watched the ruby-red liquid drip onto his overly large gut.

"I wonder how he would look gutted like a fish?" I tilted my head menacingly.

"If that will help sate you." We looked at each other, laughing evilly as we dove into our favorite pastime.

Chapter 41

Lucifer

As much as I was enjoying being with my father, torturing the souls that dared to hurt my mother, I had to return to Uriel. The bond wouldn't let me stay away from her for long, and knowing she was waiting for me, made it that much more urgent.

Father looked at me, the metallic crimson liquid dripping down his face. The evil in his smile did something to me: it made me feel less evil.

This was part of who I was, the God of Destruction. Finding a balance was necessary in my life, and Uriel came to me at the most perfect of times to help me find that balance.

Father threw the mallet that he used to hit Malachi. He nodded his head to me to lead me back up the trail of hot coals, back to the outskirts of Tartarus. "Kronos still lies in his cell," Father mentioned as we hiked up the steps. "So, we know he is not the evil we seek."

Kronos had run through my mind several times as a child after Father's many promptings and suggestions to Mother: he might try to take hold of my darkened soul. Each time Father visited, Kronos still lay in the corner of his cage, chained to the wall with magic and surrounded by darkness.

"I'll start from scratch," Father wiped the blood from his forehead. "Hera and Michael will hide, but they will be easy to find if I let your mother's home pack know we are looking for them. They will head to Bergarian, as well, in search of them. They will be swiftly turned over to Zeus for a proper trial." I grunted, reaching the top of the stairs.

"It would be easier," Father mused, "if you could retrieve the feather that Uriel's father gave her before he left. He mentioned he would come right back if she prayed to him while holding it." I stopped, wondering if I could ask her for it.

"Take care of Uriel, son. We will not make Uriel pick sides. Let the feather be, unless absolutely necessary." His hand patted my shoulder.

Fates, I loved her; I would always care for her. Being her protector was the only thing I wanted. I only wanted her to enjoy life and be happy, not force her to pick sides between her parents and me. However, I think she chose me just last night when she told me that her mother was in the room.

"Thank you." I pulled my father into a hug. He stiffened at the contact, but quickly returned it. My wings willed back into my body, and Father patted my back lovingly.

"Family," Father spoke softly. "Your mother comes from a close-knit pack and, thus, brought those values to our own family. I'll do anything for you, son." Pulling back, he put his hand on my head, rustling my perfect hair. Swatting him away, he laughed as he willed us back to the palace.

Father waved for me to go down the hall to my mate. He was already changed into his normal business attire as he sat down at the dining room table. Mother held onto Lilith until Father scooped her up in his arms, kissing her forehead.

I chuckled, watching their interaction. Mother felt my stares and gleamed with her beautiful smile. Mother, once a lonely, beaten werewolf, cured the God of the Underworld of his broken heart.

Turning my head, I walked down the hall. Leaving the calls of Loki screaming asking where Uriel was. The brat threw a fit just the night before because Uriel wasn't able to read him a bedtime story.

She was my mate. He can get his own.

Walking down the family wing, I could smell the faint smell of blood. Examining my body, it was already clean before I returned to the palace, so it wasn't me. Sniffing again, I noticed it was tangled with Uriel's scent. My heart quickened, and I ran down the hall toward the smell, stopping by my door. Uriel's heartbeat couldn't be heard.

I could recognize her sound, the way it fluttered when I'm near and slowed when she was lonely, but it wasn't there. Slamming my fist on the door frame, I followed my nose until I hit the opposite corner of the family wing, just before the guest wing began.

Taking large, heaving breaths, I approached Ares' and Mariah's door. *Why would she be here?* The door was open, and the room was dark. I peeked my head in the door only to find the, usually dark, room lit with the most glorious light.

Uriel's hand glowed like Earth's sun until she dropped it before laying on the bed at Ares' feet. The urge to run in and save her was strong, but my curiosity held me back. *What had she done?*

Small whispers and tears from my uncle puzzled me. Not once had I ever seen the God of War cry, and Uriel continued to speak to him like it was nothing. My own body twisted in on itself, listening to the doubt he had in his abilities.

The cocky god, the unbeatable warrior, had a soft side, deep inside him. I could sense Uriel's smile as she watched the two mates hold each other's embrace. Their kisses became too heated for her to watch as she tried to slide down the bed.

Rushing to her before she fell, I picked her up and put her on my shoulder. Her normal dress attire was now replaced with black leggings and a large t-shirt. "Luci?" she whined, gripping the back of my shirt tightly.

"My tummy..." I pulled her from my shoulder, cradling her like a child as I walked out. My lips found her forehead, kissing her tenderly as I walked down the hall to the dining room.

I stopped, now realizing that the blood smell tangled with her scent was strong. "Uriel," I clenched her, "you are hurt. Did you hurt yourself trying to help Ares?"

If her powers caused her to bleed, to hurt herself, I would never allow her to use them again. She was too precious and tender to allow her to do such things. Her power was growing by the day and watching her continue to use this power proved to be too much. She could stay how she is; I would work for the both of us.

"N-no," she blushed, rubbing her tummy. "I am... it's too embarrassing." Uriel hid her face in the crook of my neck. My fingers gripped around her thighs, wondering why it would be such an embarrassing matter until the light dawned on my feeble mind.

"Uriel, are you?" She whimpered, squirming in my arms. She had graced herself into adulthood and with that, her powers have bloomed. Giving her a gentle smile, I pressed another chaste kiss to her forehead.

I turned around, no longer interested in taking her to the dining room, but she squirmed again. "But I'm hungry."

"And weak," I growled as I laid her on the bed. "I'll have the servants bring breakfast to us. Now, what would you like?" I tucked her into bed.

Her eyes glowed, "I can have anything?" The innocent smile she flashed me gave away her intentions: *sugar, and lots of it.*

"Yes, bunny, anything," I cooed at her. After watching my father take care of my mother on her monthly escapades, I knew to take excellent care of Uriel. Otherwise, when a goddess gets mad while she is menstruating, it could be disastrous. Mother once shifted into her wolf and ripped his leather couch to pieces when he didn't give her his full attention.

Who knew what my sweet Uriel would do? She could deny me her body.

It won't happen.

"French toast?" she questioned, fluttering her eyelashes.

"What else?" I encouraged.

"With syrup and whipped cream," she pleaded.

Fuck, I loved when she begged. I couldn't wait until she begged for my cock.

"Of course," I kissed her forehead, leaving the bed.

"And apple juice," she added, her smile brightening. I nodded and headed to the door. "Oh, and a cupcake!" she yelled. "Chocolate with sprinkles!"

"Don't push it, Uriel," I playfully warned. She sat back on the bed, rubbing her stomach while she pouted.

Shit.

"I'll get the cupcake too," I had the door halfway shut until she yelled for me again.

"With sprinkles, pwetty pwease!"

I rolled my eyes, shutting the door before any other random food request escaped her.

For the next three days, I wanted to keep Uriel hidden away from everyone. I wanted her to rest, to keep the outside world at bay so that her power could come in slowly rather than have her use it as soon as it appeared.

That was my hopeful thought, but it never happened.

I had more visitors in my damn room in three days than I had ever received before. Uriel had Blaze and Cerberus sitting at the end of the bed near her feet. Growling at them did nothing to get them to move, but Uriel sinking into my chest as she intertwined our legs together to watch movies was nice.

Mother and Mariah came by, dropping off chocolates and sweets. They urged me to let them come inside, but I denied them. Luckily, Uriel was sleeping, so she could not argue. I was proud I managed to keep them away. When Mother and Mariah got together, they got into giddy moods, and no one could take them seriously.

Loki came on day three. Before I could spout out some foul language to get him to leave, Uriel reprimanded me by pulling out her pouty lip.

Biting my cheek, I allowed them to play a card game or two, keeping her in my lap with my hand rubbing her stomach. I knew she hurt; she hurt all the time. When she blinked her eyes, small little wrinkles appeared, her breath hitched ever so slightly, and her heart skipped a beat.

Holding her closely and rubbing her stomach while she sat on my lap were the only things that helped soothe her. My lips descended on her shoulder, letting my hot breath fan her neck. I only wanted her to feel better, to take away whatever ailed her. I could give pain to those who deserved it, but I couldn't take away the pain of those who didn't.

Loki was speaking rubbish about other deities he goes to school with in the Celestial Kingdom. He was popular amongst his peers. My brother, who is just ten years old, used his looks to get what he wanted. Many times, I saw him come home on the weekends with a smug look after visiting Earth for a movie.

As long as he didn't fuck the girls, I didn't care. They needed to wait for their mates.

He was just ten. He probably couldn't get it up anyway, but the way he was going with his bruised lips, he likely wasn't very far off.

"Go fish!" Uriel quipped as she sat smugly on my lap. The bed was littered with card games, such as Go Fish and Uno. I rolled my eyes as Loki rubbed his chin before taking another card from the deck.

"Uriel needs a nap," I growled at Loki. He took his sweet time, putting the card into the ever-growing pile in his hands.

"You can't rush these things," Loki snapped. "Besides, if you are going to hide your mate in your room all the time, I'm gonna come find her. She's my best friend, you know?" Uriel beamed as she jumped in my lap.

Holding her by the hips, I calmed her cheerful movements, so I didn't impale her sweet cupcake with my dick. "Did you hear that, Luci? I'm his best friend!" She was so proud of herself as she sat back down and called out another fish to pair.

"I thought I was your best friend?" I whispered in her ear. "The best friend that takes care of you." Kissing her neck, she shivered as she leaned back.

"Bleh, stop that!" Loki threw a discarded card at my face. "We're almost done, then I have to go pack, anyway." Thank Fates he is going to leave.

"Mom and Dad are sending me off to visit my uncle until this whole evil mess has blown over. They say I get into too much trouble around here, so they want me to go bother someone else."

Uriel's shoulders sagged. I rubbed her arms up and down, kissing her cheek. "Oh, that's so sad." Uriel looked at me, pushing out her bottom lip.

Damn it, with the lip and this woman. I think I would rather she rip up the damn couch.

"Yeah, at least visiting Poseidon will be cool. I heard he has giant clamshells for beds and tons of half-naked women running around." Uriel made a face at the reference to women running around with no clothes, but her curiosity didn't waver.

"Can we go visit, too?" Uriel's head turned to me.

Please don't give me that damn pout.

"It's like Atlantis, right? That's where he lives? I can go visit my new siren friends!" Her fingers curled around my shirt, tugging on it excitedly. My hand went to her face to deny her what she wanted, but the damn lip popped out.

"Fates," I cursed, running my hand through my hair.

"You got it bad." Loki threw down the cards and hopped off the bed.

I did have it bad. I wanted to give her everything. This, though, the thought of trillions of gallons of water hanging over me that could come crashing down at any moment, had me squirming in my seat. I wasn't afraid of water; I just didn't like the pressure of water being above me, to come crashing down, trying to burn out my fire.

Fuck, I was scared.

"Pretty-please, Luci! Just for a couple of days?" Her golden eyes twinkled with excitement as I gripped her hips just a little tighter.

"Fine," I whispered. "But you have to give me something in return when we finish our visit." Biting her shoulder, my cock rolled under her ass. Her fingers pulled on my shirt tightly.

"When it's done..." she whispered. Taking her fingers as she trailed up my neck, the sparks flew across my skin until they landed on my lips. "I want us together, forever."

Chapter 42

Uriel

I beamed at Luci, his lips gently parted as he gawked at me. Loki cleared his throat, sliding down the bed and hopping on the floor. "I'll, uh, see you," he awkwardly waved as I waved back cheerfully. Luci's lips still hadn't moved, his eyes never leaving my body.

"What is it, Luci?" I poked his cheek with my finger, giggling as non-coherent words left his lips.

I don't know why he thought this was such a shocking statement. We were mates, and he cared for me as much as I cared for him. The past few days—just lying in bed, cuddling, him rubbing my tummy to make the pain go away—had been heaven.

We watched movies, ate chocolate, and got to kiss all the time. *It was my favorite thing to do, and I really hoped we could do it some more. He was so addicting, with his s'more-tasting lips. I* couldn't help but shudder in delight when he pulled me flush against his body.

Don't get me wrong, I was scared. He had a huge thingy, and the few brief times I saw it or felt it, I swear it spoke to me. 'I will destroy your pussy,' I only used the words that Luci likes to say because I'm sure his thingy talked that way too.

It was so much fun being with Luci. He had become so playful since first meeting him. He no longer had that terrible line between his eyebrows that looked like you could stick a grain of rice between it and have it sit there and never fall out.

"You mean that?" Luci whispered, having me straddle his lap. "You really mean it: you want to be bonded?" I tilted my head in confusion, wetting my lips with my tongue.

"Of course, I do," I whispered. "Why would I not? You are everything I would have ever wanted in a man." I blushed. "You are so understanding of me," I picked at my fingers, "even with all the challenges I have had, not being a 'real woman,' you still care." Luci shook his head.

"I'm sorry, what? Not a real woman?" Luci's eyebrows made the funny line again.

Dang-it.

"Well, yeah," I muttered. "I acted, and still act, all childish sometimes." Luci pulled my head to his shoulder, rubbing my back up and down.

"I love you, Uriel. I love how you are. It brings out the laughter in me. I swear I hadn't laughed or smiled until I met you." Luci's hands cupped my face, pecking at my lips. "You are like a little sunshine that I can keep in my pocket, and I would never change that. Even if I have to share the bed with..." he paused, staring at Mr. Rainbow Farts on the other side of the bed, "with that thing."

I snorted until I fell into a full fit of giggles. I didn't need my unicorn much anymore, Luci was my big stuffy. I only had him in there because I put Dad's feather in the stuffing. It was the perfect hiding spot, so if I needed him, I could call him whenever I wanted.

"Well, I love you too, Luci. And I want to have you." Luci kissed my forehead. "I just worry if it will hurt. Will it hurt like my *lady time?*" Luci gripped my thighs, his head dipping into my neck.

"It will hurt, but a different hurt. It won't last long, and I promise you, I will make you so wet that you'll hardly feel my cock take the last piece of your innocence." My breath stopped, feeling the heat of Luci's breath on my neck.

"Now, let's go talk to my parents and see what we can do about taking you to visit my uncle."

Last night at dinner, Loki was given an extensive set of rules by his parents. Since the evil that dared to darken the skies of the Celestial Kingdom, because of the prophecy, gods and the other deities were preparing for a god-like war that hasn't been seen since Kronos was removed from power.

All the portals had been closed, even the portal that stood outside the palace had been shut down, now it only looked like a stone archway. All comings and goings would have to be done using magical carriages with pretty horses. I was excited about the opportunity to sit in a carriage. I've never done that before.

Loki was prepped, poked, and prodded with questions about how he was expected to act around Poseidon. Poseidon doesn't get out much. Loki liked to pull the joke: '*he's a real hermit,*' and laugh excessively about it. Luci sat still with me in his lap, feeding me steak, *yuck.* He was completely passive about visiting the Underwater Palace where his uncle lived.

"He's... different," Ember paused in thought. "He certainly isn't like Zeus or Hades, you will have to see for yourself. Poseidon came here once for Lucifer's baby announcement, but that was it. He stays to himself, but overall, he's very nice." Ember poked her plate, full of vegetables. Lilith sat in Hades' arms while he rocked her.

Now knowing how Luci is, his father is very much the same. He is only calm when Ember is near, and she keeps all the dark stuff away. "I thank you both for being willing to take Loki. I feel that him being with Poseidon, until this whole mess blows over, will be for the best. You know how Loki likes to cause trouble." Loki rolled his eyes, slamming his fork on the table.

Hades and Ember were heading to the Celestial Kingdom to put some feelers out on Zeus. Hermes said that Zeus wasn't acting the same. His need for revenge over my mom had clouded his vision, and now he had angels sparing so frequently that they feared my parents' wellbeing would be at stake. I shifted in my seat, not liking that my parents were in such big trouble.

"Mom, I make trouble, I'm not the one swimming in it." Ares punched Loki as he slouched over his plate.

Ares looked much better today. Mariah even gleamed at him while they fed each other. They no longer had the guilty or burdened eyes. Ares was smiling gently at Mariah instead of trying to 'get in her pants,' as Loki would say.

"I'm excited!" I chirped. "I'm hoping to, at least, see Atlantis." Luci hummed, pulling my hair away from my face.

"His kingdom is close to Atlantis. I'm sure we could make a day trip."

The next morning, Luci woke me up early. I still had the sleepy gunk in my eyes as he led me out of the palace doors. Loki was already sitting inside the carriage, looking out the window and waving for us to hurry.

I thought the carriage would resemble the ambiance of the Underworld, dark with some red. Instead, it was something I was not expecting: light brown with a tan interior, gold trimmings, and light-colored horses—except for Absalom, Luci's horse. His head turned to watch us step in. Giving him a little wave, his ears twitched back and forth until I sat on the soft cushion.

Candles lit the beautiful interior as Luci sat down and shut the door. "Are you ready?" I nodded excitedly, sitting close to the window so I could peer out.

No coachman steered the horses. They took off on their own accord, trotting ahead only to be gently lifted off the ground. Loki had a book in his hand but quickly shut it to look out the window with me. "I wish we could take the carriage more often," he mused. "They only just opened all the portals within the last twenty-five years. This used to be the only way to travel."

"Why did they change it?" I watched the palace fall further and further away. The red clouds now covered it in a beautiful, velvet blanket. "Because when Mom came along, she still wanted to see her parents and pack regularly. Hecate, Hades, and some witches helped make the portals. It took a lot of power, but it was a quicker way to travel. Poseidon never wanted a portal though, I don't think he likes surprises." Loki sat back on the opposite side of the carriage, laying down to open his book.

Stronger gods could will themselves between Earth and Bergarian quite easily but when it came to traveling between god-like worlds such as the Underworld, Celestial Kingdom, and Poseidon's Kingdom, special traveling with magic was required.

"Why would he not like surprises?" Luci rubbed his chin, looking at the now blackened sky. No one could tell if we were going up or down. We were floating in nothingness. The air chilled, but we could not feel the wind as the horses flew faster into the abyss.

"He stays to himself," Luci shrugged his shoulders. "Most of the stories that humans make up are false. He just doesn't correct them. He lets them think what they want, hell even the gods make up stories. It's a rare occasion for him to even surface from the ocean, unless he is called by Zeus, and that never happens." Luci's arm wrapped around me as the chill hit my arms.

The horses' pants, which were once barely noticeable. heightened as blue-green light surrounded the carriage. The darkness faded and the colors now became much more vibrant. Still, there was nothing to see until I leaned my head slightly out the window. Luci had his arm securely around my waist, mumbling about something or other, but the itch to investigate was too strong.

My hands gripped the side, my once loosely-braided hair now losing all the pins and bands that kept it together. Luci wrapped his hand around my hair, gently pulling me back. "Bunny, it isn't safe." He pulled me in, but my eyes never left the bright lights.

Bubbles swirled around the carriage, similar to Luci's tornado of smoke and fire, but this was much more cheerful. I laughed as bubbles flew around us and into the carriage, poking them to hear a glorious 'pop'. Loki shook his head, laughing at my silliness.

The world around us ceased the bubble tornado and spat us out at the top of a gigantic globe. The carriage jarred until our horses neighed, following the sphere's edge that held this magical underwater palace.

My eyes gazed at the beautiful structure made of coral, rock, stone, and shells. It didn't compare to anything I had ever seen with beautiful, enormous pearls that sat atop each tower. Large, opened windows with no glass held servants leaning across the edge, watching as we descended.

Wildlife outside the sphere watched as our carriage finally landed at the large roundabout with a colossal stone statue of a buff, muscular man holding a trident. He was posed throwing it at an imaginary beast. His beard was long and curled, and the lower half of his body was that of a fish.

"Holy moly," I whispered. Hades huffed as I stared at the big statue. "That's enormous."

Luci leaned over, brushing my ear with his lips. "I can tell you what else is enormous," he chuckled darkly.

Squeezing my legs together, I thought, 'it was *a terrible idea to wear a skirt.*'

Two footmen trotted to the carriage. Their bodies were littered with scales, with gills under their ears that continued to flutter back and forth like they were breathing. Their yellow eyes peered into the carriage, assessing who had arrived. Their eyes weren't round like mine but cut into slits. Their hair stood on end like they were underwater, waving with the motion of the flowing current.

"Mother said that the creatures he created need water. Poseidon has created an atmosphere where those with both lungs and gills can live together.

Muttering, "wow," I took Luci's hand to exit the carriage, my mind running a mile a minute.

I couldn't wait to figure out how he could do that.

Stepping out, I noticed the footman had fins on his forearms, his calves, and one on his back. His nostrils flared at me and the smile he gave exposed row after row of sharpened fangs. Gripping Luci's arm, he chuckled, pulling me close.

"Your Highnesses," a half-man, half-octopus approached us. From the waist down, his tentacles slithered along the smooth stoned path. Each time he moved, small suction cups grabbed and released at the same time. His top half was bare, wearing only a necklace made of seashells. I gulped, grabbing the necklace that Luci had given to me, now using it to distract me from my uneasiness.

"Poseidon is expecting you. My name is Silas, I am the head butler. If there is anything you need, I will be happy to assist you." Silas bowed, but I didn't release Luci's arm.

"Thank you, we wish to see him now," Luci's voice came out demandingly. Fresh eyes laid on me as I scooted further and further behind Luci's back. Other servants neared, their yellow eyes filled with curiosity.

Loki yelled unintelligible words while his eyes turned red, and his back straightened. When he yelled, he sounded like a bird cawing. Luci and I stared at him, confused by what was happening. "Excuse me, I don't know what came over me." Loki's suave attitude flushed with embarrassment quickly as I held out my hand to hold his.

"It's okay," I whispered.

Loki, taking my hand, breathed a sigh of relief.

What was that?

"I'm sorry, we don't get many visitors. This would be the first time in thousands of years. We aren't used to seeing such different-looking creatures."

I snorted. *They were the weird-looking ones.*

Chapter 43

Lucifer

The half-octopus male smiled brightly. His teeth pointed into fangs, but his eyes held warmth encouraging me to trust him—barely. Uriel clutched my shirt tightly behind me while Loki continued coughing violently. I side-eyed him, making sure he wasn't trying to play a joke too soon, but the way Uriel held his hand told me otherwise. Mother had given him explicit instructions to go easy on Poseidon.

"Please, follow me," Silas bowed, his tentacles turning his body most elegantly as we trod down the light-colored cobblestone path.

The palace was unlike anything I could have imagined for an underwater world. It stood tall with cemented shells that shone brightly, the most colorful corals decorated the walls. Vines, like you would normally see on lattices climbing an ancient castle, held kelp that swayed outward like it was underwater. This palace was solid, not weak in the slightest. With so few materials to construct such a fortress, I was highly impressed with its sturdiness.

The atmosphere was dense and heavy but still filled with enough oxygen for my small family to breathe. These creatures that I had neither seen nor heard of breathed it like it was water. The hair on Silas' head swayed just like it was affected by ocean currents. There must have been some power that allowed their bodies to move in the gravity that was felt around us.

Inside, deep purples, blues, and greens donned the hallway. Giant chandeliers made of white coral and filled with candles lit the way. Statues of the gods, similar to those that my father placed in his garden, stood lining the way to the throne room.

Uriel, still holding onto my shirt as I wrapped my arm around her body, looked up in wonder as she pulled a sick-looking Loki behind us. As much as it concerned me that his face was darkening, he said nothing as we continued down the blue, sea moss carpet.

"Luci! Look!" Uriel pointed upward. Instead of a decorated ceiling filled with gods, demons, and angels, it was an aquarium, of sorts. Beautiful fish swam, looking down at us like we were the ones in the fish tank at a zoo. I blinked several times, holding onto Uriel.

That thing could break and squash us.

Sighing heavily, Silas' popping of the suction cups on his tentacles accentuated the awkward silence as we approached the throne room. Clearing his throat, he turned, smiling brightly with his sharp teeth. Uriel continued to hold on to me for dear life, her body shaking as a shark swam by on the opposite wall of the hallway.

"Lots of teeth," she muttered as a sea serpent stopped to stare. Its bright-yellow eyes lingered on Uriel, putting its snout up to the glass and tapping it several times. Uriel giggled as the serpent beckoned her closer. Her hand reached out but was still too far to reach the wall. Feeling brave, Uriel inched forward, pulling me with her. Chuckling, I followed like a hapless puppy.

Putting her finger against the glass, the serpent lovingly put the side of its head to the opposite side of the glass. It pulled back and forth, moving in a motion that seemed as if Uriel was petting it. Her finger bravely left the glass, only to put her entire hand on top of the serpent's head on the other side.

"It's purring," she looked behind me to make sure I was still there. "I can feel the vibrations against the glass." Giving her hand another reassuring squeeze, she pretended to pet the, once scary, creature.

"They can feel you," Silas interrupted Uriel as she baked away. "The walls can be felt one-way. It is so our Lord can touch all his creatures to heal them if they become sick. Do not worry, they cannot hurt you." Uriel's small smile returned to the serpent that leaned against the class, begging for my mate to touch him again.

"You will have plenty of time to explore the palace. I would suggest meeting Lord Poseidon first." Reluctantly, Uriel followed while Loki stood in the same spot, staring at the throne room double doors.

"Is he all right?" Silas nodded to Loki. Loki didn't budge, and he continued to stare at the brightly-colored door with amusement. His head ticked as he caught the bright light shining on the jewels.

"I'm not sure," I spoke. "It was his first carriage ride; he may be under the weather." Silas eyed him again before opening the door.

"I must warn you: Lord Poseidon doesn't receive many guests." Silas looked over his shoulder as we followed. "In fact, he is reluctant to visit. Just be patient," he whispered as the blue moss carpet halted before the throne.

Large green coral tentacles with orange wrapped around each spire sat behind the chair. Sea anemone donned the top of the hand rests, swaying to the ocean's current. Uriel and I waited, watching the throne, but no being sat in its wake.

"He will be here shortly," Silas muttered. "I'm sure he is still preparing himself. Please wait here, and I will have refreshments brought in." As Silas popped his tentacles out of the room, Loki shook his head, rubbing his eyes.

"The hell is wrong with you?" I muttered, trying to keep Uriel from hearing my words. She had already wandered off, ascending the steps of the throne to watch the sea anemone with delight.

Loki groaned, fisting his hands to his eyes. "I don't know," he muttered. "The shiny stuff just makes me wanna stare at it, touch it, and take it. I wanna stuff all the pretty stuff in my damn pockets, and I don't know why." I raised a brow, rolling my eyes.

"This better not be some joke. Mother will have your head." Loki scoffed, still rubbing his eyes. "Wouldn't dream of it, Lucifer." Loki continued to look around the room. The gems that donned the lower part of the throne caught his eye as he ran up the stairs to greet Uriel.

"Whatcha doing?" Uriel played with the sea anemone's tentacles.

"Playing with this fun, squishy thing," she mused. "Look, it has little fishies in it!" Loki stared but snubbed his nose after he caught sight of a brightly-shining ruby on the back of the chair. He tapped it with his finger, then tried to pull it away.

"Stop that," I hissed, walking up the stairs and smacking his hands away. "You look like a damn fool doing that!"

"Luci," Uriel whispered as she got on her knees looking at the shiny jewels around the bottom of the throne.

I swear I was watching a bunch of toddlers right now as they touched everything in sight.

I didn't mind so much with Uriel, however. She was bent over, her short damn skirt now revealing her plump ass wearing lacy underwear. I leaned over to watch her crawl on the floor, counting all the diamonds that surrounded the throne.

Arranging myself so that my boner wouldn't be the first thing our uncle would see, Loki pushed me, causing me to trip. "The fuck, man?" Loki shook his head.

"I may like shiny things, but you sure do like cupcakes," he snickered, slapping his knee. He began laughing, but instead of his contagious laugh, which Mother liked so much, it sounded like cawing. Uriel crawled back around to stare at Loki.

Now her tits were falling out of her top.

I groaned, attempting to pick her up off the floor until she shook her head. "Let me count. I want to see if there are the same amount of diamonds on the throne as how long he has been the ruler of the sea. Each diamond represents fifty years, I believe." She wiggled her nose as she turned around, showing me her ass again.

Sighing, Loki hiccupped from all his laughing, spitting out a long, black feather. "Did you eat a damn bird?" I questioned until he hiccupped again, and more feathers flew out of his mouth. "What is going on with you?" I growled, shaking him by the shoulders.

"I don't know!" shaking his head, his eyes turned blood-red, his darkened hair and small horns lengthened turning into large feather-like materials. It didn't stop at the back of his head, instead, the feathers grew across his arms and covered his hands.

"What is happening to me?" he screeched as his voice changed from normal-speaking to animalistic. I've seen my mother shift plenty of times in my life as she let her wolf, Elea, run through the gardens, but this was not wolf-like. His face lengthened, morphing into a hardened beak. His clothing faded away and there emerged a large raven with small horns upon his head.

"Kronos," I whispered, stepping away. Loki, not realizing his transformation, tried to step forward, only for me to step back again. Looking down, his feet had grown enormous claws that entangled with the moss carpet. Loki's beak snapped fervently, large clacking sounds echoed through the throne room. He shrieked as he tried to escape the carpet, only to fall over with his wings flapping wildly.

My attention was so captivated by Loki that I had almost forgotten about Uriel. I turned quickly to see if her ass was still near the throne, but she wasn't there.

Instead, she was holding the hand of a burly man with bright, orange hair. It swayed along with the current while his short-ened beard stayed stationary on his face. His chest was donned with nothing but a necklace made of puka shells and he wore a seaweed wrap for a skirt.

Uriel beamed up at me like she won the lottery, but this intruder continued to examine my mate with curiosity. She tugged his hand again until flames emerged from my back as my wings sprouted.

"Unhand her," I growled, pulling her away. Uriel's eyes widened as she tripped into my arms.

The intruder dropped her hand and ran back behind the throne so fast I barely saw it. "Oh, Luci," Uriel whined as she pushed me away. "I said you would be nice, and now you went and scared him." Trying to pull her away, I tightened my grip around her more.

"Scared him? Who the fuck is he?"

The aura he radiated was that of a god, a powerful one. The only god that could radiate that kind of power would be that of the original twelve, or me. I chuckled to myself at the thought. Was this THE Poseidon?

"It's Poseidon," she muttered. "He's kinda scared. Can I go get him now?" My eyebrows knitted into confusion as I gently let her go behind the throne again. Her animated expression coaxing the god back around the throne had me rubbing my forehead in exasperation.

Mother said he was strange, but hell, this was a bit much.

"Caw"

Loki blinked his beady, little, red eyes up to me. His head ticked while he lay on his side.

Dumb fucker couldn't get up. I chuckled, walking over to the enormous bird.

"Guess you hit puberty early," I mused, leaning over my knees and staring at him. "I got my wings when I hit puberty, scared the shit out of me. Looks like you get to turn into a mischievous raven instead of having cool powers like me." Loki snapped his beak angrily at my ankles, trying to piss me off, but I quickly dodged.

"Guess Mother will have to get an enormous cage for you and change your droppings paper." I laughed loudly. This only angered Loki more, who tripped again on his enormous talons.

"Luci?" My sweet goddess before me sang to my ears, causing me to melt. "I would like you to meet someone." The red-haired god walked out, his hair flowing backward as he approached. "This is Poseidon!" Uriel's hand did a magical dance, and she bowed in his presence.

Poseidon stared at me questioningly before he gave a small wave.

The fuck?

Chapter 44

Uriel

I pried my hand away from Luci so I could get a better look at the throne. It was so sparkly and colorful with all the different shades of coral. Around the bottom, large diamonds surrounded the edges of cemented shells. I noticed they were strategically placed, all the same width apart, as I kneeled and touched each one. Luci and Loki continued arguing. I rolled my eyes at those two. I couldn't step in all the time and mediate, they have to figure out things themselves.

Loki coughed, cackled, and made weird bird noises, but I was too engrossed in counting the magical little diamonds until I reached the left side of the throne. I could hear mumbling just behind it.

Crawling around I poked my head behind the edge of the throne to discover a man with bright, red hair that swayed into the wind-like current that hovered around us. In his hand, he held a book, *The Idiots Guide for Being Social*. His eyes were scrunched, reading the fine print as his finger trailed down the page before he swiftly turned to another page. I snorted, which caused him to pause his reading and look straight ahead at the wall.

My hand covered my mouth to hush myself until his head turned to me. Just kneeling on the ground, I could see this man was large and muscular. His skin was lightly tanned while his trimmed beard held the baby-like face that must have sat underneath. His eyes held no warrior confidence like the statue outside, instead, he was completely opposite in demeanor.

Bright, blue eyes looked down at me because I was obviously smaller than him. He jumped back, his seaweed-type wrapping scraping the moss carpet.

"Hello!" I chirped, holding out my hand. "I'm Uriel, what's your name?"

The god before me looked into my eyes and back at my hand like there was some sort of disease on it, or maybe he thought I would bite him?

Loud noises came from the other side of the throne, but I paid them no mind. Poseidon, however, did, he looked behind him like he could see straight through his throne.

"Loki and Luci are on the other side. They fight sometimes, but they are nice." I mused as I scooted my bum right next to him. "Whatcha reading?" He closed the book quickly, shoving it under the throne.

"N-nothing," he sputtered.

"Do you want to come out now? We all want to meet you, you know? Sitting back here won't do any good." Poseidon cleared his throat, scratching his neck of the invisible collar he thought was too tight.

"I'm not normally around others," he whispered. "Just my creations." I hummed in thought.

"Like Silas?" Poseidon's lip curled and nodded his head.

"Yes, like Silas and the others that serve me here." I patted my lip with my finger, thinking of a way to coax him out.

He reminded me of a scared little kitten.

"I promise they are nice," I cooed at him. "I'll be with you the whole time!" The once blue eyes I saw now swirled with green, reminding me of the beautiful ocean outside the palace walls. His smile widened, and he finally took the hand that I held out for him.

My hand glowed, feeling the warmth that we both radiated. His eyes widened again and the heaviness of his body lifted substantially. "What goddess are you?" he mused, staring at our hands.

"Innocence and Grace," I replied. "Why?" Poseidon put his other hand on the bottom of our joined hands and smiled brightly.

"Your grace takes my worry away," he chuckled. "It's rather interesting." I stood, pulling him up with me, his body towered over mine like Luci, but this guy's muscles were big.

Not as big as Ares, but still... he was big.

Pulling for him to follow he didn't budge and with his size, I could not pull him out. "Come on," I whined. "They are waiting and if we wait too much longer Loki and Luci might kill each other," I giggled. Poseidon continued to look at my hand.

"You won't let go right?" He muttered.

Oh flowers, he was so cute! I wanted to eat him up like yogurt and granola.

"Nope! Just come on, I promise everything is fine." Leading him out I see an angry Luci staring at our joined hands. His wings burst from his body causing Poseidon to flinch.

Luci spouted off nonsense about 'unhanding me,' being the testosterone-driven, crazy god that he is. Maybe he did need to get 'laid,' as Ares put it the other night.

Poseidon quickly dropped my hand and ran back behind the chair. I huffed, telling Luci to be nice. By the time I brought Poseidon back from his hiding spot, Luci's wings were in their normal, resting position.

"This is Poseidon!" I announced and did a wonderful hand dance in front of the fish god's body for effect. He looked at me and then back at Luci before he gave a little wave.

He's coming out of his shell! I internally screamed at my triumph, until Luci spat out a few choice words.

"Luci!" I hissed. "We don't cuss in front of your uncle, now come here and say, 'hello!'" Poseidon eyed Luci wearily as he approached.

I stared down my mate before finally jutting out my lip. Luci sighed and went to shake Poseidon's hand. Poseidon let go of mine and was able to shake it.

Thank the Fates for that because his hand was sweaty and smelled like fish.

"Where's Loki?" I chirped. A caw was heard on the moss-like carpet on the floor several steps down from the throne. A bird lay on its side with claws stuck in the threading.

"*Caw*"

"Loki?" I squealed, running down to help him. When I bent over, Luci cursed again and stood behind me.

"Bunny, if you can't bend over properly, then you have to start wearing pants." My face turned red as I pushed my skirt back down to help Loki get up.

"What happened?" Luci rubbed his face, crossing his arms at the large raven in front of us. Loki let out another 'caw,' his wings flapping violently as his talons continued to sink deeper into the moss.

"God of Mischief?" Poseidon walked towards us, eyeing Loki. Luci hummed in agreement as he stepped forward. Poseidon's fingers went to Loki's beak, tracing the dark, silken feathers until he reached his shoulders. Pulling out Loki's wings gently, Poseidon inspected each one, walking around the enormous bird. He was in his element as he studied Loki's form.

Luci held me close until he was finished.

"You did an excellent job transforming," Poseidon spoke in barely a whisper. "If you wish to return to your god form, you will need to concentrate."

Loki's beady, red eyes blinked several times, closing only a moment until they flew back open. He flapped his wings frantically, screaming.

Poseidon chucked, waving his hand for Silas to return to the room. "My Lord?"

"Let's take Master Loki to the creation room," he mumbled. Silas took his tentacles, and one by one they helped to free Loki's talons from the carpet.

Poseidon was already walking out of the room as Silas finished. "Please follow me, Lord Poseidon will help your friend." Luci's back straightened, the entire time he had been here, he acted like a stick was up his butt.

"What's wrong?" I pulled on his arm as we walked down the hallways.

"He's different alright," Luci muttered. "It's like he never talks to people." My fingers laced with Luci's as we walked into a large, dome area.

Large cages of animals and creatures that I had never seen before sat in each cell. Some were downright scary with large teeth and eyes that glowed in the dark. Dark colors donned their skin, and signs hung on the cages.

One cage held a large horse-like creature, but instead of four legs, it only had two, and a large tail replaced the hind legs. "Look, Luci! It's a merhorse!" I giggled as its nose came closer to the cage. I rubbed it gently and cooed at the bright-yellow animal.

"It's a *hippocampus*," Poseidon spoke loudly behind us, making me jump. Luci gripped me tightly.

Clearing his throat, Poseidon stepped away scratching his head. "Sorry, it's a hippocampus. Half horse, with a siren's tail. It couldn't just be any fish," he hurried his words. "It had to be strong to be able to push through its hooves because stream-lining is nearly impossible for this animal." Poseidon turned his back and hurried away.

"He likes to talk about his animals, maybe that is where we can connect with him?" I wondered aloud. Luci only hummed, keeping a firm hand on my waist. Luci continued to take in the room around us that was full of sea creatures. I could tell he didn't feel comfortable as I felt his body shift from side to side.

Poseidon went to stand by a glass table, filled with papers, chemistry tubes, and beakers. Loki stood on the other side, his head twitching like a bird, tapping the glass as it sparkled on the conch shell desk lamp.

"Let's see," Poseidon muttered as his fingers traced a book. He scratched his chin, glancing from the book to Loki. Rounding the table, he grabbed Loki's full attention by placing a hand on either side of his head.

"Imagine the bird," he muttered. "Imagine what the bird wants to do." Loki's eyes closed, listening to Poseidon's hypnotic words. "You are now part of this animal, you breathe, you sleep, and you fly with this animal. You are the raven and the raven is you." Loki's wings went slack, now trailing the floor.

"Accept the raven, Loki. Accept that it is a part of your being now." Loki's head went slack. "Once you accept it, imagine your body morphing back to your god form. Slowly, ever so slowly, think of your head, shoulders, torso, and so on."

Loki's head now faded back to his normal skin color, his hair stayed black while the feathers of his body absorbed into his body. Finally, his talons shorted, and his body returned to its full form, fully clothed. Taking a sigh of relief, Poseidon stepped back, releasing Loki's face.

"Incredible," he muttered, stepping away to write down a set of notes.

Loki opened his eyes, feeling his face, his body, and his legs. "Thank Fates," he whispered, running towards me. I hugged him as the glow surrounded us, giving him comfort.

"Better?" I looked at him.

"Pardon my French, but that was some scary shit." I narrowed my eyes at him playfully but didn't reprimand him.

"What happened to me?" Loki directed to Luci. He shook his head, swiping his fingers through it.

"You are a god, Loki, I guess you have an animal. Ares can shift to a wolf, and you can shift into a raven. Ravens are notorious for causing trouble, so it seems fitting." Loki snickered, turning to Poseidon who was still writing notes.

"Thank you," Loki stepped forward to shake his hand. Poseidon looked to his hand and back to Loki.

"You're welcome."

Chapter 45

Lucifer

Uriel looked at Poseidon like he was a magical, unicorn cat with fluffy, red hair. Which, I guess my uncle was some sort of weird species, considering the man hardly talked and preferred to hide away in the basement of his palace.

The room was littered with creatures big and small. They were creatures that shouldn't even exist—like the half-spider beast with a torso similar to a muscular human and a face with a mix of human-like and spider-like features. Looking at it, I couldn't tell if it could speak, or if it was even anything remotely intelligent as it stood on four hind legs eating the meat of another animal. Its four 'arms' gripped it tightly while munching on the shredded meat.

I shivered. *That shit was too much, even for me. What the hell was that thing?*

"This is an *arachne*," Poseidon approached the cage. The bars were large enough for anyone's hand to slip through. I pulled Uriel away, making sure the beast didn't suck her into the cage and eat her as well. Poseidon flashed a smile as he approached it, handing the creature a smaller fish.

"They are quite gentle but can be hostile when provoked. He can speak just as well as you and I." When Poseidon talked about his creations, he acted like they were the only ones in the room. His passion for teaching us about these strange creatures seemingly eased his discomfort in speaking with us.

Uriel was right. Maybe this was the way we could get him to open up for the duration of our stay.

"Would you like to feed him?" Poseidon willed another fish from his wrap and handed it to Uriel. Uriel only shook her head, clinging to me. *Finally, the woman feared something.*

"C-can I?" Loki stepped forward and reached out his hand. With Loki's newfound raven, he felt more connected to nature now. Loki stepped forward cautiously, holding out his hand. The exoskeleton-type arm reached through the bars, leaning more heavily into it since Loki was too afraid to move closer.

"I don't bite gods, child." The spider's voice was low, causing Uriel to jump. It chuckled, taking the fish from Loki's hand and swallowing it whole. "The fish are getting old, Master," the spider clicked its fangs together as Poseidon reached through the bars, patting its thorax.

"I'm sure they are. I will have Silas go to the breeding pins today to fetch some red meat." Poseidon spoke to him like a child before he stepped away.

"I'm sure you are all hungry from your journey. Silas has prepared an early lunch for us. Come." He waved his hand for us to follow.

How could the ruler of the sea be so docile? I've read stories of the raging seas and hurricanes that strike the land on Earth. They could be fierce and deadly, killing the humans in their path and

destroying entire forests on the islands of the Caribbean. Yet this
god before me looked like he could never commit such an act.

His hands were gentle as he petted his creatures. He did not
order them, he simply requested, and they complied willingly.
Was there some kind of genetic coding that he could implement
to make them love him unconditionally?

Leading us up the stairs to a giant, dome-shaped room, he had
us sit in a room full of pillows and small tables. Pillows littered
the floor, and we had to gather them to make soft chairs as we
sat on the floor by the table.

The table held assorted underwater delicacies but also had
many foods from the Celestial Kingdom—ambrosia, nectar,
bread, fruits, and an assortment of small finger sandwiches.
Uriel immediately eyed the desserts on a three-tiered serving
tray that Silas sat down gently.

Pulling my mate closer, I whispered in her ear. "Be a good girl
and eat something of sustenance. I don't need you all sugared
up later." I winked at her as her face reddened with embarrassment.

My dick was already straining my pants. I couldn't wait to get
her back to the room. It had been too many days.

"I am... glad you are here," Poseidon cleared his throat as he
loaded his plate full of raw fish.

"Lie," Uriel whispered, popping a cucumber sandwich in her
mouth. Poseidon cleared his voice again, his face turning red.

"I'm sorry?" he muttered.

"You lied. It's okay, you didn't know that was part of my
powers." Uriel continued to stuff her face, unphased that this
god lied to her. "It's only because you are nervous. I would be
nervous too after not having visitors for so long."

Poseidon hummed, stuffing a fish into his mouth. "Yes," he swallowed. "Hades was quite... persuasive when he requested that you all come for a visit and in having Loki stay for longer." Uriel swallowed her sandwich.

"Lieeee," she sang. I pinched her thigh to signal her to stop.

"Alright!" Poseidon threw the plate off his lap, the fish flying to the floor. We all sat wide-eyed, and I pulled my mate to my lap to protect her. "Hades is unreasonable!" he grunted, pacing the room.

Loki began coughing, feathers sputtering out of his mouth.

"I don't enjoy being around people," he muttered. "I don't enjoy being around other gods—fight, fight, fight, that is all they do. Then when I have finally had enough, I blow up and throw an 'El Niño' or a 'Nor'easter' all over the Earth. The seas capsize boats or a tsunami decimates entire cities. I can't deal!" Rubbing his hair with his fist, he almost pulled out knots of hair. Uriel tried to leave my lap, but I resisted, holding her close.

"He's a ticking time bomb," Loki nudged me, pulling a feather out of his hair. "When I get nervous, this bird inside me wants to fly off."

Poseidon growled, now counting to ten and throwing scented water in his face from a nearby basin. "I enjoy the silence. I enjoy being away from it all," he huffed. "I've always been different, ever since that day." Uriel's face softened, pulling at my suit jacket as she watched. "The other gods got over being swallowed... *by their father*. I did not." He gritted his teeth. "Why am I even talking about this?"

Uriel tugged my jacket again, silently begging me to let her go. After Poseidon's outburst, I didn't want to. I held her hand, letting her slowly get up from my lap as I followed. Poseidon was now circling the floral-scented basin in the middle of the room, Uriel's hand extended to touch him. He didn't flinch when she touched his shoulder, instead, he sighed as he felt the glow from her fingers.

"Maybe it is your power that lets my walls down," he muttered. Staring at the rippling water, his voice became stronger. "I remember it all—his throat opening, swallowing us all whole, the darkness, and the burning acid. I'm not sure if anyone else does. We stayed in his stomach for years, your father, Lucifer, getting the brunt of it. I watched him suffer, burning in the acid. I watched them all. When we were finally expelled from his stomach, no one seemed to remember the lot of it. That or they were just too thankful to be free. I held onto it all; I remember like it was yesterday." His hand went to wipe his forehead of the dripping dew.

"So I stayed down here, in the ocean, away from life. Creating life forms made me happy. When I allowed it, I helped create the most amazing creatures with the other gods. I could handle them, one at a time, as they asked me to create creatures for them. I just didn't know they were doing it to destroy the humans."

Once upon a time, the gods wanted to create a species in their image without powers. They wanted to see if, without magic, they would work together, love one another, and not fight for power. It all proved wrong once they saw the evil that many humans held, killing one another for power the gods thought they would never crave. When humans were created, the gods' own evil seeped into their souls.

This made the gods want to create new creatures to wipe out the humans—vampires, fae, and shifters of all kinds. They all hunted humans down, killing them mercilessly. Until Ares eventually created the werewolves—on his own—from a group of warriors fighting to save the humans.

"You mean you helped create all those creatures?" Uriel muttered, her hand not leaving his. Poseidon's tears dripped down his face.

"That I did, and I had no idea what they were being used for." Uriel's hand dropped, and Poseidon pulled away, muttering to himself.

"Silas will show you to your rooms." Poseidon pushed his hand, spreading shells away from the doorway, and glumly walked out of the room.

"These cakes are fantastic!" Loki yelled from across the room. Silas only chuckled, his tentacles reaching for a napkin to wipe Loki's face.

"I congratulate you for opening Master up so well; that is the most he has spoken in a long while." Silas hummed, gathering the empty plates. "When you are finished eating, I'll show you to your rooms. You can go to any part of the place you like—*except* through that entryway." Silas pointed to the entryway with the seashells covering it where Poseidon exited. They still made tinkling sounds until the sway of the shells finally stopped.

"Better hold on to Uriel," Loki wiped his mouth with his arm, "because I bet money that she will go through those shells." Uriel had indeed already looked at the shelled entryway longingly. I pulled her hip closer to me and whispered in her ear.

"Be a good girl and stay with me at all times." Uriel hummed, still staring at the doorway. I knew Poseidon was telling the truth since Uriel didn't squeeze my hand when he talked about his past, but the intentions he had, I was unsure of.

Now that he has become comfortable with us, especially Uriel, did that mean he wouldn't want her to leave? I grunted, pulling my mate away. Monitoring him would be for the best.

Silas led us to our rooms, the extravagant hallway was a stark contrast from where Poseidon liked to live, much like his basement of creatures. Uriel continued to stare at everything in awe while creatures like Silas roamed the hallways. The half-fish/half-humanoid creatures continued to look at us as we did them, not understanding each other's species complete-ly.

"Are there any girls here?" Uriel piped up. "I've only seen males." Silas let out a long sigh as he stood in front of the white double door.

"Master has only created males. He says that he does not feel comfortable with the female anatomy."

"Hold the phone!" Loki yelled. "You mean to tell me that no females like you roam this place? Just a bunch of dicks walking around *and nowhere to put them?*" Uriel covered her ears while I smacked the shit out of Loki's head.

Silas chuckled, opening the door, not bothering to answer his question. "This will be your room, Your Highness." Loki walked into the room, seeing the large flat screen T.V. and various gaming consoles.

"Oh yeah! I'll be in here if you need me." Loki waved his hand for us to leave. Mother didn't like gaming consoles, *'too much violence for Loki's young mind,'* she says. I don't think she fully realized who she lived with.

"That's so sad," Uriel stood by Silas. "Do you have mates then? Of the same gender? That's okay too." Uriel smiled up at him, but Silas frowned.

"Mates?" He whispered. "What are mates?"

Chapter 46

Poseidon

Pushing the shelled curtain away, the hushed whispers of my guests fell away lazily as I took heavy steps to my quarters.

This would be more difficult than I originally thought: having to speak and partake in regular conversations with gods that knew nothing about me.

I shouldn't blame them; I should give them the proper chance to prove themselves. These were not the gods I dealt with before; they were in the past. I never spoke or heard from them again after I found out they were trying to rid the humans from Earth.

Humans were special. We took extra care creating them once upon a time. They were the first creature that all the gods had a hand in creating. Each god's personality fanning out among the lot of the first human group.

Of course, some would have more evil nature than others, that was a given. Once the final ruling, that we would not destroy our creations, was declared, I hid back under the sea where I belonged.

One by one, sneaky gods that disagreed with the ruling came to ask me to help them create a new creature. They had enjoyed seeing my handiwork with the clay and dirt when we built the humans. *That was something that I was proud of myself for: I could create life better than most gods, and I wanted to continue that work.*

Vampires, fae, orcs, shifters, and many others—with my help, these new creatures came to life, only to be swept away to live on the land of Earth. They were taught to destroy the humans, and my heart burned when I discovered their betrayal. The seas were rough in the beginning, my emotions matching the Earth's tides. Tsunamis and volcano eruptions occurred frequently as the water beneath the Earth's crust stirred.

The waters were feared for a time, but once my body calmed from the hurt of betrayal, the seas settled too. Now only the occasional sea problems arose, *but I still had to remain cautious.*

Calm, that was my middle name. Once I banned the other gods from visiting, I commenced work with my newer creations, keeping my hands busy. Since then, I have created the most fascinating creatures which many humans would consider 'monsters.'

It helped me forget, helped me wipe away the thoughts of sitting the stomach of Kronos. Gritting my teeth, I swiped the many piles of drawings off my desk, scattering them to the floor.

Letting out large breaths, I tried not to recall the darkness or the burn in my legs I often felt when I remembered it. The heaving of my breaths became ragged, banging the desk with my fist as I fought it away.

For the first time in ages, I felt calm, all for it to rush back to me once Uriel's hand vanished. Uriel's gift was phenomenal, how the oceans in my heart calmed in an instant, but it wasn't enough. It was too deeply imbedded into my brain to be removed that quickly—not thousands of years' worth of turmoil. It was not feasible to be rid of such an issue that easily.

Walking to the corner cabinet filled with various bottles of whisky, I gazed upon them in malice. They were gifts from fellow gods that wished to harm the humans. I had not once partaken in such a vile substance, but even now, I felt my gut being wrenched from my body.

With a shaky hand, I lifted the decorative shot glass, pouring a shot of whisky. My hand shook, causing the dreadful, amber liquid to spill from the brim. Touching it to my lips, I swung it down in one gulp, letting the burn fill my insides.

Repulsive. The burn trailed to my stomach, and now I could feel it all over my body.

Slamming the shot glass down, I sat in the overly-stuffed rocking chair to my right. The shark leather soothed my skin as I rubbed it absentmindedly. *Too many years I have hidden. My underwater wonderland would soon seek the light sources above the waters. Some creatures craved the lighted orbs of the night and day. I couldn't keep them here forever.*

My will to keep them safe was too strong now. Someone, or something, was out there. I felt it in the deepest parts of the ocean, in the curling of the tides, and in the wind that Zeus had no control over. Why was he not in control?

Something was there, causing the whitecaps of the ocean to crash into the shorelines of both realms. Using erosion to eat away the soil. I wasn't in control of it, and Hades knew.

Hades had a better understanding of how things worked. I often wondered why he never took to the skies as High God, but he had his reasons. Hades understood that all realms stood at risk.

Standing and walking to the window, I overlooked my kingdom. It was vast, filled with sea life that did not need the denseness of the waters. They had enough oxygen in the humid climate that I created so that both air and water dwellers could thrive here I smiled, watching the gardeners plant more kelp by the fountains.

It was peaceful here, and I wanted to keep it that way—away from the drama of the gods. Once this evil was defeated, I could return to my daily routine.

Gentle rapping at the door let me know Silas was at the door. His soft tentacles hooked to the door, letting go with the suction cup's popping sound. "Come in Silas," I waved him in, picking up the papers off the floor. I had so many more ideas since seeing Loki's wings appear. I had not thought of creating creatures of the sky like I once did.

"Master, are you feeling better?" Silas came to help pick up the papers, but I waved him off. "This is my mess. Just leave it." I chuckled, putting them into a pile on the desk.

"Your guests are tucked away in their rooms. They wish to rest for the afternoon." I sighed in relief at not having them wander the palace grounds while I continued to get my head straight.

"Thank you, Silas. You may go rest as well. I'm sure they will keep us busy later." Walking to the bed, I sat on the end, scratching my head, thinking a nap was in order to reset my social bar. Silas continued to stare at me, not walking to the door.

"What is it, Silas? Something troubles you?" I pulled the blanket to my lap, looking at him blankly.

"Master, may I speak freely?" I chuckled, shaking my head. "Of course, you can. You always can around me; you know this." Silas shook his head, looking at his tentacles.

"This might anger you, and I do not wish to do so." Standing up, I put my hand on his shoulder. The softness of his opaque skin did not repulse me in the slightest.

"You are my closest creation. You could never upset me." Squeezing his shoulder, I urged him on. "In fact, would you like a drink?" I pointed to the partially cracked shot glass. The bottle was still uncorked. "It doesn't taste great," I coughed at the remembrance. Silas only shook his head.

"What are mates, Master?"

That, I was not expecting.

Taking a heavy breath and exhaling slowly, I pinched my nose before walking away. The glass window fogged from my heavy breath streaming across the cool surface. "I was hoping you would never ask," I said guiltily.

Turning my head, I saw Silas tilted his head to the side, his tentacles drooping. "Where did you hear this?" I muttered.

"The female." I hummed in recognition.

Of course he would have heard it from her. She was as innocent as they come and didn't know social norms—when to speak and when to keep one's mouth closed—any better than I did, but this, I knew to keep my mouth shut about.

"Mates," I muttered, fiddling with my pencil, "are another part of your soul—a match," I whispered. "Lucifer and Uriel are each other's *soulmates*. They complement each other; they balance each other. Think about it: the God of Destruction and the Goddess of Innocence. Without each other, their personalities and their powers could not be evened out. You love your other half, you take care of them, and you crave them." I put my pencil back in the pencil-holder cup.

"Does Master have a mate?" Silas' eyes blinked several times, waiting for my reply.

"I might, somewhere. I'm pretty broken though—you know that." Silas shook his head.

"If you are broken, then a mate will fix you, will it not?"

After I explained to Silas how simple it was and what a mate was to another person, he hit it the nail on the head: *my mate was to fix me, but what if she couldn't? Then where would that leave me? More broken than where I was to begin with?*

"Supposedly," I looked out over the ocean.

"And what about me and your other creations? Do we have mates too?" I frowned, not wanting to tell him the truth.

If I told him he would want to leave, as well as everyone else. I wasn't ready to let go, to be alone again and forced to start new friendships with others. Silas was my constant. He was more than just a creation; he was my friend.

"You have a soul, Silas. You have a mate." Silas' fangs widened, his tentacles waving wildly on the floor until he stopped.

"But there are none like me?" He pointed to himself. "How can I have a mate?"

My mind reeled with watching those in Bergarian—how humans were the perfect blank-slates for the supernaturals. Really, all species were compatible with a humanoid appearance, but these were not shifters—the lower half of their bodies did not look the same.

"You will. Selene or Ember, who is currently pairing souls, will finds a way."

"But my anatomy..." he pointed to himself. Before he parted his tentacles any further to show me his privates, I waved my hands.

"All males have their *stuff*," I air-quoted, "and so do females. You have been made to fit inside any female. Hecate was responsible for the female anatomy when they were created."

All my creations started as male. I refused to experiment with females. I was not comfortable with the female anatomy, especially when I helped create humans. All females have thus been created from sharing DNA with their mates after being bitten and infused with the special DNA.

"Wouldn't I be too large for a human female?" Silas tried to part his tentacles again until I grabbed his arms to stop.

"There will come a time to worry about that, but not now," my face turned red. "You, as well as every creature I have created, will get the chance to find a mate," I sighed. "If you wish to leave me..." Frowning, I turned away, trying not to cry in front of my friend.

"I just wish to seek my other half. I felt like something was missing. Do you feel it too?" Silas wondered.

Rubbing my chest, feeling the emptiness, I knew the feeling. I just didn't want to disappoint a mate with my struggles. I wanted her to live a free from worries about me.

Maybe that was the real reason I hid?

"I do feel empty," I whispered, "but until this evil that threatens us all is found, I will hold you and all my creations here. Then you may go in search of your mates." Silas grinned wildly, his tentacles surrounding my body.

"Thank you, Master! I cannot wait to tell the others! I cannot wait to hold a female!" I chuckled, patting his shoulder.

"Just don't forget about me," I sniffed.

"Master, never," Silas held me again. "You have given me the greatest gift: life. Now I can share it with someone too." His head leaned on my shoulder. Patting him on the back, I hummed.

"Yeah, maybe one day, I'll get that too."

Chapter 47

Uriel

L uci pushed me in the door after I asked Silas if he had a mate. *I mean, Silas could have a male mate if he wanted to. Why not? I know shifters leave marks on each other's shoulders,* but I didn't see one on his. *Maybe they have a different way? It was a perfectly logical question.*

Luci turned the lights on in the dim room. The palace was so far below the sea that it made it hard for the light sources to penetrate. Bioluminescent plants lit the area of the gardens and there were torches in the rooms.

"Uriel, asking him that was unwise," Luci loosened the collar of his dress shirt, untying the knot of his silk necktie. His fingers threaded it through, causing me to watch intently as he wrapped it around his fingers.

Why was that so hypnotic to watch?

Luci's dark eyes stared up at me, seeing that I was watching how he folded the tie around his fingers. "I don't know if those monsters can have mates." I gasped, breaking myself from the trance of his tie wiggling between his fingers.

"But they are alive? They think, speak, and move, surely, they have a soul?" Luci walked towards me, still threading the tie between his fingers.

"I never thought of it that way," he mumbled, but his steps did not falter as he stood before me. A dark shadow cast over his face as the flame on the other side of the room danced through the current.

"You are such a smart little bunny, aren't you?" My bum almost twitched like a bunny's tail, so excited for Luci to see how smart I am.

"Even so, that is something Poseidon needs to talk to his creations about." I hummed, feeling Luci's fingers trail below my chin and down my collarbone, his tie leaving tickles in its wake. My breath tethered, feeling the smoothness of the silk brushing between my breasts.

Good day for a low-cut top.

Luci hummed, continuing to raise the tie, slowly letting it weave out of his fingers before pushing me to the bed. The back of my bum hit the top of the bed as he crawled over me, and I crawled backward until I hit the pillows. His tie continued to dance on chest.

Small tickles made my body erupt in tiny little goose bumps. Luci's eyes became sinister, my breath catching each time I met them. "Luci," I whispered, only for his index finger to part my lips.

"It's been days since I've been able to touch you." Luci hovered over my body, without touching me. Taking his tie he placed it over my eyes, tying it around my head.

"W-what are you doing?" my voice barely left my lips. Luci hummed, continuing to tie it tightly.

My world became dark, my hands reaching out to touch anything on the bed beneath us. From what my poor eyes saw before Luci caught me in his web of seduction, it was a beautiful room filled with whites and creams. No large clamshell bed like Loki had previously joked about. Now there was nothing I could see, the darkness of my eyelids begging for light.

My hands moved above my heart, trying to find Luci's chest that was hovering just above me. "Patience, my good girl. Patience." My legs tightened together, feeling the heaviness of Luci leave the bed. Soft pants of his breath, the rustle of him unbuttoning his shirt, and the belt buckle that clinked in my ears had me whimpering.

"Don't you want to be my good girl?" He chuckled darkly as I heard his pants hit the floor. "Don't you want to show me how well you listen?" My nipples perked at his husky words while I tried to stay still.

The bed dipped again. His deep, heavy cologne hovered over my body, causing it to push down chest. I wanted to speak but was silenced with something so utterly soft it made my lips part.

Something velvet with a hint of rose scent touched my lips. It traced down my lips to my neck. I lifted my chin higher so I could feel every petal and every curve of the flower that touched my collarbones ever so delicately.

Luci's hot breath fanned my cheek. I could not see his stare, but I felt it. It burned into the side of my head until it followed the path of flower he traced between the valley of my breasts. Continuing to tease me with the delicate flower, his finger pulled down the cinched part of my dress that covered my chest.

"Exquisite," he hummed, taking the flower and tracing around my nipple. I reveled in his words—telling me how beautiful I was, how perfect I am in his eyes, how I was all his. I loved how he talked and how he praised me. My fingers itched to move, begged to grab on to him and not let go.

"I know what you're thinking, but you better keep those hands down. I will tie you to the bed if you are naughty," I whined. He chuckled huskily, now pulling at the strings of the short, corset sundress I wore. Laying the long-stemmed rose on my chest, he tenderly and ever so slowly pulled the dress down. I felt the silk fabric trail down my stomach, thighs, and finally my toes.

Luci parted my legs, so I was completely exposed. Somehow, he had removed my underwear along with my dress. I gripped the soft duvet again, trying to keep my hands still. "I think your breasts have gotten larger," Luci growled. The vibrations from his lips left my nipples aching.

"Please, Luci," I begged. "Please?" I waited for an answer, but it never came. His breath hovered over me.

"I love it when you beg for me," he whispered, now taking his warm mouth and sucking my hardened nipple. My hands couldn't stay still. They slid into his hair, pushing him further into my breast, forcing him to take as much of me in his mouth as he could. The other breast didn't go unnoticed as he switched between them, taking his hand and pinching the previous wet peak.

I moaned his name. My hips involuntarily tried to find the friction I desperately needed until his rough hands pushed my hips back into the mattress. The tingles were unbearable.

"You're so greedy, bunny." His cock rubbed against my leg. That long beast of a monster. That was the only monster I knew in this palace—not those creations that Poseidon created.

Lucifer took the flower that laid beside my body, his breath still fanning my nipples, now cooled from the remnants of his mouth. The rose trailed along my hip until it brushed the one particular area that needed attention. I grunted in frustration, trying to wiggle my hips.

Pushing on the stem of the rose, he guided me to part my legs again. My heart lit with fire as his body trailed down mine. He took his time. He liked to do that to me, watching me wither under him. It was his own sweet torture he liked to give me. He wanted his bunny to know that she needed him.

And I really did.

His tongue parted my folds, licking my clit, and I instantly fell. I knew it wouldn't take much and there it was, the bed wet beneath me. "That's a good fucking girl," he forced with gritted teeth, lapping up the juices between my thighs. Mini aftershocks elicited my moans, gripping his hair as he finished.

I removed his tie from around my eyes before laying it on my stomach. Lucifer's head popped up in a state of confusion.

I don't disobey Luci. I don't like to because I wanted to be his good girl, but this was important. Super important.

Surely he can't stand it either. Each time we touched, even flying down to the Underwater Kingdom, he had to feel it. The sparks just holding hands became unbearable. The pull of our bodies needing to be together was so strong I don't know how other gods could stand it.

My pussy clenched, feeling his fingers still near my entrance. *He hadn't even put those fingers inside me in days,* unable to stretch me for the beast I was about to ask for.

"Lucifer," I breathed. Luci now sat up on the bed, his naked body coming up next to me. He pulled my head into his shoulder until finally I was in his lap. His thingy was at attention, sitting at my thigh, and I felt my pussy pulsate with glee.

"Too much?" his voice was pained, pushing his thumb over my cheek. Shaking my head, I glanced into his big, beautiful, dark eyes.

"Bond with me. Make us one." Luci froze, the lust from his dark eyes was washed away with the waves of the realization of my request .

"What?" He barely breathed, atypical for his normal demeanor.

"I mean it." I licked my lips, staring at him adoringly.

This god was my mate. I didn't know anything about this new life, but he helped me every step of the way. He's shown me things that I had only ever dreamed of. He showed me the Underworld, took me to the beach, and even brought me to Poseidon's Kingdom. He would do anything to make me happy. Flowers, he told me he loved me, and he has done so every night since as we fell asleep in each other's arms. I can't be separated from him, not ever.

The God of Destruction lowered his walls for me, just a little goddess who had the mind of a child. Luci helped me grow. Why would I not want to be with him? He's gentle with me, he protects me, and there would be no other person I would rather be with.

Luci's breath halted, his body still hovering over me. I wasn't not sure if he was still breathing. "Lucifer?" I whispered his full name again.

It didn't feel foreign like I thought it would. Luci was just so easy to say, but this was not the time for nicknames. No, this required a name that grasped his attention, taking in all of him—not just the loving side he shares with me but all of him. In spite of all the torment he can cause, I was there to help soothe his storms, and he was there to create them in me.

"Lucifer, make it official. Claim me. Claim this body because you have already claimed my heart."

Luci cleared his throat. Watching his throat bob only made me squeeze my thighs together.

He was everything I ever could have wanted. How didn't I fall at his feet the very first time I met him? I'll never know.

"Uriel," his voice went dry. "We can wait..." his voice trailed as the bright smile I had on my face faded. It didn't take long before Luci saw my disappointment, and his lips grabbed hold of mine, kissing me with wild abandon.

It was hurried, forceful even, like an inner beast inside him had been unleashed. Parting my lips for a gasp I had to take, Luci's warm tongue slipped into my mouth. His fingers, now sporting claws, dug into my hips as he rubbed on top of me.

His harsh kisses softened; my eyes opened to see the firm placement of his brows soften as his gentle pecks cooled my aching lips. Luci's heavy lids opened to reveal the fire in his eyes. His face dropped below my jaw, and I felt the light feathery flutters of his lashes.

"Are you sure Uriel? This... this would bind us together, *forever*. I have my many flaws; you have to see that. I can lose my temper so easily. What if I become too rough?" Luci's voice cracked, his hand wrapping around my neck, giving a gentle squeeze. "I just don't want to hurt you. I don't know how much control I have." My nipples tightened, reacting to the warmth of his arm across my chest and the feeling of his calloused hand around my neck.

The grip he had on my neck was a warning. It was his way of letting me know he could really hurt me. The tightness of his grip should have frightened me. It was such a vulnerable spot for a hand to grip. He had the control. He had the upper hand. He was the dominant alpha in this pairing, and I was just the submissive omega who enjoyed getting the praise that I craved. His words could break me more than the hand that was around my neck.

It made me instantly wet.

"You would never hurt me," I whispered. My fingers brushing the unruly hair from his forehead. "We were made for each other, remember?"

Chapter 48

Under the Moon

Hades grabbed Ember around the waist, his lips touching the top of her head as she held Lilith close to her chest. Taking the chariot ride up to the Celestial Heavens had been rather unpleasant. The once smooth ride through the dark void between worlds had become rough and uneasy. The carriage to tossed and turned while Hades' hell horses screamed into the blackness. Hades tightened his grip around Ember, rocking his mate and daughter back and forth.

This was supposed to be a quick trip to speak with Zeus to understand the plans he had for Hera and Michael, who were indeed still missing. There were no signs the goddess and angel were willing to return to the Celestial Heavens to face trial. Their time was almost up, and soon, there would be no chance for redemption.

Hades hoped to talk some sense into his younger brother. This ruling for the trial was going by the laws of the High God. Zeus considered Hera to be the most trustworthy goddess—the one who he had loved for so long and lost. As such, Hades hoped a lesser punishment would suffice.

Once the carriage finally landed on the pearly streets, Ember pushed its door open, not bothering to wait for the footmen to help her down. Lilith grumbled, feeling her mother let out a harsh breath.

"Why was the ride so terrible?" she muttered as she looked up at the sky.

Hades put his arm around Ember, who was now stunned, before also examining the scene overhead. The skies were black with bolts of lightning weaving between the darkened clouds. Rain poured from the clouds but always evaporated before landing on the god and goddess' heads.

"Let's hurry inside," Hades urged, trudging down the pearled stone path. The typical brightness of the Celestial Kingdom had receded, and now, all that remained were dark, grayed clouds that hovered over the lands.

Angels outside the palace doors were donned in their battle armor, busily sharpening their swords and daggers. Hades shook his head as they arrived at the once bright, white doors. Now they barely hung on the warped hinges, unable to shut properly to obstruct the weather. The servants opened the doors with a loud crack and whine as the hinges fought to support their weight.

Ember stayed quiet, gripping Lilith who had been lulled back to sleep by the rumbling thunder, her thumb slipping into her mouth, suckling as if it was her mother.

"Stay close to me," Hades ordered. Ember dared not question her mate. She knew that was best for her and her child, given their current circumstances.

They both walked down the previously golden carpet, now stained with black burn marks from the lightning strikes. Some pieces of the carpet were still aflame as they walked past. Rubble and pieces of the ceiling now covered the marbled floor around them. Servants tried to clean as quickly as they could only for more debris and dust to fall when the palace shook again.

Angels, wearing their helmets and body armor, held deadly-looking spears, standing to form several rows before Zeus' throne. All were ready to attack anyone on a moment's notice, even Hades.

Hades chuckled, thinking to himself, *'what could those useless angels do to him?'* Hades was undoubtedly stronger, but the thought of his mate being helpless had him seething internally.

'How dare Zeus have so many guards ready to attack him, of all people? He was here to help Zeus. Why would he do such a thing?' Holding tightly to his mate, they approached the bottom of the steps. Trying to uphold the peace, Hades and Ember bowed in reverence.

For the first time in millennia, Zeus sat upon his throne instead of greeting his guests when they first arrived. His mood was ever-brooding as he now wore dark, gray robes instead of his pristine, white ones. His white hair was disheveled, and his beard had grown. His once, blue eyes now burned deeply with embers of fury.

"What do you want?" Zeus' voice was eerily calm for the atmosphere that surrounded the palace, while angels and servants appeared nervous before the High God.

Hades stepped forward, still not relinquishing his hold on his mate. "I've come to speak with you about the treason committed against the goddess, Uriel, by her mother and father."

Zeus had a sparkle in his eye as he leaned forward, taking one elbow to prop his head up in amusement. "Right," he hummed. "Pray tell me, why *you* wish to speak with me about it?"

Hades, taken aback by Zeus' normally playful behavior, raised a brow. "I think we need to hold a meeting with the Twelve to see if we can come to some sort of an agreement. We both know why Hera did it—to save her daughter. She was scared and—" Hades was cut-off by a mighty, red lightning bolt that struck right behind his mate.

Lilith cried out, holding onto her mother as Ember buried her head into Hades' arms.

"That is enough!" Hades growled. "I'm trying to be diplomatic about this, but you are being unreasonable!"

Zeus merely smirked, leaning back on his throne. His finger motioned for one of the celestial fairies to grace him with a platter of grapes and cheeses. Popping one purple grape into his mouth, he let the juice flow down his lips and onto his robe.

"Is that so?" He chuckled, now rising from his throne. Descending the stairs theatrically, he flared his robes in a prissy manner as he reached the bottom and stood nose-to-nose with Hades. Hades would not back down. His nose touched his younger brothers, and he let out a huff.

"If even *one* god deems it necessary to call upon the Twelve, then it should be granted. You know this. My reasoning should be heard. You are biased in all this because you still harbor contempt against Hera," Hades growled.

Zeus squinted his eyes.

The loud roars of the thunder had Gabriel, who stood in the background, shudder. His weight shuffled from foot to foot as he waited to hear what the two powerful gods had to say. Gabriel thought of his mate Persephone, who was at home with their youngest child. He hoped that she was alright. Persephone was no stranger to thunder, lightning, and rain since she grew up with her mother in the Earth and Bergarian realms. However, it was the thoughts that may plague her mind as a result, reminding her of her mother's absence, that worried him.

"Are you implying that I am unfit to rule judgement over this matter?" Zeus challenged, daring Hades to say another word.

Hades tutted, still not backing down. "That is exactly what I'm saying. Your close relationship with Hera will impede your judgment. You could pass judgement out of spite from losing her, from not having a mate of your own, and being jealous that Uriel is not *your* daughter."

Zeus threw his head back and laughed. The roaring thunder ceased, and for but a moment, the skies parted and let what little light was present to shine on Ember.

Zeus' finger pointed straight at Ember. "If anything, I should blame your mate, don't you think? She is the one who paired Hera with Michael."

Ember held her child to her chest, stepping back nervously.

"You keep my mate out of this!" Hades put his hand in front of his mate. "It isn't simple to find your soulmate. You know this. Maybe the Fates don't want you to have one yet, in hopes that you would redeem yourself for your foolishness of cheating on someone who dared to love you."

Zeus rubbed his beard, smirking. Shaking his head, he stepped up to Hades, who still did not back away. Hades was ready for a fight, knowing this may be the time when he must overthrow the Sky God.

"I don't give a flying fuck about Hera," he sneered. "I am ready to seek judgement on the parents who dared to poison the Goddess of Innocence. Who is it to say that they are not the evil entity that threatens her and that's why they tried to taint her?" Zeus turned, ascending the stairs back to his throne.

"They are not." Ember defended Hera and Michael.

As much as she despised what they did, they only did it to protect their only daughter. If something ever came to pass where such a prophecy hung in the air for their own children, who is to say she wouldn't do the same? Hades was powerful. Everyone knew that. She would not hesitate to hide her children from such a fate, especially if they did not know what evil sought them out. Hera had every right to fear Zeus.

"Zeus, what happened to you?" Ember pleaded. Putting Lilith in Hades arms, Ember walked halfway to the throne. "Uriel soothed you, just the other day. You seemed so happy once she relieved the burden you carried. I felt the warmth in your heart that one day, soon, you would have a mate and feel their love. Uriel gave you hope." Ember's lip wobbled.

The empathy power she held was so strong now she could feel the roaring waves of turmoil of every soul within a one-hundred-foot radius. With Athena's help, she learned to block them out, but now, the walls were crumbling with a need to decipher what Zeus was feeling—there was *something* different.

Ember tried to break down his walls, like she could so easily do with all the other gods, to delve within their souls to feel their emotions. This time, she couldn't. She couldn't break the barrier that surrounded his heart.

"*Something is wrong,*" Ember mind-linked Hades. "*Something, is very wrong.*" Ember grasped her chest, walking backwards, her eyes fixed upon Zeus.

The skepticism in Zeus' raised eyebrow had Hades stewing in his stance. Handing his daughter back to Ember, he stood in front of her, shielding them.

"Hold a trial, Zeus. You still have the final say." Hades taunted, "You are the High God, correct?"

Zeus' head ticked higher, liking the sound of that. "Yes, I am. Glad you didn't forget." Zeus sat back down in his seat, thrumming his fingers against the arms of his throne. Suddenly, an hourglass appeared beside him, the sand almost running out completely.

"I'm afraid, their time is up," he muttered. "But... I will grant you your request. I am *most* merciful in that regard." he sneered.

Hades gritted his teeth, his sinuous smoke tendrils slithering from his body.

"I do, however, have a request of my own," he taunted. "Uriel *must* be here for the gathering of the Twelve and remain for the duration of the trial." The weight of Zeus' 'request' filled the room, ensuing silence between the gods. Ember shook her head in deprecation.

"Is that really such an abhorrent request? To have the victim present for the proceedings?" Zeus' voice was still eerily calm, not unlike the calm right before the biggest of storms.

"Her mate won't like that," Ember whispered to herself. Covering her mouth at her blunder.

Zeus stood abruptly with his fist clenched. "A mate?" Zeus growled lowly. "Since when did the Goddess of Innocence get a mate, and why was I not informed?" Zeus resumed tapping his fingers on the arms of the throne, the wind picking up to blow his beard.

"It just happened recently; don't you remember? With Uriel being so sheltered, we have taken it slow with her. She just found out what mates are—" Ember was interrupted by a bolt of lightning gathering and striking at her feet.

The sudden shock of realization flashed before Hades' eyes. This was not his brother, it was clearly another entity that was inhabiting Zeus' body.

Ember screamed in fright, holding onto Hades, who had now lost his temper. Smoke engulfed them. His mate was completely covered in the black haze until the smoke lifted her and his daughter from his presence and carried them to the far side of the room.

Hades sprouted fur, using the ability he gained from his mate's genetics to shift into the most ferocious wolf. He had only shifted a handful of times, but when he did, he was unstoppable.

Zeus stared at him in disbelief, watching the acidic saliva drip and burn the once perfect carpet. His claws crushed the steps as he stalked toward the High God. Giant padded feet ignited the entire area as Hades, the hell hound, snarled murderously in Zeus' face.

"You forget who is more powerful." The sulfuric breath of the monstrous hellhound forced Zeus to lean back in his throne.

Lightning struck beside the throne, but Hades did not flinch.

"You forget how powerful a mated pair can be, now you listen here, brother." Hades licked his maw, the left-over spit dripping and burning holes in Zeus's robes. "You straighten up your act or I will take back what is rightfully mine. Your days of bullshitting are over, Zeus."

Zeus nodded his head, zipping his lips while Hades backed away, his eyes never leaving Zeus. "Prepare a room for the pair." Zeus waved his hand, wiping his forehead.

Hades continued to glare at Zeus while he gathered his mate and daughter from the protective smoke.

"And send invitations to the Twelve," Zeus commanded again. as Hades—the hellhound—and Ember left the room.

The doors slammed behind the departing couple, and the servants fled the room to attend to Zeus' commands. The light dimmed, and thunder rolled above Zeus' head. He chuckled, planting his fingertips against one another as he strummed them. His chuckle turned into sinister laughter, his teeth turned into sharp fangs and his eyes glowed red.

"This will be most interesting." Black sludge encrusted the corner of his lips. Wiping it away gleefully, he sat back on his throne, waiting for the fun to begin.

Chapter 49

Under the Moon

Hades maintained his wolf-like form with his head hung low, growling at the celestial fairies. He wasn't sure if they were working for Zeus out of loyalty or fear. Their wings shuddered as they opened the guest room doors. The brightly lit guestroom was surprisingly immaculate, unlike the rest of the palace which was crumbling to pieces. Within a day's time, Hades worried the entire palace would crumble.

Ember graciously thanked the fairies and sat down on the bed with a sleeping Lilith. "I can't reach—" Hades' maw snapped, silencing Ember, who glared at the overly large hellhound.

"*We shouldn't speak aloud,*" he mumbled through the link. "*I'm sorry I snapped at you.*"

Ember hummed, looking over her shoulder at the hellhound who looked across the Celestial Kingdom. Clouds were darkening by the minute, the sunshine was completely gone, and pellets of ice jumped playfully on the ground.

"*I can't get a read on his feelings,*" Ember spoke, still upset her mate would snap at her. She didn't reprimand him, knowing a lot was on his mind. "*It's like a steel wall is there, blocking his emotions from me. Hades, I think he really is the evil that is after Uriel.*"

Hades growled, baring his teeth while he rounded the bed. He laid his head on Ember's lap, nuzzling into her. Lilith woke from the movement, staring down at the beast that should scare any child. She only giggled, pulling on the fur atop Hades' head.

"Da," she spoke.

Ember smiled, looking at her wolfy mate. "I forget how fast they grow as gods." She hummed, bouncing Lilith.

"*We need to warn Lucifer.*" Hades continued to look up at his daughter. Hades shut his eyes, trying to contact his son, but a wall stood firm, blocking the connection. Hades growled, trying to push through, but he could get nothing.

Ember bit her lips, reciprocating Hades' frustration. She was trying to push through as well, but to no avail. "It's no use," she whispered. Another crack of lightning flashed through the sky, and large hail pounded into the homes of neighboring angels and gods.

"We are at the Fates' mercy," Hades growled, wrapping his body around his mate.

Uriel

Luci hovered over my body, as I laid beneath him. His broad chest bore no hair. His pectoral muscles fluctuated as I told him of my one desire. I wanted to be his, bound to him, forever.

Plus, I really needed all these tingles to go away, like yesterday.

"Are you sure?" His voice lowered, his hands turning black with ash which slowly crept up his arm. Letting out a shaky breath, my fingers climbed to his face, gently tracing the strained lines of his face. "Because once it's in, you're mine."

I giggled, almost crying at the excitement until he crashed his lips onto mine.

His darkened hands tangled into my hair, pulling at the back of my curled strands giving him ample access to my neck. He sucked staggeringly hard, leaving marks all over me. His lips trailed down my neck to my chest, where he grabbed me lustfully over my nipples, pinching one hard. I cried out in both pain and ecstasy.

His shaft lodged outside my lower lips. The heat of his shaft was so intense sitting right there. I wanted nothing more than for him to slide it in, to connect my body to him, not by fingers and tongue, but by parts of our bodies that were made for this.

"I'll be gentle." He gritted his teeth. His cock left little wet trails of cum on my thigh, making my body twitch with excitement as he tried to position himself.

My Lucifer wasn't gentle. He was a beast of a god. He was the God of Destruction, and I wanted him to destroy the last part of my innocence. I was made for him to destroy, now and for the rest of eternity. I hummed, trying to agree to the outlandish claim that he would try to be gentle because I very well knew he would not.

His finger trailed between my lower lips, testing to see if my body was ready for him. "You are always so wet, bunny. Always so ready to take me."

My legs spread wide for him. I felt no shame in letting his beast enter me. His fingers pushed inside me, using two to thrust inward. I cried out, feeling myself stretch from his fingers. Pulling his fingers away, he licked the remnants of my essence and hummed with delight.

While one arm leaned over me, he prodded my overly wet opening with the other. He groaned, crushing his hips into me. The beginning wasn't so bad. The heat of his angry head pushed inside me. Slowly, his wings unfolded behind his body. The burning embers at the tip of his wings hovered overhead as they stretched, shielding me from the window, hiding me like I was some sort of special secret.

Lucifer intently watched his shaft enter me slowly. I hitched my breath, feeling him take this last part of me, which I was eager to give him. His eyes filled with fire as he laid his other elbow near my head. My eyes instinctively closed.

"Look at me, bunny," he growled as I felt him nudge inside me again. My eyes burst open at his command, fluttering as a sexy smirk graced his face. "I want to see you filled to the brim with my cock." Letting out a breath, he reared back, forcing his shaft inside me.

Half squealing in surprise, half moaning, I gripped hold of Luci's shoulders with my nails.

"Fucking beautiful," he groaned, drawing out and pushing back into my body. "You are so fucking tight." His shaft continued to move. Whimpering, I moved my hips to meet his thrusts. "Made just for me," he grumbled. "Mine to destroy. I'll destroy this part of you, heal you, and force myself inside you to destroy it again." Luci lurched forward, his chest looming over my head as he jerked. "I smell your innocence all over my cock, it's fucking invigorating," he groaned.

Moaning his full name, I wrapped my legs around his waist. His wings beat behind him, pulsing to the rhythm of his thrusts. I felt so full. There was no more room for him. As soon as he hit the back of my womb, my chest would lift, provoking him to bite down harshly against my breasts.

"Lucifer!" I screamed. The bed shook, and I swear I thought the tides of the oceans changed.

The room became darker, and the ash from his wings dripped to the bed, dissolving into nothing. Using his wings to propel his body into me faster, harder I felt my own wings emerge. They smoothly unfurled from under my back and pushed their way outward. The golden tips of my wings outshined the small fire on Luci's wings as our feathers somehow entangled.

"This is all mine," Luci growled into my neck, nipping at me with his teeth. "All fucking mine. You are mine forever, bunny. You can never leave me," he panted. "I'll find you and hunt you down."

"Yes, sir" I whimpered, gripping my legs tighter around his waist. "All yours. All yours," I whispered, feeling the heat of his shaft rubbing the insides of my body.

"I'll find you and then fuck you for having ever tried to leave me."

"I'll never leave," I whined.

My body suddenly relaxed. Luci's did too—or so I thought. Instead, when I opened my eyes, could see the faint outline of Luci. He stared back at me while our bodies below us were still entangled in the throes of passion. His finger pushed a piece of floating hair away from my face while his chest burned wildly with light.

"Soul bonding, my sweet Uriel," he murmured, kissing my lips.

I sighed, still feeling the strong buildup between my thighs as our bodies continued their assaults below. I felt a bright burning sensation in my chest. Luci held my face to him, so I could not see what was happening. We both spasmed in the space above our bodies as we screamed each other's names.

My back arched as the piercing heat soared through my heart. Luci's hold only intensified as he grunted, releasing a warm liquid into my body. My eyelids parted as I laid back on the sheets, panting heavily from the haze of that amazing orgasm.

Our wing feathers were still entangled with one another. My fingers rested on Luci's head, stroking him lovingly as he lay with his face buried between my breasts.

Was this all a dream? Were our souls hovering over our bodies?

Pulling my hand from Luci's curls, I looked at my fingertips. I certainly felt different. The buzzing throughout my body energized me in ways that differed from usual. My spirit felt light and happy, and the tingles that I hoped would go away, only intensified.

I guess this is how it will always be.

I hummed, proud of our accomplishments when Luci lifted his head. His eyes, half hooded, looked at me with such love and adoration, my breath hitched when I looked down at him.

"I love you," I whispered. His smile widened, and he leaned up to kiss me so sweetly.

"Are you alright?" He cleared his throat.

His shoulders bore bloody marks from my fingernails. I bit my lip in worry that it would scar his perfect skin. Luci's fingers pinched my chin, making me stare back into his eyes.

"I liked it," he growled. "You can inflict as much pain as you want." I half snorted, half giggled then immediately covered my mouth.

That didn't sound ladylike.

"I love you too, Uriel."

My wings glowed in the cocoon we shared. I stared in awe at how bright it had become. The warmth in my chest glowed and burned. It was feeling everything I could have ever felt for Luci—all-encompassing, undying love.

"I feel you here," I touched my chest, which gave me a deepened feeling. My fingers brushed across something slightly raised and indented on my skin below my left collarbone. I glanced at my chest to see an image burned into my skin—a flame. It formed a dark red flame, almost like a fireball over my heart.

"My mark," he spoke with pride, gently caressing it.

Shots of pleasure ran straight through me to the core. I moaned, causing Luci's cock to twitch inside me.

Luci bit his lip. "I'll save that information for later," he chuckled.

"What does your mark on me look like?" he questioned, lifting his body off of mine. His cock slipped out of me with the movement. I almost cried, no longer feeling full. My eyes fluttered to Luci's chest where my mark resided. It was a beautiful, small lamb hovering just over his heart. I giggled, seeing the God of Destruction with a tattoo of something so precious and innocent looking.

"A little lamb." I touched it.

His wings shuddered, shaking my wings from its hold. Luci went speechless, holding his hand over it.

"My sweet, innocent, little lamb," he whispered. His wings dipped and his body wrapped around mine holding me tightly.

I bit my lip, readying to ask the one question that I desperately needed to be answered.

"So, does that mean we can do it again?"

Chapter 50

Lucifer

Uriel propped her head up on her elbow with her wings laying delicately across the pillows, shimmering in the light. A few of my feathers still entangled with hers from when they had intertwined with one another. Her glow was undeniable; the shimmer in her eyes held such warmth that I wanted to scream to the world that I had claimed her.

Her finger traced my chest, traveling everywhere but to the lamb that sat right above my heart. *How ironic that a lamb, an innocent lamb, was put on my chest.*

She was the one who calmed me, the sacrificial lamb who was destined to be bonded to me.

I couldn't believe we had come this far. She sat beside me in all her naked glory with her pink tits pressed against each other. She had no shame as she continued to stare at my body. Chuckling, I pushed aside a dark curl that dared to disturb my view of her beautiful face.

"You want to do it again, huh?" I pulled her by her ass, rubbing my, already hardened, cock against her puffy, pink pussy. My hips rolled, and her head dropped back, falling into the pillows and giving me an ample view of her chest.

The fire blaze branded on her chest reminded me that I had claimed her and bonded our souls together. I would forever know where she is, my heart always seeking its other half.

My tongue stretched out to her mark, licking one side of her branding. Her body tensed as she giggled with pleasure. Her giggles were music to my ears and had me fisting my cock, ready to impale her again.

"Oh, sir?" Her sultry voice pranced through my ears

She did not just pull that on me right now.

I grabbed her cheeks as her puffy lips formed a beautiful pout. "Do you really want to go there, bunny?" I licked the tip of her nose. Her feathers shook, not in fear but anticipation.

"Maybe." Her words were a sexy combination of airy and melodic. My lips crashed into hers, gripping her ass, grinding my erection against her mound. I rolled over on my back, willing my wings back into my body.

I need to get those damn things under control for what I'm about to do.

Uriel shook her head as she saw me lay on my back. My erection standing at attention as she eyed it longingly.

"Ride my face," I growled, jolting her from her trance. The quick movement of her head whipping flung her beautiful, long hair over her naked body.

I need to get her a hair tie.

I growled out again, pulling her to my chest. "Ride my face," I spat.

Uriel's eyes grew wide. Biting her lip, she got on her knees and crawled to me.

Fuck, she looked good crawling to me with her tits swaying like they were.

"What a good bunny you are, listening to your sir." She stopped; her cheeks flushed pink as she continued to place her knees on either side of my head.

Staring up at her, I got a full view of her beautiful face, her hair cascading behind her back, and her expanded wings that kept her balance.

"Watch me," I commanded her while my eyes never left her wide-eyed expression. Her mouth gaped while she lowered her beautiful lower lips to my face.

Lifting my head, I pulled her ass closer to me. She relaxed upon feeling my tongue fucking her core. My bunny's wings spread outward, stretching far across the bed.

She looked so damn glorious. It was clear that no angel or goddess could ever top my mate.

As I sucked firmly on her clit, her back arched and her eyes left me.

I'll forgive her this time. Her body is not used to the pleasure I can give her, yet. One day, though. One day I'll edge her until she begs for release.

A high-pitched scream left her lips as her hips lowered deeper into my face. I ate greedily as she ground her pussy into my face. My tongue curled up into her sucking her again with vigor.

"Too much!" she cried out, trying to leave her seat, but I held onto her plump ass eating my fill.

"Do it again," I ordered her. "Do it for me, bunny. Make me proud." A whine left her lips, and the pink of her cheeks brightened as she rode up the mountain quicker than expected and damn squirted in my mouth.

Fuck I'm good.

"Luci!" she cried, trying to get off me again, but I pulled her back down, positioning her pussy at the base of my cock.

"I—I didn't..." She shook her head frantically.

She must have thought she pissed herself it was that good.

"You taste divine, my little bunny." I nipped at her lip before I kissed her, allowing her to taste the remnants of her body on my tongue.

"Are you ready to work for me?" Her panting calmed, and her beautiful mound was so damn swollen.

"Are you sure you are okay, bunny?" Putting my hands to her face, I brought her forehead to mine, determining whether this was too much.

"I would like to do more for you." She blushed, and her little, shy smile caused my cock to twitch. "Especially if it feels like that." Her breath hitched at the feeling of my cock pushing beneath her.

"Tell me if it is too much." I kissed her lips. As much as I wanted to devour her and make her obey my every command, she was my mate, and I needed to be sure she was eased into my rough ministrations with her. There was no rush, we would share eternity together.

"Now, I want you to take my cock,"—Uriel blushed again, snapping her hand over her mouth—"and I want you to slowly slide it into your pussy and ride me."

Uriel looked behind her where my cock settled between her ass cheeks. She hummed, backing up, getting on her knees, and almost damn well standing to get it inside her.

Fuck, she was either too small or I was damn impressive.

I groaned, feeling the wetness of her cavern and watching her wings keep her steady. She was the epitome of beauty, taking my cock while her mouth opened wide as I stretched her canal.

"Good girl," I purred, crushing my hips against hers. I panted at the tightness of her pussy and the building anticipation. "Now, trust your instincts. Show me what you want to do."

Uriel didn't hesitate; she bounced up and down on my cock, and I gripped her hips until she bounced the ever-living shit out of me. Her face now red with her branded chest glowing brightly, I roared from the sensation, slightly upset that I was going to come so early. Grabbing her waist, attempting to pro-long her pleasure, I arranged her on all fours. Her wings spread out, hanging limp on the mattress.

Holy fuck, built-in handlebars!

Probing my cock, I watched her wetness trickle down her leg.

"Fuck, fuck, fuck," I whispered easing into her.

Do not blow this

"You look so good taking Sir's cock. Does it fill you up? Hmm? Does it fill you inside?"

She moaned, gripping the pillow and burying her face in it. Chuckling, I gripped hold of her wings as I positioned myself at her opening.

If she has anything near the feeling I had when she touched my wings, she is gonna blow her shit.

She screamed as my hands gripped the base of her wings, and my cock pushed all the way inside her. Using her wings as leverage I thrust into her over and over again. Tears ran down her face while she clutched the headboard.

"Holy fuck! Such a damn good girl, bunny."

She cried out; her orgasm lasted far longer than any other time. I grinned as my thrusts became sporadic.

I held out as long as I could and gave my mate the best I could muster. Ropes and ropes of my seed coated the inside of her body, dripping from her core, pushed out by her constant stream of orgasms. She let go of the headboard, collapsing into the pillows with her ass still in the air, letting me finish emptying my seed inside her.

Fates! That was indescribable.

Pulling from her gently, holding her back end up, and slowly laying her on her side, I pulled her to me. I was so damn exhausted but looking at her, whimpering, sweating, with an undeniable mess between her legs, I swelled with pride.

I took care of her.

"My sweet bunny," I cooed in her ear. She barely hummed, her poor eyes not even opening.

"I'm going to clean you up." I kissed her forehead. She didn't flinch or try to reach for me.

I chuckled. *I finally wore my little mate to pieces.*

Both of our wings merged back into our bodies. I carried her naked form to the ensuite bathroom, filling the tub with warm water, and dumping in some of the finest oils I have ever smelled. The oils mixed with the soap, causing the bubbles to form faster than anticipated.

"Shit—shit." I switched off the water just when the bubbles almost overflowed the tub.

If Uriel was awake for this she would be so damn excited.

"Bunny?" I nudged her, trying to wake her.

She mumbled something incoherent as I sat us down in the hot water. Stirring slightly, her eyes fluttered.

"Bubbles," she mumbled in the most blasé tone. I chuckled, rubbing my hand through my hair.

Next time then.

Washing her body thoroughly—her hair, her arms, and between her legs—I made especially sure to soap up her ample breasts. A good handful and my cock instantly jumped to life.

Counting to ten, I calmed myself before reheating the water with my hands so she could soak her aching muscles. I lowered us both into the steamy water. She was neck-deep, straddling my waist as I laid her head on my chest. Her soft little pants tickled me as my calloused hands rubbed the side of her head.

If someone told me months ago that I would find my mate and fall madly in love, insanely fast, I would have called them crazy.

The darkness within me was too much for most women, but lo and behold, I didn't have a woman—I had a damn innocent girl prance into my life, turning it upside down.

Uriel hummed, wrapping her arms around my body. Kissing the top of her head, I had a terrible realization: *Uriel's symbol is a lamb.* It sits with its legs folded underneath itself, looking straight at the person before it.

What if she was the sacrificial lamb, not her gift of innocence?

What if she is the sacrifice that is required to save the innocence of the realms and the Celestial Kingdom.

Gripping her tightly, I threw the thought away. *Surely, she could not be—she could not be the sacrifice needed to keep the prophecy at bay.*

I had her now. I would protect her, and with the Fates warning, I will be prepared. I'd keep my mate hidden away, away from the evil that 'lurks in the sky'—as her dream indicated.

The torches in the bathroom flickered; a blowing wind chilled the room.

"Hello?" I growled out.

Uriel continued to sleep in my arms unfazed, but the presence I felt in the room now was different. The entire atmosphere changed. Picking up Uriel, and letting my wet body drip across the floor, I covered my mate with a towel and carried her to our bedroom.

Entering our bedroom, I found the lights were out and only the bioluminescence from the garden outside shone.

"Lucifer?" My body stilled, turning slowly toward the voice. It was, none other than, my father.

"Shit, son why the hell are you naked in a dream?" Father covered his eyes, quickly turning around.

Clutching Uriel tightly, I carried her to the bed, tucking her in. Then, I returned to the bathroom to retrieve a towel for myself.

"The hell is wrong with you? Creeping the shit out of me in a dream? Why didn't you just link me?" I shook the excess water from my hair.

My father walked closer to the bed, but with my quick reflexes, I pushed his chest and shoved him away from her. He landed on the opposite side of the room, rubbing his head, seemingly unaffected, and stepped away from the now dented wall.

"Ah, you have mated. Congratulations." His smile lit up the room, and my fist which was ablaze softened to black. "I'm proud of you."

He kept his distance until I ran to him and hugged him. He paused briefly, only to grip me back with a tightness that I've longed to feel since I was a child. I wasn't angry; I wasn't having trouble controlling my anger, and the deep darkness within my soul was gone. Uriel had filled it with light.

Don't get me wrong, though, I'll still kill a fucker.

"As a joyous of an occasion as this is, I'm afraid I bring disturbing news." We released our embrace, but my father kept both hands on my shoulders. "The Twelve have been called

to assemble to help rule judgment against Hera and Michael...
Uriel is expected to be there."

Chapter 51

Lucifer

"Excuse me?" I gritted my teeth, feeling a burn in the back of my throat.

"I didn't link you because I can't, Lucifer. There is a ward restricting communication inside the Celestial Palace. I'm not sure who created it, but I need you to get a message to Ares. Ares and Mariah haven't slept, so I haven't been able to reach them, and I need to get a message to him." My father paced away, rubbing his stubbly chin. "I need them to check Tartarus"—Father paused, glancing over his shoulder—"to see if Kronos is still locked in his cell."

My mouth fell open at his words. "You don't think...?"

Father's jaw ticked, nodding his head. "I think he's out. I'm almost sure of it. This power—this evil someone is using, it is stifling."

Stepping back to the bed, I pushed Uriel's hair away from her face.

I can't let her get caught. I can't go up there.

"She can't leave here," I muttered. "I won't let anyone take her."

My back stiffened at Father's careful steps to the bed. "And we won't either. She is family. She will be protected once the Twelve arrive to overpower this evil being. However, if you don't willingly take her to the Celestial Kingdom, I'm worried about what Zeus will do to get her there." Father sat at the end of the bed, disregarding my glare. "It isn't just us; the humans and supernaturals could be at risk too."

"Zeus is doing this?"

Father shook his head, rubbing his mating mark. "It is the body of Zeus... at least I think it is. Either that or it is Kronos impersonating him." I sighed heavily, looking at Uriel.

"Get the message to Ares," Father spoke firmly. I hummed in agreement as he left the bed.

Before I knew what was happening, I was laying in the tub again with Uriel on my chest. My eyes blinked, adjusting to the dimming torches in the bathroom. Night must have fallen, and we had spent the entire afternoon in the tub with my body heat keeping the water warm.

I sat up with Uriel who continued to sleep soundly. Drying her and putting her in the bed, I tucked her in and planted a chaste kiss on her forehead. Her body leaned into me, ready for me to slip beside her, but I had work to do. Arranging one of my shirts over a pillow and sliding it towards her, she grabbed it instantly and hugged it close. Chuckling, I left the room, locking it and casting a magical ward to keep her safe.

I'll know if anyone comes in or out of that room.

Crossing the hallway, I found Loki, with the door still open, wearing a headset and playing a video game. His yelling and cursing were loud enough for the entire hallway to hear. I yanked the head set off his head; he growled as his horns and feathers sprouted from his head.

"Come on featherbrain. Father has given us an assignment."

Loki groaned in annoyance, but he knew never to mess with Father and the duties he delegated to us. As we walked down the hall, feathers spilled to the floor as he shook out his arms. "Dumb, stupid feather shit," he grumbled as we went to find Silas.

We heard Silas' tentacles popping through the main entryway. He busily prepared a floral arrangement filled with bright flowers and sponges. His hands moved smoothly and slowly like he was actually underwater. As we approached, Silas turned and gave us a fanged smile which then faded upon registering our determined faces.

"Silas, we need your help."

Uriel

I hugged the source of Luci's smell again, only to find it super squishy. I mean, really squishy, and my Luci was not squishy. I opened my eyes, looking at the black pillow covered with Luci's shirt. I huffed, throwing it to the ground.

He left me here after we just 'did it.'

The sheets flew over the bed. I was clean, and my hair was slightly damp. I realized I was clean from the evidence of our 'activities.' I giggled, running to the closet bum naked to change into a long yellow dress. It had capped sleeves and fell just above my knee.

I really love the dresses that Ember picked out for me.

Prancing to the door, I pulled to open it, only to find it extremely heavy. Grunting and straining, I managed to pull it open just enough to slip through, and it slammed shut as soon as I squeezed through it.

That was super heavy.

Dusting off my hands, I went exploring since Luci wasn't around.

I mean, seriously: he left me in that room and didn't cuddle me at all.

I should have been super mad, but the enormous light-blue halls and deep-green, squishy carpet were something to behold. My toes squished into the sea sponge material so much that I could almost bounce around the hallway. Following the hallway in the opposite direction from which we came, I stumbled upon a hallway full of doors with chatter and laughter billowing behind one of them.

Being one for laughter, I cracked the door open to see a ton of creatures just like Silas and that crazy spider guy. This time, there were also some centaurs, a minotaur, and a satyr! I thought they were all made-up fairytales, but here they were, right in front of me!

My wide eyes caught sight of the big minotaur who was drinking from a large bucket because his hands were too large to hold on to a regular-sized glass. His body was that of a hairy beast, taunt with large thighs and hooved feet. A tanned leather skirt covered his man parts and his slightly hairy six-pack crept up to a normal human face. Horns sprouted from his head and he had a ring in his nose.

"Well, there she is—the woman we have been talking about!"

I squeaked, shutting the door hastily, turning, and running back to my room. As I pulled on the door handle to my room, the pounding of feet and hooves on the carpet neared. I panicked as I tried to pull the door open again.

"We will not hurt you." The little satyr—who had the top half of a human and the bottom half of a goat—put his hand on my arm. His eyes looked like those of a goat with funny slits in them and he had curved horns coming from his head.

"He's right, we would never." The minotaur's gruff voice was muffled by the huge ring in his nose. His eyes narrowed, appraising me. "She's quite small. Do you think Silas was right, and we are to have one of these as a mate? I think I would break one."

"Oh flower," I whispered. "I—I have mated already!" I chuckled nervously at the hisses from the snakes and the loud goat neigh from the satyr

"Not you," the minotaur boomed.

"Silas found out what mates were, and once we are allowed to go to the surface, we will all find ours!" the satyr clarified hurriedly.

The minotaur said he was friendly, but he looks absolutely terrifying. I can't believe those poor women had to be mated to these monsters.

"Come now, we are celebrating. Why don't you join us?" I gulped as the Satyr pulled my hand. "I'm Rhos." He flashed me a fanged smile.

Why does everyone need fangs?

"I'm Uriel," I muttered as they pulled me down the hall.

Everyone was so excited to see me, their names came to me in a blur. The minotaur said very little, he just clopped his hooves against the ground while some snake-like creatures sat near him. The rest of the creatures—the nicer-looking ones—stayed near me trying to comfort my beating heart.

"Thanks to you, we get to leave this place. Not that it is terrible here. We love working here, but we always felt like something was missing."

The monsters hummed in agreement as they brought me into the room I peeked in earlier. It had televisions, pool tables, a food buffet, and games spread out on the tables.

"We were celebrating!" Rhos pulled me to the couch and sat me down. The snake people used their massive tails, which began at the waist of their human-like torso, as a make-shift chair. Their slitted eyes on their human faces looked me up and down as their forked tongues slinked out of their mouths.

I covered my mouth with my hand. *I'm going to puke.*

Rhos laughed, bringing me a plate of food piled with raw meat and grass. "I was not sure what you would like, so I got a little of everything."

I stared at the plate, taking much too long to take it from him, causing an awkward silence before I finally accepted it. I forced out, "T-thank you," and put it down on the table. "I just ate though, I'm very full," I lied, rubbing my stomach. It rumbled, betraying me at just the right time, and the Minotaur chucked in the corner with his bulging arms crossing his body.

"She eats like Master, not like us." The spider we saw earlier squeezed his legs through the door. His dark exoskeleton clicked as six of his legs alternately hit the floor, two of the shorter legs were nestled near his body, and his arms were almost as long as his legs.

I froze, watching his sharp chelicerae which clasped in the front of his face horizontally. He could open and close them like pinchers. "Flowers," I whimpered.

Rhos sat close to me, and at that moment, I really wanted Luci here. I knew they would not hurt me, but they gave me the heebie-jeebies!

"Goddess Uriel?" The spider came closer, and I leaned back into the couch as best I could.

"Uh, huh?" I hummed, barely.

"Master has yet to give me a name, and with the new information about gaining a mate, I would like to have a name that would attract one." His chelicerae pinched together; his mouth barely moved, but the hint of teeth on the inside of his mouth made me think he was smiling. "Will you give me a name?" The other monsters in the room quieted. One even dropped the bucket he was eating out of in the corner.

"A name?"

The spider lowered himself to my level, leaning over the table. He was certainly different and exuded no ill-intent as he rubbed his hands together. "Please?" he twilled.

"That isn't fair," one centaur said. "He will get the upper hand with a better name!" He threw his hands out. The monsters growled for him to hush as the room went silent again.

A name so special it makes his mate want him?

I don't know one woman alive that would want to be mated to this creature. My mom hated spiders; in fact, she had a special ward cast around our house to keep the creepy crawlies out.

As they all patiently waited, I ran through names in my head, searching for something that a woman would find attractive. It was all on me. My hands went to my face, feeling the burn as everyone watched.

"Little goddess, I will not blame you if my mate rejects me." His long arm stretched to touch my shoulder. He pulled it back after using his finger to test my skin. "So soft," he muttered as the door burst open revealing my fuming mate.

His wings extended from his body and there was a fire in his footsteps as he entered. The room grew dark, and Loki stood at the doorway in awe.

"Look at all, you guys! You are outstanding!" Loki raised his fists in triumph. "Anyone wanna play some video games?" A feather flew out of his mouth as he coughed in excitement.

Luci wasn't scared of the big spider guy at all. He pulled me up and gripped me around my waist. "Listen here *spider*, she's mine," he growled. His heavy pants blew my hair in front of my face as I spat it away.

"Arachne," I whispered.

The spider clicked his chelicerae in agreement, and Luci's eyes caught mine.

"He is an arachne, and his name is Galen." I smiled up at the not-so-scary spider. He leaned backward, sitting back on his abdomen. The noise in his throat chittered and squealed as he backed away.

"It means 'calm,' in Greek. I think your mate would appreciate that." I hummed, pulling Luci back to me. Now that he was here, I felt safer, wrapped in his arms. Luci sighed heavily, pushing his hair back.

"Why do you even put shirts on?" I questioned him. "You always rip them off. What does your mom say when you do it all the time?"

He chuckled, pulling me into a kiss. "You're something else, you know that?" He shook his head. "And I guess since we are bonded now, my wards don't work on you." Luci's attention was drawn to Loki who was trying to take Rhos out the door to play games. Rhos' loud hooves against the granite did nothing to conceal their actions.

"Loki," Luci barked, waving him back in. "We have a mission. Now isn't the time." Loki rolled his eyes, walking back in.

"Well, can we at least take these guys?" Loki indicated to the monsters behind him with his thumb before he moved to poke at one of the snakes.

Luci cocked a smile and nodded. "I don't think it would be a bad idea at all."

"No!" Poseidon stated as he strolled in, wearing his full god-like battle attire. It consisted of a sheeted white cloth held to his body with a thick eel leather belt. He held a triton in one hand and a ball of water in the other.

Chapter 52

Poseidon

The afternoon carried on quietly as I stared out from above in the highest tower. No one could find me here, not even my most trusted friend, Silas, who was now tending to the needs of our guests.

My hand gripped the railing, and the fish flew by like birds in the sky. I gazed at their streaks of colors that blinded my peripheral. The bioluminescent colors of the garden sparkled, letting me know the surface was losing its light.

How many years has it been since I had surfaced and graced the sandy shores with my feet? Far too long and yet, not long enough.

My cold feet felt the coolness of the hardened stone tower, the small torch radiating enough light that I could feel the burn on my back.

They shouldn't be here. My guests would be far better off hiding somewhere amongst Bergarian, in the palaces of the supernaturals there. I wasn't here to entertain and protect. I couldn't. It brought up too many sour memories of the many times I had sought comfort in fellow gods only for them to use my gift of molding new life to their advantage.

Hades stayed away too. He sunk into the abyss of the Underworld and gave me no reason to hate him, but I distrusted them all. How terrible of me to believe that, but my heart couldn't take another betrayal.

A fire erupted fifteen feet away from me. It wasn't large by any means, but the fire gave way to small electric sparks that made me growl in frustration. The last time I received a letter like this was when Zeus had tried to put a stop to me creating new beings. Of course, I did not listen, and they all hide here beneath the waves, but the creatures that I have made were nothing but honorable towards any other living creature.

They weren't made with the evil that many of their predecessors exhibited. They were taught to have their own opinions, their own mind, and to discover the life of lies, deceit, and truth. The one thing I could not show them, or have them understand, was that of love. Because I did not even know what that was like.

The lightning sparked the scroll, launching it towards me, pushing it through the thick air as I grabbed hold. The lightning static dissipated, leaving me nothing but a scroll baring Zeus' wax seal in hand. Grumbling, I pulled it apart, finding something I hoped I would never see: a summons to the Celestial Kingdom for a trial, or a pre-trial of sorts, to determine if a trial was agreed upon by the gods. Reading further, I found that Uriel's parents, Hera and Michael, had deceived Uriel by keeping her hidden, poisoning their own daughter because of a prophecy—a prophecy that hangs in the balance between life and death of all creations. I grumbled again, pinching the bridge of my nose.

I had not been to the Celestial Kingdom since Zeus had taken over. I wouldn't even know the proper etiquette that was required.

Do I wear clothes that humans wear? A suit with a tie? My original robes?

Pushing away from the banister, I turned hastily and trotted down the stairs. My feet hit the cushion of the mossy carpet as I trekked further and deeper into the palace. I did not understand why such a convening was necessary. It should be quite simple: Uriel was poisoned by another and it demanded punishment.

As I rounded the steps, hushed arguments flowed from Lucifer and Loki as they spoke to Silas. Every detail I had questions about spilled from their mouths. Silas' mouth hung in shock at the accidental poisoning and the prophecy that rode on Uriel's back.

Leaning against the wall, I eavesdropped like a coward instead of walking straight into the conversation. I was the God of the Sea, the one who controlled the mighty waves and all the creatures within, yet I could not face my brothers and sisters in such a manner.

Lucifer whispered hurriedly, explaining that their message needed to be sent to Ares within the next hour: to find out if Kronos was still in Tartarus.

Kronos?

My heart clenched in my chest. *Our sperm donor was alive, and now they feared he escaped from his prison.*

Gasping for air, I sunk to the floor as the world around me became fuzzy. I don't know if I could ever face such an evil entity. He stole everything from me. He stole my younger years. The fear lives in my nightmares every night, and now he could be walking amongst us, or worse yet, ruling over all the gods.

I shivered, burying my face in my hands as I fought to regain my composure.

What kind of god am I?

Silas took the message, walking down the hallways with his tentacles popping steadily. Stopping, he turned his head over his shoulder and asked Lucifer, "Are you going to stop him?" Silas' eyes softened. "Are you going to stop the madness, and help heal our Master of his nightmares?"

My heart capsized again in my chest.

How could he possibly know? Am I that loud when I sleep? Does he hang by my door, listening to me cry into the night?

Embarrassment flooded me. I was too scared to even close my eyes because it would remind me of the darkness of the pit of my father's stomach.

"I'll do more than that," Lucifer growled. "I'm going to destroy every piece of matter that created him." Lucifer's heavy promise halted my panting. His words held truth, and his determination radiated throughout the room.

Loki backed away, seeing Lucifer's smoldering red hands. "I will do it for my mate, and in turn, if that helps Poseidon, so be it." Lucifer turned, glancing at Loki as he trailed behind him down the hallway.

Shamefully following down the hallway, hoping to not be seen, I watched as he opened the door to the lounge room where all my creatures relaxed. Once the work was done around the palace, they went there to play, love life, and talk amongst themselves.

Sometimes I would join them to play their card games as to speak among them. I did not once feel judged by them. Many had been around for hundreds, if not thousands, of years. Many even roamed the Earth realm for a time until I recalled the ones that were not tainted by evil that wanted to destroy the humans before they were destroyed.

They craved the sunlight, but this was where they were safe. I would keep them safe for as long as they let me.

That moment was now. I would not let my children be taken from me. I will be a better creator and father to them than my own father ever was to me.

Uriel sat in the middle of the sofa. Her golden eyes gleamed when her mate strode into the room. She did not fear him, not one furious step he took toward her made her cower. Uriel looked at him with such love and adoration, it made me yearn for something like that.

"Maybe we can take these guys." Loki waved his thumb around the room. His eyes filled with mischief as he poked at one of the *nagas*—a creature I created who had the top half of a human and the bottom half of a snake.

"No!" I stepped forward. My body took on a mind of its own, donning me in the battle attire that I had not worn for thousands of years: my trident in hand with my belt tightly woven around my torso.

My creature's eyes glanced toward me, shocked by the anger was now spilling from me. They had never before witnessed this side of me.

"They will not help you," I grunted, pointing my trident to the rest of the room. "They are my children, and I will not dare risk them being harmed."

"But won't harm come to us if you lose?" Rhos whispered. "We can help, and we can—"

"I said no!" I bellowed. My eyes turned as red as one of the scales on the coral naga's tail. "I will protect you."

A fire burned in my belly that I had never before felt. The drive to protect what I called my own and ensure they would be safe—that the future would be safe from Kronos—strengthened my resolve.

"Silas tells you too much." I gritted my teeth. "What do you know?"

Silas peered in the doorway. His eyes blinked, filled with guilt. "They know why the guests are here: to hide Uriel and to protect the princes from the evil," he spoke, gripping the floors with popping noises. "They deserved the truth. They deserved to know what's happening, what evil this is, and now that it sounds like it might be—" Silas abruptly stopped his words, looking at the marbled floor. He knew not to bring up Kronos' name.

"Who might it be?" Rhos spoke again, his soft clicking of hooves across the floor echoed into the silent room.

"Kronos," Uriel whispered. Her eyes shone bright, looking into my eyes. Stepping forward, she dragged her mate with her as she held out her hand for me to take. I looked at her and her hand; she smiled, pushing it forward more encouraging me to take it.

Before I took her hand, a dark, red mark peeked out from her low-cut dress. Lucifer also had a mark on his bare chest; I could see the full picture of her mark there—a kneeling lamb staring right at me.

"Fates," I whispered, not daring to put my hand in hers.

This prophecy that was briefly mentioned in the letter was falling into place, and they dared to try to stop it? She was a sacrifice, an innocent sacrifice.

Did Lucifer not know, or did he dare not try to see?

I placed my hand in hers to appease her. My shoulders slumped and the tension in by back fell away with the bright, soothing glow of her hand.

"Ares has received the message, and he plans to arrive by midnight, Master." Silas interrupted the glow from Uriel's hands. She pulled her hand away, and Lucifer pulled her to his side as she smiled up at me.

"You are stronger than you think, you know?" Uriel ticked her head. "Your heart was actually shining brighter just now," she mused. "I'm still learning my powers; they are still growing, I think." Lucifer pulled her closer, nuzzling his nose into her neck as he kissed her shoulder.

"If you can strike a fire to protect all your 'children,'" she giggled, "then I think you can manage to do that for yourself. Don't you want to survive this? This evil is supposed to be so powerful that it could wipe us all out?"

My fist tightened around the trident, tapping it on the floor. "I do not care for my own life," I muttered.

"Well, you should," Uriel snapped, causing me to stand back in shock.

This tiny little goddess has more fire in her than I thought.

"If you don't save yourself, who will save your mate?"

My jaw dropped at her words, surely waiting for a fish to fly into my mouth. The heavy breathing from the minotaur caught my attention. His eyes narrowed, and his arms flexed.

"They all want this to work so they can find their own mates. They want their own happiness, and everyone here deserves it, even you. Even though you struggle to be around others."

Uriel stepped back into Lucifer's arms, looking up at him with pure adoration. "My mate takes care of me, and I take care of him. Now, I don't get those scary dreams. Why would you deny your mate something like that if she, too, suffers from something?"

My breath caught, and I was unable to breathe. This woman, as innocent as she is, had my mind turning.

"You are so smart, bunny." Lucifer's fingers trailed down her cheek. "Such a good girl for me." She nuzzled into his chest, gripping him around the waist.

They certainly were complete opposites, and they complimented each other so well.

"So, what are you going to do now? Let them help? Will you fight for you, fight for a gift that is granted to every god and goddess now?"

My back straightened, and my grip tightened on my trident as it stood tall.

This little goddess had a point. Who was I to deny my mate whom I had not met? If the worlds came to an end, we would never find each other. My creatures would never find their happiness, either.

"We wait for Ares' word," I spoke with confidence I thought I would never know. "Then we decide a plan of action."

Chapter 53

Under the Moon

The sweat on Ares' brow dripped down between Mariah's breasts. He had been relentless ever since Uriel's saving touch brought his inner turmoil to the surface. Now he was able to express his feelings more deeply. His fears, his worries, his insecurities—Mariah now knew it all. She only looked on with him more love than he ever thought she could give him.

Ares's body heaved into Mariah again. Missionary wasn't his favorite position, but it was the most intimate for him. He was able to stare into his mate's eyes as she felt his seed bury deep inside her womb. He made sure her eyes always stayed open. She wasn't even allowed to roll her eyes in pleasure. Ares wanted not only his cock inside her but his very soul.

Mariah looked on with him with love filling her hazed eyes. The soft curves of her muscular arms and her long legs had him quivering beneath the prominent v-line she loved so much. Mariah always commented how large he was, even though he was the first cock she had ever allowed to grace her body. She writhed beneath him, begging for more. His cock was never flaccid around her; it was always ready to plummet himself into his mate.

"I love you." Ares nuzzled his nose into her neck, kissing the mark he etched on her shoulder. Even with his mark on her chest, a wolf's head, from their soul-bonding, it wasn't enough. Ares would mark her repeatedly if he could. Leaving no part of her skin untouched by the beauty of his marks.

"I love you too, my alpha warrior." She hummed in contentment. "You don't have to keep doing this," she giggled. "We have been at it for days; you need a break."

Ares grumbled, putting his lips to her breasts. His cock already stirred again, ready for another round. "I cannot help it. My need to be inside you, to connect with you, is too strong." He bit her nipple, causing her to arch her back and moan his name. "As long as you find me worthy, I'll always want to be deep inside you," he mumbled with his lips around her breast.

"You have always been worthy. I just wish you had spoken to me about this sooner." She ran her fingers through his hair, closing her eyes as she felt his tongue's caresses soothe the ache of his bites.

"I know. You are just perfect and—" His voice was interrupted by a knock at the door.

Loukas banged on the other side, urging Ares to dress and open the door. Growling in annoyance, Ares slipped his raging cock from Mariah's core. She winced, feeling the heat of his body leave hers. Ares covered her body with the thick furs and stomped to the door in the nude.

Mariah watched the rippling of his muscles in his lower back and ass. They were her favorite parts of his body. She loved seeing the claw marks she left as she pulled him tighter into her aching cavern.

"This better be good," Ares growled, opening the door.

Loukas stood stunned, looking the God of War up and down with a smirk plastered across his face. "Never a dull moment with you two, I swear. Nora is getting upset with you not joining her for dinner the past few nights."

Mariah awed in the corner. "Tell her we will be there tonight," she yelled out the door.

Ares grumbled, rolling his eyes at his mate's tender heart. He wanted to fuck her more, and make sure his seed was fully implanted into her womb. Now that he felt worthy to be a father, it was all he wanted.

"I'm afraid you won't have time for that." Loukas' expensive shoes shuffled on the floor. "This letter came for you. We are having trouble with communication between realms right now, and this has been marked as urgent from Poseidon's Kingdom."

Ares gripped the letter from Loukas, his cock bobbing as he turned around to hastily open the letter. Loukas stood in the corner, his tail flicking side to side as he waited for Ares to read.

Ares read silently; he never did like reading aloud. It took him time to read, the letters often jumbling together, and his excitement to know what was happening between words, made concentrating difficult.

Mariah, understanding the dilemma her mate was having, wrapped herself in one of the blackened furs. Taking care that her body was covered, she padded over to her mate. Looking up at him, he smiled softly at her as he shared the letter with her. Mariah's eyes widened at the words on the parchment.

"What is it?" Loukas crossed his arms. He felt his impatience in his horns, making them ache.

"It's from Lucifer," Mariah spoke slowly. "Hades and Ember are stuck in the Celestial Heavens and it looks like the Twelve are being summoned for a pre-trial for Hera and Michael. They can't send out communication unless through dreams." Mariah bit her lip as she read on.

"The old-fashioned way," Loukas mused. "That can make it hard to send word when the two of you haven't slept." Loukas snickered. Ares shot him a glare to silence him while Mariah blushed with a giggle.

"Hades believes it's Kronos." Ares tightened his fists around the letter. It burst into flames, leaving nothing but ash on his hands. "Mariah, I must visit Tartarus to make sure Kronos is still locked away."

"I'm coming with you," Mariah went to the bathroom to dress.

Ares instantly threw on his battle regalia—the leather skirt, the sword at his side, and the shield on his back. Combing his hands through his hair to get rid of the tangles as his mate emerged from the bathroom. The leather bindings on her forearms and calves made Ares' cock twitch with excitement. He loved the outfit she chose for herself, making sure to match her mate with her own leather skirt, sword at her side, and a shield of her wolf sat on her back. She braided her hair quickly before she threw it over her shoulder.

As much as Ares wanted Mariah to be with him, he shook his head and put both hands on her shoulders. "I need you to remain here," he muttered in her ear. Mariah's eyes knitted into confusion as her mate looked on to her with adoration. "Just in case you are with child." A small slip of a smile broke through his tough demeanor.

"I'm coming too, Ares. You will not face that monster alone." Mariah didn't even stomp her foot in protest. Her mind was made up, and her fingers curled around Ares' arm. "We do this together, or not at all." Her voice never wavered as Ares nodded.

He would not fight with his mate; she was a warrior—the Warrior Wolf-Goddess who he loved so much.

With the snap of Ares' fingers, they all stepped into Tartarus. The screams and howls of pain from those damned to torment for the rest of eternity begged for mercy. Mariah kept her head tall, her jaw tight, and her eyes straight forward. She had yet to grace the bloody soil of Tartarus. Ares always made sure she trained with the warriors that surrounded the palace rather than enter a disgusting place like this. His mate may be strong, but he liked to think he was saving her from the emotional torment that anyone could endure after seeing such a place.

Mariah never faltered in her steps. Loukas stood alongside the two, his tail waving back and forth as they passed the torture demons. Their appearance was hideous enough to make anyone's stomach churn—melting skin, protruding bones, and forever-rotting muscle.

The stench of Tartarus was far worse than the rotten-egg smell of sulfur, burning bodies, and rotten infections. It kept their pace quick as they descended to the depths of the pit. The pit that held the worst of the worst: the pedophiles, sexual traffickers, murderers, and worse all lined the cave-like walls. Each condemned soul had a personal demon to ensure that not one of them had a moment of rest.

"This way," Ares grunted, traveling further into the pit. Down deeper than the layers that contained the Titans that once roamed the Earth, there in an opaque box, sat one lonely Titan. His disheveled gray beard hung to the floor, hair tangled and matted with dirt and debris. Blood, feces, and urine caked the bottom of the box. His head hung low, and his chained wrists hung above his head.

Ares pounded the box, waiting for the diseased Titan's eyes to rise to meet his. It took some time, but with a slow ascent, his gaze met Ares. "What ails you?" Ares taunted. "Is the box not to your liking, Titan?"

A few minutes passed which felt like forever to Mariah as she waited for this infamous Titan to open his mouth.

A cracked, bloody smile appeared on Kronos' lips as he looked from Ares to Mariah. "Can't even plant a seed into your mate, I see." His was voice low and calculating, each word was deliberate as he spoke, careful not to give away any emotion.

Ares' fists gripped tight, but Mariah soothed him with her other hand, tickling his forearm covered in tattoos. "Don't mind him," Mariah whispered. "Is this Kronos?"

Ares put his hand to the box, feeling the aura inside. It was overpowering and stifling. The box—constructed by Hecate and Hades, and later, reinforced by Vulcan with his magical wielding—confirmed that Kronos had not left his prison.

"It is Kronos," Ares muttered. The few times he had visited with Hades only solidified his conclusion that this was the same Titan. "I don't know what evil has gripped hold of Zeus, but Kronos is definitely here." Ares continued to walk around the box, inspecting it thoroughly as Loukas followed close behind, serving as the second set of eyes.

"Maybe we should call upon Hecate?" Ares directed his question to Loukas who only shook his head.

"She's been summoned to the Celestial Kingdom already. I tried to reach her, but only got static. My fire-letters cannot even reach her."

Ares released a breath. "She must not have known the danger when she received it. As is most likely the case with every other member of the Original Twelve."

"Besides you," Loukas spoke louder. "You know now. Zeus needs all of the Twelve for whatever he has planned. Poseidon has not traveled there yet either, and who knows if Hera and Michael have even been found."

Ares rubbed his chest, shaking his head. Zeus had never been the smartest god, but this newfound evil that has invaded his heart was clearly powerful. He devised a complex scheme to maneuver the assembly of the Twelve, quickly and quietly. Ares was never book-smart, but when it came to battle, he could devise a plan of attack with the most complex and comprehensive strategy. Every tiny detail was implemented, and now, Zeus seemed to have taken a liking to planning his next steps carefully.

The question was, what did he want? Revenge for Hera for not staying with him? Revenge for not having a mate of his own? Or did he simply want all the realms to suffer as he has for so long?

Assured that Kronos was rotting away in Tartarus, sitting in his own filth, Ares gripped Mariah by the waist, plotting their next move. Kronos kept his lips sealed, looking at the ground vacantly—that in itself seemed terrifying. He issued no taunting words, nor did he bang the chains, demanding to be let free. He just sat there, silent, unmoving, with his eyes closed.

"We will travel to Poseidon's Kingdom," Ares spoke to Loukas, "and deliver the news."

Chapter 54

Uriel

Luci laced his fingers between mine as the monsters in the room trailed behind us, walking down the soft carpeted hallways. We all met in the receiving room. Silas had servants, who were similar to his form and others with more fish-like qualities on two legs, bring in food and drinks.

Poseidon sat in the overly-large, decorative chair colored with turquoise, shades of blue, and hints of orange. One hand supported his red beard as he leaned on the arm. Loki eyed the food before stuffing his face like he did earlier. His skin turned dark and his eyes began to glow red.

"When you get excited," Poseidon muttered, almost to himself, "your animal wants to surface. Remember the techniques I've taught you if I am not around."

I shoved Loki to make sure he said a proper, 'thank you.' He stopped and smiled with an enormous pile of sandwiches in his mouth. Playfully swallowing and muttering his thanks, he shoved another mouthful in his mouth.

Before I pushed him again, Luci grabbed me and put me on his lap, far away from Loki. "Don't worry about him," Luci growled in my ear.

I giggled, nuzzling up against Luci's neck. "You are just jealous that I was giving him attention." I traced the lamb on his chest, causing him to shudder. Grabbing my hand in his, he rubbed my knuckles and brought it to his lips to kiss as he leaned us into the couch.

Poseidon and Luci talked while the monsters gathered around the sitting area. My eyes began to drift closed. It had gotten late, and I was sure it was well past midnight. A few snarls and growls filled the air while I continued to nod off, but I only found them soothing to fall asleep with.

With Luci by my side, along with my new friends, which I had gathered in just a short time, I felt safe. With the darkness looming and the future now becoming the present, the time spent with my mate and my family felt extremely important. My heart was hanging heavy, but Luci's gentle touches moving my chin upward to plant a kiss on my forehead had me cuddle closer to him.

The whispers became murmurs, and I woke to find everyone talking excitedly. Ares stood tall in his ancient armor alongside Mariah, whose hand was intertwined with his. Her head stood erect; and her free fist balled in anger as Ares spoke.

"Kronos is in Tartarus still. I saw him with my own eyes." Poseidon shook his head, his internal anguish was oozing out of him.

There was no use in hiding when someone said that dreadful Titan's name.

"I felt his power through the bindings. This is Zeus we are dealing with, not Kronos."

Poseidon winced again, standing at his full height, leaning on his trident. Luci's gaze fell to Poseidon, who now stood overlooking his underwater kingdom. Poseidon's inner turmoil over what to do called to me. I sat up straight, wanting to go over to comfort him.

"I've been summoned now," Ares growled. "I received my letter as soon as I returned from Tartarus. Waiting much longer to answer will draw unwanted attention. Especially for you." Ares nodded to Poseidon.

"We all go then." Luci sat me back on the couch. "All four of us at the same time. Zeus is trying to assemble the gods in mismatched times so as not to be taken head-on by multiple gods at once. It's strategic; it's smart." His eyes gazed at Poseidon, Ares, and Mariah, all with determination on their faces.

"Five," I stood up, narrowing my eyes at Luci. "There are five of us." Luci shook his head, brushing a lock of hair away from my cheek. "Four, bunny. You aren't coming with us. I will not allow you to be taken from me," he growled. The torchlights flickered in the room, and the monsters who stood close by felt Luci's aura leak from him. Luci's towering form hovered over me as the lights dimmed to a quarter of the light previously emitted.

"You, Loki, and Silas will remain here. Poseidon's creations will accompany us with the rebellion. I will not have you walk into the lion's den." Luci gritted his teeth, his hands gripping my arms. "I love you too much." A low growl rumbled in his chest. The sweet kiss he put on my forehead melted me, but I had to do something.

"What about my parents?" I muttered. "Maybe they aren't even there yet! Maybe there will be no trial!" Ares chuckled, crossing his arms.

"Zeus has your parents. He was waiting for Hades, perhaps the strongest of the gods, to walk right into the front doors to question him so he could be captured easily." Ares let go of Mariah's hand, who only looked at him longingly. "Why do you think neither your mother nor your father have contacted you since?" Gone was the typically playful war god. His hips bent down to reach my height, and I felt so small and helpless.

"They are trying to protect me," I muttered with my lip wobbling as I stepped away.

Luci pushed Ares back. "Back off," he snapped at his uncle.

Ares chuckled, walking away. "I'm trying to put things into perspective here. Hera hasn't even visited you in your dreams now, has she?" I shook my head, pulling at my dress.

"My father came to me in a dream. Why couldn't Hera visit Uriel? What is the difference?" Luci replied. Ares kissed Mariah's lips, holding her close.

"Because her power is weakening," Poseidon whispered, still looking out the window. "The longer you are bound by a god's power, the harder it is for you to fight it."

Ares grunted. "I was going to say that she was being tortured to stay awake, but I guess that works, too."

I gasped. *Both of those circumstances sound awful.*

"I said enough!" Luci yelled. The lights went out in the room, the only visible light was from the small bioluminescent barnacles that decorated some of the walls. Poseidon's armor was full of the glow, and it swayed as he sat back in his seat.

"They are safe. I know they are!" I snipped, holding back tears. Pulling out my father's feather, which I kept between my boobs, I held it up for all to see.

"Damn," Ares chuckled, and Luci stared down in shock.

Shrugging my shoulders, I clenched it. "What? I didn't have any pockets in this dress."

Luci grabbed my waist, pinching it gently. "Bunny," he growled until I started praying with the feather wound between my fingers.

I prayed for my father to come find me, to answer me, to let me know he was alright. Seconds turned to minutes, and once the silence of ten long minutes had passed, Luci grabbed the feather from my fingers. Everyone was sitting, and my eyes fell to the floor. They all waited and watched, but nothing happened at all.

"Let's go," Luci grabbed my hand. The feather was carelessly dropped to the floor as he led me out of the room. The inside of the palace's lights brightened as Luci imposed his darkening aura upon the gardens. Small fish that could be the equivalent of birds on Earth and Bergarian swam away from us.

Kelp and sea anemones swayed with the current until Luci backed me up against the garden wall, hidden from the decorative path. His eyes were ablaze and his knee pushed between my legs, which filled me hot with need. I would do anything to fulfill that need, but right now, the thought of my parents being trapped in the, once bright, palace filled me with despair.

I caused all of this. If I was never born, none of this would have happened. All these gods, humans, and supernaturals endangered because of some stupid prophecy that involved me. I wasn't anything special, just a tiny, little goddess who barely had control over her powers.

Luci's hardened face, softened upon seeing my weepy eyes. "Oh, bunny." He silently cursed, pulling me into a hug. I wrapped my arms around his muscular waist. "I'm sorry about your parents." His cheek lay on the top of my head. "We are going to get them back. That is why the whole plan was created. Ares, Poseidon, Mariah, the monsters, and I will be plenty to take him on. Zeus won't know what hit him."

I sniffled into his shoulder as he pulled away slightly. "If I was never born—" Luci's hand latched around my neck. The small squeeze melted me with the reminder of how powerful he was. My hands fell from around his waist, gripping his wrists.

"My bunny shouldn't talk like that. My good girl doesn't talk like that." I whimpered. "My good girl does whatever she can to please me."

I almost purred, forgetting about the horrible whispers running through my head: *If I just wasn't here, everyone would have been happier, and no one would be in danger.*

"If you were never born, bunny"—Luci's lips broached the shell of my ear. His hot breath flowed down my neck causing my nipples to pearl against my dress—"you would have never saved me."

I gulped as Luci's thumb caressed the side of my neck. His grip tightened and loosened again, letting me know he was still there.

"I would be living in a box beside Kronos, slowly destroying myself because I was afraid of destroying the surrounding worlds." The front part of Luci's body pressed flush with mine as his heavy breaths had me grip his shoulders. "Without you, Uriel, I'd be a broken god."

I sniffed, wiping away the lone tear streaking down my cheek.

"You see, I need you. I need you more than I need air, and you telling me that you aren't worth it gives me a rage I've never experienced." Biting my lip, I mustered enough courage to investigate his fiery eyes. "Now tell me, bunny, how are you going to make this up to me? How can you let me know you will never think like this again, and will go back to being the good girl who has such a spark for life?" Luci's grip loosened, and his thumb tickled my chin. A sparkle in his eye glimmered, and my hands fell from his shoulders.

Luci helped me forget all about my worries with just his touch, his words, and that deep feeling inside my chest that could suffocate me at the same time. The bond between us grew tenfold since we mated, and I couldn't wait to explore this beautiful gift his mother gave us. I quickly dried my tears. I knew my Luci wanted to see the playful me, not the one that wished life was never given to her.

And I wanted nothing more than to please him.

My fingers fiddled with each other, picking at my fingernails. Luci's impatient growl had me pushing my thighs together. Surely, he didn't want to do something *out here?* Biting my lip and pulling it with the bluntness of my teeth, I traced his silver belt buckle, tugging it with one of my fingers.

"Bunny..." His low growl went straight to that clit thingy he likes to play with.

My knees fell to the soft sand that outlined the stone wall, cushioning to my knees. Luci was groaning, his hand falling to my head and squeezing for me to hurry. Butterflies erupted in my stomach as I peeled away layer after layer of fabric that kept his thick shaft from me.

"So good," he hummed, petting my hair.

With a newfound excitement, I pulled it out. It was already hard, thick, and angry as it stared back at me. Taking my tongue, I licked the leaky tip. Luci's hissing didn't go unnoticed. Licking him from tip to base, and holding his balls with one hand, I nipped the underside of the tip. He used one arm to lean up against the wall.

"Bunny," he growled with his hand gripping my hair.

I smiled, fluttering my lashes as I graced his cock with my lips. He tried valiantly to muffle his growls. We were outside, and servants walked through the garden tending to the foliage. It felt so naughty to be out here like this, but the excitement running through me pushed me forward. I soared with this new level of confidence.

"That's it," he whispered huskily. "See how much power you have over me? Fuck."

My mouth continued to swallow him; his body shook and his grip on the back of my head tightened. My hand reached around, grabbing his bum, which had me arch my back enjoying his tight muscles. He muttered something with his face turned away from me, but I didn't care. I wanted to make him spill himself. His shaft touched the back of my throat and I gagged. Suddenly, I was pulled up from my kneeling position, my mouth releasing with a pop.

"My seed is for your pussy, you understand?" I moaned, feeling his tight grip around my hips.

He pulled my top down, dropping his mouth to my breasts, biting them with his teeth. "I love these." Both breasts spilled from the elastic of my low top. "They are all mine. You're mine, you understand?" I whimpered, running my hands through his hair.

"No one will take you from me. No one will dare touch you." Luci's frantic hands bunched my skirt up, revealing my lack of underwear. "Fucking hell, bunny. If I wasn't so damn hard, I'd spank your ass." I giggled. He gripped one cheek with his hand and the other pushed his tip to my core.

"Mine," he growled into my mouth before he thrust into me.

Chapter 55

Lucifer

"I'd like to say I taught him that," Ares whispered to Mariah while my mate sucked my cock.

The damn fucking god can't lay off.

"Leave," I growled, feeling her tongue swirl around the head of my cock.

After they left, I took Uriel the way I wanted. I pulled her legs up, and slid her dress above her thighs. Growling into her ear as Uriel's neck dipped to the side. My teeth grazed her neck, leaving bites and sucks across her silky skin. My teeth grew, biting into her neck and pulling at her delicate skin. Uriel's leg tightened as I slipped into her dripping pussy. She liked a little pain, which I was more than happy to give her.

My forehead pressed to hers. I pushed not only my cock inside her but myself into her mind. I had yet to read her since the first time we met, to see if she had ill intentions. Low and behold, the small devious plan she had stewing in her ignited my range. Pushing my hips deeper, letting one of her legs fall, I stretched her legs to the limit. They parted widely as I rammed my cock upward by bending my knees.

With sweat on my brow, I silenced Uriel's loud moans with my hand. "My bunny is trying to get into trouble," I growled in her ear. Pushing my cock inside her deeper, she whimpered, while holding onto my shoulders. Pushing her hands above her head so she could not touch me, I forced my way in.

"What are you planning to do, bunny?" My mate's pussy clenched, getting closer to her orgasm. "Don't you dare come. Do you hear me?" I pulled my cock out, stopping my assault. As much as I wanted to thrust into her again as my balls tightened in anger, I stopped. Her nails gripped my chest, scratching right down my torso.

"Bunny," I growled. Her thick lashes were coated with her glittery tears from ramming my cock in her mouth. "You are going to stay here like a good girl, right?"

Whimpering, she pushed her pussy back onto my shaft. Groaning, I pulled out of her, my cock dripping with her essence.

"Luci, please." Her hands dropped to my hips, pulling me closer.

"Now you are a needy girl, huh?" Her lip pouted. If I wasn't so worried about her safety, I would force myself back inside her. "You will stay here, won't you? You are going to be my good girl, right?"

She didn't answer. My hand went straight to her leg that was curved around my hip, slapping it harshly. Her body shuddered with her breasts pushing forward.

Oh, she was my little pain bunny. Fuck, this was so good.

Groaning, I pulled her chin up, forcing my tongue into her mouth. "Answer me," I spoke between changing the position of my head to bite her lip. "Are you going to be good? Are you going to make me so proud of you?"

I was using her pleasure, her kink, of wanting to please me to my advantage, but it was for her safety. I wasn't about to let her go near the Celestial Kingdom.

"Uh-huh." Her fingers went around my cock, stroking it. Feeling her wetness and her hand stroking me, I jerked my hips.

Fuck, she felt so damn good.

My forehead leaned into her, and her plans of committing a sin against me dwindled down to nothing. "Good girl." I pulled my cock from her grasp before probing her cavern. "You will stay here," I grunted, pushing inside her. "You will stay safe. You will not allow any harm to come unto you."

She yelled as my cock hit the back of her cavern.

"Shhh," I pushed forward, hearing the slick of our bodies slapping together. Lifting both of her legs, I ground my pelvis into her. "That's it, take it, take my cock. Milk me dry," I muttered into her neck.

"Luci..." Her nails pierced my back as my wings sprang forth. Her hands gripped the base of my wings, pulling on the sensitive feathers. "Can I come please, Luci?"

I hummed, coming closer to my own release. "You stay here," I mumbled into her shoulder. "You stay safe." I bit her shoulder again causing her to cry out.

"Yes! I will be safe!" She fell apart in my arms. Her hips thrust along with mine as her orgasm rode out long and hard. I held myself back, feeling her wetness fall from her cavern and all over my cock. The slickness fueled the fire for me to finish inside.

She was a fucking squirter.

"Damnit Uriel." With her pulling my feathers, I came undone. My ass clenched as her hand went down my pants holding on to my tense, muscular cheeks. Her nails scratched while her lips stroked my neck. Shivers ran down my spine, and my feathers shook with the aftershocks. My seed spilled into her, and her body fell limp as I held her to the wall.

"I can't lose you. Do you understand?" My lips kissed her now bruised and love-bitten neck. "I would destroy everything in my path if anything happened to you."

"You won't lose me," she muttered, her head resting on my shoulder. "I just want you and everyone safe too," she whispered, tears springing to her eyes.

"That's why I'm here, to take care of you." Kissing her temple, I sat her down on both her feet, straightening her dress. She pulled her hair behind her back while I buckled my pants. Her body was weak from the exertion, so I picked her up and carried her back to our bedroom.

The lights were already dimmed, obscuring the monsters in the hallway strapping on their battle armor. Silas stood outside the bedroom that Uriel and I shared with a spear in hand. Loki stood with him. His horns now looked longer, stronger, and dare I say, he looked taller?

I laid Uriel on the soft sheets. She whined, feeling me sit on the bed rather than lay beside her.

"I have to go," I muttered to her. Her eyes were heavy.

As much as I wanted to curl up with her in my arms and take care of her, over and over, through the night, I had to do this for our future. I had to protect her, keep her always, and make sure that the future was still bright for the innocent. If Uriel were taken, all the innocent lives of the world would disappear.

"Please don't," she whispered. "I can't lose you either, Luci."

I chuckled, a smirk forming on my lips. "Do you have that little faith in me?" Her eyes widened for a moment, but my lips silenced her before she could speak.

"I will be back, and until then, you can feel me here." I touched the flame mark on her chest. "Normally a bonded couple spends weeks together to solidify the bond further, but if this isn't taken care of now, there may not be a future for us to share."

Uriel nodded in understanding, her hand taking mine and kissing my fingers. "Come back to me." She cried, pushing herself off the bed before she wrapped her arms around me.

My wings drooped, my heart aching with the pain of leaving her here in a different realm. To be separated from her would hurt us both, but I would protect her at all costs.

"Do as I say," I whispered in her ear. "Be my good girl." Feeling her small kiss on my shoulder, I stood up from the bed. "Sleep, Uriel. It will all be over soon." Taking my hand and putting it across her eyes, her body slumped with her eyes closed, and I tucked her into the bed.

Backing away, I headed to the door, taking one last look at my sleeping mate before locking her in and creating a ward that no one could penetrate.

Hopefully, she will stay there and not venture out.

"Take care of her," I growled to Silas. His narrow slits in his eyes only looked to the ground, bowing with his arm over his chest.

"And you..." I investigated Loki's eyes. They were not filled with the playful look he normally had, they held only fear of the unknown. "Keep you and her safe." I put my hand between his horns, ruffling his hair.

Loki didn't argue back. He jumped forward, pulling me into a hug. "Bring Mom and Dad back please." Loki sniffed. "Tell them I won't cause mischief anymore."

Grunting, I kneeled to the floor. He had grown a head taller since arriving to Poseidon's palace. It could have been his raven emerging or the fact he was getting older, but I now looked up at him, holding his hand.

"You know Mother and Father don't want you to change, right?" Loki's head cocked to the side reminding me of a bird. Smirking, I squeezed his hand. "The God of Mischief is who you are, they don't want you to deny who you are. They have been hit with giving birth to our sister while worrying about me, and now Uriel's prophecy and our bond. They have not forgotten you. It's a hard transition from adolescence to a teenager."

Loki sniffed, shuffling his feet. This was the most I had spoken to him our entire lives. I'm sure it was uncomfortable for him.

"Loki, you are my brother. I've dealt with a lot over the years, things that I kept inside to keep away from you so that you did not have to feel the burden. As you brother, I care for you, I will protect you, and our family. That is all that our parents are trying to do for us as well. Never change, you were made in their image, as was I. You will find yourself such as I have, once you find your mate."

Loki squeezed my hand as I stood. He slung his arms around my body, and his head almost reached the top of my chest. Rubbing his head once more with my calloused hands, I turned to Silas. The unspoken words we exchanged only confirmed he would protect my family with his life.

My slow walk down the hall to the receiving room was filled with tension. Snarls of nagas, centaurs, and minotaurs, and Poseidon's other creatures echoed through the room. Each creature held their own weapons, some of which I had never seen before. Turning my head in question to Poseidon, his head tilted to the open doorway to the god whom I had seen only a handful of times.

His reclusiveness with his mate only made me smile at how vehemently he rejected the idea of living amongst the gods. He preferred the simple life, living with my grandparents in the Black Claw Pack of Earth.

"Vulcan," I muttered, walking towards him.

His arms outstretched, pulling me into a hug. "Just because I like to stay away from the drama of it all doesn't mean I don't know things." He patted my shoulder.

"How is Tamera?" I smiled at him.

"She is well; pregnant with triplets." Vulcan puffed out his chest. "Two girls and a boy" Ares' eyes softened in the corner, holding onto Mariah. "Due any day, but with this new threat, I believe I should be here to verify their safety." Vulcan's stance grew hard.

"So, these weapons will give Poseidon's creatures a fighting chance?"

His smile widened. "It felt good to forge again." Pulling a sword from behind his back, he held it with both hands, one on the blade and one on the handle. "This is for you," Vulcan then whispered. "This will pull your powers into one single blow."

Gripping the handle, the heat from my charred hands channeled into the handle until the entire blade smoked with its heat.

"It will withstand your power. It's the only weapon of its kind. Even stronger than the Demon Sword I made all those years ago for your father. Use it wisely." Vulcan narrowed his eyes. "I cannot make a weapon such as this again. It has taken many years to perfect it for your use."

"How did you know I would need it?" I questioned. "How could you possibly know if you didn't know about Uriel's prophecy?"

"I didn't." He shook his head. "I just knew that if the Fates allowed you to be born with such power, you would do great things. And great things need a suitable weapon, they should not just rely upon the power in the hands."

I released a breath as the gods circled around me closer.

"It's time." Poseidon's trident glowed. "Everyone, gather close. It will be a rough ride between worlds," Poseidon muttered.

Everyone's hand touched the shoulder of the one beside them, forming a chain of warriors. Poseidon closed his eyes, tilting his head back. "May the Fates be with us," he whispered before we were sucked into darkness.

Chapter 56

Lucifer

T raveling as a group, we all held onto each other's shoulders. The dark void between realms was strikingly chaotic compared to the normal stillness one could find here. The silence no longer greeted us, as we ascended to the highest realm. The wind blasted through the crowd as we all tried to escape from the darkness.

Growls and grunts emanated from monsters as their grips loosened, their eyes widening in the cold, harsh wind.

"They won't make it," Poseidon yelled out. His voice was barely audible over the wails of the wind. "There are too many of them, and there is a ward preventing passage from anyone who is not a god."

Ares gripped Mariah tighter as a Minotaur held steadfast to his other arm.

"Send them back!" I yelled. "We do this alone." Before Poseidon's power breached the ceiling of the blackness with us, all of his creations let go, falling back into the dark abyss.

Poseidon wielded his trident automatically, the blast came forth mightily as it tried to capture the monsters slowly fading into oblivion. The grip on his trident wavered with the wind pulling it from his hands. Taking his other arm and latching onto it, lightning struck the base of the three prongs, causing it to burst into bright light. The force of the red lightning bolt made Poseidon fumble, dropping his trident which promptly fell into the black interstice.

Ares pulled Mariah tighter by the waist. I pulled my sword from my back. Vulcan gripped hold of me, shielding the sword from any prying eyes as the bright light of the Celestial Kingdom came into view.

"Put it behind your back," Vulcan ordered as we landed.

It was just the five of us. Vulcan carried his axe before him as we ascended the steps leading to the pearly gates. The sky cracked with bright red and blue bolts of electricity. It looked as if the Apocalypse was already upon the Celestial Realm. The palace was in shambles, crumbling in on itself, and darkness obstructed the formerly bright clouds creating a dark gray sky.

Poseidon looked back over the steps, back down into the abyss that engulfed his creations, separating them from us. His throat bobbed, his fist tightening on itself in the absence of his trident.

"I will forge another," Vulcan put his hand on his shoulder, pulling him away. An upheaval of wind pushed Poseidon back toward the void.

"I don't care about the trident. What of them?" His voice was barely above a whisper. "They are my family." Mariah pulled Poseidon away, helping Vulcan.

"They are still there; we will find them." She patted his arm. "But we won't be able to find them until we fix this." Mariah's glare shifted to the tops of the crumbling palace towers. Ares unsheathed his weapon as his mate did the same.

The sword given to me hung on my back, clear from view until it was absolutely necessary as we advanced, donned in our traditional armor. My body was covered in black leather bindings with a corset-like vest which sat low in the back to permit my wings to spread. They emerged automatically, my deep black wings dripped ash and red embers of flames as we scaled the granite steps.

"Looking badass, little nephew." Ares looked me up and down. "Never thought I would see the day where you could control it."

I grunted in agreement. "All thanks to my mate, she centers me," I muttered, my eyes not leaving the unhinged doors of the once magnificent palace.

My mark burned hot as I entered the palace, we were becoming sacrifices ourselves. We had no other plan than to face Zeus head-on. Even without Poseidon's trident, we expected to succeed. This many gods fighting against him at once should surely beat one of the Original Twelve, even if he was High God.

I surveyed the area as we walked forward. The crumbling walls and the cracked floors all held black ash; the entryway was completely dark as we edged towards the throne room. If Zeus was going to be dramatic about all of this, of course, he would sit upon his high and mighty throne to try to belittle us.

Angels stood sentry by the walls. They no longer displayed bright white wings; their attire was instead that of gray robes and pallid skin. As I saw Gabriel with the light faded from his once golden eyes, my fists clenched the dagger in its holster on my thigh. They had all succumbed to whatever evil Zeus let possess his body.

"I'm waiting!" The taunting began as soon as we entered. The strongest of the gods all were held in chains, securely bolted to the floor. My father, who was bound next to Zeus' throne, was chained with both hands on the floor, hunched over. His red eyes blazed with fury as he fought to free himself from the shackles.

"Curse the Fates," Ares growled. "What the fuck happened? Something isn't right," he whispered harshly. "Mariah, get out of here."

Mariah, as stubborn as her mate shook her head. "Through thick and thin, my love." Her hand reached for his squeezing it tightly.

"This feeling"—Poseidon clutched his heart—"I've felt it before. I know it." Poseidon tried to retreat, but I pulled him closer to me by his arm.

"Where is Uriel?" Zeus waved his hand, standing. "This trial is regarding her parent's treatment of her. I would expect her presence since she is the prime witness." Zeus descended the throne, his blackened robes skimming each step.

"Why are they chained?" Vulcan spoke up. Holding his axe close to his chest, Zeus walked toward his son.

"My son." His hand reached out to cup Vulcan's cheek.

Vulcan ripped away from his touch and spat at his feet. "Hades is more of a father than you."

Zeus' eyes didn't even acknowledge the statement, only chuckled as his attention went back to me. "I'm waiting," Zeus hummed.

"And I want answers," I growled. "Why is my father chained to your throne and why are all the gods being held against their will?"

Zeus stepped back, snapping his fingers. A light shone on the darkened corner of the room. My mother sat in a cage with Lilith in her arms.

"Luci," she whispered, shaking her head. "Don't bring her here," she sniffed. "Don't bring Uriel or it will be death—" Zeus hit the cage with a bolt of lightning, and the cage rattled shooting electricity up my mother's body. Lilith screamed briefly at the intensity, but Mother's scream didn't falter.

"You bastard, leave my mate alone!" Father rattled the chains, dark smoke pooling down the stairs. "I'm going to rip you to pieces," he hissed. Hair sprouted from my father's back, but his shift was incomplete, he could not shift into his beastly hellhound with the restraints on his body.

"Time is wasting—"

Before Zeus could finish, I slung my arm behind my back to procure my specially forged sword. My hands heated as I wielded it channeling my power into the iron as I buried it into Zeus' chest. Every bit of my power was concentrated, pouring into the hole of his heart.

Cracking a smile, Ares pulled his sword from his sheath only to be slung to the floor by a snap of Zeus' finger. Darkened angels pulled Ares and Mariah away as my sword lodged firmly into Zeus' gut. Vulcan, going for Zeus' legs, was also pulled away by the sallow angles.

The angels' eyes glazed over black, revealing they were not in control of their bodies as they wrestled with the strongest of the gods. Angered by my sword's inability to be dislodged from Zeus, I let go, lengthening my claws and expanding my wings to their massive height. What was left of the light that hung in the room was obscured by the mass of my burning feathers hovering over the God of the Sky.

He calmly looked up at me as I floated over his body. My claws ripped through the air with a high-pitched whistle. Zeus caught my wrist mid-air as he rose above me. His hand was strong enough to crack my wrist, but not enough to stop the red plasma that ran through my veins from singeing his hands.

"My, my, what a strong one you are," Zeus muttered. "Your power even exceeds that of your father," he tutted. "I guess it isn't so surprising though. You are the cause of the destruction of all the realms." Growling, I pulled my hand away, but bindings of red lightning gripped my wrists. They were so heavy, that they dropped me to the floor with their weight.

"But not strong enough," he chuckled. My wings sprawled across the floor. I heard my mother crying in the corner with Lilith clinging to her tightly. Heaving ragged breaths, I reviewed every plan that formed in my thoughts.

While Uriel slept in my arms, we thought, we planned for every possibility of what could happen with Zeus. He only carried so much power; he was just one god. If even three gods stood together, surely, we could easily take down one, even if he was the High God.

My father, strongest of all of the gods, now sat on his knees at Zeus' feet. His fangs dripped with black acidic venom as he watched Zeus, his younger brother sit back on his throne. Zeus pushed his robes away, hitting my father in the face. He chuckled, dragging his index finger mindlessly on the arm of the chair. His unamused face had me seething. Poseidon was still standing beside me, doing nothing, paralyzed in fear.

Zeus rolled his eyes, flicking bits of electricity toward Poseidon's way. "Such a scaredy-cat, aren't you?" The dark angel, Gabriel, gripped his arms to pull him away. "Or maybe you are simply pathetic, like those creations of yours that couldn't even make it up here?" Zeus laughed loudly with thick, black tears running down his face. He flung the tear toward Poseidon.

Poseidon growled, and his descending fangs reminded me of a shark. "You won't get away with it," Poseidon yelled. "Hurting them, hurting us, you won't get away with any of it!"

Gabriel blinked his black eyes twice before his hand covered Poseidon's mouth. All around the room, angels were covering gods that sat in chains on the floor. Hecate's eyes brimmed with tears at the sight of this evil, this power, that was too powerful for even her to control.

"What the fuck happened to you?" I snapped. "What happened with being happy and ruling over the sky? Why do you have to go and fuck with people's lives? What the hell happened to you?" I rattled the heavy bolts of electricity holding me down. "Uriel healed you of your burden. You should be fine!"

Zeus' eyes narrowed, pounding the armrests. "Enough!" His body lay back on his throne. "Maybe I was tired of not having a mate; maybe I was ready for a change. I'm no longer the 'lost god' that takes orders from some woman who only *seems* to have her life in order."

Zeus' hand waved, beckoning for a chained woman and angel to enter—Hera and Michael.

They were worse for wear. Their bodies were blackened with scorch marks from the lightning that tortured them, and they were further humiliated with their forced nudity. Michael tried to shield Hera, to keep her body covered but his wings had been severely charred, so they didn't do much.

"Now that the goddess of Marriage and Family failed in her domain not once, but twice"—he paused for effect—"for one unable to please her partner and two, not able to protect their daughter, I think it is high time for her to face a suitable punishment. I just need the girl of the hour and then we can witness Hera's third failure"—Hera sobbed in the corner, looking to the ground—"the daughter she couldn't control. The daughter she couldn't keep hidden away to protect the innocent souls of the realms. The lives of every creature lay in her hands, and I will give her the ultimate choice." Zeus threw his head back to laugh.

"She will get to choose; she can save the gods—her family—she can save the helpless humans, or she can save the supernaturals. Only one realm will be permitted to survive; it will be the most exciting thing to witness." Zeus rubbed his hands.

"You have gone bloody mad!" I roared. "What the fuck happened to you? You twisted—" A slap of lightning jolted through my face. My mother screamed, begging Zeus to stop. The bolts continued to rain down upon my face. Blood pooled to my collar bone before dripping down my torso.

"In fact, I'm even going to give *you* a choice, son of Hades." Zeus pulled me up by my neck. He darted his head to my mother in the iron cage and back to me, while his sinister grin leaked an oozing black tar from his lips. "Summon Uriel here. If you don't..." he paused looking at my mother, "your baby sister and beloved mother will pay the consequences."

Father's chains rattled as he howled in pain. "Don't you fucking touch my mate!" Part of the chain ripped from the bolted floor. Five angels hurdled towards him, pushing him down, and quickly muzzling the snout he spouted.

Gritting my teeth, I rumbled through my own thickened chains. They sizzled, burning deeper into my flesh with every movement.

Zeus bent down, looking me in the eye. "Summon her."

"Don't listen to him!" Mother screamed. "Don't bring her here! We will be fi—" Mother's cries were silenced when the lightning struck the cage, causing a loud crash.

"The choice is yours," Zeus hummed. "Bring her here, or they will pay the consequence."

"I'm here." A beautifully sweet, soft voice echoed through the chaotic halls. All eyes turned behind us.

Fates don't let it be her. Not her. Not here. Not now.

Why the fuck didn't she listen to me?

"You wanted to see me?" Her voice rang out quietly as Zeus' sadistic grin widened on his face.

Chapter 57

Uriel

"Get up."

A thunderous crack rang through the room. My chest rose heavily while I tried to sit up. My mark burned my fingers as they probed its form on my chest. Looking about the room, my tangled hair caught in my face. Brushing it away, I flung off the covers that Luci had meticulously tucked around my body.

Did he leave already?

The mark burned furiously with my thoughts of Luci running through my head. Dread swept over me the moment I rounded the bed. My bare feet slapped the wooden floors, and my hands pulled at the handles of the bedroom door. The heavy door cracked with a long whine; the pressure of its weight became unbearable.

"Hang on." Loki's voice came through the door. The combination of my pulling and his pushing forced the door open enough for me to squeeze through.

"Lucifer wants you to stay in there. The ward will keep you safe. I'm surprised you can move it so well," Loki looked me up and down. Loki's appearance was starkly different than before he first transformed into a raven. He was already taller than me despite only being ten years old.

Silas cleared his throat, his tentacles popping on the floor. "Goddess Uriel, your mate and the others have already left for the Celestial Kingdom. Our orders are for you to remain here with us."

Silas' small smile only made me grind my teeth. Sure, I wanted to be Luci's 'good girl,' but if we were dealing with Zeus, I could help him. I've helped Zeus once before, and I could do it again. Having everyone else fight my own battles, over a prophecy about me, seemed silly.

Aren't I the one able to change my own fate?

Silas' lips frowned, as his non-existent eyebrows raised on his forehead. "Surely, you do not plan to—" Great thunder from outside the palace roared. It wasn't the normal sound of thunder; it was more muffled like the loud sound filtered through a thick pillow.

"I didn't think you could hear thunder in the sea." Loki mused, walking down the hall to the first window.

I didn't think so either.

The waves could be rolling on the surface of the water, but beneath the waves and the heavy currents, the ocean floor should remain untouched. This was not the case when we looked outside into the garden where the kelp was being uprooted, even though it was inside the large atmospheric bubble of Poseidon's Kingdom.

"Master has our home mimic those conditions outside of the sphere." Silas twisted his lips, his hand sitting on the window frame. "The ocean must be in great turmoil if the plant life here is being uprooted."

"Imagine the surface," I whispered, grabbing Loki's hand. "It could be ten times worse above the water."

Loki shook his head. "No, surely not. Maybe Poseidon is angry and that's why the waves move."

Silas stepped away from the window, motioning for us to follow him down the hall. It was eerily quiet as we entered the room we were forbidden from before. Silas parted the shells, but Loki and I remained outside. "Come." Silas waved again.

We squeezed our hands together as we walked inside. The dim room was filled with purple and blue lights, and a round table sat in the middle. Loki and I huddled near the clinking shells of the doorway way as Silas put his hands on the table.

"Poseidon cannot control the seas as well when he is out of his element. If there is a raging storm on the surface causing the forceful waves, it is being created by something else."

Stepping forward, I let go of Loki's hand and silently walked to the table. It wasn't really a table at all, it was a map of all the oceans. On one side was Bergarian where white caps trailed across the seas of both the East and West. Earth was no different, the Pacific and Atlantic oceans were riddled with hurricanes, waterspouts, and tsunamis. There were even huge storms that swept across both ocean and land.

"Zeus," I muttered. "He controls the sky. If his storms are powerful enough, they can invade the water." Silas only hummed in agreement.

Biting my lip, my thoughts went spiraling down into a dark place. As much as I loved spending my time with Luci, as much as I loved the life around me, the only way to stop this was for me to face the evil myself.

If I don't follow Luci to the Celestial Kingdom, the worlds will end, and innocent lives will continue to die. The fate of the realms was in my hands, no matter how much Luci wanted to protect me. If I didn't go many would die. Even if I did, we still may enter the same fate, but I had to try.

What could I possibly do to make this madness stop?

Gripping the table with my head hovering over the moving picture, a tear dropped into one of the oceans. It rippled, calming the white caps, ceasing their travel over the ocean. Each tear that fell rippled, all the way into the next realm, calming the seas and the storms. My innocent gasp as I watched the map of the world calm had me grip my fist.

"Go." A gentle voice echoed in my head.

"Go."

My eyes glanced around the room. I only could see Loki and Silas watching the moving map before me still.

"Go." Each voice was different, more determined than the last.

Go? Go after I promised Luci that I would stay?

My fingers played with each other, interlacing with one another until finally, with a determined spirit, I made my decision. I knew what I had to do. I knew exactly what was required of me. Looking to my hands, I traced my fingertips that once touched a lying soul. I sucked the lie right from their body and it turned to ash before dropping to the floor. Even with my powers still weak, I was able to pull the guilt from Zeus when he was burdened.

I was no warrior. I could barely lift the weights Luci used every day to strengthen his body. I could barely reach the top of the bed without jumping. In every sense of the word, I was weak. Weak in body, but I wasn't weak in the mind. Luci made up for my weak body, and in return, I would use my newfound power to help him, the gods, my family, and the realms.

"We have to go," I muttered, still looking at my hands. Loki put his arm around me, hugging me to his chest. "Please," I spoke more boldly.

Loki's smirk grew, and he brushed his fingernails against his black shirt to polish them. "I've never been one to follow rules, and I'm not about to start now." Loki grabbed my hand to pull me outside when Silas' tentacles gripped my ankle.

"I can't let you do this; I promised my master. I promised the Prince of the Underworld to take care of you." Silas' tentacles lifted his body to twice the size of Loki. "I have to keep my word," he growled.

"There will be no Master if I don't go." I pulled at my leg. "There will be no more gods, no humans, no worlds of fantasy. If I don't go, we all perish. If I go, we may have a chance."

Silas held onto my leg. The inner battle he had was enough for his body to sink back down to eye level.

"No more worlds mean no more mates. No chance of finding the other half of your soul, Silas."

Silas stiffened, and the fluid movements of his tentacles ceased. A heavy sigh left his body as he loosened his arm, freeing my leg. Silas said no other words of opposition; he just gripped me into a tightened hug.

"Do what you must, and when you return, please save me from your mate's wrath."

I giggled pushing him away. "Everything will be fine." I spouted the lie from my lips.

I wasn't sure if everything would be alright, but I had to try.

"Getting there might be difficult." Loki broke the awkward tension. "No carriage to go between worlds."

Silas chuckled, crawling to the massive bookcase beside the bed. "You won't need it. You have your animal, the raven." Silas flipped the pages of an old book, opening up to a section on the gods who could shift. One was Athena who could turn into an owl. She was able to fly between realms with ease with her wings.

Loki gripped the book, reading it with intensity. "This first flight is going to be a bitch," he muttered his feathers beginning to sprout from his body.

"Language," I whispered.

For the next thirty minutes, Loki worked with Silas at the front of the palace. His raven had doubled in size since the first time he transformed. Mighty horns stuck out from his head; his wingspan was nearly equal to Luci's. The more he flew around the courtyard, the better he became. His large wingspan gave me hope that we would be able to fly between worlds and arrive in the Celestial Kingdom, in time to help. The pain in my chest was growing by the minute and I feared we may be too late. Loki's feathers ruffled as he tilted his head behind him indicating he was ready for me to mount his back.

Silas looked on worriedly, clutching a bag in hand. "At least take this," he muttered, pulling my hands securely around it. "It is purified sea water, only available in Poseidon's personal pools." Peeking inside the bag, there was a small glass vile shaped like a mermaid which held the liquid. "It can heal small wounds, but I'm not sure it will work with the power you face."

"Thank you," I whispered. As I tried to mount, Silas stopped me, pointing to my necklace.

"What is this?" He pointed to the small black pearl. My bright white manta ray leather was a stark contrast against the pearl Luci found on the beach.

"Luci gave this black pearl to me. On our first date on the beach." I admired it, still feeling the pang in my chest. I prayed to the Fates he was still alright.

Silas studied it, the suction cups on the tips of his fingers playing with it. He hummed, gently placing it back on my chest. "There is a human story from the Tahitians of Earth. The God of Peace and Fertility, Oro, fell in love with a Tahitian princess. He offered a black pearl as a symbol of his love."

My shoulders slumped, feeling the heaviness of the necklace. "Luci gave me this the day he told me he loved me," I sniffed. Smiling at the tiny pearl, I took my leg and swung it over Loki.

We will win this. I'm not sure how, but we will.

"Are you ready, Loki?"

"Caw"

Silas stood back, crossing his arm over his chest in salute.

With heavy wings, Loki lifted from the ground with me on top of him. My small wings would be no match for traveling between the realms. Loki let out a mighty 'caw' before pushing himself upwards towards the sky.

I was going to get our family back with the little plan I devised. I prayed to the Fates it would be enough.

We landed just outside the gates. My home wasn't the same as it was before. Lightning and thunder rolled through the eerie sky, buildings toppled over, and rain poured from above. My heart stopped as I heard screaming from my mate.

Loki ruffled his feathers, grabbing me by my arm with his claw.

"I know. Remember the plan," I whispered to him. He hopped along the ground three times before jumping into the sky. His large form went unnoticed with the rain and ice spilling from the darkened sky.

Not wasting another moment, I ran up the stairs with my two small daggers at my side. I paused noticing my wings barely met half the height of the dark angels that lined the hallways. They were looking straight at me, but not seeing me. My hand waved in front of their faces until I heard a scream.

Ember.

Running forward, hiding behind the unhinged doorway, I watched as Zeus leaned over Luci who was chained to the floor—everyone was. Athena's neck was pinned to the ground, Hades was half-shifted into his wolf bound to the throne, and so many others were clearly in pain.

"Don't listen to him!" Ember cried from a cage in the back corner. She held onto Lilith who was screaming in terror. "Don't bring her here!" Ember cried out again just before lightning hit the cage, silencing her.

Zeus's words echoed through the halls demanding Lucifer to bring me or have his mother and sister pay the consequences.

I will not leave that guilt on my mate.

Stepping forward with my head held high, gripping the black pearl around my neck, my judging eyes hit Zeus. "I'm here... You wanted to see me?" My voice shook more than I wanted. The pad of my shoes drug on the marbled floor.

A malicious grin settled on Zeus' face. My face paled seeing the dirty complexion. This wasn't the same god I saw at Lilith's party, nor the one who laid on the floor of Hades' throne room wallowing in his guilt. There was no guilt in this imposter; there was only hatred and lust for revenge.

My calculating steps were too slow; Zeus shoved Luci back to the floor while wails from the goddesses pleaded for me to leave. I held my ground with my hand gripping the dagger that would do me no good.

Zeus' heavy breath fanned my face as he encroached. Brimstone and rot filled my lungs. His eyes were full of fury, no longer the pale blue seeped in regret they were before.

"W-who are you?" I forced my breath.

"Zeus. Who else do you think I would be, little goddess?"

The pang in my body hurt so much at his tremendous lie. Luci yelled for me to run, to save myself.

How could I save myself when half of my soul was chained to the floor? How could I leave knowing that all the realms would be destroyed?

"Lie," I said aloud. Ember gripped Lilith tighter, and Luci's mouth hung open as I stepped forward.

'Zeus' stepped back, his brows furrowing.

"You are *not* Zeus, God of the Sky."

Chapter 58

Under the Moon

Uriel's small body barely reached mid-chest of the mighty Zeus. His towering form held a dark shadow over her as she clutched the handle of her dagger at her side. In no way, shape, or form, would this dagger do her any good, but the small amount of comfort it gave her steadied the quiver of her shaky breath.

Lucifer, still held to the floor by the thick lightning restraints, growled. He was livid that his mate would dare disobey him, but most of all, he was worried for her safety. The prophecy was unfolding in front of his eyes. His beloved Uriel was hanging by a mere thread, just a helpless little lamb ripe for Zeus to slaughter.

Lucifer grunted, fighting against his restraints, his wings breaking free, and his claws scratching the already ruined floor. Angels fought back, pushing him lower, the electrical bands holding him tightly to the floor only grew stronger as Zeus looked over his shoulder, smirking.

"Pray tell, who do you think I am?" 'Zeus' lulled his head to the side in amusement.

This tiny goddess in front of him had him laughing from within. She came so willingly, so easily, because she had already bonded to the God of Destruction, making it so easy for her to find him. His once complicated, meticulous plans were paying off. His back straightened with the confidence building inside him.

"I'm not sure." Uriel glanced at the god with her golden eyes. Her position wavered when she saw his eyes go from the deepest navy to a bright blue. Those bright blue eyes she remembered from so long ago when her touch healed Zeus from his burdens.

Hera and Michael shivered in the corner as their naked bodies were incessantly poked and prodded by the darkened angels. Their torn skin dripped golden blood to the floor, but they did not dare to make a sound as they watched the scene unfold. Just like Hera and Michael, all the other gods held quietly onto their souls watching Uriel's interaction with the Zeus look-alike. News had traveled fast of Uriel's prophecy and how their lives, along with the lives of all living things, hung in the balance with the fate of this tiny goddess.

Meanwhile, the gentle tapping of small claws hopping along the floor neared the cage that held Ember. In the short time Loki had discovered his raven, his skills had grown exceedingly. He was able to manipulate his size in just a matter of minutes after he studied the books Poseidon had in his library. His now small body hopped between the bars, pecking lightly on his mother to get her attention.

Ember stared down at the bird, immediately knowing who it was. "Loki?" she whispered in her shaky voice. His head rubbed against Ember's thigh in greeting. "You need to let your father free," she whispered hastily. "Luci is out in the open, but your father, you could help him."

Loki opened his beak in understanding. The vile around his neck that Uriel had given him would help heal his father's wounds so he could help Lucifer. Loki got to work, gently hopping across the floor. No god or goddess paid him any mind, assuming he was just a lost, stupid bird.

Uriel's eyes remained on Zeus, making sure his attention never diverted from her. "You are something different," Uriel mused, trying to get the mighty god to talk. Zeus stepped closer to her, and Lucifer shook the chains now covering his wings.

"That's right." Zeus' dirty bare feet slapped the floor.

"Something different entirely." Uriel scratched her face with her hand. Trying to buy time. She had to stall until another god or goddess was free because she knew her physical strength was no match against this god.

"Time is of the essence, Uriel." Zeus backed away from her. "Come."

Walking with Zeus, since she had no other choice, she walked past her mate that lay on the floor. The helplessness in his eyes was overshadowed by the rage fueling him to get to his mate.

"Don't even think about it."

Zeus didn't even look over his shoulder when Uriel stopped to stare at her mate. Lucifer's glare at Uriel, warning her to leave, didn't make her budge. She mouthed, 'I love you,' before turning back to follow the God of the Sky. Lucifer's breath hitched. It was not that he didn't appreciate the sentiment, but he knew those words had a double meaning—they meant goodbye.

Uriel rounded the table, rather similar to the table back in the Underwater Palace. This time it was folded into a scene of Earth—New York City, a place where heavy populations of innocent people lived, and children played.

"Time," Uriel muttered to herself, watching fire drench the skies from above. Glancing back to Lucifer, she saw the darkness in his eyes as the bright red electricity engulfed him further.

"I'm channeling his power of destruction," Zeus explained, "sucking him dry of the power he holds inside and putting it here."

With a wave of his hand over the table, fire rained from the sky of the city displayed, causing countless buildings to go up in flames. Women and children ran from their homes into the streets only to succumb to the fire raining from the sky.

"No." Uriel shook her head. "You can't do this. They are innocent. They did nothing to you!"

Zeus chuckled, not moving from his place. His eyes danced across the apparition on the table. "Oh, they aren't dead yet," he scoffed. "But soon, it will happen. This is just a glimpse into the future. In time, this is what the Earth will look like." Zeus' hand waved over the table, changing the image to show the entirety of Earth and of Bergarian. Both worlds were enveloped in flames. Terrible screams of pain and terror rang in Uriel's ear, begging for mercy.

"Make it stop!" She cried out, her ears bleeding from the innocent screams. "You cannot do this to them! They did nothing!"

Zeus rolled his head back in laughter. "Oh, but I can, and I will!" he growled. "I am time. I control the patterns of life. I dictate the life and death of people that my sons and daughters have created. I am the true ruler of all the cosmos."

Uriel took her hand from her ear; blood stained her fingers as the screams finally ceased. "Father of time?" Uriel muttered quietly.

Remembering her studies, she knew of the Titan that was said to be the Father of all the Cosmos. Her research ran deeper when her mother was gone, uncovering a name that had been wiped away from all the history books of the Celestial Kingdom. Only the humans still had such history written.

"Kronos," she muttered. Zeus stood back from the table, rounding it to come closer. "You are Kronos," she said, louder for all to hear. Shouts escaped from the gods who had broken free from the angels' grips but were quickly silenced again by darkened hands over their mouths.

"You are smarter than you look." Kronos smiled wickedly with black tar falling from his mouth.

Uriel pursed her lips, not liking the undertone of his voice. "That is impossible," she added.

Ares broke free from the angel's hold on him, stumbling to the ground. "I felt you in that damn box!" He hissed. "There is no way—" Kronos used Zeus' power to wrap red lightning around Ares' mouth.

Uriel's eyes widened looking at Mariah. She was held against the wall by three angels, hands bound above her head, but a certain glow to Mariah's stomach didn't go unnoticed. Bright light radiated from the depths of Mariah's womb in a rhythmic beat.

"Flowers," Uriel breathed. This had to end quickly, for the sake of everyone, especially the new innocent heart that fluttered in Mariah's belly.

"Oh, I assure you, it is quite possible." Kronos touched the face that he had disguised himself with. "I am the father of the God of the Sky. I am within all of you." His hand waved around the room. "I am the Father of the Cosmos, and the things that live within. I am the Titan of Time; ruler of when things should be and when they should not."

Uriel looked to Lucifer. His face was red with fury, trying to fight the bonds that strapped him down. His black wings convulsed while he struggled to get to his knees. Lucifer looked at Uriel pleadingly. "Leave," he mouthed. "Don't." He shook his head.

Uriel wanted to listen to her mate, but this was her battle to bear, even if she was scared to death. She was not the Goddess of Bravery, Fighting, or Courage. She was just the Goddess of Innocence and Grace; the one that wanted to protect the lives of those who had done nothing wrong and did not deserve this sort of death.

"It took time," Kronos continued. "but I figured out a way to connect with my children. All magic grows over time, and no one even saw me coming." Kronos walked to Hera, picking her up by the back of her hair. "Especially this one." Kronos' drooled tar ran down Hera's cheek.

"I planned this from the very beginning. I planted the seed for you to keep Uriel hidden so her powers wouldn't develop," he whispered. "She is now too weak to defend those she holds so dear." Hera sobbed as Kronos dropped her to the floor.

"Taking Zeus' body was no problem. My spirit can mingle between any of my children, but since Zeus was the one that ultimately destroyed me so long ago, I felt some revenge was in order." He shrugged his shoulders. "I can freely move my spirit between both of our bodies."

"Maybe you shouldn't eat your children, then they wouldn't have to rise against you," Uriel spat. The fire she felt in her mark had her snapping in ways she never thought she could. She wanted nothing more than to end the arrogant Titan, but how was she to do that?

"Listen here, granddaughter," Kronos sauntered his way to Uriel. His robes danced across the floor until they stood chest to chest. "I am the King of the Cosmos. I will wipe everything that my sons and daughters have created, and then I will create a new era, a new world that lives by *my* rules." Kronos gritted his teeth.

Uriel felt a surge in her body. Her proximity to the Titan had her seething at the maliciousness of his darkened soul. He was teeming with sin, fraught with an evil that repulsed her little body and compelled her to extend her hand to utilize what little power she thought she had.

"NO!" Lucifer screamed from the sidelines. Uriel grabbed Kronos' hand, her golden eyes looking into the depths of Kronos' soul.

Kronos only smirked, watching the glow of his hands. "What are you going to do, little goddess?" Kronos watched with a smile on his face.

Uriel's mouth set into a firm, thin line as the warmth grew hotter. Her other hand cupped the same large hand of Kronos until Uriel's hands turn black. The mocking smirk on Krono's face vanished upon seeing the change in Uriel.

Loki, who had been working at the throne pecking away the chains restraining his father, finally released the last one. Hades completed the shift into his monstrous hellhound, but was still weak from his powers being drained. Loki shook the vile necklace off his neck, pushing it towards Hades. He picked up the vial, swallowing it whole. The thick fur sprouted on his back stood on end as the healing power surged through his body rejuvenating him.

Hades lunged forward, knocking over the angels who were immobilizing Lucifer. His fangs sliced into wings, causing feathers to fly around him. Angels scattered away upon noticing the fury Hades unleashed now that he regained his full strength. Hades' razor-sharp teeth ripped into the electric chains, dropping them to the floor in shambles.

As soon as Lucifer felt the chains extricated from his body, he burst forth using his wings at full speed, covering half the length of the room in a flash. His hands charred black, dripping molten plasma to the floor. Lucifer was going to end Kronos. He would eviscerate the Titan once and for all. The rage built inside him once he darted his eyes to Uriel. Half her body had been encrusted with soot, and black smoke was being sucked into her lungs as her hands held steadfast to Kronos.

Black tar no longer ran down Zeus' face. The gray hair of his beard brightened back to the typical white. Kronos fought against Uriel's hands to free himself, but Uriel stood firm, staring at him with her golden eyes.

"It's finished, Kronos." her whisper echoed through the walls.

More black ash worked up Uriel's arms and her neck. Lucifer growled, seeing his mate's white skin soiled. It cracked, leaving hints of red underneath her. Lucifer grabbed the mark on his chest, feeling the lamb on his chest burn bright.

The evil power was fading in the room. Angels knocked out of the stupor with their wings turning back to the glorious white and their eyes returned to their normal lustrous color. Confusion ensued in the room as Ember burst from the cage after her mate set her free.

"Kill him now!" She directed her cry to Lucifer.

Vulcan, holding the sword he forged for Lucifer, pushed it into Lucifer's hand. Vulcan studied Kronos, whose borrowed form had become weak. It no longer looked like the evil still saturated Zeus' body, but one could not be sure.

"It will destroy what is intended!" Vulcan hurried his words.

In the seconds that transpired, Lucifer had already flapped his wings, pushing Kronos' hands away from Uriel with a mighty gust of wind. Kronos laid on his back with Lucifer straddling him. His dark navy eyes were disturbed as Lucifer raised up his sword.

"I am the God of Destruction," Lucifer hissed, "and it is this day that I end you." Pushing the blade deep within Kronos' chest, black tar oozed from the wound and covered the sword. Lucifer wasn't satisfied, so he raised his sword again to plummet it into Kronos' head. The crack of bone had Ember whine from afar, Hades holding his mate tightly.

Lucifer pushed Kronos away from Uriel; her body sucked enough evil from his body which caused her to sway. Vulcan, seeing Uriel begin to fall raced to her side, holding her with his arms. Gently he sat on the floor holding her. Vulcan pushed his long beard away to look upon her face. Both were Hera's children, but with different fathers. His half-sister stared at him with heavy eyes.

"Is he gone?" Uriel choked. The blackness continued to rise above her neck and to her cheeks.

"Yes, he's gone, you did it." Vulcan wiped away a tear. "You did a great job."

Uriel chuckled, trying to raise her hand to touch Vulcan's bearded face. "Your eyes"—Uriel paused—"look like my mom's." Uriel choked on her words. Her head rolled back, unable to hold the weight of her head.

"Uriel?" Vulcan took his other large hand, cradling her head to his chest. "That's because I'm your half-brother," Vulcan's voice cracked.

Uriel's faint, forced smile had her dimming eyes brighten for a moment. "I've always wanted a brother." Her eyes fluttered closed as Lucifer rushed to her side. Still covered in the black tar-like blood.

"Uriel, you wake up, damnit!" Lucifer took Uriel from Vulcan's hands. Vulcan's eyes never left his sisters. "You can't go to sleep." Lucifer's frustration came out as tears. Gods and goddess surrounded the recently mated couple, feeling the goddess' soul fading deep in their hearts.

"You wake up right now," Lucifer gently shook her.

"Are you okay, Luci?" She coughed. "Are you hurt?" Her eyes closed prompting Lucifer to shake her gently.

"I won't be if you don't stay awake!" His tears turned to sobs. The pain in his chest growing so intense, he thought he would die.

He *would* die. He would die without her if she left him here alone. He would go on a rampage, begging the gods to take his life, to help him leave this world to meet his mate amongst the stars.

"I'm just so tired." Her hand reached for Lucifer's cheek, but fell short, dropping back into her lap. The black sludge coating her body crusted over. Her dried skin began flaking in the gentle breeze. "My parents?" she whispered, closing her eyes.

"They are fine," Lucifer sobbed into her chest. "Fates don't let her leave me damnit! Please, Uriel, stay with me."

Chapter 59

Lucifer

"For fucks sake!" I gently shook Uriel, jostling the black ash so that it began falling out of her shining hair. Her body was covered with filth; all the dirt and sin she pulled from Kronos consumed her body.

"Someone do something?" I had never felt more helpless in my life, holding my mate in my arms, watching the light in her soul fade. Her breathing was slow, barely detectable, the rise in her chest became shallower with each breath.

"Hecate!" I screamed for her to come near. The gods parted, looking down at us both with tears in her eyes.

"I—" she began but I quickly yelled at her.

"Don't you say you can't help!" Boiling tears ran down my cheeks, dripping onto Uriel's skin. "Don't you dare!"

Hecate walked backwards; her hands folded over her lap backing away. My eyes searched the crowd.

"Athena!" My voice cracked.

Many gods and goddesses looked away in pain. They couldn't even look upon my mate; the pitiful sniffles leaving their weeping faces did not compare to what I felt. My soul was breaking; my Uriel was fading fast preparing for her soul to join the stars.

Athena walked forward, daring to kneel beside me. Putting her hand on my shoulder, the sympathy in her eyes only told me one thing: she could do nothing.

"NO!" I roared, bringing Uriel's body closer to me. Her neck lacked any support; I held it to my chest, grabbing her face to look into my eyes. "Come on bunny," I whispered in her ear. "You can't leave me, not now."

Burying my nose into her neck, it smelled of nothing but sulfur and sin. I kissed her neck, anyway, trailing it until I reached her beautiful, chapped lips. It was the only part of her body not charred with black.

"I will see you soon"—I petted her hair—"because I can't live without you. Not now, not ever." I shook my head, my tears falling on her ashen cheeks.

Hera and Michael sat at the feet of my mate; Hera's sobs barely drowned out my own. Michael held onto Hera with one arm and rested his other hand on his daughter's ankle. Vulcan held one of Uriel's hands, rubbing his thumb across her flaking black knuckles.

The cries continued for what felt like it could have been hours before my mother knelt down beside me. Taking her finger, she brushed the messy hair from my face. "You've mated," she whispered. "I can see that now that my power is returning." Her tiny hand pulled down the front part of Uriel's dress, exposing my mark.

"We haven't had time to enjoy each other." My voice cracked. "I always wanted her, even when I didn't know that I did." Gazing into Uriel's discolored face, I pulled her head close, cupping her cheek. Slowly, I pressed my lips to the only skin that was left uncharred.

Expecting my calloused lips to feel cold from her pouty lips, since the warmth was leaving her body, I was stunned to feel warmth flow into her. Pulling back momentarily, I noticed the charred ash around her lips faded.

Noticing the same, Mother gripped my shoulder. "Kiss her more," she urged, "more!"

Not hesitating, my lips slammed back to Uriel. I didn't just leave my lips on hers; I kissed those lips with unabated breath, sucking her lips, pulling at whatever evil tainted her soul. Her face warmed slowly. My eyes slid open watching her beautiful face emerge from under the ash that was flaking away. Rubbing her face, more flakes fell away from her.

Rosey cheeks, fluttering lashes—her face had become completely clear. I wanted to pull my lips away to see the beautiful face before me, the face that has soothed me since the first day I laid eyes upon her. However, I dared not let go, not until I took every bit of that suffocating evil away from her.

Gasps echoed through the crowd; Hera screamed for joy as I felt Uriel's arms slip around me. Her fingers ran through my hair until she gripped hold of my neck. Utter joy raced through my body, and the bond burned bright into my chest.

There is no damn way I will ever let go now. I would never let my lips leave hers again so she would stay alive.

Here, in my arms, is where she will stay forever. Never again will I let her out of my sight. I will never leave her to face any danger, and she will touch no one with any evil within. I will snuff out all the evil that dared try to take her away from me.

Uriel giggled, trying to push me away, but I held on tighter. Her heavy sigh let me force my tongue into her mouth to taste every part of her. The sulfuric smell lifted from her body as gardenias and vanilla replaced the rotting stench. My mate was here, she was moving with her heart beating steady in her chest. My hands roamed her body, feeling the softness of her skin. The top she wore was pushed aside so I could feel the tempting curves of her body.

By the Fates, she was alive.

"Luci." Mother nudged me. "There are other people present," she whispered.

"Tell them to close their eyes," I mumbled, ready to grab ahold of Uriel's breasts.

Someone's continued throat clearing had Uriel stop kissing me, and I pulled away only to look her in those golden eyes. "You're here," I whispered in her mouth. "Never do that again."

My bunny's shy face shook her head, her curls coming down her face. "I won't. I'm sorry." I pecked her lips, clenching her to my body.

Mother nudged me again. "I think her parents would like to see her."

I growled, holding onto Uriel. "She's mine!" My body covered Uriel as I kissed her up her neck. Uriel petted my hair as I kept my face buried to her shoulder.

"Hi." Uriel's hand left my hair to wave at her parents who still held her feet. "Are you guys okay?" she muttered.

Hera cried out, now holding onto Uriel and me; her father followed all of us into one gigantic pile of gods.

"You scared us so much, my sweet." Hera petted her hair. "I'm so sorry for everything."

Michael kissed Uriel's cheek, his wings engulfing the lot of us. I grumbled, irritated with the feeling of other bodies on top of me.

"I'm fine now." Uriel rubbed her eyes. "Luci saved me."

Sitting up, still holding Uriel on my lap, I kept my arms around her while the other gods continued to watch. "No, Uriel; you saved me. From the very beginning, you saved me." Uriel and I stared at each other, our hands cupping each other's faces.

"What just happened?" Poseidon stood over us, filled with curiosity. "How was Lucifer able to suck the evil from her?"

Mother stood with Father's arms wrapped around her while Lilith slept in the crook of Father's arm. "Once you are bonded, you can take on some of the abilities of your partner. That is why Hades can turn into a wolf."

Poseidon shook his head in disbelief. "I clearly know nothing of bonds then," Poseidon chuckled. "They seem strange."

"Well, you should know more about them." Ember nudged Poseidon, who only raised a brow. Mother had her way with her bonding secrets, and I recognized that spark in her smile.

"It's interesting"—Athena touched Uriel's skin—"that it took Lucifer's lips to pull the evil out of her, and it barely affected his body. It was like you ultimately destroyed the evil inside her once you pulled from her." Athena's finger touched my arms, which did not hold the darkness that Uriel had on her body. "The God of Destruction can destroy the evil drawn into his mate."

"So, I can suck out evil with my hands, and then Luci can suck the evil out of me with his mouth?" Uriel verified cheerfully.

"That's what she said." Loki sauntered up, still spitting feathers from his mouth. Mother pulled him into a hug.

"My big boy!" Loki now stood a head taller than Mother, his horns now permanently on top of his head. "You have a raven!"

Athena stood by in the corner, even with her disheveled look, torn clothes, and bare feet she pulled a notebook from her suit jacket and began writing things down. Shaking my head, I pulled Uriel into my arms.

The entire palace was in shambles, the roof had fallen in, black tar coated on the floor, and hunks of stone lay out in the open. With the evil of Kronos now vanquished, it would take time to repair what was left.

Angels had already begun cleaning out the throne room, and celestial fairies used their magic to repair the small cracks in the floors. The one thing in the room left untouched was the body of Zeus. We had all been too worried about Uriel, worried she would perish, and that I would follow. So, we just left the body lying in the middle of the floor.

Zeus' hand flopped on the floor. He was still covered in the tar-like substance that held him to the floor with the sword embedded into his head. "I have a splitting headache," he groaned, trying to move his head. "Is there a fucking sword in my head? Get it out!" His arms waved around dramatically.

Hades chuckled, walking barefoot across the floor before pulling it out with one swipe.

"Damn, you could have warned me," Zeus complained, rubbing his forehead. The wound began to close, along with the one in his chest. The once gray beard that Kronos donned while in his body was back to the usual white blonde. His bright blue eyes surveyed the surrounding room.

"What the fuck happened? Did I miss a party?" His shoulders slumped. "Sheesh, I know I've been a terrible god all these years, but I swear, I'm trying. Not getting invited hurts, ya know?" His head slumped while his elbows rested on his knees.

Hera, gracefully went to Zeus and pulled on his hand to help him stand. Michael's dislike for his mate touching a former partner didn't go unnoticed, and Zeus backed away respectfully.

"Your body was possessed by Kronos," Hera said softly.

Zeus coughed, rubbing his chest as the rest of his body healed. "Fates," he cursed. "I—I did not know. The last thing I remember was Uriel helping me in the Underworld." Zeus smiled at Uriel, who waved shyly. "Then I went through the portal, and then... nothing. That is the last I remember until I woke up with the sword in my head."

"Kronos' spirit entangled into your soul," Athena explained, "and I am afraid we are not done with him just yet. Lucifer may have destroyed the connection, but you need his body and soul to fully exterminate him."

Uriel grabbed onto my wings, pulling them around her body. I shook, feeling the sensation her fingers elicited on my feathers. Now that I got her back, I needed her more than ever. Her heart raced rapidly in her chest. The flutters of her fear had my anger swell within me again.

Hades pulled Zeus to the throne, both side-by-side for the first time in centuries. "With your permission, brother, I say we take a trip to Tartarus and end this once and for all."

Zeus' face passed over the crowd. They all watched the High God in a different light as Father gave his blessing for Zeus to rule, yet again.

Zeus gritted his teeth, nodding his head in agreement. "To Tartarus, to destroy the threat of the gods."

Chapter 60

Uriel

Luci gripped me tightly, keeping me sitting in his arms. Hushed whispers from the other gods filled my ears as they gathered around Zeus. They were most likely discussing the next plan of action. My mom had settled back at my feet, rubbing them as her tears dropped onto my ankles.

"Mom?"

She raised her head, tears still streaming down her cheeks. "All along, I should have asked for help." She gripped the blanket covering her body tighter around her neck. "I had no clue the paranoia and those deep, terrible insecurities were from, *him*."

"Mom," I whispered again. Luci let the tight hold around my waist loosen, although his eyes were still red from his own tears. My arms wrapped around my mom, who muttered, 'thank you' to Luci.

Dad kept his wings wrapped around our family. The small family that I had known all of my life now included Luci and Vulcan, who hovered outside Dad's wings over us. My head glanced upward to see the large, bearded god in his battle attire. Stretching my arm out, I beckoned him to join us. Dad let him in gladly as Vulcan moved to hug me tightly.

"You've got a lot to explain, Mom," Vulcan joked. "I understand why, but damn. My therapist will not believe this."

Mom let out a sob gripping the both of us. "How about a big family vacation, with mates and all," Mom muttered. Luci growled behind me, pulling my waist to seat me back in his arms. "As soon as Lucifer and Uriel have their alone time, of course." She winked at my brooding mate.

He didn't smile, instead he unfurled his wings, encasing us into our own, private cocoon. Away from prying eyes, Luci's forehead rubbed against my cheek. His fingers became impossibly tight around my neck. The control he craved was back in full force as the tickling of his claws sparked my desire to listen and be his good girl immediately.

"Are you okay?" I sniffed, huffing a laugh.

Luci shook his head, unable to speak for the longest time. His wings shuffled until they shuttered completely around us. "You're asking if I am okay?" Luci scoffed. "You were the one dying in my arms just moments ago."

I smiled, pressing my lips to his, my legs already straddling his hips. "You sucked up all that yucky stuff." I half giggled. "You don't seem yourself."

Luci's hands roamed my body, not out of lust or desire, but just feeling me as if confirming I was actually here. I was still sitting in front of him. I wasn't going anywhere.

I knew what I had to do when I first stepped foot in the palace. I was to touch Zeus' body and take whatever evil sat in him. I just couldn't fathom how powerful it was, and once I touched his hands, I knew it was over for me. A god or goddess dying was unheard of, but if my mark being a lamb was any inclination, I knew it was what the Fates had in store for me.

I touched Luci's mark, and he shivered under my touch. His cock rubbed my clit as he groaned. "Bunny,"—he pulled me to his chest—"you can never leave me." His grip tightened. "I'll always find you."

"I had to help," I softly argued. "It was about me, you, and the rest of the worlds. We have to work together, right?" A tear ran down Luci's cheek. I caught it with my thumb. "Mates are stronger together," I whispered.

The palace was restored piece by piece, and the darkened clouds in the sky departed. The land was healing itself; the fire and lightning that rained down on the heavens ceased and now new foliage sprouted across the lands.

One goddess, who I assumed was Persephone, was twiddling her fingers around vines, plants, and shrubs near the palace, holding a little baby in her arms. Gabriel, who had just awoken from the evil that consumed him, rushed through the gaping hole in the wall to embrace her. One arm slipped around her while the other caressed the young baby's head.

Luci gripped my hand. My white leather outfit was still littered with ash as we stepped down the palace steps. The road home would be easier than getting here. Hades stood before us, his back straight and his pants ripped from shifting. Ember stood by him, her hand in his as Lilith screamed with excitement.

"Da!" Her hand reached out to Hades. The brooding face he had set before, now donned a smile as he picked her up.

Baby gods and goddesses must grow fast because I swear, she looked almost one-year-old by human standards.

Within a blink of an eye, we all landed back in the Underworld Palace's foyer. Luci gripped my hand, pulling me away from the group of gods who traveled with us.

Resisting his pull, I shook my head. "What's going on?"

Luci brushed away his dirty hair, the dried blood flaking off his body. "They are going to take care of Kronos," he gritted his teeth. "We are going to our room."

Trying to hold back a smile, I pursed my lips together, holding in the excitement to be alone with him again. "Don't you want to end him, too?" I asked, making sure.

Luci's vision trailed back to the group of gods, who were in a heated discussion. Luci pulled his sword off his hip, dropping it to the foyer floor. The loud noise it made as it bounced away from him didn't even warrant a glace from the gods.

"This is between them and their father." Luci's hand squeezed mine as he rushed us down the halls. My feet weren't carrying me fast enough to keep up with his long strides, and before I knew, it he lifted me into his arms, cradling me like a child.

"Luci!" I gripped his neck.

Blaze hopped out of our room, his bright, flaming tail waving brightly. Chittering, he ran down the hall before Luci could approach him.

"You are scaring him!"

Luci only grunted in reply before he kicked the double doors open to our dark room. Assuming he was going to deposit me on the bed, he surprised me as he went to the bathroom door. The entire bathroom was lit with hundreds of candles with red rose and gardenia petals scattered intermittently between each candle. The candles adorned each open space on the counter, the floor, and even the windowpanes, only the path that led us straight to the shower that was already running with steam was excluded. Water droplets cascaded down the glass from waterfalls that erupted from the gold ceiling.

Before I could comment on how beautiful or magnificent it was, Luci had me in the shower, pushing me up against the glass. My clothes became drenched with water, and my breath heaved at the proximity of his mouth to my neck.

His touch wasn't forced or rushed. It was gentle as his fingertips pulled my clothes down my body. With each newfound inch of my skin he released, he placed a chaste kiss, starting at my shoulder and trailing down my arm, until he kissed every single finger on my hand.

"Luci," I whispered.

He didn't reply as he repeated his affections on the other side of my body. I wanted to believe he was toying with me, trying to make me beg, but the way his lips touched my skin—how soft, how slowly he rubbed his face against each part of my body—it showed a new side to my Lucifer. The brooding god, who dared to defy all odds of conquering his anger, let me into his heart. The god who knew nothing but destruction, and who feared my demise based on a prophecy, saved me, just as much as I saved him. The water cascaded down my body as I felt the heat of the water trickle down my breasts. Luci's tongue licked between them as he lifted his head to meet my lips with his.

Tangling our bodies with each other, his hands roamed my backside. Both of our eyes were partially opened, staring at each other. As odd as it may seem, it was so intimate just the way we kissed, as if afraid one of us would disappear from existence—because we almost did.

"My beautiful mate," he moaned, pulling my hips into him. His erection rubbing against my stomach burned a new desire into me. I wanted to be closer, I wanted to never leave his body.

Lucifer's emotion filled my heart to the brim, spilling over into my soul with the love and affection he wanted to show me.

The hint of residual fear in his emotions spurred hot tears to spring to my eyes. The emotion that ran through the both of us was so overwhelming only actions could sate it. My fingers fiddled with what was left of his pants. They fell to the floor with a thud. Dirt, ash, and whatever sin was left over washed down the drain.

"I need you," I muttered through our kiss. "I need you now," the crack in my voice rushed my mate.

Instantly, he transported us to the bed; our bodies were still wet as he laid me in the middle. The room that was once bare of any light was filled with candles. The aroma of roses, gardenias, and a hint of sunshine on a spring day filled my lungs.

No words were spoken between us as he lined his cock to my center. His forehead touched mine as he slid in with no resistance. My body was heavy with need when he slowly entered me. Both of us moaned, and my neck leaned to the side so his lips could suck the most erotic place on my body. My hands wrapped around his back, feeling the rhythmic thrusting of his body. Muscles tightened on his back, and small grunts left his mouth as he slid his enormous shaft into my weeping core. Moaning his name in encouragement, his rhythm pushed harder, faster, deeper.

"Bunny," he whispered, giving me that extra surge of pleasure as I came around him. The spark in his eyes and the smirk on his face that appeared as I reveled in his sexy voice fueled me. "Such a good girl," he cooed as he pushed deeper into me. My legs wrapped around him. He wasn't done with me, not even close based on the look he had in his eyes.

"You take my cock so well, bunny." Shivers ran through me again. My eyes rolled at the sensation of his cock twitching inside me, as I grinded more against him. "Your pussy was made for this." The rhythmic pulsing had me moaning his name.

"I love you," I cried out as another orgasm ripped through me. Luci's eyebrows pursed together; his rhythm now ruined with sporadic pushes into my body as I sunk deeper into the mattress.

"You are fucking mine, Uriel." He growled with his wings sprouting from his body. They hovered over us, the red embers on the tips burning holes into the mattress. "You will always listen to me. You will never put yourself in danger again." His hot breath fanned my neck.

I hummed, feeling his pelvis roll against me.

"Words, bunny," he panted.

Biting my lip, my lashes fluttered and I stared into his dark pools of lust. "Is that the best you can do?" I quipped back.

His thrusting slowed briefly, and his eyes widened at my defiance.

I smiled, pushing my hand towards my clit.

His lip curled in amusement before throwing one of my legs over his shoulder. "You asked for it, bunny." His voice wavered.

His rough hands pushed down on my shoulders as he ravaged me. His wings propelled his thrusts deeper and harder until we both came undone and stars brightened behind my eyes. Luci's sweat dripped on my breasts as ropes of his cum filled me. My body was utterly spent. He rested his forehead against the side of my cheek as we panted.

"You will never leave my side again. I hope you know that." His hand reached around my throat, giving it a light squeeze. My head rolled to the side, kissing his cheek.

"I never plan to."

Chapter 61

Zeus

"We go now." I rubbed my itchy beard. My body was a mess. Never in my life have I ever felt this weak. It was like a damn tick sucked of all the life essence from my body. My body felt itchy and sick, and the black tar that coated my body where Kronos bled out of me remained.

"Maybe you should clean up first," Ember offered, but I shook my head. We needed to strike now while he was weakened and be rid of our father, who dared tried to attack us, for good. Next time, we wouldn't be so lucky. Kronos only grew stronger as the years went by, and he was close this time—too close.

The gods all looked to me to lead the attack. For the first time since my numerous betrayals against Hera, they looked to me for what to do. Their eyes were stern, holding a grudge against our father. They could all do what they willed. They could go down and destroy them together without my permission, but they didn't. They waited for my word. My apprehension made me mumble to myself, questioning why this would be.

Hades put his hand on my shoulder. "You've defeated him before," Hades spoke loud enough for all to hear. "You can do it again."

I shook my head, not feeling the confidence I once had—when Rhea, our mother, told me I had the power to do so. Yet they still looked to me as Hades continued to bolster my confidence. He could do all of this without me. They all could. Yet Hades continued to promote me as some sort of leader.

I had changed much since I last fought Kronos. I was no longer the heroic god that came in on a white stallion to gut the belly of Kronos—I was different. I had feelings of regret and guilt still swarming my soul from when I let being the High God go to my head. It was true, that Uriel had taken away much of my guilt, but I still had one person I needed to talk to if I was to properly assume the position that I have failed at for all those years. I would do things better moving forward, the way that I should have done them since the beginning.

"Hera, may I have a word?"

The goddess stood in surprise at my sudden outburst. Their murmurs of planning how to go about destroying Kronos ceased as they all stared at me. Glancing around the room, my eyes all met theirs, and I shook my head. Hera beckoned me to follow her to speak in private.

"No, this will be done in front of the others."

If I was to gain any respect from my fellow brethren and sisters, this needed to be done publicly. If Hera refused my apology as she has rightfully done in the past, it would paint me as a tainted god, and therefore, I would relinquish my title.

"Hera, I want to formally apologize," I raised my hands in surrender as Michael approached, his wings covering her face. "I'm not plotting anything," I sighed, pulling my hands down. "I have been a fool, and I wanted to publicly apologize for embarrassing you, hurting you, and downright spitting in your face as the Goddess of Marriage and Partnership. I got a big damn head and took whatever I wanted all because I thought, I was powerful." Hanging my head low; the silence of the foyer had my own thoughts echoing in my head.

"I've been jealous for a long while, ever since you found your mate," I swallowed. "Even more so when I found out that you had a daughter and still didn't tell me, despite us working together for so long." Daring not to look to anyone but Hera, I got on one knee. The surrounding gods gasped, but the murmurs and whispers escaped my ears because my focus was on Hera.

I bow to no one, and they all know that.

"I've failed you and the rest of our family. I beg for your forgiveness for betraying your trust, and I offer my most sincere happiness for you and your mate, Michael."

Michael's stance softened with his wings falling around him. Pulling Hera from behind his body, he gave a nod of approval to approach me. My knee was still on the cold foyer floor, and the rest of the gods looked on as witnesses as Hera approached. She had been through so much with her family over the past twenty-five years with Uriel, and she didn't feel comfortable enough to even tell me of her problems, all because of my jealousy.

Now I have finally pushed Hera away from my heart, knowing she is mated to another, and hopefully, one day, I would be blessed with the a gift of a mate. Until that time, I will spend the rest of my days trying to make up for my transgressions.

"Zeus, thank you." Her voice was so low, I barely heard it. "And I thank you for your apology. I hope you find what you are looking for in a mate one day."

I cleared my throat, wiping my brow. The silence of the room broke as Ember snickered in the corner trying to cover it up with a cough. Hades shook his head, but said not a word as his mate's face turned bright red.

"Sorry," she whispered, putting her face into Hades' chest.

As much as I wanted to run to Ember and beg her for what she knew, I kept my mouth closed. It was time to show some humility, take my faults, let go of any bitterness in my heart, and become the High God everyone expected me to be.

"Friends?" I held out my hand to Hera. who took it gladly, shaking it. Michael came to her side, wrapping his arm around her shoulders. My hand extended to Michael, who also took my hand gladly.

My half-smile flashed around the room before I willed my battle attire to replace my tattered robes. With lightening in my fist, I nodded to the rest.

It was time to end this once and for all.

The Twelve were the only ones allowed to descend into Tartarus with Persephone taking Demeter's place. Michael and Gabriel were reluctant to part from their mates but conceded to stand outside of the pit. Ember stayed within the confines of the palace with Blaze and Cerberus by her side. Hades willed his torture demons away, knowing many could not stomach their gruesome appearance. The stench alone was making me choke on my spit.

Our shallow breathing sounded much louder than it should during our silent walk to the depths of the pit, even more so with

Poseidon. His unease ran down him like waves of thunder as he walked alongside me where the three high male gods stood together as a unit. Falling back, I nudged Poseidon whose body stiffened. I frowned at the weakness hiding in his eyes. He was the creative one, the one with the best ideas when we created the humans, suggesting we made them in our image. Poseidon even warned our darker sides would eventually show in them.

"Poseidon?" My voice whispered, trying to keep the conversation between us. "How are you?"

He raised his brows in confusion of why I would even talk to him at my simple question. Okay, sure, I was a prick for a long while, but I was trying to do better now. I was trying to finally understand the guy instead of writing him off as a lost cause or weird for staying away and hiding from us in that underwater bubble he liked to keep himself in.

"I'm fine." He rubbed his beard. "Just ready to get this over with."

It wasn't a secret that Poseidon had issues stemming back to the days when he sat in darkness of Kronos' stomach. He vividly remembered the stomach fluid eating them, causing mental scars, and weakening their powers, but Poseidon was never normal. Then again, I guess I didn't really know what his 'normal' was because he was older than I am.

Pulling Poseidon aside, I wanted to rectify some of what he went through. If it was any inclination, a lot of his problems extended to his memory of everything that had happened on the inside. No one else remembered, and no one else talked about the years they sat there. Poseidon only brought it up once when we sorted through the positions we would have in the Celestial Kingdom.

The group formed a circle around the opaque box that held Kronos. Inside, black sludge coated the glass, inching its way to the bottom. It looked like a giant explosion of tar coated the walls. Hades and Ares cupped their hands to look inside, only growling in disgust as they stepped away.

I looked to Poseidon. "I want you to land the final blow."

Poseidon's fear emitted from him as I gave him a choice. Standing back to hit the blackened cave walls, he shook his head. "I don't want any part of it." His voice shook. "I just want to be left alone in peace."

"Will you get peace?" I stepped forward, grabbing his shoulders. "Will you ever get peace if you don't have a hand in it? Look what he has done to you." I looked up and down as he leaned his head back against the wall. "Look what power he has over you, and he hasn't touched you for thousands of years."

My brother shook his head again, trying not to spill the unshed pain in his eyes. I could not imagine what he went through, what he still goes through in the night, in the dark. He didn't deserve it. Out of all the gods, he was the one that most deserved nothing but good. Sure, he created creatures behind my back, but Fates, he did it out of love. He only wanted to have companions he could trust after so many of us used him for his creativity, just to create creatures to destroy. Poseidon only did it for friendship.

Fates only knows if he has ever laid with a woman.

"This is an opportunity for you"—Hera and Athena's heated stares on my back comforted me. As heated as those stares were, I knew they only expressed concern over my forcefulness of Poseidon—"to know that you ended him, and he will never manifest again." I turned, pointing to the rest of the gods. "To know that he will never return to hurt you or any of them again," I said louder. "He has hurt you most of all. It is your time, Poseidon."

Dropping my hand from his shoulder, I grabbed Hades' hand. The circle was almost complete. Each god glowing brightly, radiating their power. Eleven gods stood before the glass box, ready for our souls to destroy the one that help created us. Hades squeezed my hand, his head nodding for me to pull Poseidon once more.

Even if Hades and I had our issues, he surely is a good brother.

My hand outstretched, beckoning Poseidon. Kronos' screams from within the box could be heard loudly. Cursing, yelling and more black tar inched down the box as Kronos tried to break free. Kronos' face leaned against the glass, watching Poseidon step forward.

"Oh, the God of the Sea," he hissed. "Dare he try to destroy me? Don't worry, I'll always be with you in your dreams." Kronos chuckled. The deep rumble in his voice quaked the bloodied soil beneath us. "All of you are nothing but worthless pieces—"

Poseidon grabbed my hand, placing his other in Hera's. The radiating smile she gave him only encouraged him to let his power flow as we channeled our powers to him. With a loud roar, he unleashed the magnificent surge of power with a blinding light, draining us all as he poured it into Kronos.

The box contained the loud explosion of dust and tar. It was so loud and heavy that cracks of lightning echoed until one final explosion had the entire box stop in time. Tiny particles of dust halted with the lightning frozen in a perfect picture. We all stared in awe at the new piece of art before us. Seconds passed by until it all dropped to the floor in a heap of ash and dirt that littered the ground with what was once Kronos.

Chapter 62

Uriel

"You look beautiful, Uriel." My mom pulled a curl away from one of the whisps who was curling my hair. My hair was a fluttery mess as at least fifty of the little blue balls of light continued to pull and braid. They were common in the world of Bergarian; they fluttered around the mates mostly and liked to cause trouble for the men, frequently teasing them.

I giggled as my mother tried to swat one away until they released the entirety of my hair and began working on my mom's. Sitting down on the bench beside me, she sighed dejectedly.

"I guess there is no use in pushing them away is there?"

I hummed a quick 'no' and stared at my reflection in the mirror. My hair was perfectly curled, styled down as Luci preferred. A small crown of white and gold roses adorned my head while my dress was filled with fluffy tulle and sparkling diamonds around the bodice that glowed through the skylight of the magnificent tent. My white toes continued to peak through the oatmeal-like sand particles where they were buried into the sand.

Mom's hand brushed my hair to the side, looking down at the upper part of my chest. "I still can't believe, in that short amount of time, he marked you." Mom's eyes closed, letting out a slow breath. "If I had known he was your mate when I left you—"

I grabbed her hand, squeezing it gently. "You never would have left me there," I whispered.

It had been well over a week since Kronos had been officially destroyed, by my new friend, Poseidon. He walked out of Tartarus a new god, and his eyes actually sparked while Zeus hugged him around his shoulders. Hades even had a newfound lightness to his steps when they entered the palace.

A celebration took over that night, Luci and I heard the yells and roars of praise as the twelve gods and their mates danced into the night. I wanted to go out to see the commotion when we entered our bedroom bidding them goodnight, but Luci kept me huddled in bed and gave us our own party, even having the servants bring in the finest desserts.

Luci's hand never left my body. He even dared to pull me to the bathroom with him when he needed to wash. I giggled with him all night as our bodies intertwined with each other. We didn't leave the room for a full three days when we finally heard banging on the other side of the door. Mom stood there with her hands on her hips while Dad looked on in horror behind her.

Mom said it had been enough time and we needed to grace the rest of the gods with our appearance. Luci didn't like that and growled at her as he pulled me back around his body. I giggled and Mom's eyes only softened before shrugging her shoulders.

"I didn't think it would happen so soon," Mom uttered again as the whisps finished with her hair. Her beautiful updo had tendrils of beautiful curls framing her face, making her look much younger, dare I even say look the same age as me?

"My little girl grew up overnight and got a mate, all without me. I didn't even get to give you dating advice," she whined.

I laid my head on her shoulder, smiling into the mirror. "Would you have *really* given me dating advice? Or would you have just told me to stay away from him?"

Mom's mouth pursed together, humming in thought. "You're right; I would have told you to stay away." Her finger traced my jaw until my father walked into the gorgeous tent.

The enormous glass chandelier swayed as the flap of the tent opened, showing Dad in his beautiful angel ceremonial garb which was slung over his chest. His wings dusted the sandy floor as he approached. As I stood up, my dress came to just tea-length on my legs and swayed as I gave him an enormous hug.

"Hi Dad," I wrapped my arms around his neck.

"There's my sugar!" He kissed my shoulder letting me go. "I'm surprised your mate isn't standing outside the tent. He hasn't let you out of his sight since last week."

Dad rolled his eyes as he let go of me to kiss Mom on the cheek. "How are you, my goddess?" Mom only pulled him down for another kiss, tugging on his robes.

"Yuck," I muttered.

I still couldn't get used to Mom and Dad being all smoochy in front of me.

"Loki is keeping him busy," I added to break the awkward passion developing between my parents. "Loki has some new power he discovered which permits him to talk to other birds."

"Oh?" Dad looked up in surprise. "And why does that interest Lucifer?"

I shrugged my shoulders, not really knowing. *Maybe he just wanted to get closer to his brother now that he had his anger under control.*

"Knock, knock?" Luci's mother walked in, she was wearing a light blue dress that cut off at her ankles, and her feet were bare like everyone else. Sweet harp music began playing in the background.

I smiled, running to the opening of the tent only to have Ember stop me. "Not so fast!" she sang, pulling me away. "There's someone who wants to see you first."

My head tilted in question until a big god with a slight twitch in his eye and a long, groomed beard entered. "Vulcan!" I squealed running to him, putting my arms around him.

"I'm surprised you remembered me." His voice cracked. His hand came up to my head, petting it gently. My head barely reached his mid-chest, and his beard tickled my chin as I gazed up at him.

I hadn't seen Vulcan since my near-death; he had taken it upon himself to help find all the missing monsters that had fallen into the 'in-between' world. It was dark and cold, and the wind had settled there. Poseidon spent most of the week with Vulcan as they extracted every single one and brought them back to the Underwater Palace to heal.

"Of course, I remember!" I squinted at him playfully. "How could I forget my favorite big brother?"

Vulcan smiled his pearly white teeth which were a sharp contrast to his unruly black beard. The sentiment made his eyes glassy when Mom and Dad walked up around us. The large group hug felt warm and familiar like it should have always been this way.

"Remember what I said? Family vacation with mates and children once things settle down," Mom reiterated.

Vulcan's mate, Tamera had given birth to the triplets just the day before. and busy was pretty much an understatement in our family right now. The two girls and one boy were dubbed Amaryllis, Alexandra, and Angelos. I loved the names instantly and couldn't wait to cradle at least one baby in my arms. The way gods healed so quickly after birth, Tamera was more than happy to bring the new family of five to the bonding ceremony today. Now I could finally meet my new sister-in-law at the party and play with the babies to my heart's content.

"Watch out, you might give Uriel baby fever," Mom warned. "I'm not sure she is quite ready for that." Mom eyed me warily.

That was true. I wasn't ready to have a baby, just yet. But having fun with other god's babies made me feel all gooey inside.

"I only want to be Luci's good girl right now," I said absentmindedly, trying to look out the tent flap and listen to the music playing outside. "He tells me all the time what a good girl I am taking his—" Vulcan slapped his hand over my mouth, I still tried to mumble the word though.

Mom's eyes widened. "Excuse me?" she choked.

Vulcan removed his hand, shaking his head.

Hanging my mouth open, I glanced back at my parents who were visibly disturbed. "Umm," I patted my lips with my fingers, trying to figure out something else to say—but I had nothing.

Mom continued to stare at me until Ember broke the tension. "It's starting," she whispered, ushering Vulcan out of the tent.

Mom and Dad silently stood on either side of me, my arms hooking in with both. "She's mated now, Hera," my dad whispered to her. I smiled, remembering that I was already mated.

Luci was mine and I was his, and there was nothing, or nobody, to ruin it.

"Yes, we are definitely mated. We mated like..." I held my hands up trying to count just how many times, but Father shoved my hands down quickly with a nervous chuckle.

"She doesn't need to know. Your mother is always going to see you as her innocent little girl, so let's not remind her so much."

I shoved out my lip. My mom was still tense at the thought that I was mated. Dad is the one who should be more over-protective—that was how it worked in all the stories and movies I had watched. Dad looked at Luci with such pride now though. Maybe it was because Luci had saved me, and he knew we matched each other so well. Mom, even with Kronos influencing her decisions, deep down always thought of me as hers, and hers alone.

I shrugged my shoulders. *She just has to get over it.*

"Ready?" Ember whispered, opening the white leather flap.

The salty air filled the tent, and the beautiful lull of the ocean sent a calming wave of ease as Mom took a breath. Squeezing my arm with hers, we stepped out into the light and the privacy of the Isle of Dragons.

The rows of beautiful, white, padded seats held not only the gods but most of the werewolves from Ember's home pack, including her parents—former Alpha Wesley and Luna Charlotte.

Enormous white and red flower petals lined the aisle, the smoothness of the petals mixing with the grainy sand sent a rush of happiness through me. Before we took the next steps to meet my mate, who I had yet to see, four little hands pulled at my dress.

To my surprise, Thalamere and Alyssa, the prince and princess of Atlantis whispered my name. "Goddess Uriel!" Their faces lit up like a thousand stars. Letting go of my parent's arms I hugged them both tightly.

I never even thought to invite them.

My eyes, which had been firmly planted on the sea of rose petals in the sand, glanced at the end of the aisle. Luci, who normally is in black attire, was wearing sandy-colored dress slacks and a white button-up shirt with the top button undone. His face was clean-shaven, and his hair was gelled back to perfection. My eyes watered, looking at how handsome he was. He graced me with his handsome smile as he stared.

"We have to go back now." Thalamere pointed back to the row with his parents, the King and Queen of Atlantis.

"Kiss him good!" Alyssa kissed my cheek while I giggled watching them meet back with their friends, Manta and Scurry, on the seats that were far too large for them.

Standing back up and taking my parent's arms for support, I looked to my God of Destruction once more. The darkness that had surrounded him when we first met was completely gone. His hand left his pocket, holding it out for me as my parents, knocking me out of my stupor, pulled me down the aisle. But my eyes never left my Lucifer.

Chapter 63

Lucifer

She paused, kneeling on the soft sand, finally looking up from her thick lashes as the Atlantean prince and princess got her attention. It was the first time she saw me. She was too busy looking at her parents and thinking about how happy it made her that they were there, and alive.

It had been a long week, with most of it spent in our room. When we did eventually emerge, I had to pacify the soon-to-be in-laws by convincing them that I would forever take care of their daughter. Michael must have seen something inside me—that I would lay down my life for his daughter, my mate—because he pulled me into a hug without hesitation. Hera was still leery of me, as anyone should be. However, I was Uriel's mate, and in the end, I helped save her, sucking the evil that dared try to taint her soul of innocence using the bond we shared.

As much as she put on a brave face for her family after her near-death experience, she reverted to her child-like ways during the three days we spent together huddled in our bed. I spent a significant portion of that time constantly reassuring her that she was fine; she was safe, and that never again would the prophecy rear its ugly head, because she had saved us all. Uriel's craving for sweets and decadent chocolate increased during that time as well. Of course, I was happy to spoil her until her cravings subsided. Luckily, it was only for those few days, just her way of coping as she worked through the turmoil of almost losing everything—her parents, me, the life of all the innocent—if she had died. It was a lot to handle, for any goddess.

What would have happened if we didn't mate before then? What would have become of my bunny?

I threw the thoughts away harshly, not daring to contemplate what it felt like to lose someone you were so deeply in love with. In the most vulnerable moments, when I held Uriel's fading body in my arms, when she almost met the stars, something changed in me. As much of a possessive bastard as I was already, it had increased tenfold since that day. Uriel saw it as a new life, a new hope, not just for us but for the entire Celestial Kingdom.

The urge for destruction still ravaged my soul, but when near my mate, she calmed the stormy seas of my aching heart. She was my drug, and I didn't care who knew it. Despite my possessiveness over her, I did leave her for one hour to talk with my brother. Loki and I had many issues to work out as brothers, and I wanted them settled before I took my mate on the ultimate adventure of her life.

Uriel had confided in me how much she wanted to travel the worlds, to know everything about them, discover every land and sea. I was going to give it all to her—showing her the humans of Earth, the forests of Bergarian, even deep down into the depths of Atlantis she loved so much.

Uriel's eyes fluttered as she let go of the King and Queen of Atlantis' children and turned her gaze back to me. They ran to their seats as Uriel slowly put her arms in the crook of her parents' arms. She was dressed in a beautiful tea-length dress, the beautiful white fabric in contrast to her ebony hair. Her golden eyes glittered in the sun as the rays warmed her skin.

I smiled, and that smile was only for her as many hushed whispers in the crowd awed at my emotion. *Uriel* was *my emotion; the only emotion that I dared to crave for the rest of my life.*

Uriel's steps faltered as she stared at me, surely not understanding the attire I chose to wear. Black was my signature color and now I faced her with a white shirt and light-colored pants. I wanted her to see that she had not only healed the sin from those around her but me as well. Pulling my calloused hand from my pocket, it reached out to her. Her parents nudged her to walk to the slow thrumming rhythm of the harps playing music along the side of the crowd.

As she took her small, timid steps, I smiled brighter, watching her wings unfold behind her back. Her nerves radiated within my soul as she finally reached the make-shift altar my mother prepared.

"We've come to give you our blessing," Michael spoke loudly for all to hear, "for taking our daughter as your mate." It was very well known that I would have taken Uriel without their permission—because I already had—but the formalities of the gods showing interest in our mating humbled my heart further. I was honored that they would want to witness our union.

Extending my hand to Uriel as her warm hand slid into my own, I guided her to the platform. Pulling her waist closer to me, I kissed her forehead. The whisps never left Uriel as they hovered over us while we stood before my mother, the officiant.

"You look beautiful," I whispered.

That was a lie. She looked damn fucking radiant beside me.

"Greetings and welcome to all who appear here today." Never being fond of public speaking, Mother squirmed behind the small table placed before us as she held up the Sphere of Souls. The deep navy sphere hovered over her hands with small swirls of white smoke orbiting just above its surface; some moving fast, while others moved slowly.

"Two souls in the Sphere are now missing." she smiled at me, softening her eyes. "The Goddess of Innocence and Grace, Uriel, and the God of Destruction, Lucifer, have now joined their souls together, making the perfect match."

Father's lip curled as he gazed upon Mother's ethereal radiance. Lilith, still clutching to Father, pulled on his beard cooing at him. Mother continued with the ceremony, describing how soulmates came to be, how Selene blessed first the werewolves with mates, then other supernatural, until eventually, the Gods were granted the same gift.

Uriel clung to every single word that left my mother's lips, but my full attention was on my mate. The beautiful tendrils of hair swept her face, the small freckles that danced on her skin as the light sources peppered her with kisses.

She was all mine.

The sphere finally rested upon the deep purple pillow before us. Mother waved her hands until I pulled Uriel close to me. Uriel leaned into me, the pink tint of her cheeks glowing into my dark eyes.

"You're officially mine now," I whispered as Mother continued with the ceremony.

"I thought I was always yours?" She titled her head. "Ever since we mated—"

I hushed her lips with my hungry mouth. Pushing her back, holding on to her lower back, I forced my soul into her in front of the crowd. Rounds of applause roared through the crowd as Uriel clutched the front of my shirt.

Loki flew overhead in the form of his raven, casting a dark shadow that passed over the crowd. Uriel mentioned the idea of having birds fly overhead during our searing kiss. As fucking cheesy as it was, with the help of my brother, we arranged something better—the birds of Hell.

Dozens of Phoenixes took to the air overhead with their flaming tails of fire exploding, scorching the sky. Feathers dropped from their wings and tails, only to ignite and fizzle out just before hitting the crowd, dusting the crowd with ash as white as snow.

Breaking away from the kiss, Uriel's eyes widened as the ash floated down around us. "It's so pretty," she whispered, holding out her hand for the ash to collect in her hand.

The phoenix only reminded me of my love for my mate: the fiery passion we had for each other, the explosion of the pain of almost losing her only to find her as pure as the first rains that descended on the worlds. We had started anew, and this time I would be sure to cherish every moment.

Tracing my finger across her cheek, her head turned back to me. The pink lips I assaulted with my teeth curved into a breathtaking smile. As I ran my finger across her lip, she surprised me by sucking on one of my fingers. I groaned as she twirled her tongue around my finger.

She has more of me in her than I realized.

"Better watch it, bunny," I growled. "There are many people around us. I'd hate to embarrass you."

Uriel snickered, kissing my cheek. "I dare you." She nudged me.

Grinning wickedly at her, I pulled her playfully to my chest as the crowd dispersed. My finger trailed up her dress only to be interrupted by her parents. Groaning in displeasure, I looked to Hera who stood there glaring with her arms crossed.

"I hope you both can behave during the reception," Hera chided. The sweetness she held for Uriel was still alive, but the undertone was a warning for me.

Grabbing Uriel's ass, I squeezed it, eliciting a sweet squeak from her. "We wouldn't dare to ruin the perfect party that was planned for the gods," I smirked.

Hera opened her mouth to speak, but Mother intervened before Hera could utter another word. Laughing awkwardly, Mother pulled my mate and me away back to the tent and quickly pushed us inside.

"Alright, get dressed." Mother slung a dress to Uriel. It was a tighter-fitting gown that would hug her curves and show off her beautiful skin. "You two"—Mother pointed to both of us before motioning to her eyes and back at us with two fingers—"have fifteen minutes." She winked before she left, closing the flap of the tent behind her.

I shook my head at my mother who was trying to help us address the sexual tension between us before we tried to bump and grind on the dance floor. Uriel hooked her finger, curling it, beckoning for me to come to her.

My bunny had grown a spine, and I loved it.

I lurched forward to grab her, but she hopped away, going further into the tent. The back of the tent was covered in pillows and reminded me of the first time gave her genuine pleasure. My cock hardened in my dress pants, already trying to break free of them. Uriel giggled, throwing a pillow at me and stopping my movements. Growling, I leaped forward, only for her to jump away again.

"I don't have time, Uriel," I taunted her. "When I catch you, I'm going to have to punish you."

Uriel stopped in her tracks, her hands on her hips. "Well, do you want a good girl or a bad girl then?" Her innocent smile and her fluttering lashes had my palm over my cock. The desire in her eyes had her biting her bottom lip as I gripped hold of my growing shaft.

Fuck, I get to choose?

"How about a little bit of both?" I raised a brow.

As she continued to stare at my hand gripping myself, I moved quickly, pushing her down into the pillows and ripping the front part of her dress. She squealed in excitement, filling the tent with her giggles. Her glorious breasts greeted me as I kissed them tenderly.

"Suck my cock like a good girl."

She stopped giggling. Her teeth released her lip as I rolled her over. She meticulously took her time, pulling my belt buckle out slowly. I growled, sitting up and gripping her neck. The pressure had her moaning instantly.

"I said to be a good girl. You are becoming bratty, huh? Do you know what brats don't get?"

She hummed with a faint smile on her lips.

"My bunny doesn't get the cummies like she wants."

Uriel's eyes widened at that as her fingers rushed to unbutton my pants. Her desire filled the air, causing my wings to unfold slowly from my body. I leaned back. She pulled my pants off as I unbuttoned my shirt, letting my chest feel the salty air. The laughs and cheers from outside faded away as her fingers gripped hold of the base of my cock. Her sweet lips descended on the head, and she finally sucked the living shit out of it. My hips bucked as my hand gripped her hair.

"Such a good girl," I growled.

She hummed at the praise. Her fingers trailed down her dress, slipping between her legs. Letting her suck until she was almost pushing me over the edge, I pulled her away, only for her to groan in disappointment.

"What?" I growled in her ear. Ripping the back of her dress, her wings unfolded from her body as I put her up on her knees. Her glorious, silky ass bounced right in front of me. "Did you not get to come?" She whimpered, wiggling before me.

Pumping my cock several times, I laid down under her pussy, pulling it to my face. "Ride my face," I barked at her. Her hips shook as they rolled into my mouth.

Fuck, she tasted so damn good.

She came so close, too close, as her desire dripped down her legs. She winced again as I pulled away before she could climb to her orgasm. I slapped her ass, making her scream.

"Did you like that, bunny?" Her head only bobbed up and down, still on all fours.

Slapping her ass harder, I hovered over her ear. "Words, bunny. It makes me so happy when you use your words."

Barely a whisper, she agreed, "Yes, sir."

Damn.

Pushing my cock inside her, I gripped the base of her wings; they shuddered before me as she screamed. "That's it, bunny." The tension softened in her back as she met my thrusts greedily. "I want you to cum all over your sir's cock."

My praise had her coming down faster than expected, but I wasn't far behind. Gripping her wings, I thrust into her harder, my wings engulfing her body to hold her up as her legs shook with pleasure. Her convulsing pussy walls sucked my cock dry while I thrust into her deeper.

Feeling every ridge of my cock being tickled by her fluttering walls had me clutching her pump ass as I slid in and out of her. My cock disappeared into her body as I became one with her, grunting when my hips couldn't keep up with the rhythm. My body frantically shoved as much cock as I could to fill her.

I fucking love her body; I fucking love her, and she is damn well mine.

"Mine!" I yelled as launched my seed into her body. I came so damn hard that I swear I saw the Fates all smiling at me. This was how it was supposed to be, how Uriel's life should have always been.

We both crumpled to the pillows, hearing the shouts of Dionysus yelling for more alcohol.

"Bunny," I whispered, pulling her tangled hair away from her face. She panted, rolling over to look at me. "I love you."

She smiled again, her finger tracing her mark. "And I love you," she murmured.

Kissing her forehead, I tried to get up to find her dress so we could go to the party. *We could not be late, or Hera was going to barge in the tent.*

"We still have three more minutes." She smiled coyly.

Chapter 64

Uriel

I pouted as Luci led me out of the tent. He cleaned me up like I was some little child and made me put on the white dress that hugged my body like a second skin. In the back, a big white bow sat on the curve of my lower back which roused an illicit groan from Luci.

"Stop pouting, or I'll give you something to pout about." He slapped my bum and grabbed my hand, now leading me out to the sands of the Isle of Dragons.

The light sources hung over the horizon, and the pretty mason jar lights hung around the gigantic structure that held a bamboo dance floor. Everyone's feet were bare. The slapping of their feet and the twirling of all the pretty dresses led me into an enchantment that was straight out of a fairy tale.

"Uriel!" Silas waved to me. He was sitting on the pier that led right to the dance floor on the sand. His tentacles dipped into the ocean as he sat with his body leaning on his muscular arm. I waved frantically, happy to see one of my new friends.

Pulling Luci's hand, he stopped to see where I wanted to go. "Can I go say hello?" I tugged Luci's hand again, but his mom called him too.

Luci squinted his eyes in a glare cast toward Silas. An arm went over Silas' chest in some sort of silent agreement. Luci let me go.

"Stay with him," Luci muttered in my ear, "or I'll punish you out in the open." I snickered. His lips touched my forehead, and he let me go running down the pier.

"You're here!" I ran to hug him. His tentacles popped along my skin as I sat next to him. I slid my feet into the warm water, watching the fish swirl around us both. "Did Poseidon bring you?"

Silas' fangs poked out through his smile. "He did."

"And when do you get to hunt for your mate?" I clapped my hands excitedly, watching the twinkle in his eye. His skin was dry from his torso up, but his tentacles continued to pull water from the ocean to wet them. He didn't have the stinky-fishy smell that I would think he would have.

"Soon," he muttered, looking at the last light source. "Master wants to try and give me legs."

I gasped, putting my hands to my chest. "Can he make that happen?"

Silas chuckled, pushing the curl out of my face. "Of course, he can. He is the Master of his creations. However, I think I will only be able to have my legs for so long before I revert to my original form. I won't be able to stray far from the ocean."

I tilted my head, studying the sorrow in his eyes. "That means your mate will have to travel to the ocean to see or find you." He hummed in agreement. "If she is your soulmate, then she will find you," I chirped back. "Fates have a hand in everything, and if you want something bad enough," I paused, pursing my lips, "the Fates will change the tides for you to have it."

Out of all people, I should know this. I wanted nothing more than to live when I saw my mate bolted to the floor. I wanted to save him, save my family, and save every innocent who didn't deserve the fate Kronos planned. I wanted to live, and I fought for it.

"I hope you are right," he muttered. I nudged him playfully.

He was as solemn as Poseidon could be.

Repetitive clicking shuffled down the dock until I saw Galen, the enormous half spider trill beside me.

"Is Silas being grumpy?" Galen clicked his chelicerae together near his face, lowering his body to see the both of us. His legs were so long they went behind my back.

"He just wants a mate too, now that he knows he can have one." I rubbed his back.

Galen tilted his head, his eyes squinting accusingly at Silas. "The one called Ember will make it so. You should not worry so much."

The constant trill from Galen comforting his friend was nice, but he still gives me the heebie-jeebies. Maybe he will be mated to an arachnologist so they can be creepy together!

"Uriel!" Athena waved for me to come down to the dock. Silas slid back into the water, his head and shoulders still hovering on the surface.

"It will happen," I told Silas again.

Silas' tentacles stuck to my leg. "Thank you, Goddess." He smiled one more time before he sunk into the ocean.

Galen helped me up. The little hairs on his legs brushed my shoulders, and I shivered involuntarily. "Sorry I repulse you," Galen hung his head.

These monsters Poseidon created were all so sweet. I sure hope their mates think the same.

"I don't find you repulsive, Galen." I pulled his head closer to me, trying not to wince. "You just remind me of the smaller ones that don't have a big heart like you do."

Galen's stiff smile had him chittering until Athena called me again.

"Don't forget to come dance," I chided.

Galen twilled his voice. "Most cannot dance with two feet, let alone six. I shall watch from the tropical canopy."

Smiling, I ran down the dock where Athena greeted me. She wore Bermuda shorts and a tight-fitting tank top and held a tropical drink in her hand. "Here, you must try this." She handed it to me. The cold, yellow substance with a pineapple slice on the side and a pretty, purple umbrella had me giggling in excitement.

"What is this?" I squealed, taking a large sip.

Mmm... I rolled my eyes in the back of my head at the taste.

"A piña colada." Athena grinned.

I sucked half the thing down in under ten seconds. "It makes my tummy all warm." I paused, only to drink the rest down.

"Want another?" Athena laughed, and I nodded my head frantically. "Here." She waved her hand, and it filled right back up to the brim.

Athena led me back to the crowd. Tons of Ember's family members were dancing and mingling with the gods. My parents sat talking to Vulcan in the corner of the room, playing with the new babies. I sucked down the rest of my piña colada only for it to magically refill.

This is the best juice cup ever! I'm never letting it go.

"What are you doing?" Warmth tingled behind my back. Turning too quickly, I fell into Luci's arms, who raised a brow. "I told you to stay with Silas until I came back."

My eyes widened as I sucked down more of my drink. "Athena came and got me." I innocently replied, playing with the umbrella. Athena winked at Luci before she giggled and walked away.

"Have you tried this? It's freaking amazeballs!" Sucking some more, Luci suddenly took it from me.

"Noooo, it's mine!" I tried jumping, but Luci took a sip.

"Uriel, do you know what this is?"

I groaned. Leaning my head back, watching him take another sip. "Piña Coladaaaaa, duhhhh." I rolled my eyes, which earned me a hard smack on my bum. "Owie!" I poked his chest.

"Gimmie it! Athena gave it to me. It is the coolest gift ever!" Snatching it back, I emptied the glass again as I tried to run away from Luci.

It was easy, I was small and light. I went under some dancers' legs, who squealed in surprise. They all laughed as they saw my tushie wiggle through the crowd heading for the middle of the dance floor. Luci called after me. His worried voice had me laughing so hard, some of my drink spilled.

Realizing I was making a mess, I stood up and pranced to the other side of the crowd, where I saw Ares grinding on Mariah. His hands were on her butt and his hips ground hard into the front of her body to the beat of the music. Lights strobed around us as I stopped in front of them both—just staring at them.

I wish I could dance like that.

Still sucking on my straw, they stopped dancing and stared down at my short stature.

"What do you need, little goddess?" Ares smirked as my straw tried to suck up the last bit of my drink. The loud slurping noise echoed when the music paused between songs. Slow music played, and the warmth in Mariah's eyes had me smiling.

Hades grabbed my arm with his enormous hands and pulled me to his side, about to scold me. Before he got a word out, I blurted, "So, when is the baby coming?" I slurred.

Ares and Mariah's faces fell, looking at each other.

"It takes time sweetheart." Mariah brushed a hair away from my face. Ares looked to his mate, his forehead touching hers.

"It has to be soon, though, right? Because that light coming from your stomach is a lot brighter now." My hand rotated to touch her stomach, feeling the warmth it protruded and even the baby's tiny heartbeat.

"Thump, thump, thump..." I muttered, swaying.

"What do you mean, little goddess?" Ares pulled away, his hand touching Mariah's stomach.

"There's a cute wittle baby in theressss," I cooed, putting my ear up to her stomach. "I saw it before I sucked all the icky stuff out of Kronos. That's when I knew I had to save all of you. That innocent little baby gave me courage."

Hades pulled me away. "Bunny, you're drunk," he whispered before looking up at his uncle. "I'm sorry, Ares." Luci's look of disappointment in me had my stomach churn.

"No!" I ripped my arm away. "There *is* a baby! In her tummy!" I pulled Ares down to my level, forcing his ear to her stomach. He sighed, gripping ahold of Mariah's hips.

I swear I saw a tear. Whether it was one of happiness or sadness, I wasn't sure, but Ares' eyes sure did light up.

He heard it.

"No way," he whispered. Mariah tried to pull Ares up by his shoulders, but he just lifted her up with his ear still plastered to his stomach. "Baby, you're pregnant!" he boomed.

"That's what I've been saying!" I yelled over the music. The crowd stopped, looking over at the God of War holding his mate up in the air.

His face turned, kissing her stomach. "We're pregnant!" Ares roared again, twirling Mariah around the dance floor.

She was crying.

I felt bad.

Wait, she was crying? I thought she wanted to be pregnant?

The crowd roared with applause, many laughing and taking drinks. "I'll drink to dat!" I held up my drink only for Luci to take it away.

"You have caused enough trouble," he whispered in my ear, pulling me away.

"But sir, I'm not done." I giggled again, trying to give him the best fluttery lashes.

He liked that the most—the whole innocent look. Even though I was beyond innocent in the mating department, I like to think I still had that power over him.

"Uriel, what's going on?" Mom's glide through the dance floor was elegant and full of purpose. Dad's wings were so large that the crowd had to part for the both of them. "Is it true that Mariah is pregnant?"

I nodded frantically, waving my hands around. "Yeah!" I wobbled and fell right into Luci's arms. "And I bet you aren't far off yourself!" I did an over-exaggerated wink. Mom's eyes of horror only made me giggle some more.

"Hey Luci," I clung to his white dress shirt. Holding me up by my elbows, he eyed me warily. "Is your dad the muffin man?" I snorted, trying to keep the joke to myself until just the right moment.

"Uh, no?"

"Are you sure? Because you sure give me the banana cream filling!"

Mom's eyes rolled back in her head. Her beautiful wheat-colored hair now turning stark white. I was sure it was in laughter until she fell asleep, and Dad caught her.

"Wow. She must be tired," I mused, tilting my head.

Dad stood there with his mouth gaping, but all I did was cackle in laughter. Even Luci started snickering, pulling me away from my parents. Somewhere between the scuffle, my cup fell to the floor. I whined to go back, but Luci continued to carry me away.

"No more," he laughed, throwing me over his shoulder. "Let's get some food in you. Fates, you are going to get me in such trouble with your mom."

Chapter 65

Lucifer

Gently taking Uriel off my shoulder and sliding her into my arms, I sat her down at the small wooden picnic table. Uriel was adamant that this party was to be fun, 'like one big, giant, birthday party,' and not done over the top. So, it was exactly that: simple with the fun party features that Uriel was deprived of all her life.

Chocolate fountains, cupcake mountains, cookies, candies, a hot chocolate bar, and of course, normal food for the rest of us were in endless supply as the celestial fairies continued to bring in more food. Dionysus, of course, was in charge of the whole celebration: checking the bar, the food, and the drinking games. He even set up a damn beer pong table that humans like to play. My grandparents' wolves were all playing that game, launching hoots and hollers even over the large bass of the music.

Humans got one thing right—music. I couldn't imagine the gods trying to bump and grind into a bunch of harps and flutes.

"I'm tired," Uriel's mouth slurred as I had her sit on my lap.

She needed some carbs and fast, but the only way I was going to accomplish that was to give her a damn cupcake.

I found one that was black, with hints of gold sprinkles on top. "A danger cupcake!" she giggled, licking the frosting.

Her tongue licked it innocently, but my eyes darkened, watching her twirl her tongue around so gracefully against her lips. Part of the frosting stuck to the side of her cheek as she devoured the rest that was in her hand. My finger swiped it away, holding it up to her mouth. She didn't think twice about sucking it down with my finger. My cock twitched as she continued to suck when there was nothing left.

"Bunny," I growled, but her poor little lashes had closed shut. Slumping into my body, I pulled her head into my chest. Her little, tiny breaths evened out as I situated her against my body.

Damn Athena, she knew what she was fucking doing.

Athena was too observant for her own good. She knew damn well Mariah was pregnant, and she knew Uriel could see it too. Ares is just too busy trying to get pussy to pay attention. So he doesn't use his wolf abilities to smell her or even listen to the extra heartbeat thrumming in her. She wanted Uriel to make a scene, and she about broke Mariah's heart.

Payback is a bitch when you make Athena pass out from vulgar sex talk weeks prior.

I smiled, watching Athena drinking from the fancy glass. She held it up to me, sending me a wink.

As I left Uriel to visit with Silas, I was pulled away by my mother. She was prancing on the balls of her feet as she brought me to a drinking table. Poseidon was holding a glass of punch, swirling the spiked drink, smiling at it.

"As we all know, Hades had the 'chance' to see his mate in the pool." Father flinched but Mother only put her hand on his.

"Since Selene allowed this one time in her life, I figure that I should be able to do it, too."

Zeus grabbed Poseidon by the shoulder, pushing him forward to a large punch bowl.

"Now are you sure, Zeus?" Mother tilted her head to question him. Her eyes fluttered with her smile breaking across her face.

"I'm sure. I'd like the Fates to lead me to her. I need some time to sort things out. Especially since Hera is stepping down from ruling beside me to concentrate on her family."

Hera did a lot of the work, even when Zeus knew he could never get her back. This time the High God was taking ruling into his own hands.

About damn time.

Mother hummed in agreement until her fingers touched the surface of the punch in the bowl, causing the liquid to ripple. Poseidon walked closer, glancing back at Mother. "Poseidon, I'm giving you a glimpse of your mate."

Poseidon stepped back, shaking his head. "No, you can't do that. Can you?"

Mother giggled. "Uh, duh. Of course, I can. You've been through a lot, Poseidon, and I think you need that extra boost to push you in the right direction, especially if she is human. She won't live forever until you've bonded with her."

Poseidon hung his mouth, gripping his cup. "What?"

"If I didn't show you your mate, you would just continue to hide yourself away down in your Underwater Palace now, wouldn't you?" Mother scolded.

Poseidon pursed his lips, hanging his head in shame. His deep red hair was combed back, and dare I even say, he trimmed his beard? He had taken more pride in his looks and had done a lot better being around the enormous crowd of supernaturals and gods.

"Now, look." Mother pointed inside the drink.

A girl with deep, thick hair and intensely tanned skin appeared inside the swirl of pink, holding a long surfboard in her hand. She was laughing loudly, waving her hand for someone to follow her. She was maybe in her late twenties. Her body was definitely womanly, and I wasn't sure how she could keep her chest on a surfboard when she paddled into the surf. Deep brown eyes and a spark of joy ran through her as she headed towards the oncoming waves into the setting sun.

Poseidon reached out to touch the picture until the liquid stopped moving, and the projection of his mate disappeared. His hand dropped his drink, and his hands ran through his hair.

"Uh-huh!" Mother made a high pitch squeal of satisfaction. "Just strung you two together, so now you have to go find her," she winked.

Poseidon shook his head and rubbed his chest. "Where is she?" He pleaded with her, but Mother only shook her head.

"You have to find her. That means you have to leave your palace," she giggled.

"You are evil." Father patted her ass. "I kind of like it." A growl left his throat, and a scream of laughter burst from Lilith who sat on the sand playing.

Mother turned to me, now pulling me away from a disgruntled Poseidon, who was marching off into the sea. "I wanted to show you that"—Mother paused, looking back at Zeus who continued to talk to Hades like best friends—"I can usually find souls to match, and I worried for you for so long when you became of age." She rubbed my arms. "I didn't realize anything could cloud my ability to see souls. With those plants blocking her, Uriel was right under our noses, and I never even knew it. I just hope you don't think that I kept her from you."

Shaking my head, I pulled my mother in for a hug. "I—I never thought that." My lips kissed her cheek. "You have tried to help me for so long. I'm sorry I wasn't able to be a better son for you."

Her brows furrowed before she shook me by my upper arms. "Are you crazy? You are the best son I could have ever asked for! I just hope you don't think I kept things hidden from you... those plants—" I hugged my mother again.

She thought too much. She cared too much. Her abilities to understand feelings were far too strong.

"I never thought that, not once. I know you would not purposefully keep things from me." Hugging her once more, I left her with Father, finding my precious mate, who was currently drunk off her ass.

It wouldn't take long for Uriel to sober from her brief drinking experience—that would never happen again. I grabbed a nearby blanket and carried her down the dock she insisted we built. Her body shifted with her nose breathing in my now opened white dress shirt. Everyone was pulling off their nice dress clothes. Aphrodite was half-naked in a hot-pink bikini while Dionysus sported a speedo. I shivered, thinking about what else was going to happen as the night progressed.

Sitting in one of the padded chairs, I leaned back, getting the perfect view of the stars. The pier was far enough away that the bright lights of the party didn't disturb the perfect view of the sky. Traveling to the surface wasn't something I ever did, too worried I would get pissed off and fly off the handle. I stayed underground, in the Underworld, with those fake stars Father put up for Mother to make her feel like she was in a happier place.

He does everything to make her happy, and she smiles at him with such love and appreciation. I couldn't wait to do that for my mate, taking her on adventures between the realms, showing her things, letting us both experience lives we never thought we would have.

Uriel hummed, her eyes fluttering open until those bright gold eyes looked up at me. I swear she could light up any darkness with those eyes. "I'm sorry," she yawned. "I didn't mean to fall asleep. Is the party over?"

Shuffling on my lap, she stirred my cock back to life and she giggled rubbing it with her hand. "Sorry." She shrugged her shoulders.

"You are not damn sorry," I playfully growled at her.

"Language," she whispered. Chuckling, I pulled her back into my arms.

Life could not get any better.

A slow song played loudly from the beach; Uriel began humming to the tune.

"Dance with me," I ordered her, standing up.

"You can be nice, you know?" She giggled.

I pulled her arm harshly, slamming her body up against me. "I'm not a nice guy," I growled in her ear. One arm snaked around her lower back, and the other behind her neck, keeping her close to my body. We swayed to the slow music until I felt those unbelievable lips kiss up my neck.

"But you are nice to me," she whispered with her voice dropping an octave.

I swear that damn lusty voice she has will be the death of me.

"And if you need to let out some anger sometimes, you know I'm here."

I smirked, feeling the heat of her blushing face on my chest. "Like angry sex?" Biting her lip, she nodded as I kissed the top of her head. "That's good to know, bunny."

"And even if you aren't angry, it can be rough too," she muttered.

The fucking hell did this all come from?

"Is that so?" My hand slipped down to her ass to give her a squeeze. Her laughter filled the air, her head rolled back, and the sweet curls of her hair dangled past her hips to stare up at me.

"Uh-huh, and I'll love every minute." Her lips came to meet me allowing my teeth to bite her lips gently.

"How did the Fates get this so right?" I muttered into her lips.

Her fingers ran up my chest, finally landing in my now messy hair. "I don't know, but I'm sure glad I have you, Luci." Her breath hitched as I wrapped her legs around my torso. Her squeal sent chills down my spine. I would do anything to hear her laugh for the rest of eternity.

"And I'm glad I have you, bunny." My hands ran up her bare ass, and my eyes widened. "When did you take your damn panties off?"

Uriel bit her lip, her eyes full of mischief. "I think I left them on the dance floor somewhere when I was crawling away from you," she snorted.

Shaking my head, I slapped her ass. "Then I think we need to get you punished."

Her face brightened, trying not to smile. "Oh, that sounds bad." The twinkle in her eye made her squirm in my hold. "Is there any way to get out of it?"

"You can suck my cock under the table in front of your parents. How about that?"

She pouted her lip. Waiting for her to protest, she leaned in and whispered in my ear. "Can I still get my spanking, too?"

Epilogue

Under the Moon

"**B**aby!"

Lucifer wrapped his arm around Uriel's waist. True to his word, there was never a moment he let her out of his sight. Uriel often complained but secretly, deep down, she loved his possessiveness and how he took care of her. He took her worries away when she was around him, and she felt absolutely comfortable being herself.

Uriel and Lucifer reappeared in front of the portal of the Underworld. Uriel freed herself from her mate's embrace before dashing ahead in her excitement. The dark stones and the beautiful flowers that Uriel had stared in awe at just seven months before waved into the breeze she created as she skipped along the stones. Luci's wings helped him catch up to her before grabbing her by her waist.

"No running," Lucifer grumbled in her ear, "or that ass is going to be a brighter red than the sunburn on your cheeks."

Uriel snickered. She wasn't at all afraid of Luci's threats. In fact, Uriel had found a whole new side of herself since the night of their ceremony, after discovering that she had more than just a playful side, she also had a bratty side—and she liked it.

"Is that a threat, sir?" She snickered again, wiggling out of his hold.

"Damn right," he growled in her ear, nipping it harshly, "and don't even think that I won't do it in front of all these people."

Hanging torches set the Underworld Palace alight, and the red moon cast a glow of mystery upon the palace grounds. It was nothing that Uriel wasn't used to now. Although she and Lucifer explored Earth and Bergarian during the week, they spent every weekend in the Underworld. They had just returned to the Underworld for the baby announcement after visiting the Hawaiian Islands with Poseidon who was trying to gain favor with his mate.

"I can't believe Mariah had the baby already!" Uriel could barely contain her excitement.

The War God made such a fuss over Mariah during her pregnancy. Ares had been the perfect father-to-be, albeit a bit more overbearing than was necessary. She wasn't even allowed to walk after the night her pregnancy was revealed. He carried her everywhere and procured every random food craving. He washed her, massaged her feet, and eagerly read stories to her stomach every night before they went to sleep.

Ares even attempted to remain celibate, refusing to make love to his mate. It came as no surprise that the attempt didn't last long. He caved on the third day when Mariah experienced a spout of absolute horniness and begged for his cock. He couldn't deny her, so after plenty of encouraging words from Ember assuring him that it was perfectly safe, they made it a daily occurrence—sometimes three or four times daily. He found her pregnant body insatiable.

The crowd settled in the foyer with a drink in everyone's hand as they toasted to how well the Celestial Kingdom fared after Kronos's attack. The palace was rebuilt, Zeus had been diligent in his duties, and the gods praised how well he had handled it all. Now he regularly visits all the realms, ensuring the worlds are running smoothly. He even ventured so far as to help Hades expand his special demon task force to include angels, aiding the endeavor to snuff out any evil being inflicted upon innocent humans.

The ceremonial party for the baby announcement excited the entire Celestial Realm. Ares ensured that the party was going to be out of this world. He even insisted that Dionysus was present to assist by setting up drinking games, a smoking bar, and even a playground for any kids that may show up.

Green and yellow streamers hung throughout the hall, which was filled with balloons, cakes, alcohol, and food. Ares even arranged for pink and blue t-shirts to be provided at the door for people to wear, indicating whether they thought the baby was a boy or a girl. Zeus had a bright, pink shirt slung over his body, proclaiming to everyone he thought a baby girl would grace their presence, while Athena wore blue.

Uriel stuck out her lip in annoyance. "I don't want to wear a shirt," she whispered to Luci as she stood at the bottom of the stairs.

Lucifer looked over to the overflowing buffet table where he met his mate mere months ago. He smiled, thinking about their first meeting and how silly it was to think he almost let her walk out those double doors.

"I don't want to cover my dress." Uriel looked down, admiring her light-yellow lace-covered dress. It had pockets at her waist which she often would slip her hands into, swaying her dress to and fro.

"Then don't." Luci kissed her temple. "We aren't exactly rule-followers, anyway."

Uriel stuck out her lip again. She was hoping to get a rile out of Luci, but that didn't seem to work. She would figure something out later. Luci willed an amber liquid into his hands, swirling it as he looked down into the tawny substance. The ice cubes clinked, almost summoning Athena to them.

"Would you like a drink, Uriel?"

Uriel's head popped up from examining her lacy dress. Her pretty porcelain skin was now tanned with a hint of a sunburn on her cheeks and chest. Athena held out a strawberry liquid. It too had an umbrella just like the one at the big party after their bonding ceremony months earlier.

Uriel's golden eyes widened. "Yes!" she squealed, but Lucifer promptly grabbed it from Athena's hands before she could retrieve it.

"Uh no." He took it away, putting it on a servant's tray as it passed by.

Uriel whined, stomping her foot, "Why! I haven't had one in a long time." Her lip stuck out, provoking Lucifer to land a firm swat on Uriel's back side.

"Owie."

"Watch it," he warned, raising a brow.

Athena watched the two, finding their dynamic utterly amusing. "Here, this is one without alcohol." Athena willed another strawberry-flavored one, and Uriel took it gladly.

"You're lucky I can detect lies now," Lucifer commented, drinking from his glass.

Athena chuckled as Ares and Mariah stepped to the top of the stairs, holding a baby in a silk yellow blanket. Two cherubs floated around their bodies, blowing horns for everyone's attention.

"This is ridiculously excessive," Hades groaned, stepping up beside his son. "Fucking cherubs," he muttered.

"Are you sure those are cherubs?" Uriel mused. "Those *things* have horns on their heads."

It was true. The cherubs were specifically created for the baby announcement. Hades had a terrible time assembling them. He made them the lightest shade of red he could, trying to appease his friend but he couldn't fully curtail his stylistic flare. The result was chubby, little, red-tinged babies with horns and black wings.

"Those aren't cherubs. You should have asked Zeus to assist you." Athena looked on in disgust.

Ares looked down into the crowd, narrowing his eyes at Hades. He wanted everything perfect, but as he watched those things flutter around his head, all he could think was, *'I asked for damn cherubs and this was what I got? Hades somehow came up with this twisted demonic version of a cherub. He had a seriously sick, dark sense of humor.'* He scoffed silently, shaking his head

Hades snickered as he noticed Ares' glare at the same time Athena commented, "Those things look like demon hell babies." He covered his mouth to suppress his laugh as Ember nudged him, shaking her head.

Lilith ran by both her parents, babbling and eating a turkey leg with one hand. The cute, pink dress with little frills that Ember dressed her in did not reflect her personality. Despite her beautiful, strawberry-blonde hair which was so reminiscent of her mother, Hades' strong genes were evident in the permanent scowl on her face.

Ares cleared his throat, and the devil-demon babies floated away and dispersed into thin air. Hades wasn't keeping those around—that was some creepy shit, even for him.

"We would like to announce..." Ares paused for effect, giving the perfect view of the massive black t-shirt that said, 'Best dad of all the realms.' Some laughed, but Ares continued to stare at his mate with pride as he took the baby from her arms and finished, "our daughter, Agape."

The claps from the crowd thundered through the room, startling the newborn baby girl into a fit of cries. Ares clutched her to his chest, and she instantly soothed into his touch.

Uriel was bursting with excitement, ready to see the little baby as the new family descended the stairs. "Can I go see?" Uriel gasped, holding her hands over her mouth.

Her child-like personality had still not left her, and Lucifer hoped it never world. He hoped their children would be just as adorable—but that wouldn't be happening anytime soon. He had too many things he wanted to do with his little bunny, *alone.*

"Go but come right back."

Uriel nodded frantically, rushing over to the little baby who glowed so brightly in Uriel's vision that it almost hurt her eyes. "So pretty," she cooed, trailing a finger down the baby's cheek. Warm light trailed Uriel's finger as Agape's little head turned to see the Goddess of Innocence staring at her. The baby smiled, yawned, and quickly went back to sleep, none the wiser.

"What did you do?" Mariah asked as she looked over her baby, clutching her to her chest.

"I blessed her with grace," Uriel hummed. "I'm not sure what form it will come in, though, since she's just a little baby."

Uriel's powers continued to grow. She could suck lies out of little, naughty children and then give them the guilt until they prayed for forgiveness, which she would instantly grant. When she blessed someone with grace, it could come in a warm feeling of being loved and cared for. However, for the few people of the artistic nature she had blessed with grace, their movements became more fluid and their paint strokes more emotional. Uriel still had a lot to learn, but she knew she should use her newfound skill to help little Agape in her life.

Meanwhile, Loki was busy working the crowd. He had uncovered a new level of charisma since he became the raven. The she-wolves from Mariah's pack all showed up for the event, and they were enthralled with him. With his dark hair and deep green eyes, he looked nothing short of the Prince of Darkness he was as his charisma drew hungry teenage girls to his feet.

"He's going to get in trouble one day," Lucifer muttered to his father.

Uriel looked at both Hades and her mate, watching how they both looked at Loki with disappointment. 'Flowers, they looked so much alike with their jaws tight and their eyes narrowed.'

"What I've learned about being a parent"—Hera stood by her daughter, wrapping her arm around her—"is that you can only guide your children so much. It is up to them and the Fates what they do with that guidance" The sweet smell of honeysuckle tickled Uriel's nose and she, immediately, hugged Hera and rubbed her mother's growing tummy.

Ember hummed in agreement, intertwining her fingers with Hades. "That is true. I just hope he remembers he has a mate, and she may not be so forgiving."

"She'll be strict," Uriel chirped. "I bet his mate will deny him at first, and he will have to work for her affection. I mean..."

Everyone looked at her to finish her statement, but she lowered her head and buried it in Lucifer's chest.

"Go on." Lucifer nudged his mate. She was so smart; she didn't need to hide from them.

"Like... she won't put up with his shit."

Hera stood back, staring at her child, '*How dare she just curse like that?*'

Lucifer only chuckled, he didn't like how his little bunny cursed but if it was any consolation, he loved that it got Hera riled up. '*Payback is a bitch,*' he thought to himself.

"Uriel!" Hera finally chided, but Uriel shrugged her shoulders.

"Got to make my own decisions about my life, Mom." She winked.

Subscribe to stay up-to-date on new releases! Click Here

Current Series and Books

Under the Moon Series

Under the MoonClara and Kane's Story

The Alpha's KittenCharlotte and Wesley's Story

Finding Love with the Fae King Osirus and Melina's Story

The Exiled DragonCreed and Odessa's Story

Under the Moon: The Dark WarClara, Kane, Jasper and Taliyah's story

His True Beloved: A Vampire's Second Chance Sebastian and Christine's Story

Alpha of her Dreams (Coming Soon) Evelyn and Kit's Story

The Alpha's Broken Princess (Coming Soon) Melody and Marcus' Story

Twinning and Sinning From Mutts to MatesDax, Dimitri, and Seraphina's Story

Under the Moon: God Series

Seeking Hades' EmberHades and Ember's Story

Lucifer's RedemptionLucifer and Uriel's Story

Printed in Great Britain
by Amazon

20384489R00312